PROLOGUE:
TALES FROM PARIS: REPETITION

Created by: Thomas Astruc
Comics adaptation by: Nicole D'Andria
Written by: Nolwenn Pierre
Director: Neil Ruffier Meray
Storyboarder: Fabrice Ca[...]
Art by: Angie Nasca
Art arranged by: Cheryl B[...]
Lettered by: Justin Birch

D1400959

CHAPTER 1:
ADVENTURES OF LADYBUG AND CAT NOIR:
REPLAY

Created by: Thomas Astruc
Story by: Bryan Seaton
Scripted by: Nicole D'Andria
Art by: Brian Hess
Letters by: Justin Birch
Colors by: Darné Lang

Bryan Seaton: Publisher/ CEO • Shawn Gabborin: Editor In Chief • Jason Martin: Publisher-Danger Zone • Nicole D'Andria: Marketing Director/Editor
Danielle Davison: Executive Administrator • Chad Cicconi: Akumatized • Shawn Pryor: President of Creator Relations

ZAG Miraculous *Miraculous* is a trademark of ZAG - Method. © 2015 ZAG - Method - All Rights Reserved. MIRACULOUS: ADVENTURES OF LADYBUG AND CAT NOIR Volume
1, DECEMBER 2017. Published by Action Lab Entertainment. No part of this publication may be reproduced or transmitted without permission. Printed in Canada. First Printing.

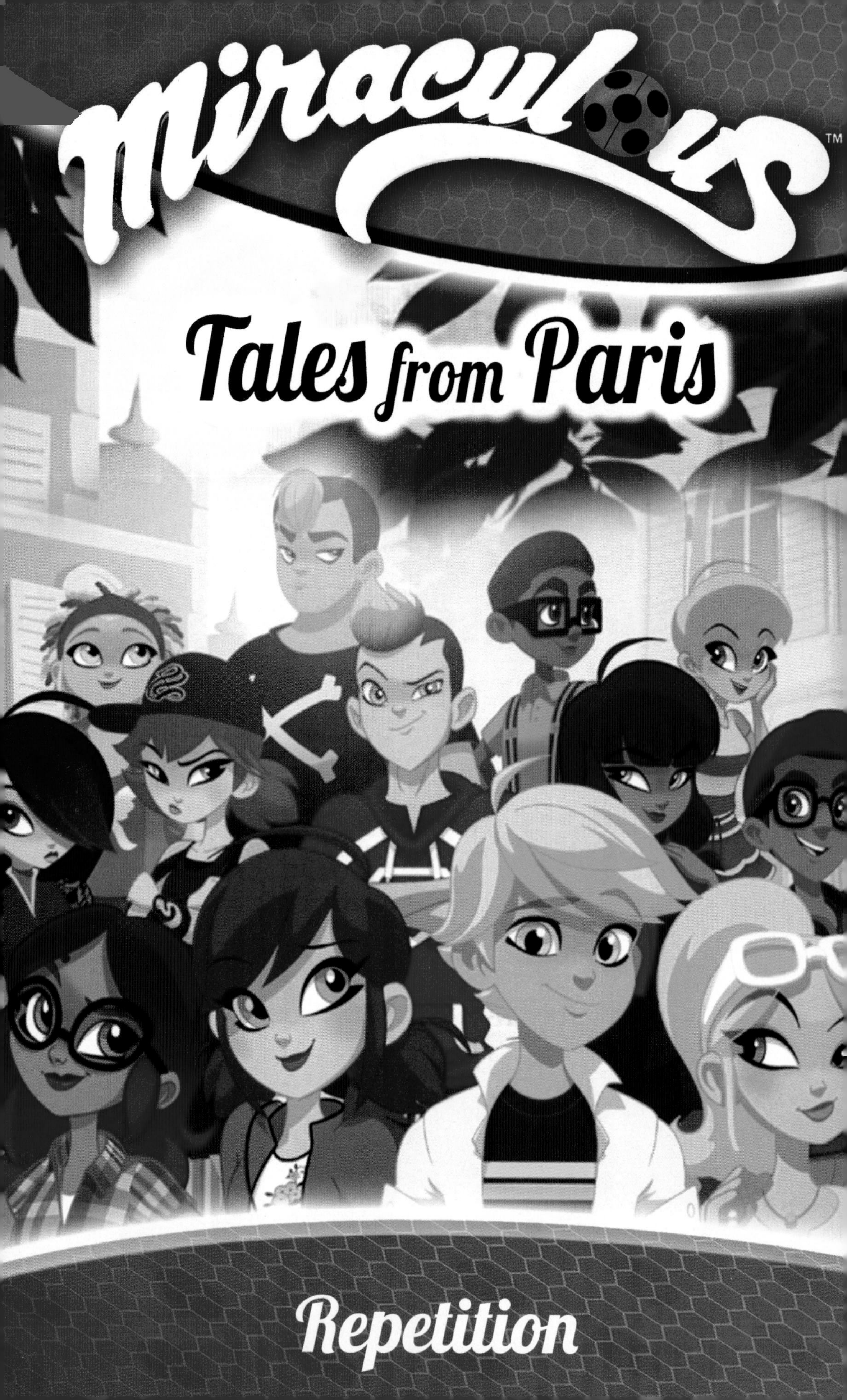
Miraculous™
Tales from Paris
Repetition

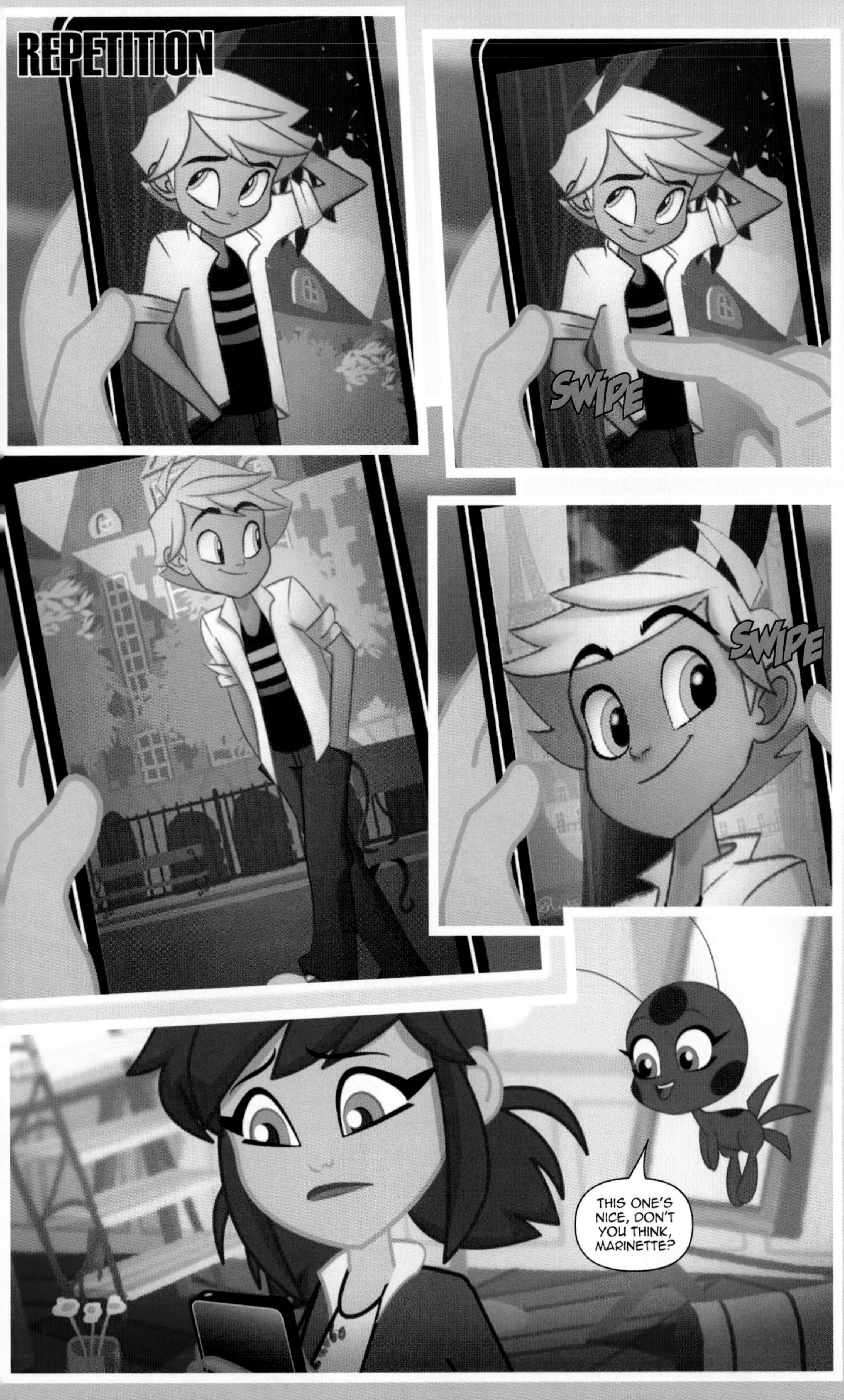
REPETITION
SWIPE
SWIPE
THIS ONE'S NICE, DON'T YOU THINK, MARINETTE?

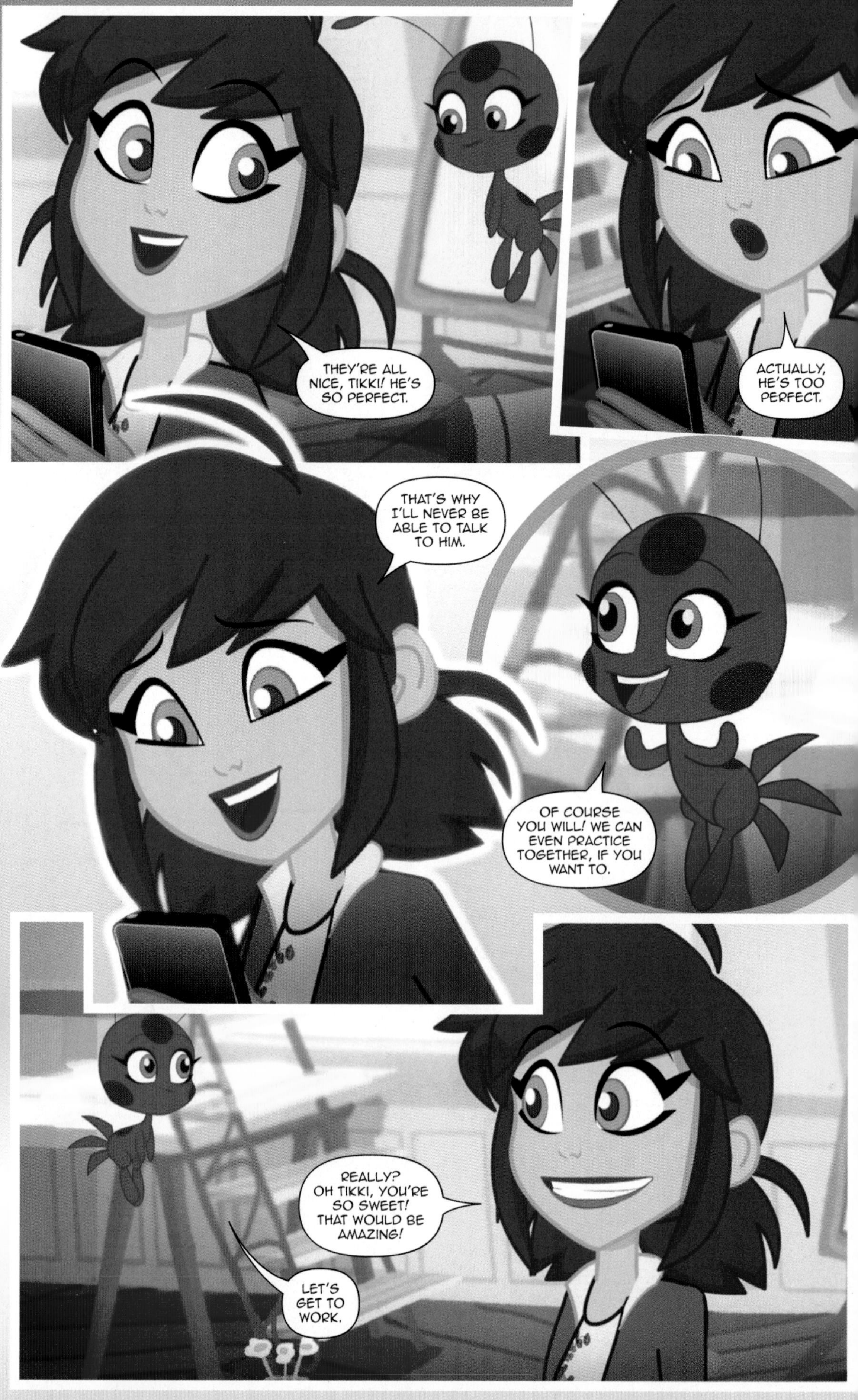
THEY'RE ALL NICE, TIKKI! HE'S SO PERFECT.
ACTUALLY, HE'S TOO PERFECT.
THAT'S WHY I'LL NEVER BE ABLE TO TALK TO HIM.
OF COURSE YOU WILL! WE CAN EVEN PRACTICE TOGETHER, IF YOU WANT TO.
REALLY? OH TIKKI, YOU'RE SO SWEET! THAT WOULD BE AMAZING!
LET'S GET TO WORK.

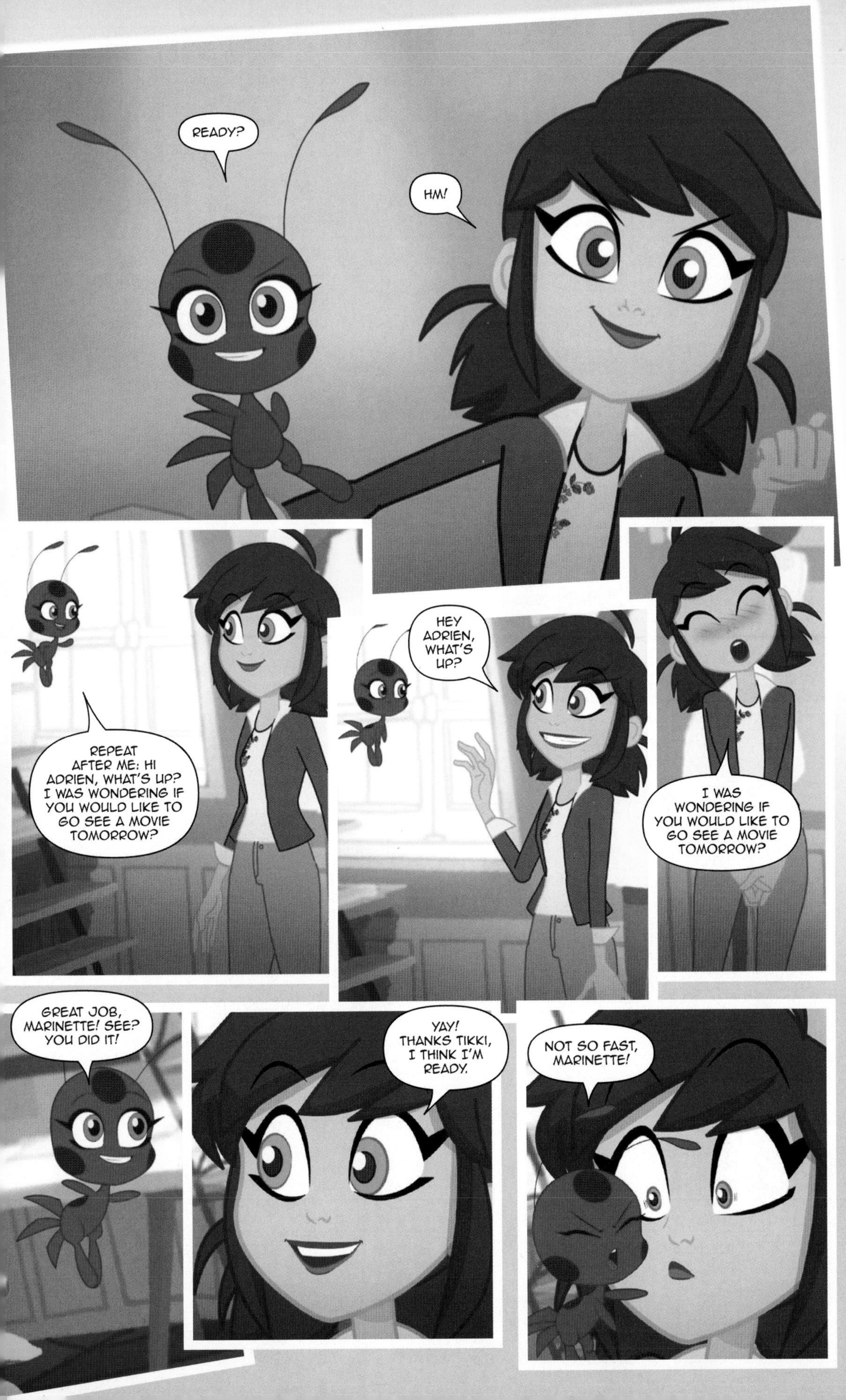
READY?
HM!
REPEAT AFTER ME: HI ADRIEN, WHAT'S UP? I WAS WONDERING IF YOU WOULD LIKE TO GO SEE A MOVIE TOMORROW?
HEY ADRIEN, WHAT'S UP?
I WAS WONDERING IF YOU WOULD LIKE TO GO SEE A MOVIE TOMORROW?
GREAT JOB, MARINETTE! SEE? YOU DID IT!
YAY! THANKS TIKKI, I THINK I'M READY.
NOT SO FAST, MARINETTE!

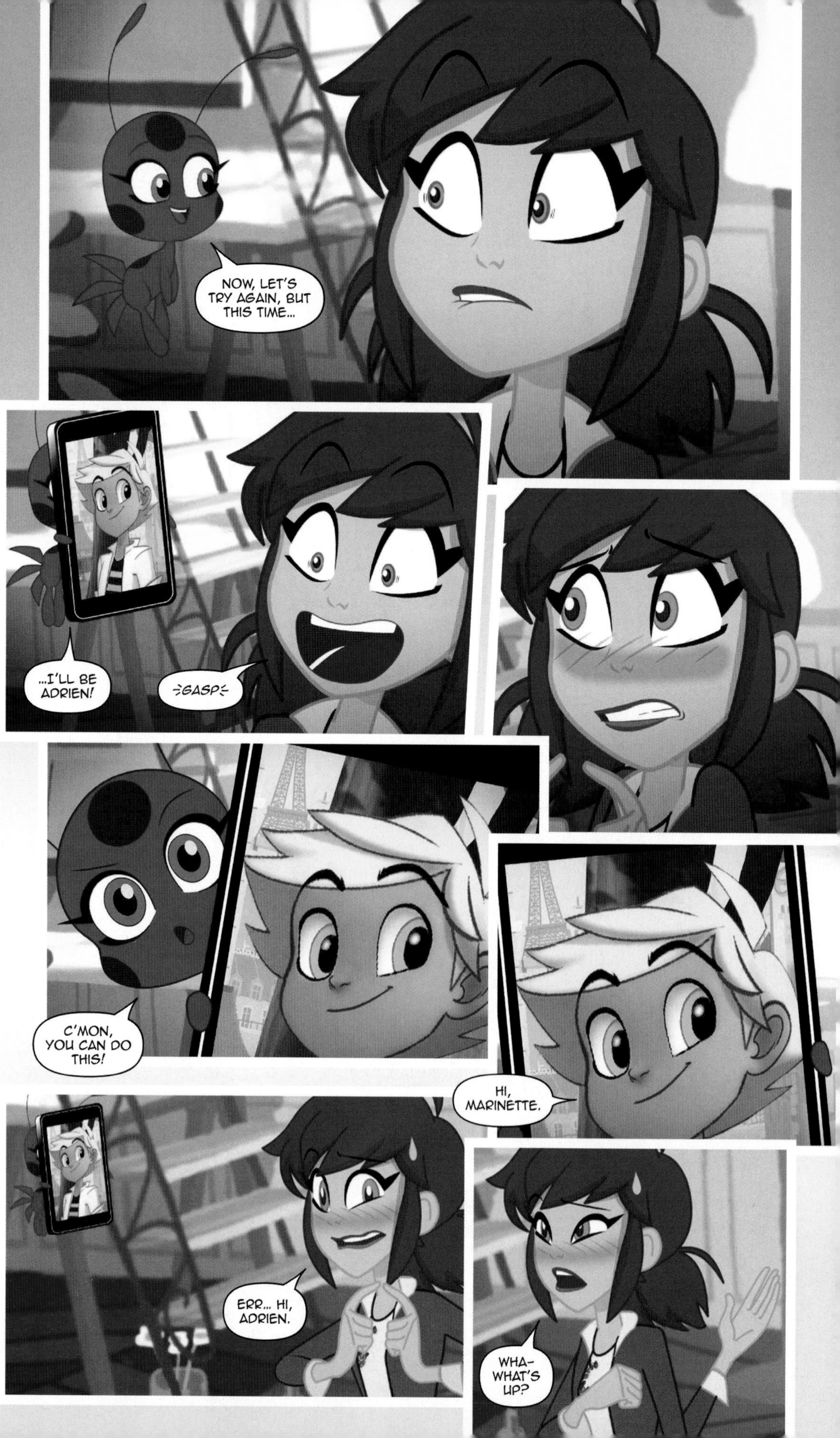
NOW, LET'S TRY AGAIN, BUT THIS TIME...
...I'LL BE ADRIEN!
GASP
C'MON, YOU CAN DO THIS!
HI, MARINETTE.
ERR... HI, ADRIEN.
WHA- WHAT'S UP?

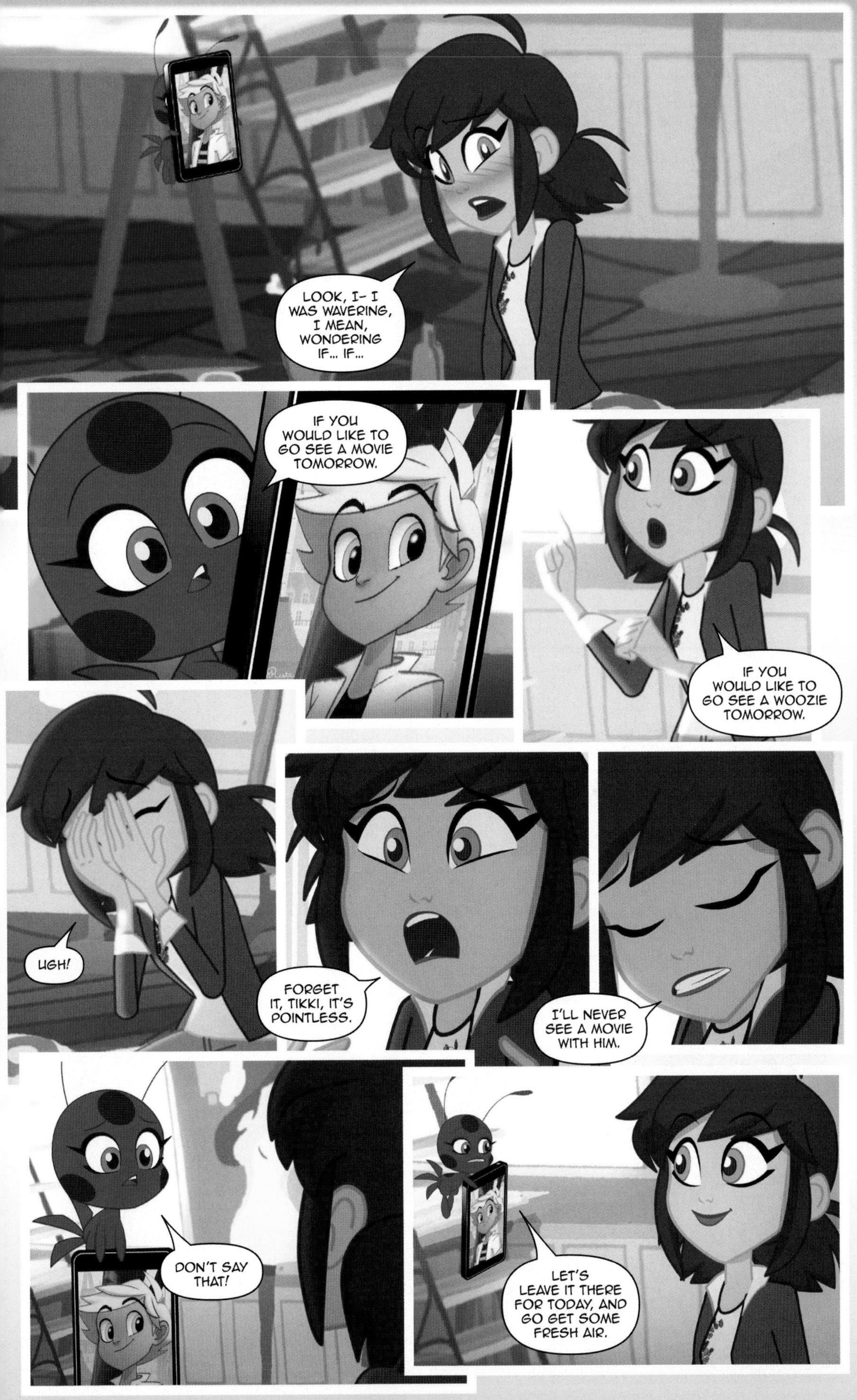
LOOK, I- I WAS WAVERING, I MEAN, WONDERING IF... IF...
IF YOU WOULD LIKE TO GO SEE A MOVIE TOMORROW.
IF YOU WOULD LIKE TO GO SEE A WOOZIE TOMORROW.
UGH!
FORGET IT, TIKKI, IT'S POINTLESS.
I'LL NEVER SEE A MOVIE WITH HIM.
DON'T SAY THAT!
LET'S LEAVE IT THERE FOR TODAY, AND GO GET SOME FRESH AIR.

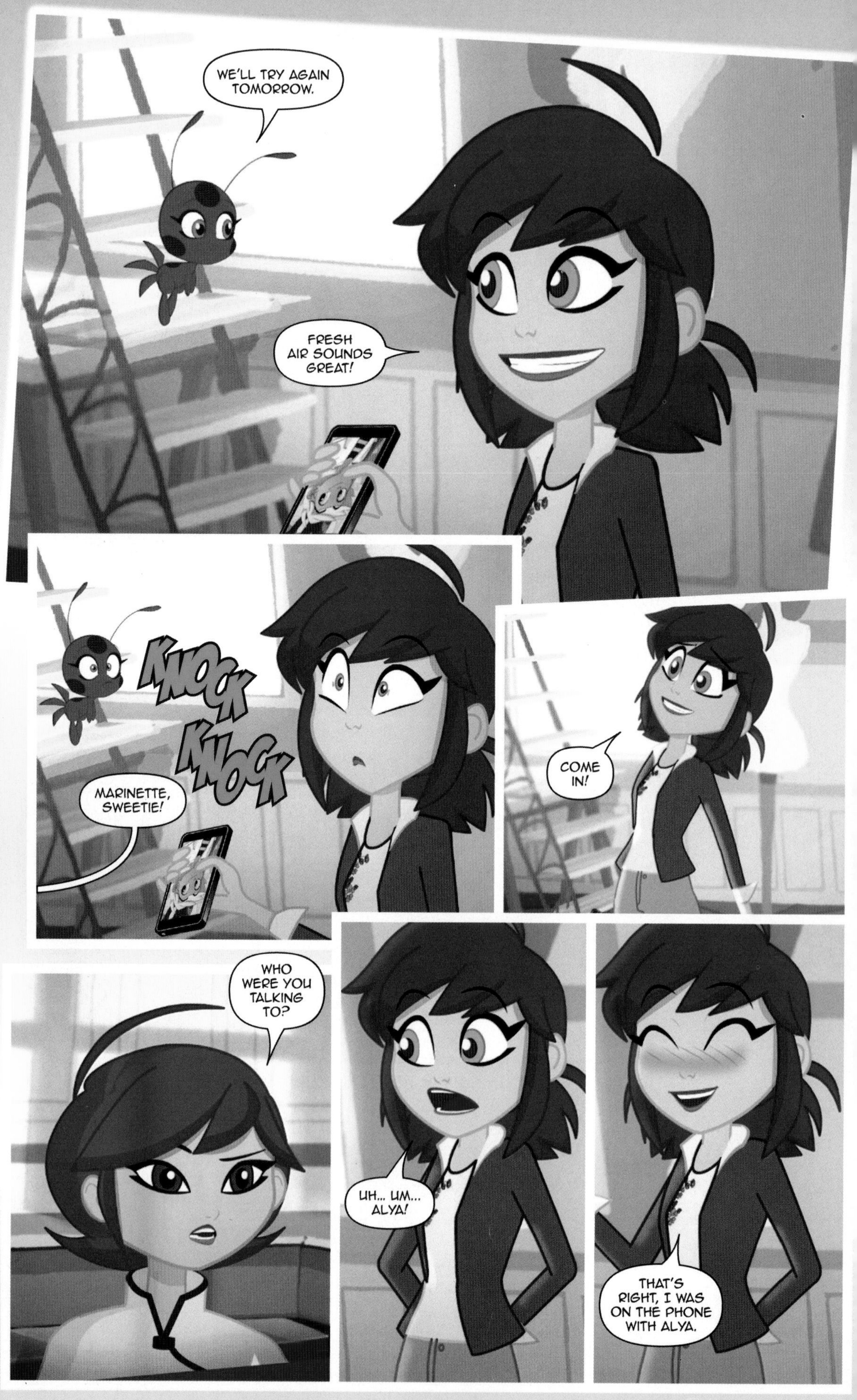
WE'LL TRY AGAIN TOMORROW.
FRESH AIR SOUNDS GREAT!
KNOCK KNOCK
MARINETTE, SWEETIE!
COME IN!
WHO WERE YOU TALKING TO?
UH... UM... ALYA!
THAT'S RIGHT, I WAS ON THE PHONE WITH ALYA.

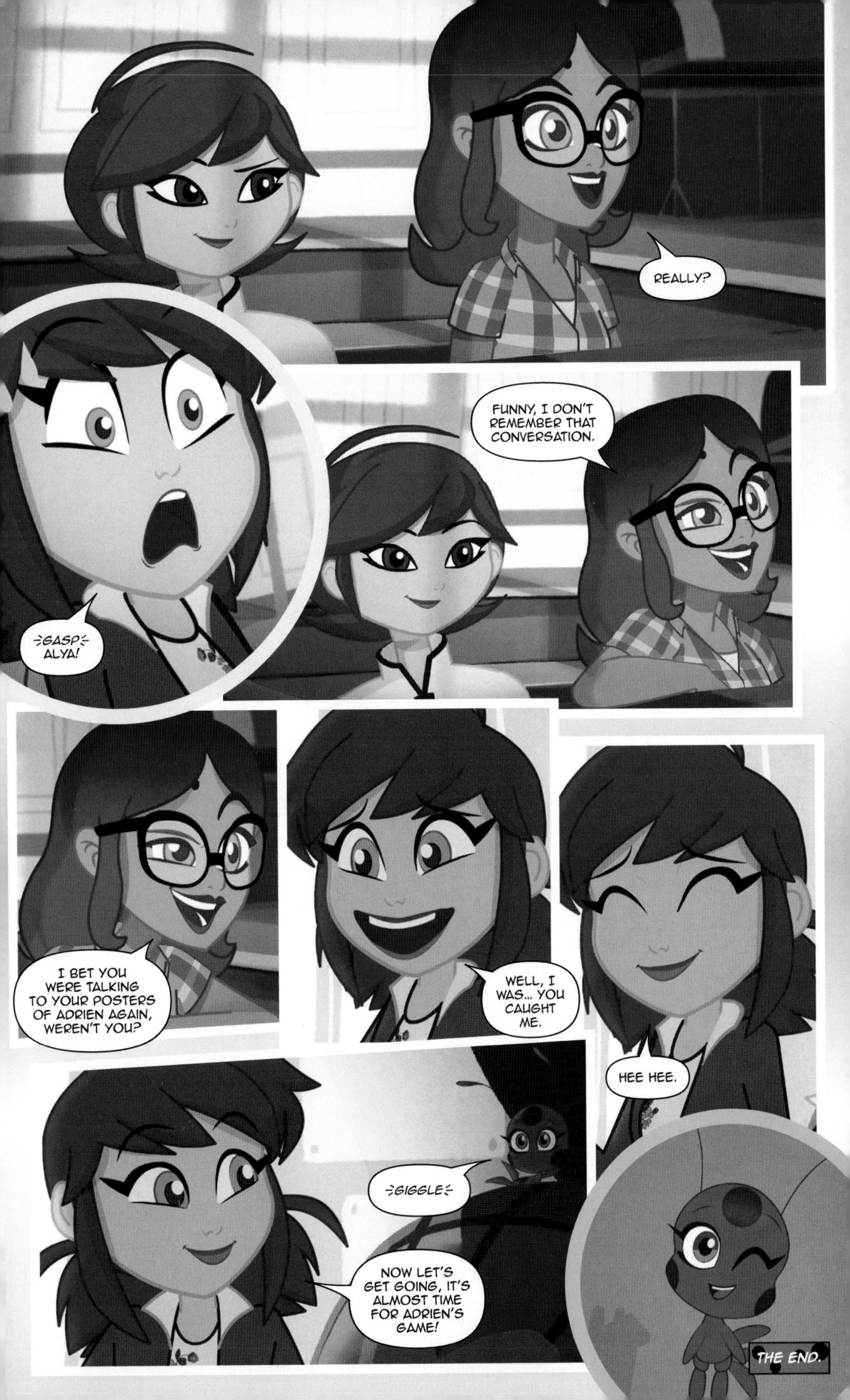
REALLY?
FUNNY, I DON'T REMEMBER THAT CONVERSATION.
-GASP- ALYA!
I BET YOU WERE TALKING TO YOUR POSTERS OF ADRIEN AGAIN, WEREN'T YOU?
WELL, I WAS... YOU CAUGHT ME.
HEE HEE.
-GIGGLE-
NOW LET'S GET GOING, IT'S ALMOST TIME FOR ADRIEN'S GAME!
THE END.

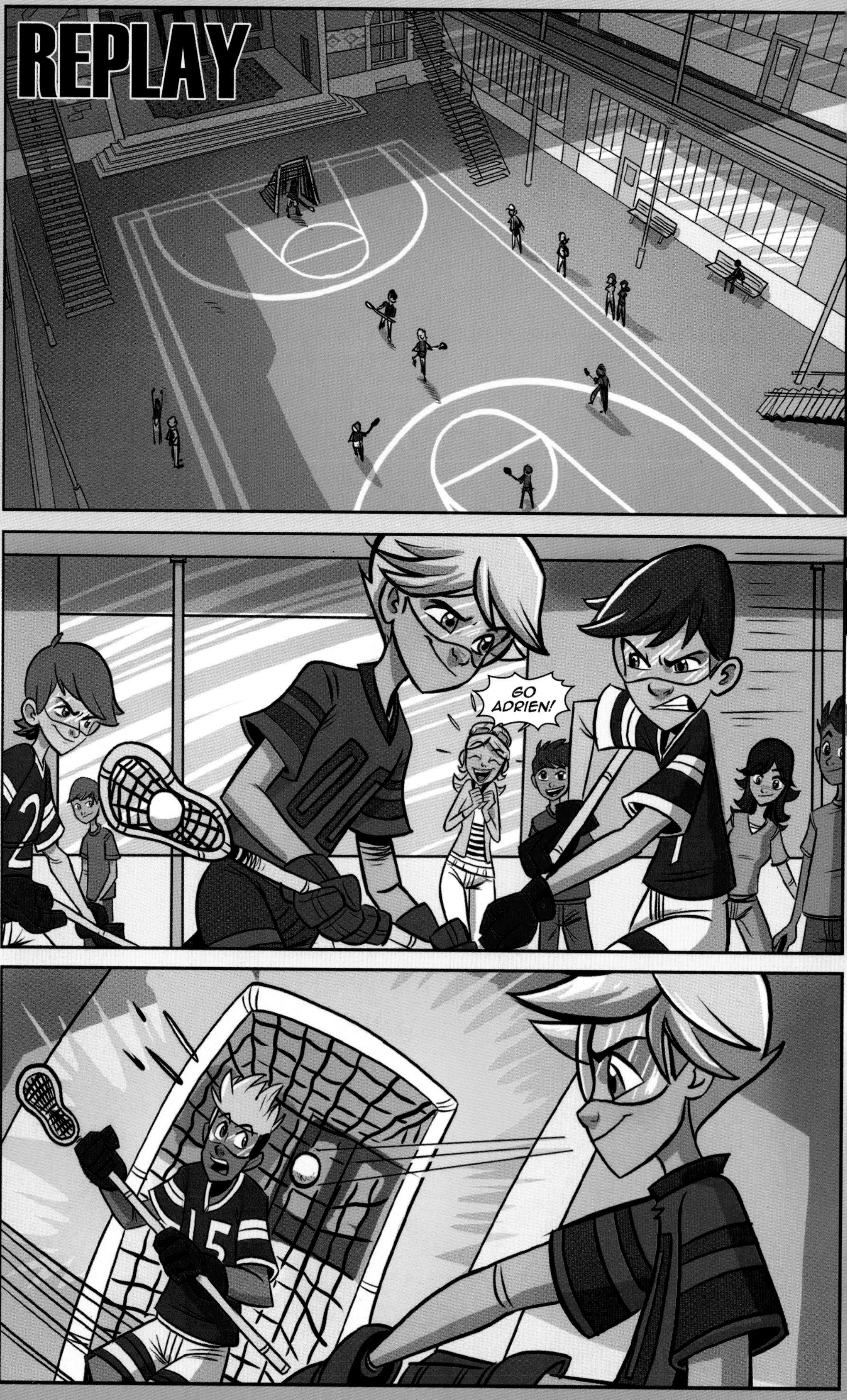
REPLAY
GO ADRIEN!

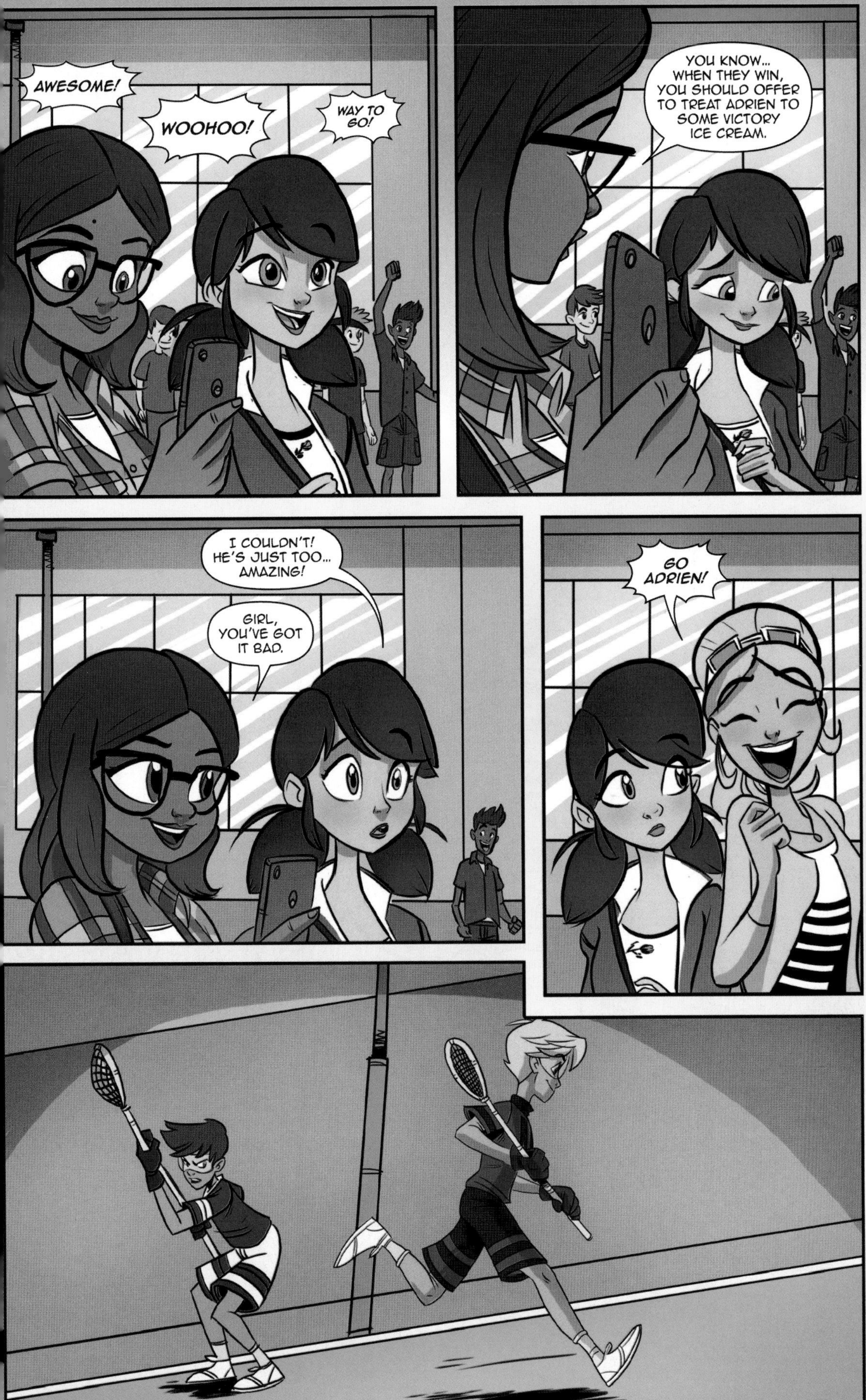
AWESOME!
WOOHOO!
WAY TO GO!
YOU KNOW... WHEN THEY WIN, YOU SHOULD OFFER TO TREAT ADRIEN TO SOME VICTORY ICE CREAM.
I COULDN'T! HE'S JUST TOO... AMAZING!
GIRL, YOU'VE GOT IT BAD.
GO ADRIEN!

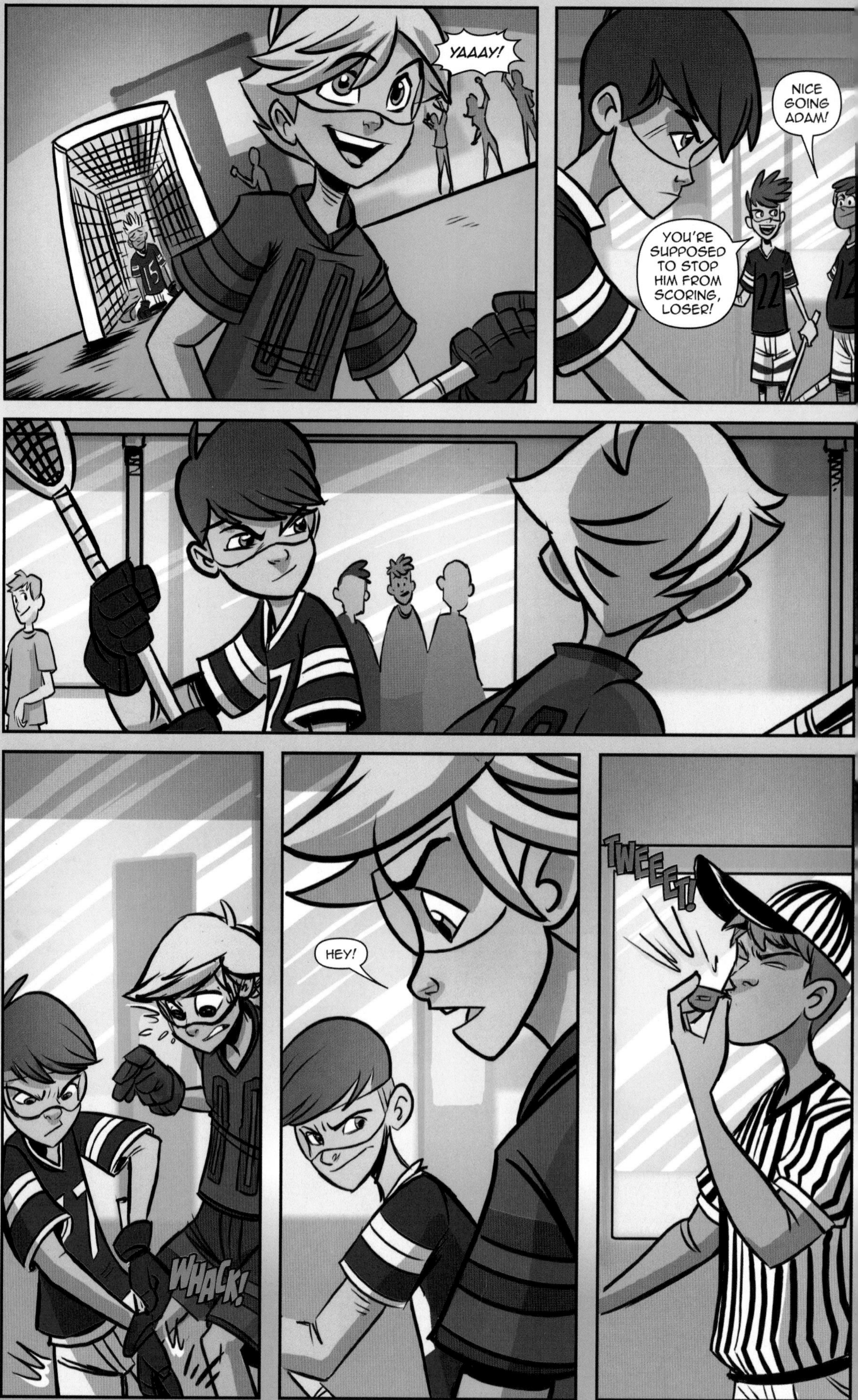
YAAAY!
NICE GOING ADAM!
YOU'RE SUPPOSED TO STOP HIM FROM SCORING, LOSER!
WHACK!
HEY!
TWEEEET!

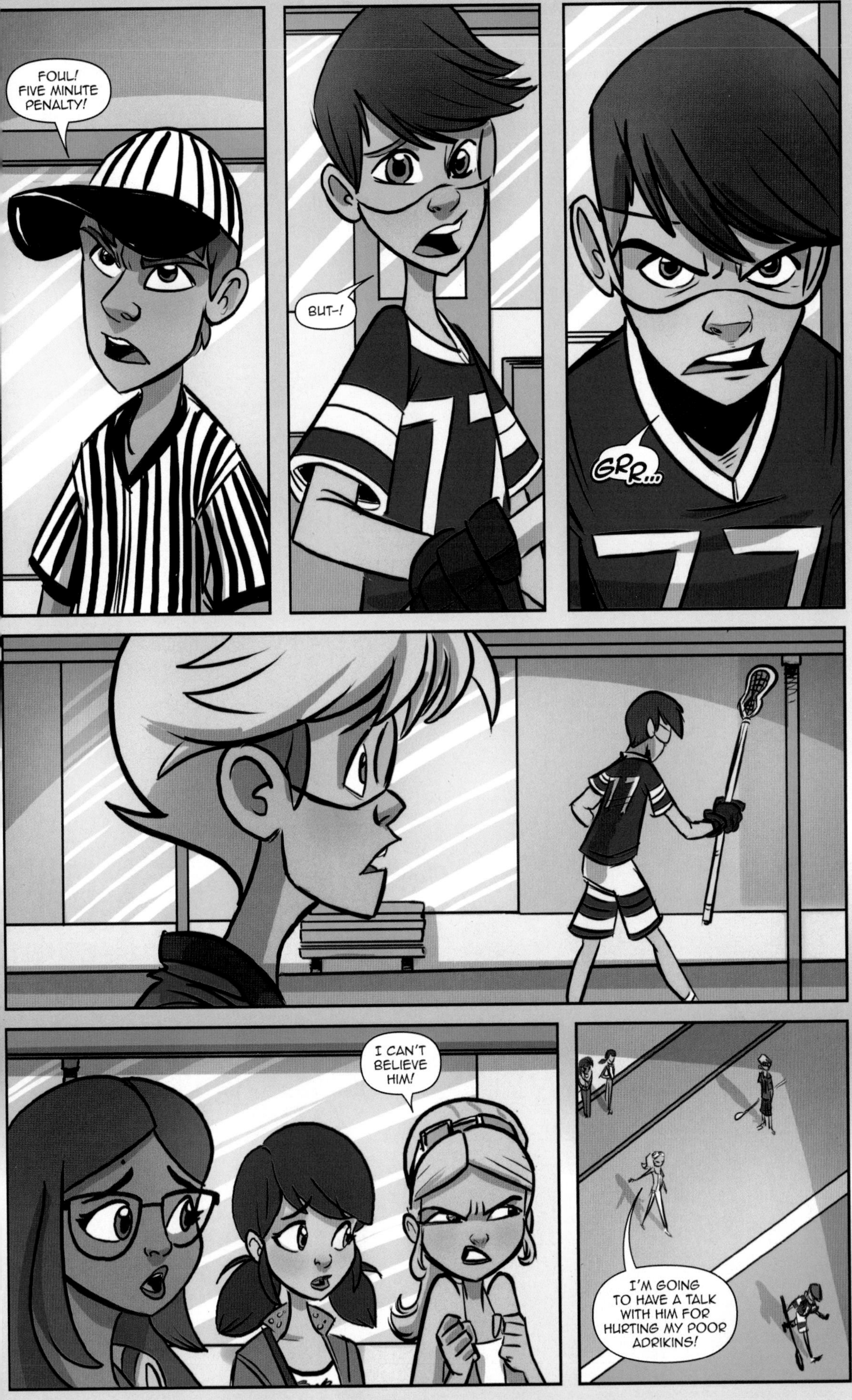
FOUL! FIVE MINUTE PENALTY!
BUT-!
GRR...
I CAN'T BELIEVE HIM!
I'M GOING TO HAVE A TALK WITH HIM FOR HURTING MY POOR ADRIKINS!

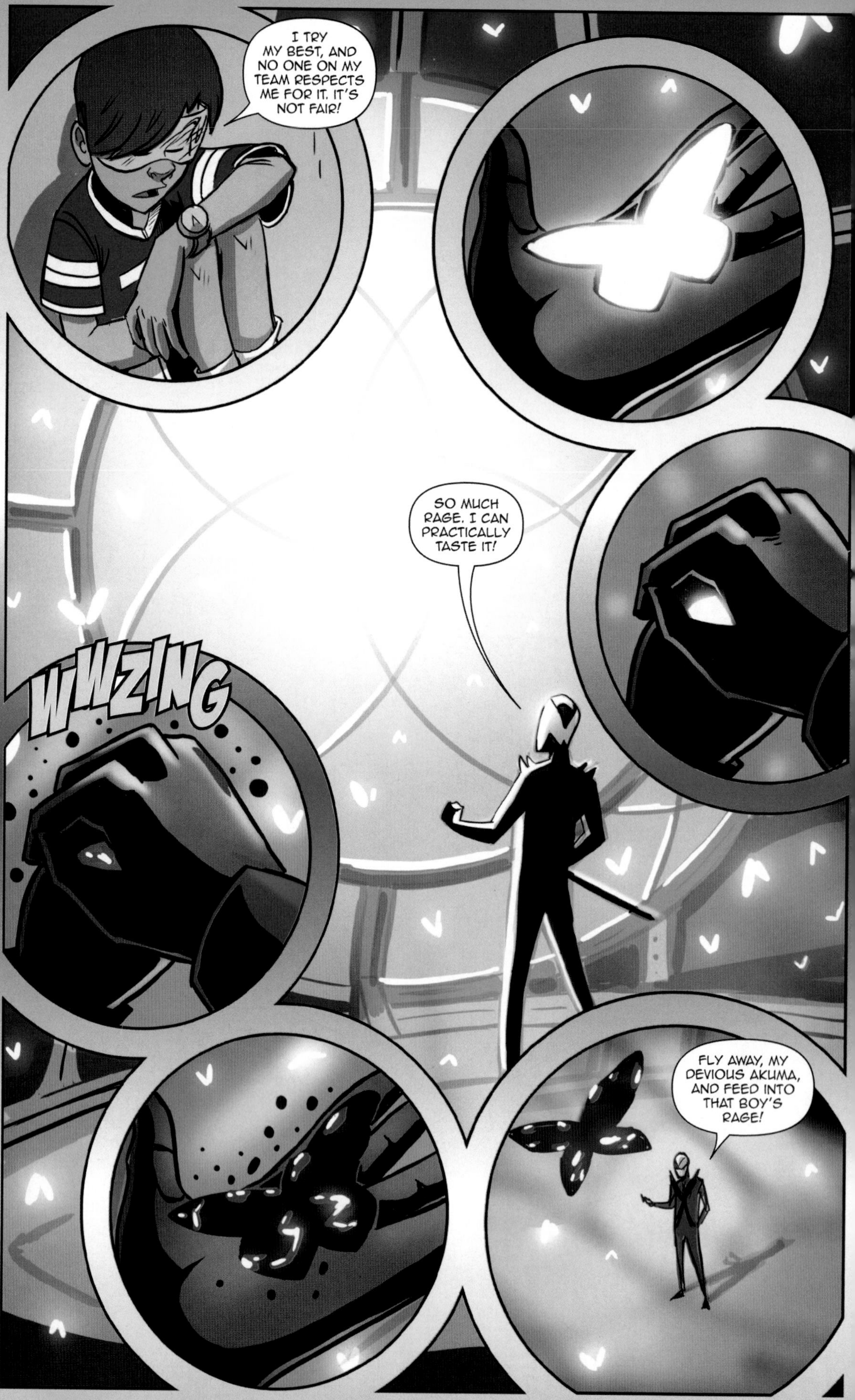
I TRY MY BEST, AND NO ONE ON MY TEAM RESPECTS ME FOR IT. IT'S NOT FAIR!
SO MUCH RAGE. I CAN PRACTICALLY TASTE IT!
WWZING
FLY AWAY, MY DEVIOUS AKUMA, AND FEED INTO THAT BOY'S RAGE!

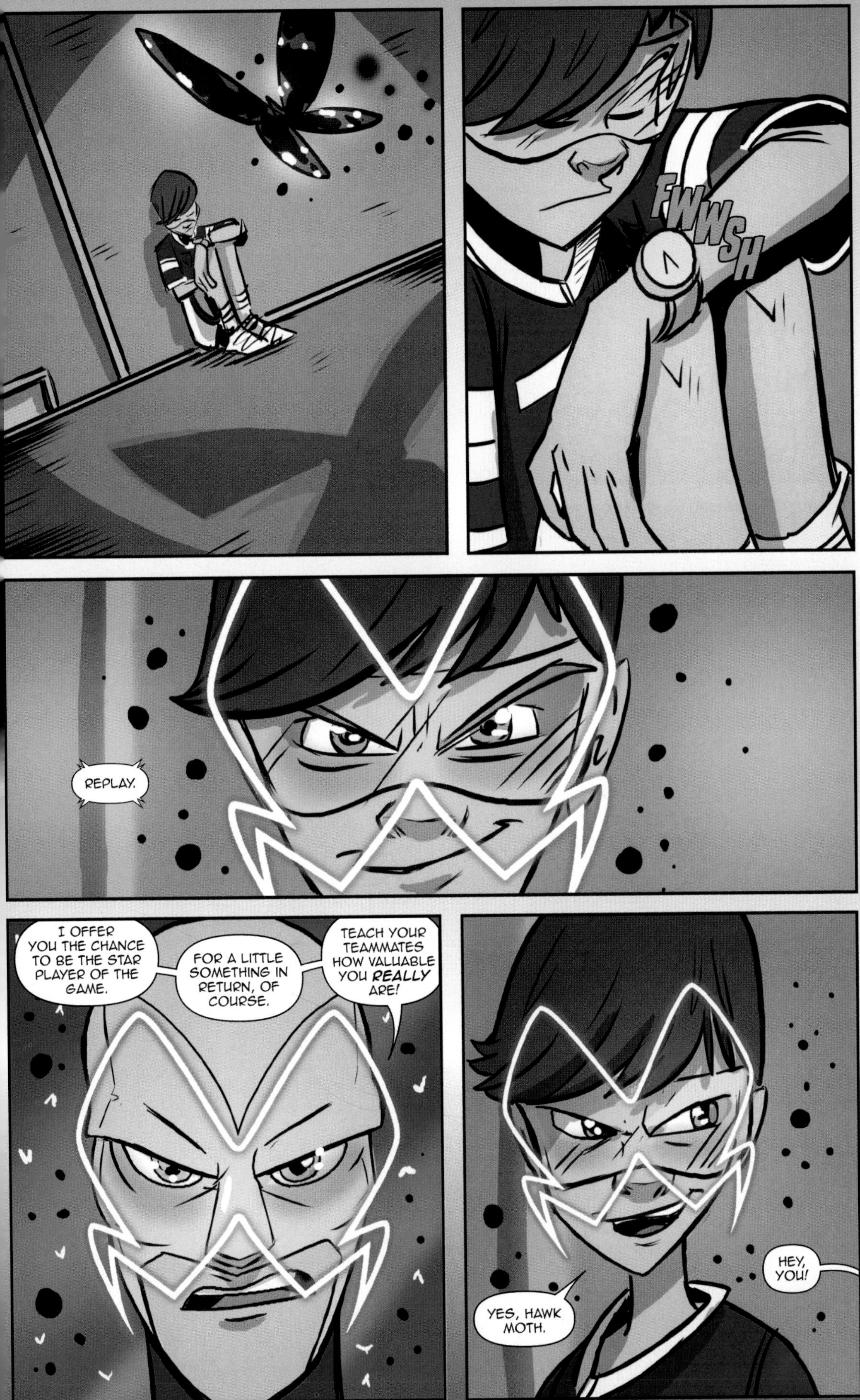
FWWSH
REPLAY.
I OFFER YOU THE CHANCE TO BE THE STAR PLAYER OF THE GAME.
FOR A LITTLE SOMETHING IN RETURN, OF COURSE.
TEACH YOUR TEAMMATES HOW VALUABLE YOU **REALLY** ARE!
HEY, YOU!
YES, HAWK MOTH.

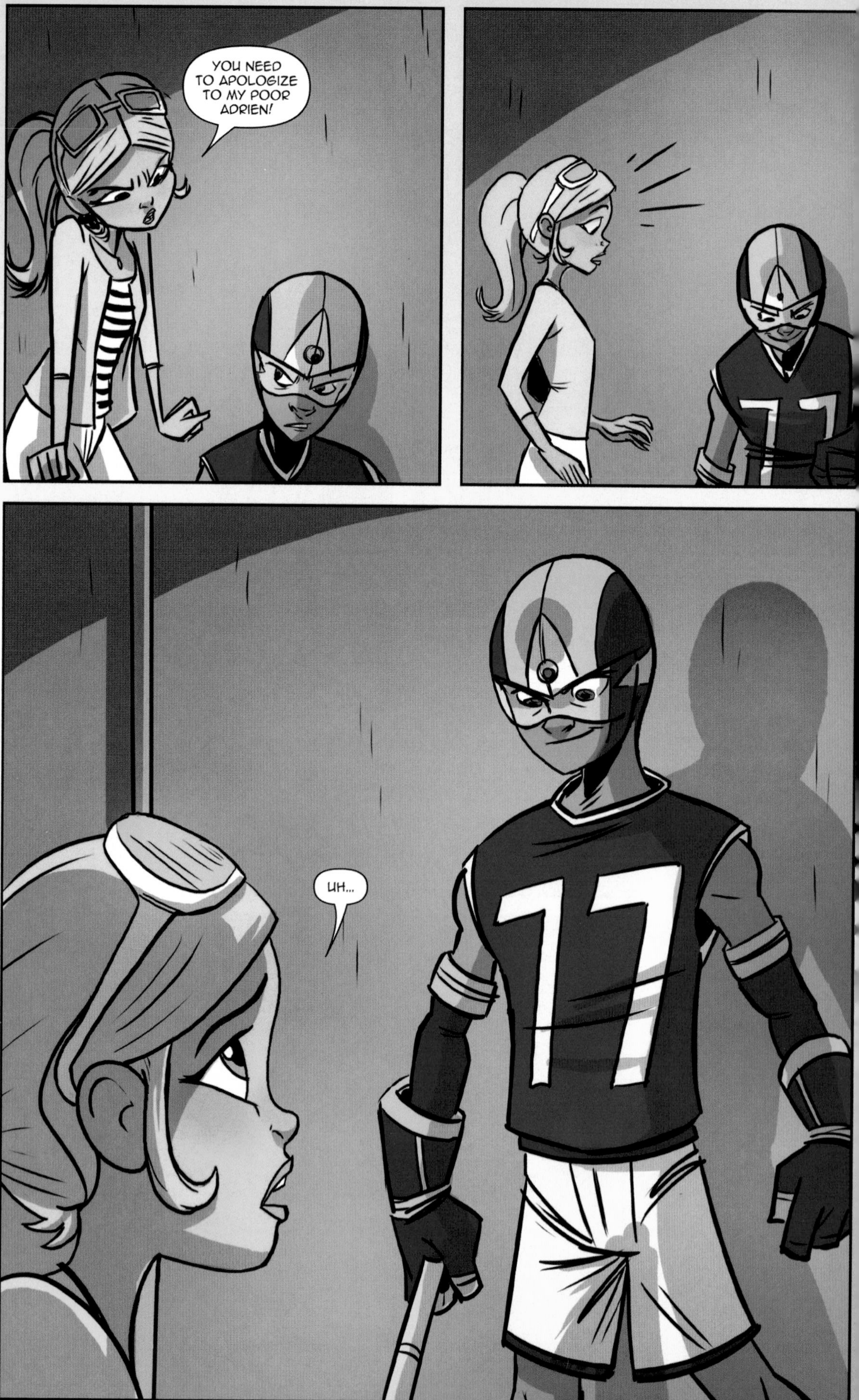
YOU NEED TO APOLOGIZE TO MY POOR ADRIEN!
UH...

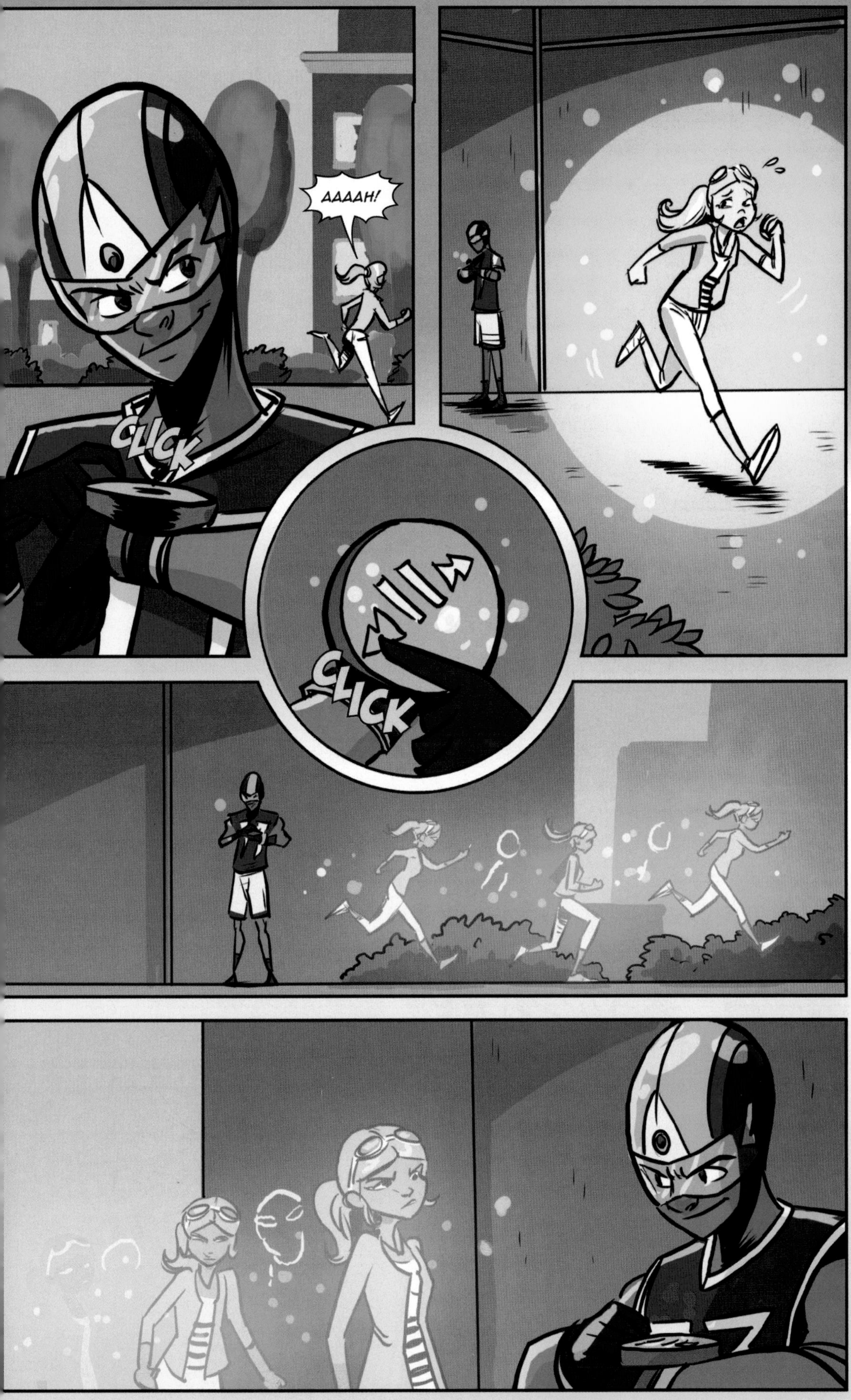
AAAAH!
CLICK
CLICK

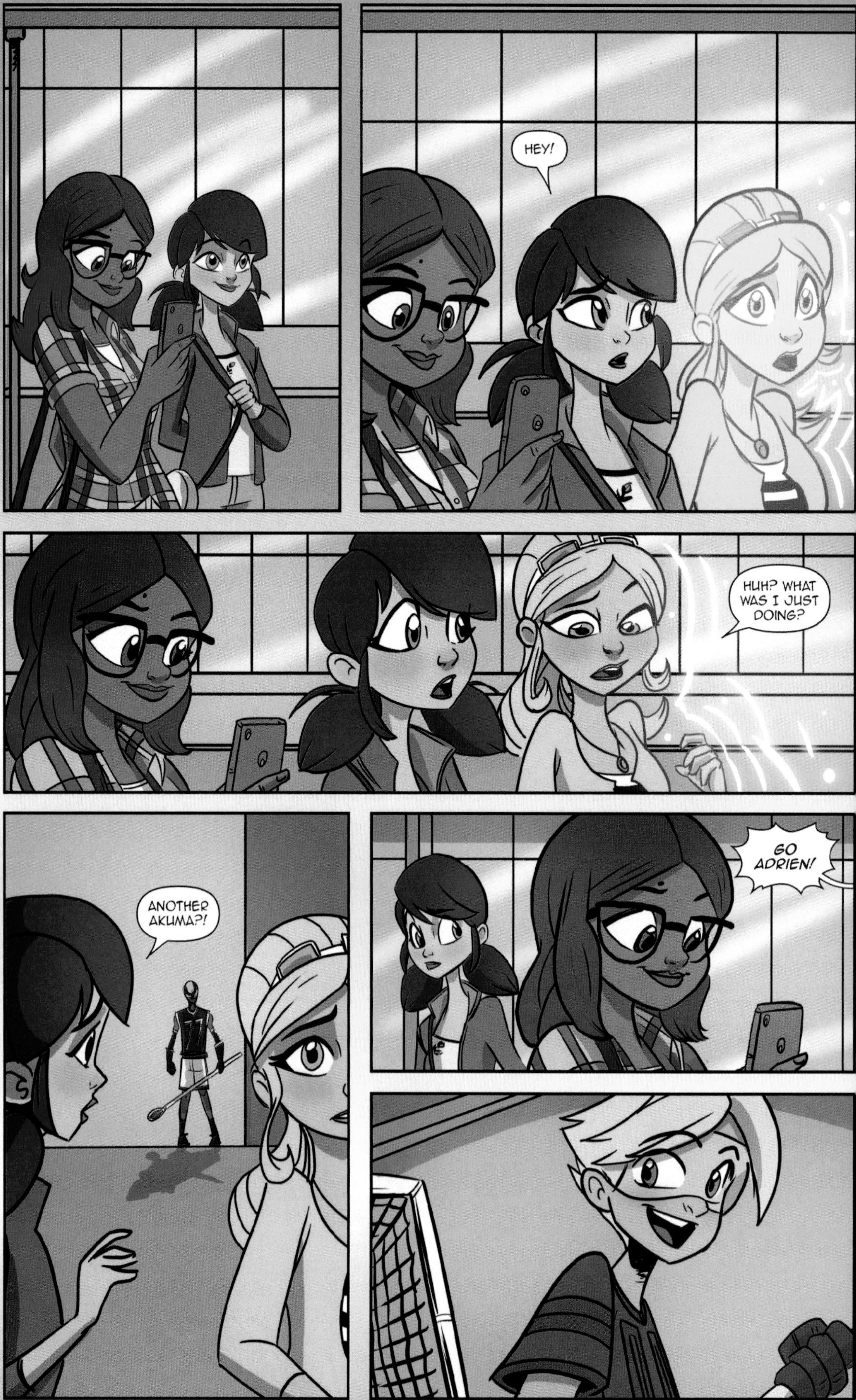
HEY!
HUH? WHAT WAS I JUST DOING?
ANOTHER AKUMA?!
GO ADRIEN!

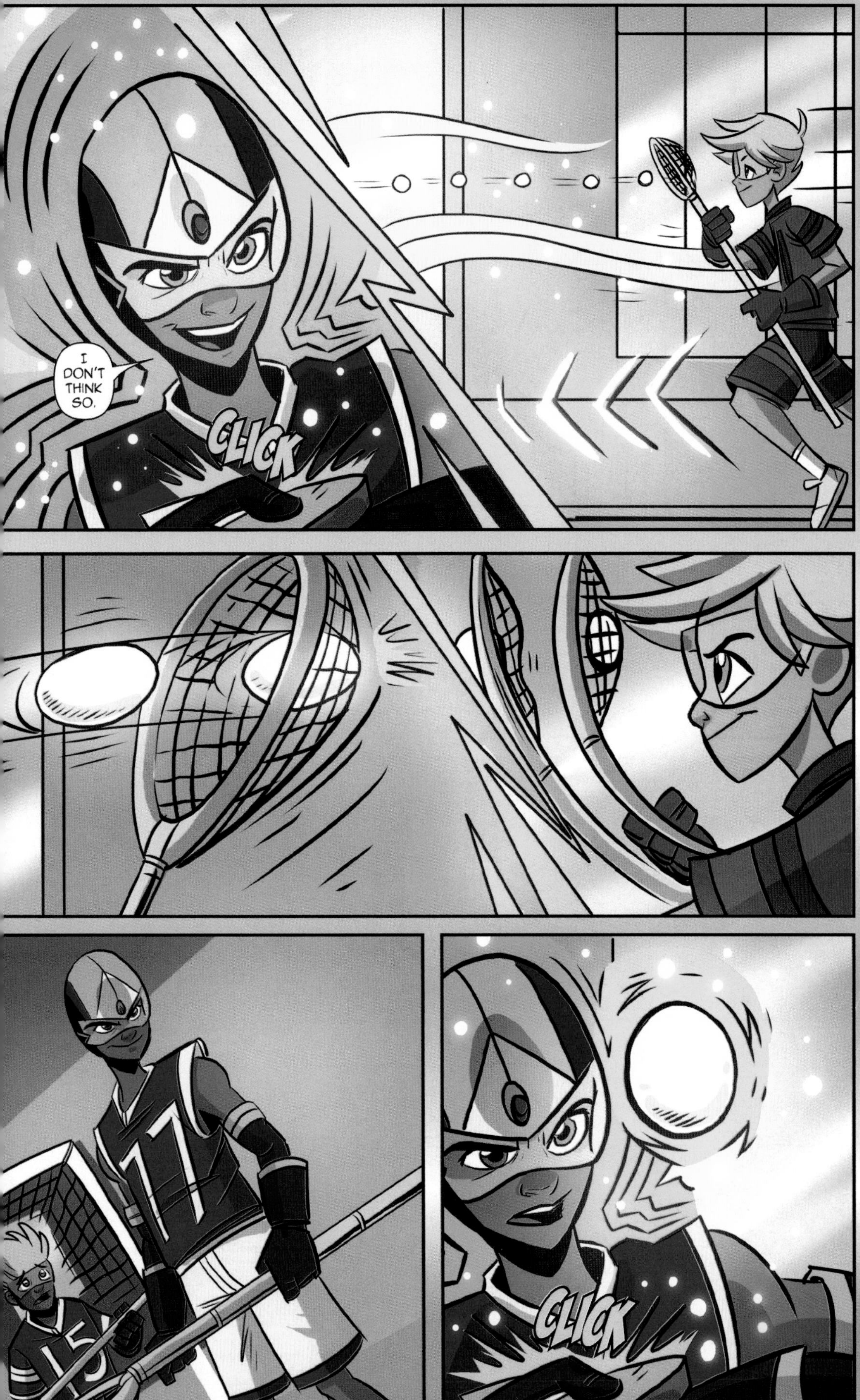
I DON'T THINK SO.
CLICK
CLICK

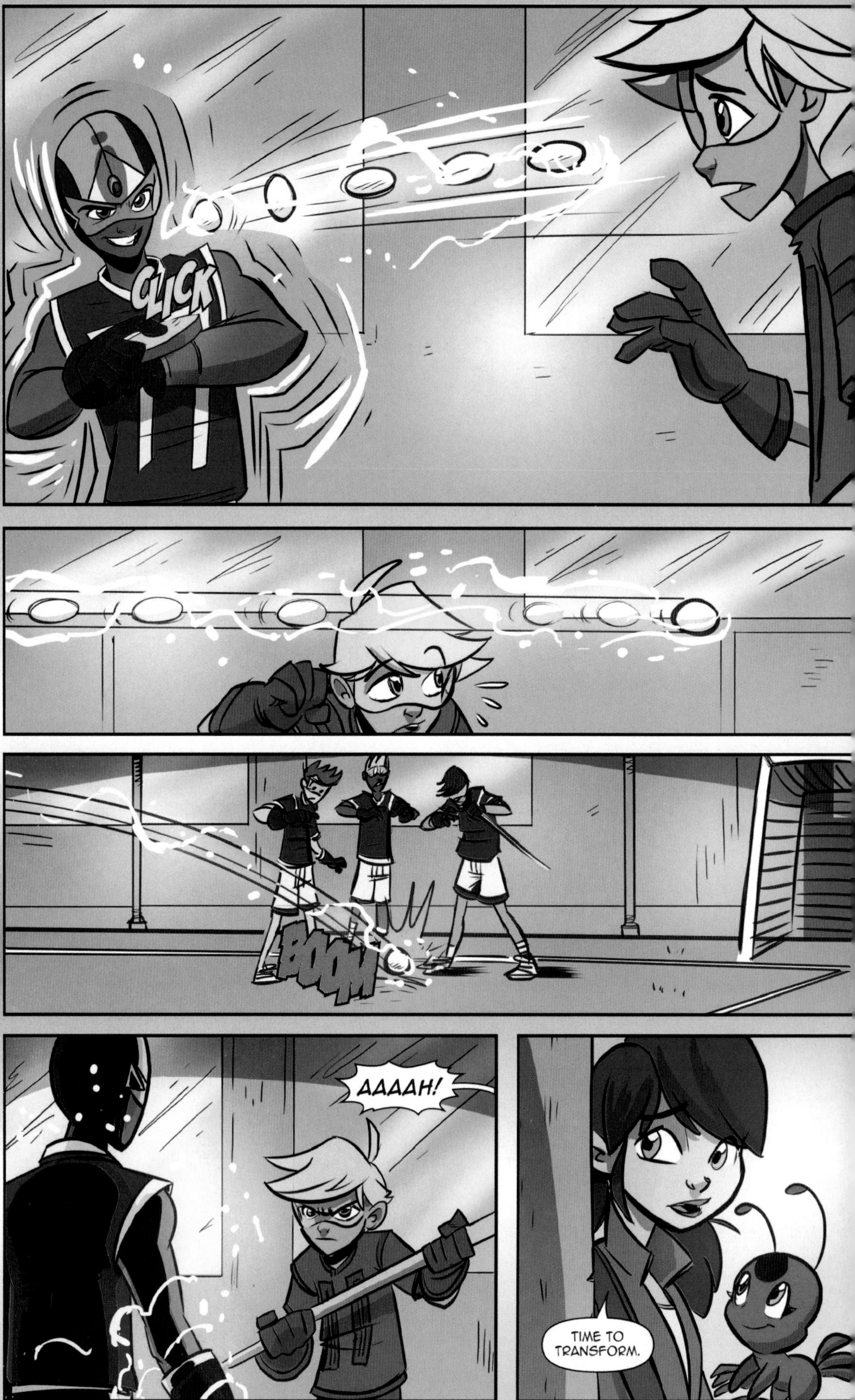
CLICK
BOOM
AAAAH!
TIME TO TRANSFORM.

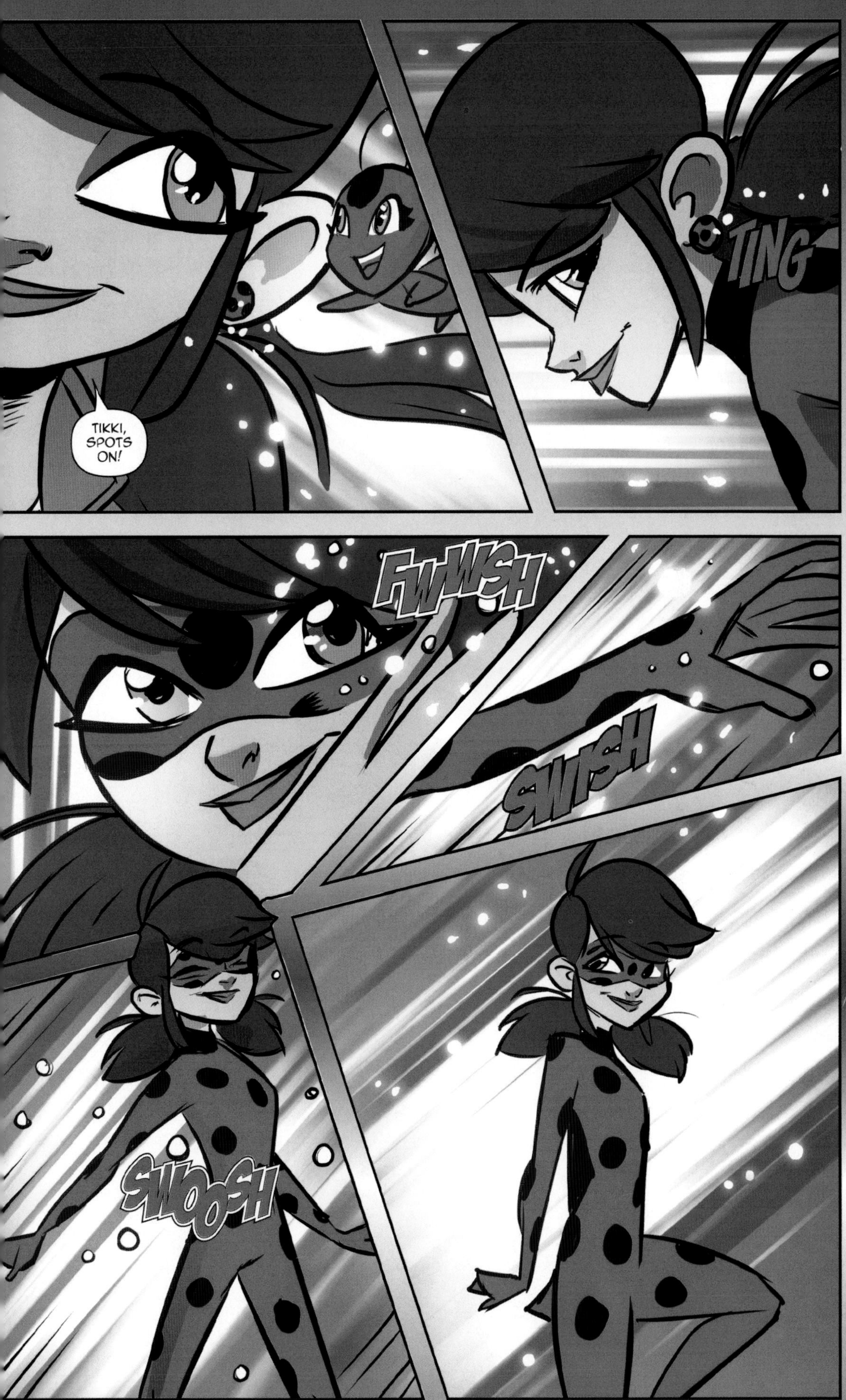
TIKKI, SPOTS ON!
TING
FWWISH
SWISH
SWOOSH

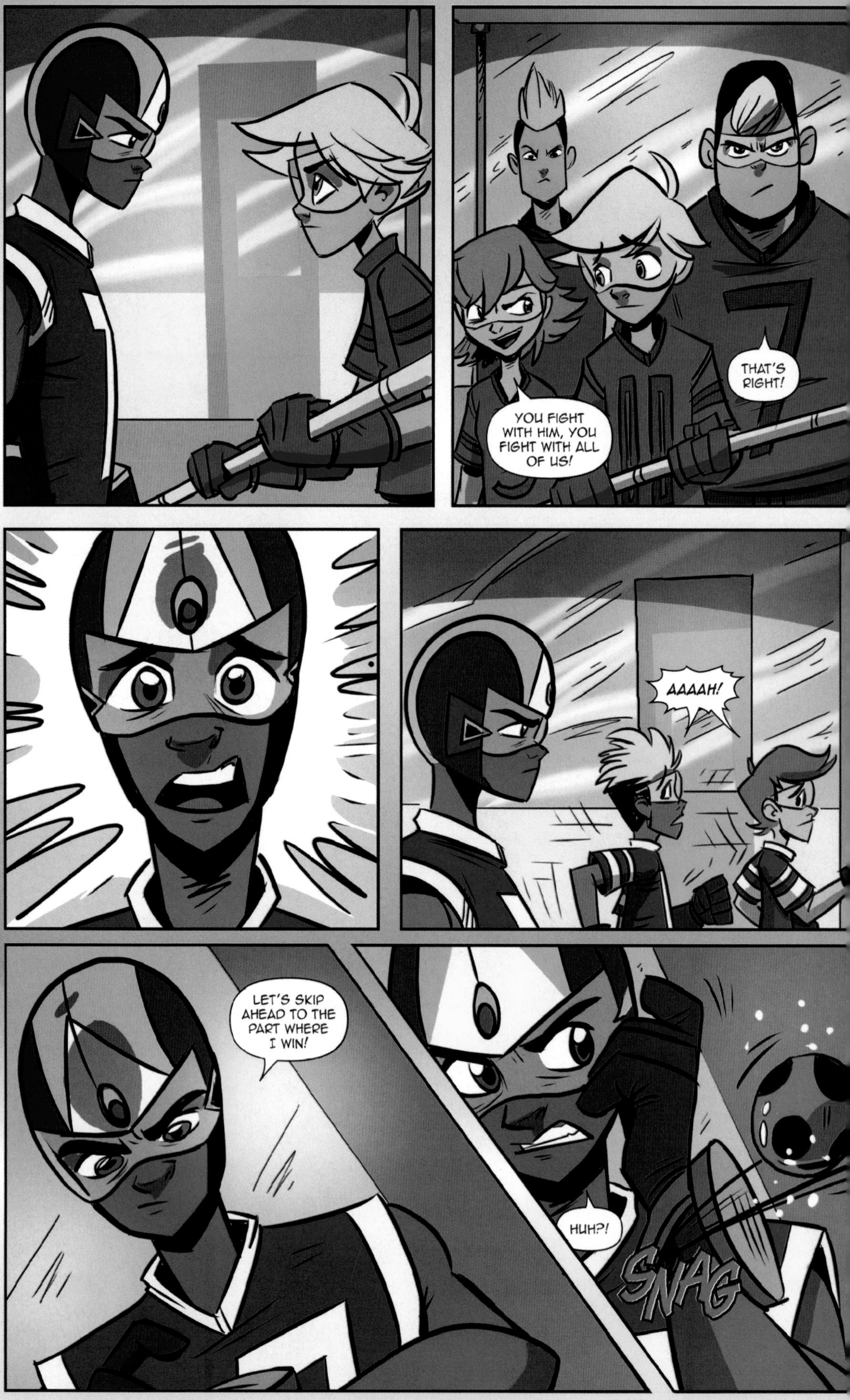
YOU FIGHT WITH HIM, YOU FIGHT WITH ALL OF US!
THAT'S RIGHT!
AAAAH!
LET'S SKIP AHEAD TO THE PART WHERE I WIN!
HUH?!
SNAG

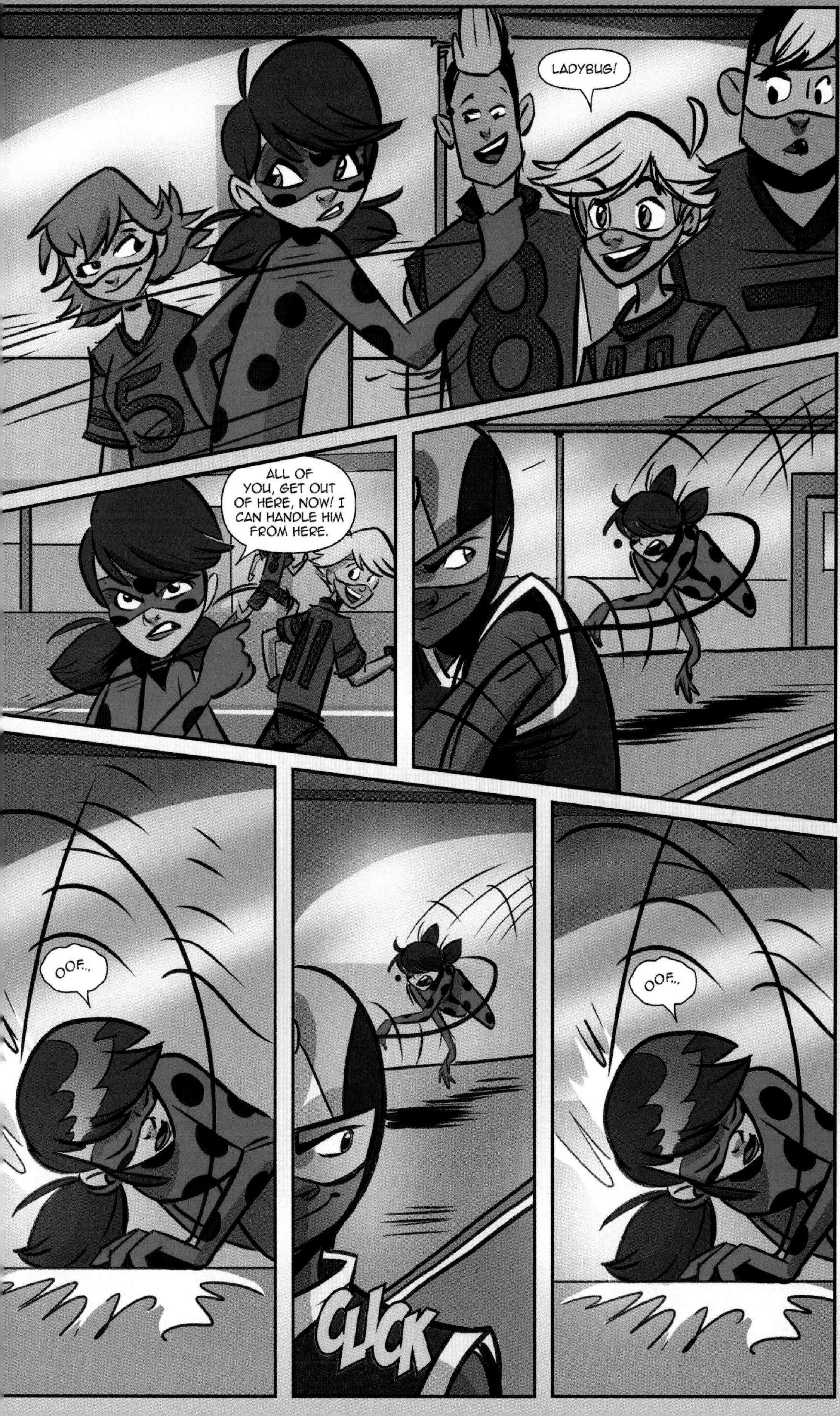
LADYBUG!
ALL OF YOU, GET OUT OF HERE, NOW! I CAN HANDLE HIM FROM HERE.
OOF...
CLICK
OOF...

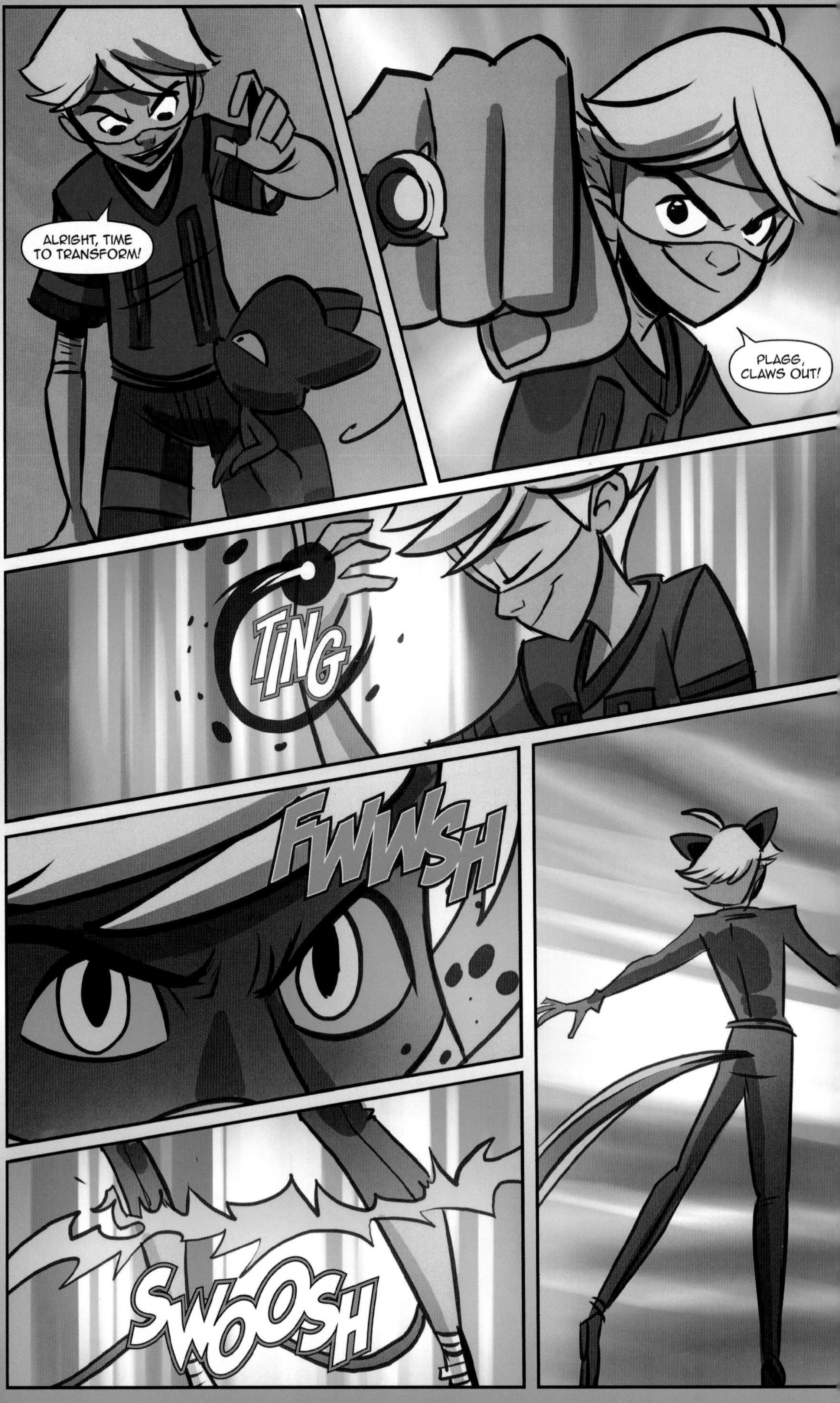
ALRIGHT, TIME TO TRANSFORM!
PLAGG, CLAWS OUT!
TING
FWWSH
SWOOSH

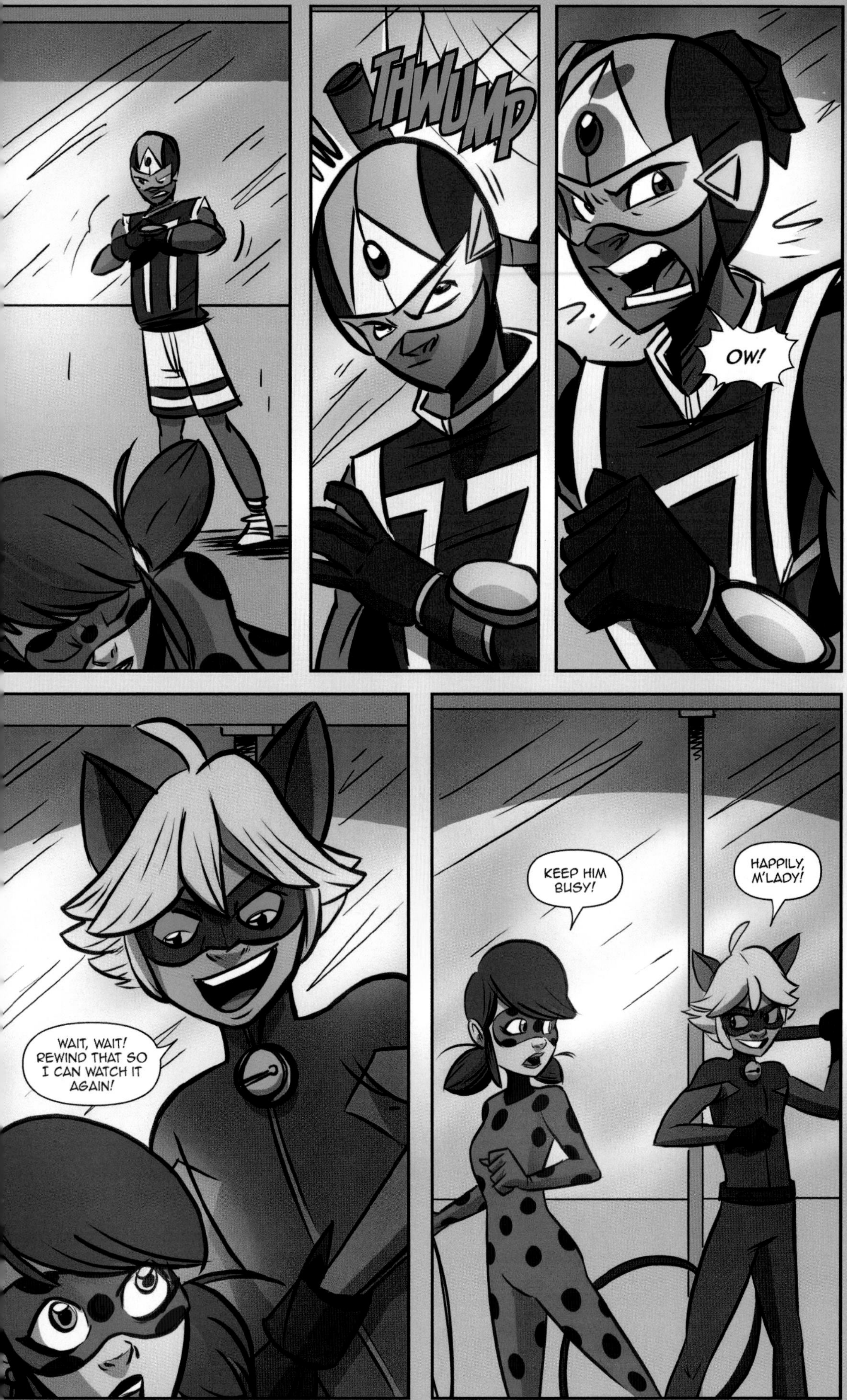
THWUMP
OW!
WAIT, WAIT! REWIND THAT SO I CAN WATCH IT AGAIN!
KEEP HIM BUSY!
HAPPILY, M'LADY!

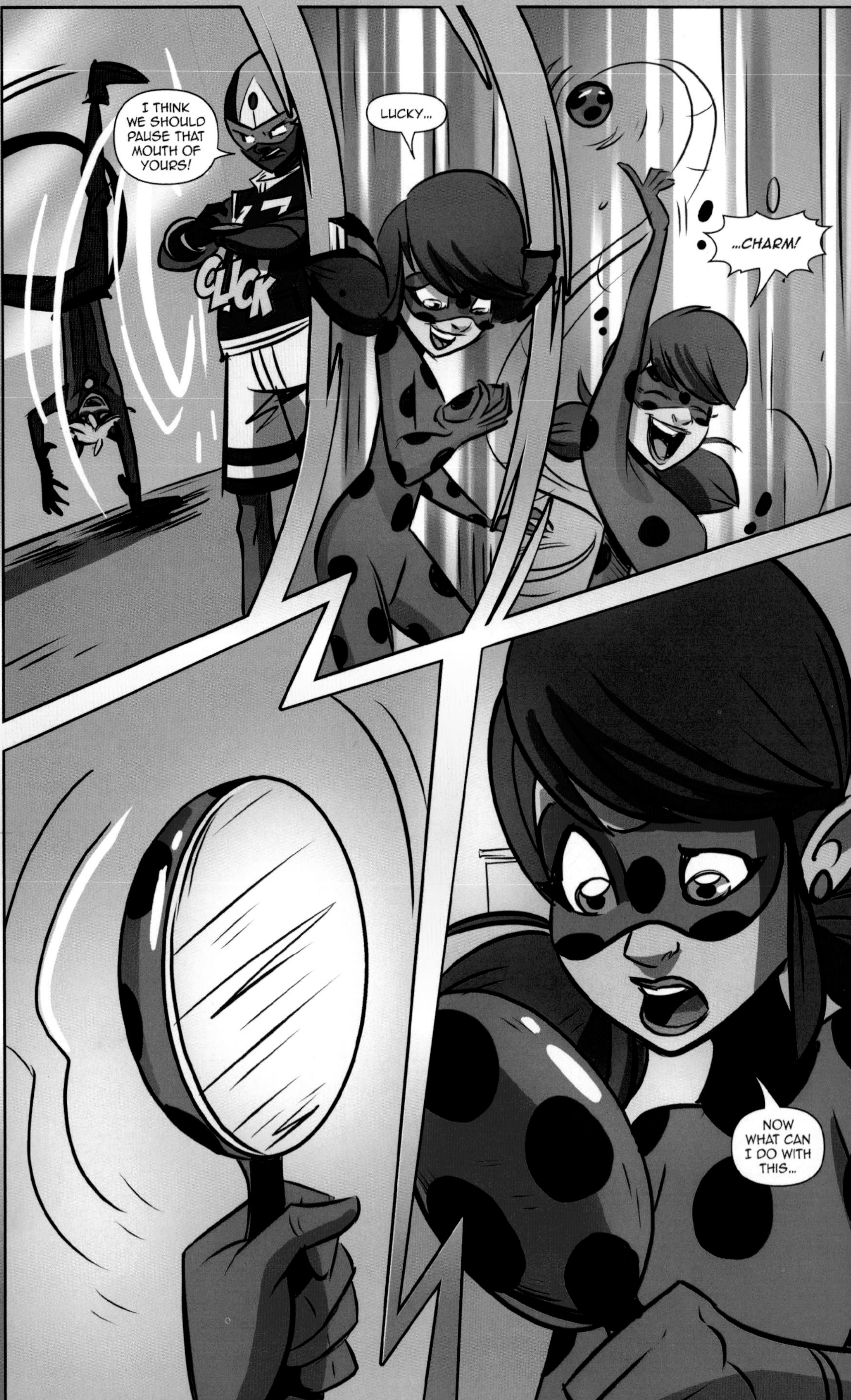
I THINK WE SHOULD PAUSE THAT MOUTH OF YOURS!
CLICK
LUCKY...
...CHARM!
NOW WHAT CAN I DO WITH THIS...

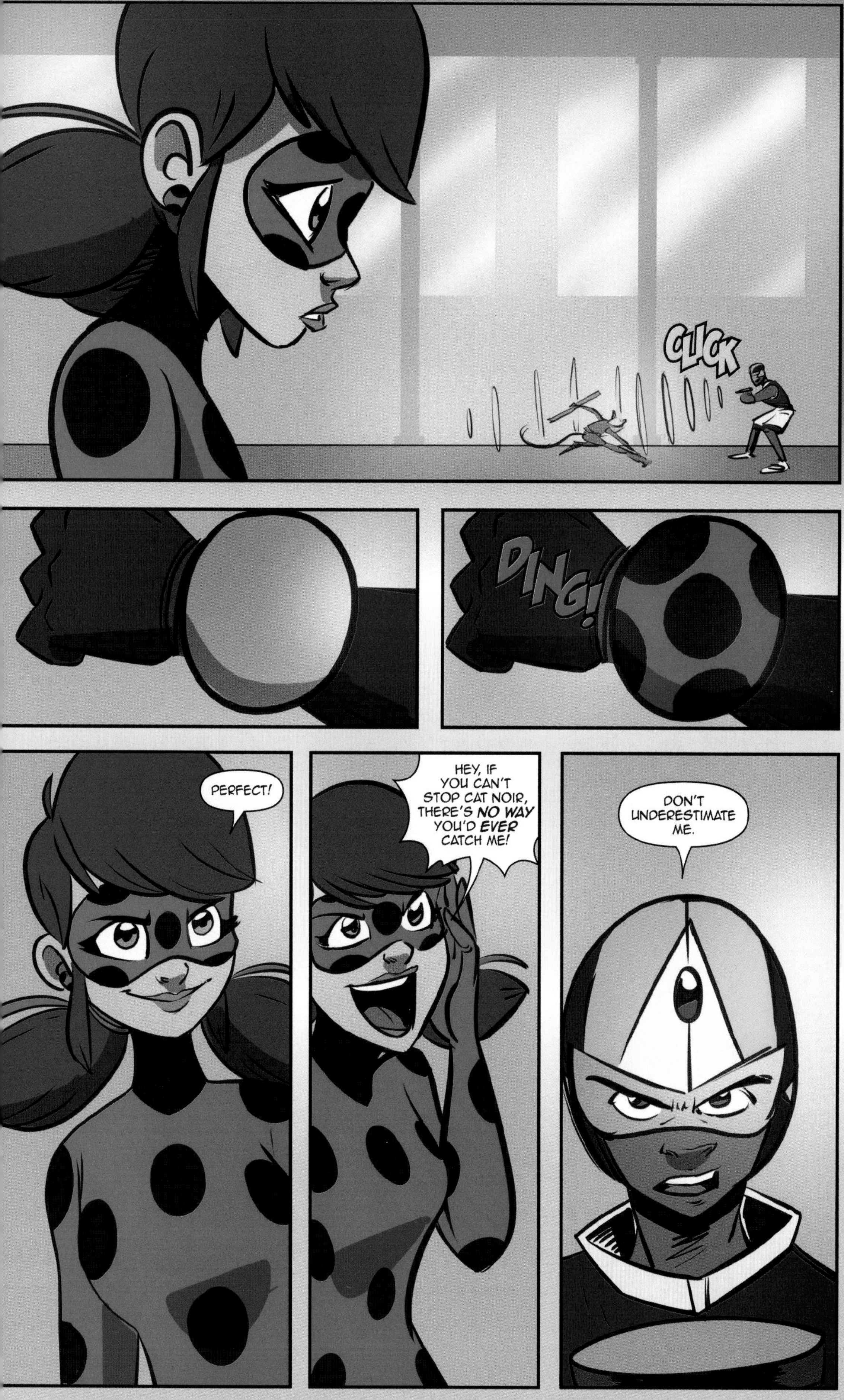
CLICK
DING!
PERFECT!
HEY, IF YOU CAN'T STOP CAT NOIR, THERE'S NO WAY YOU'D EVER CATCH ME!
DON'T UNDERESTIMATE ME.

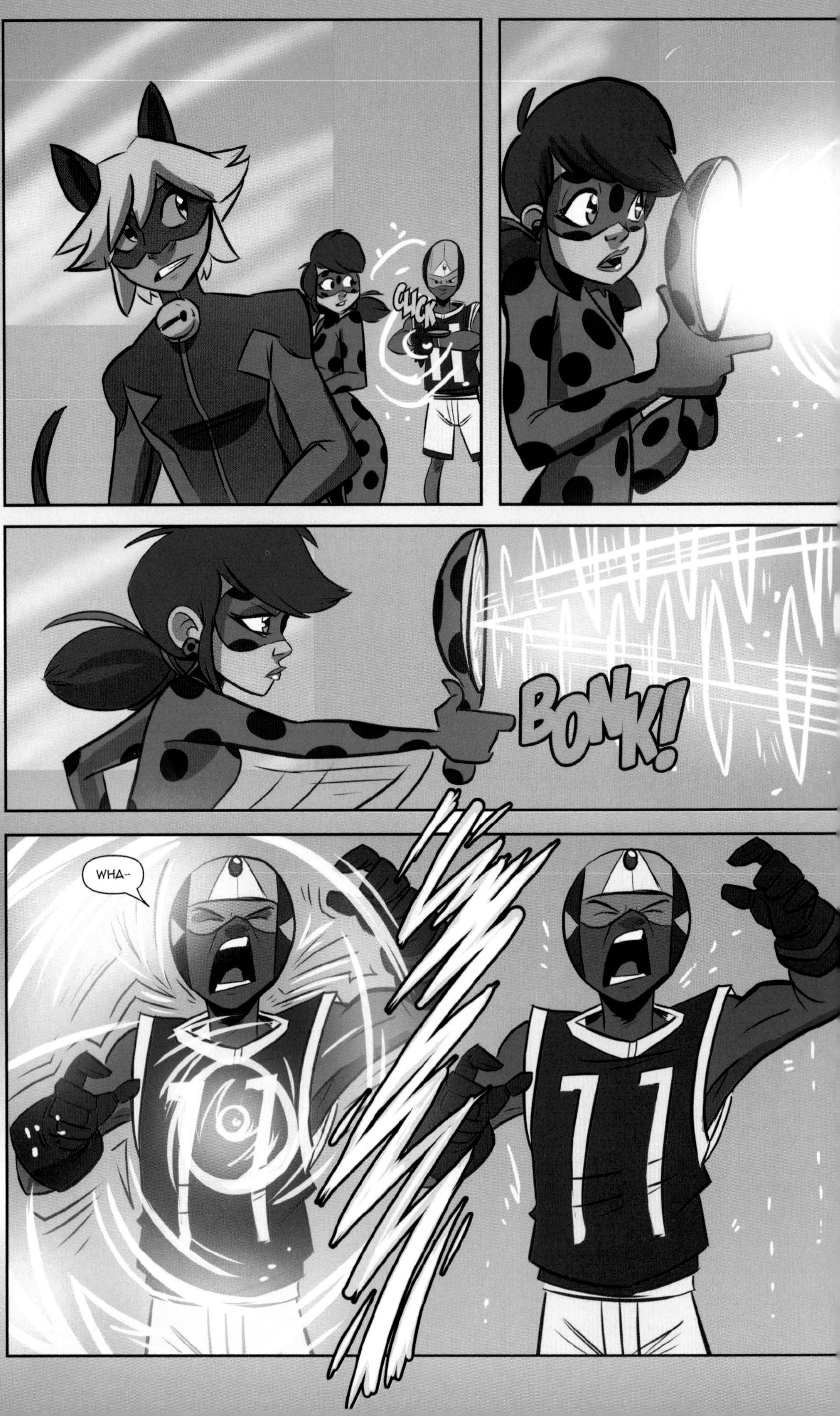
CLICK
BONK!
WHA-

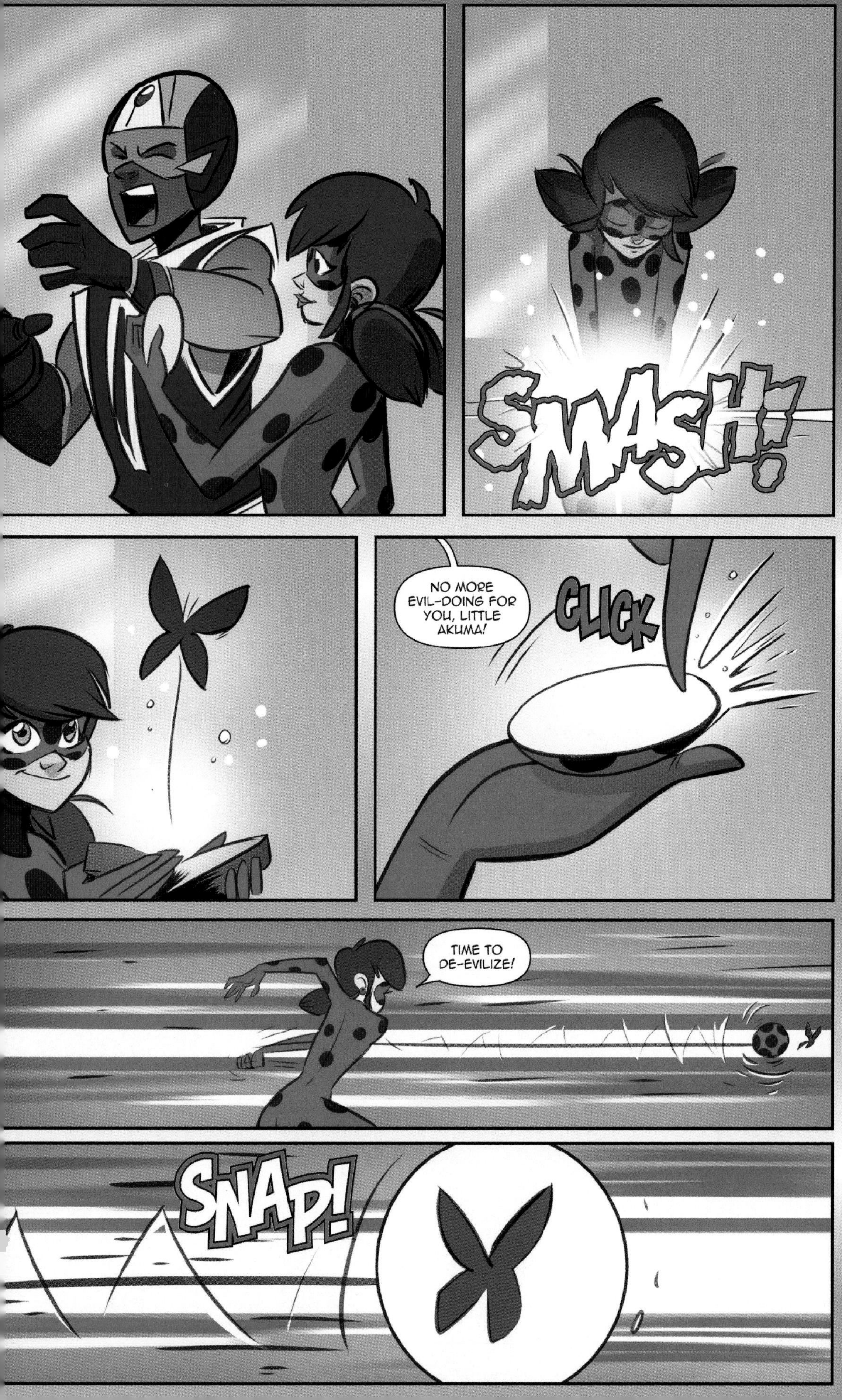
SMASH!
NO MORE EVIL-DOING FOR YOU, LITTLE AKUMA!
CLICK
TIME TO DE-EVILIZE!
SNAP!

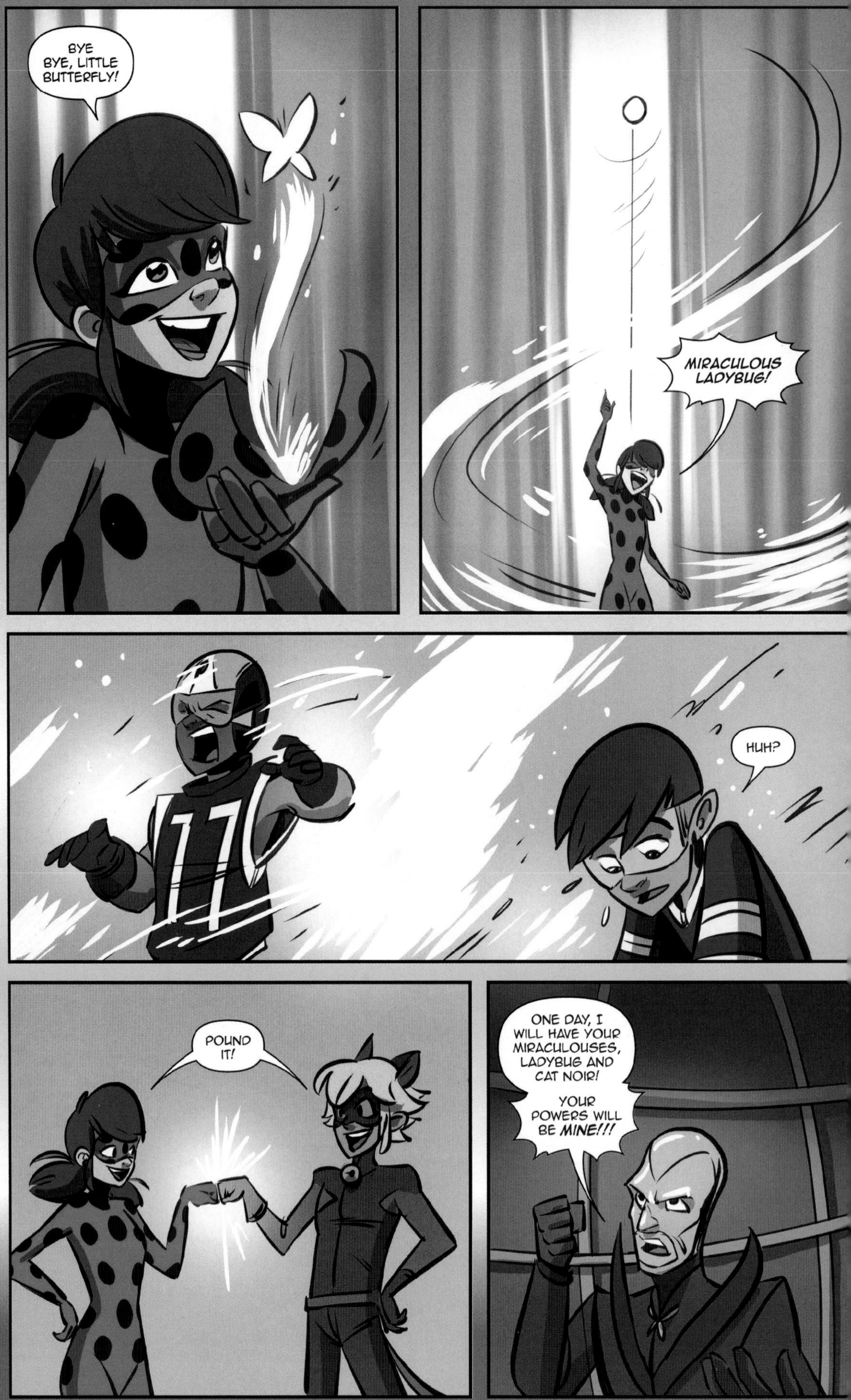
BYE BYE, LITTLE BUTTERFLY!
MIRACULOUS LADYBUG!
HUH?
POUND IT!
ONE DAY, I WILL HAVE YOUR MIRACULOUSES, LADYBUG AND CAT NOIR!
YOUR POWERS WILL BE *MINE!!!*

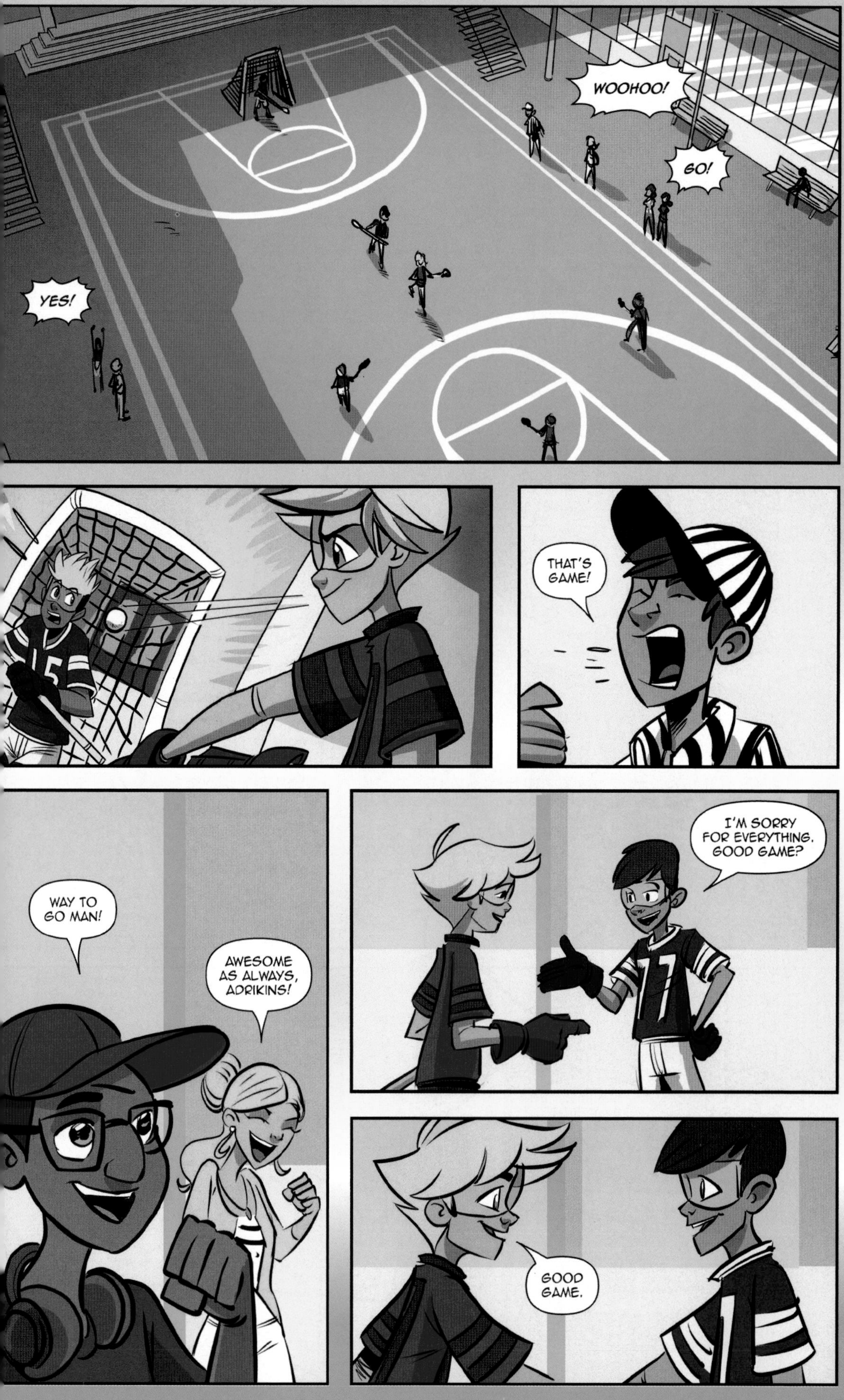
WOOHOO!
GO!
YES!
THAT'S GAME!
WAY TO GO MAN!
AWESOME AS ALWAYS, ADRIKINS!
I'M SORRY FOR EVERYTHING. GOOD GAME?
GOOD GAME.

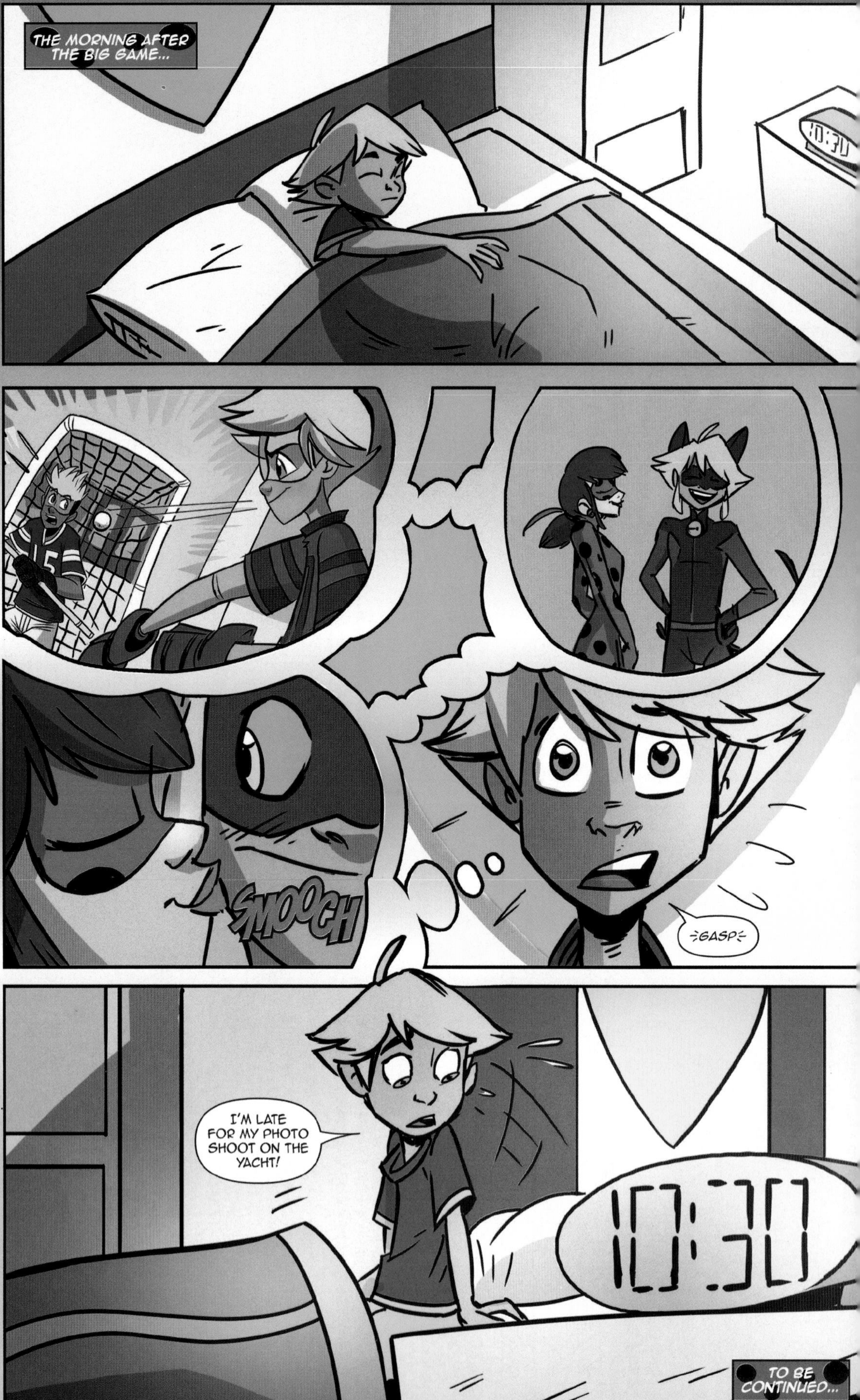
THE MORNING AFTER THE BIG GAME...
10:30
15
SMOOCH
GASP
I'M LATE FOR MY PHOTO SHOOT ON THE YACHT!
10:30
TO BE CONTINUED...

CHAPTER 2:
THE TRASH KRAKKEN:
SILURUS

Created by: Thomas Astruc
Written by: Thomas Astruc, Mélanie Duval, Fred Lenoir, Sébastien
Thibaudeau & Bryan Seaton
Art by: Brian Hess
Letters by: Justin Birch
Colors by: Darné Lang
Editing by: Nicole D'Andria & Bryan Seaton

**Comic art style based on the
Webisode art style of Angie Nasca**

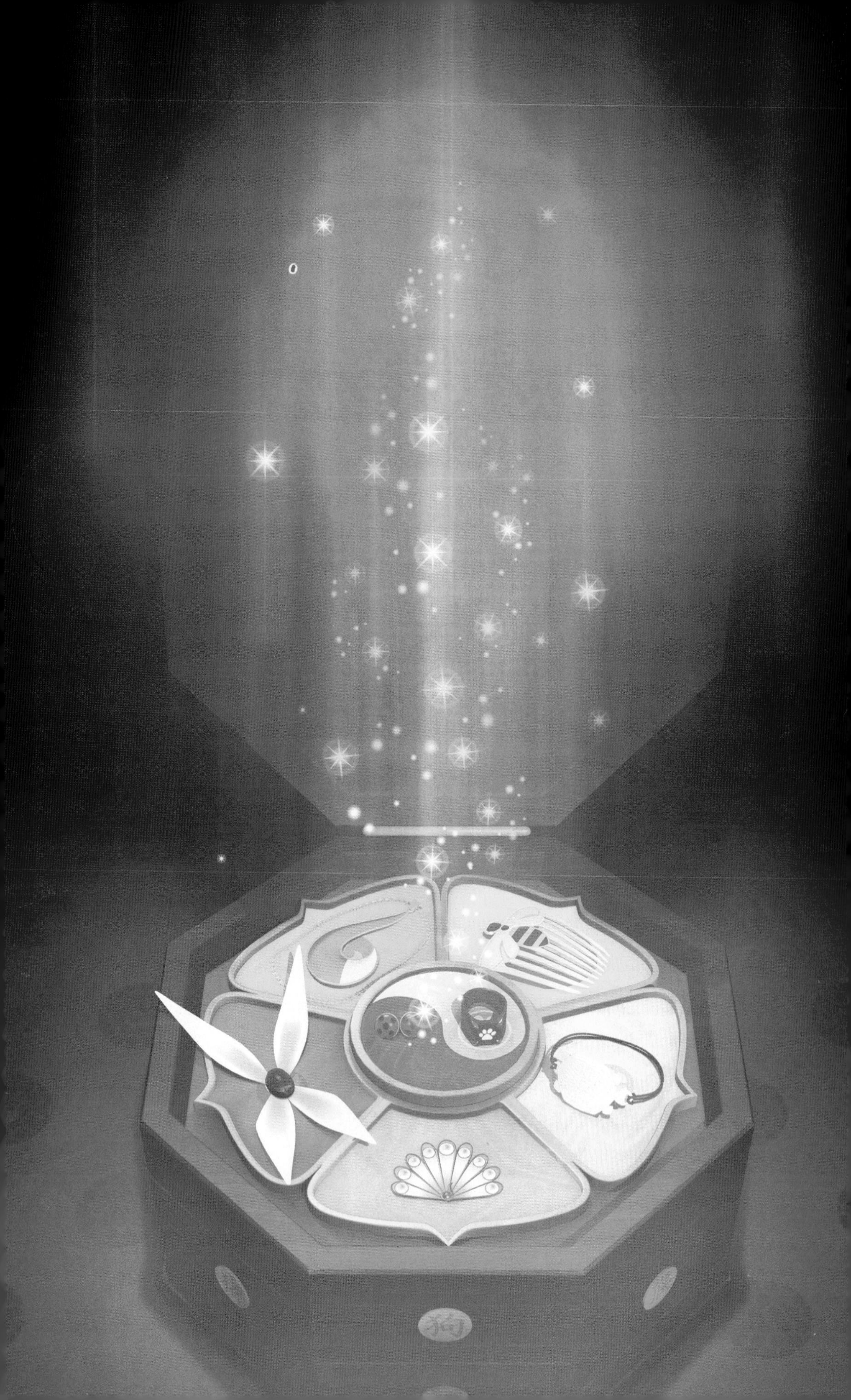
狗

The Trash Krakken
Silurus

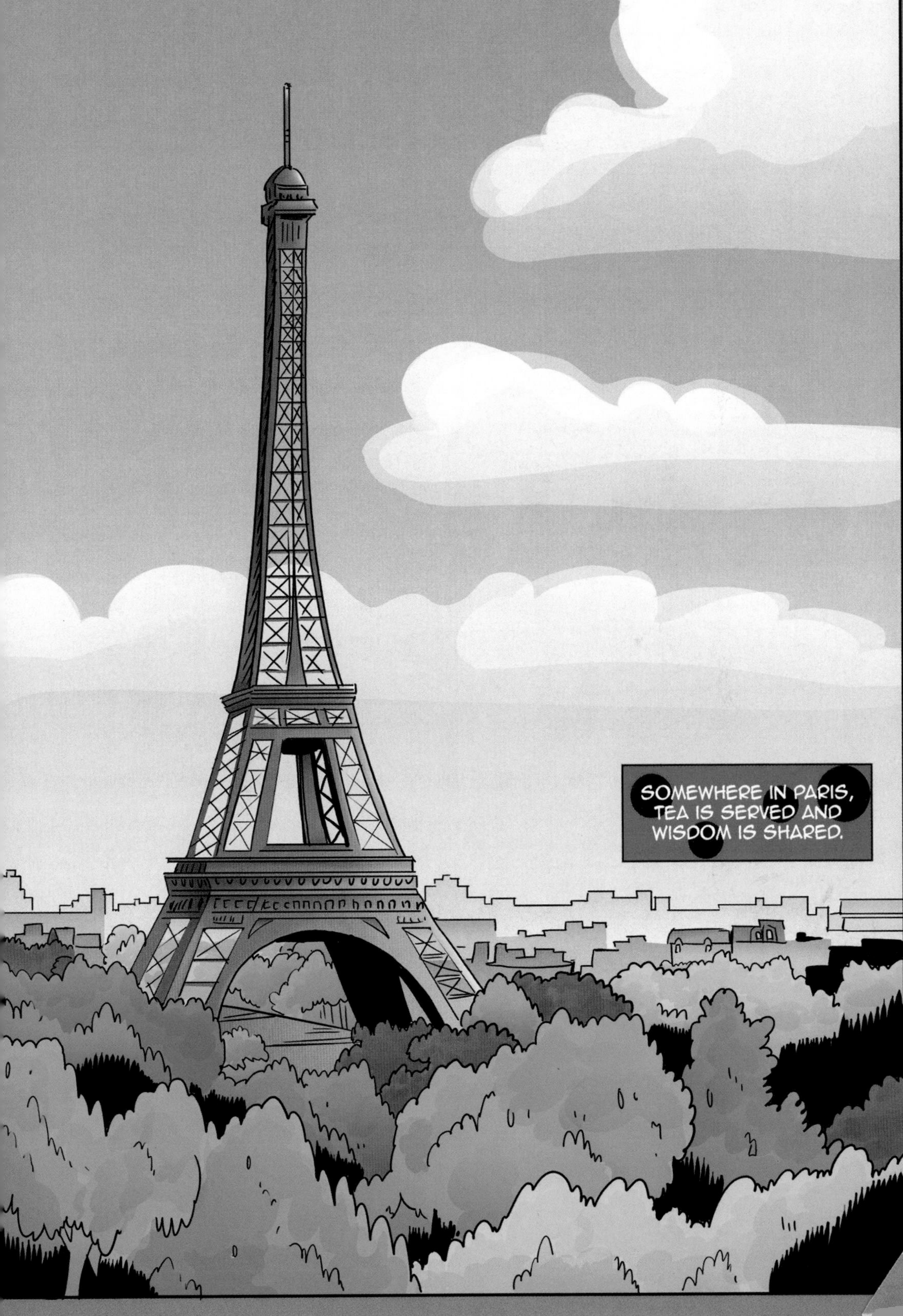
SOMEWHERE IN PARIS, TEA IS SERVED AND WISDOM IS SHARED.

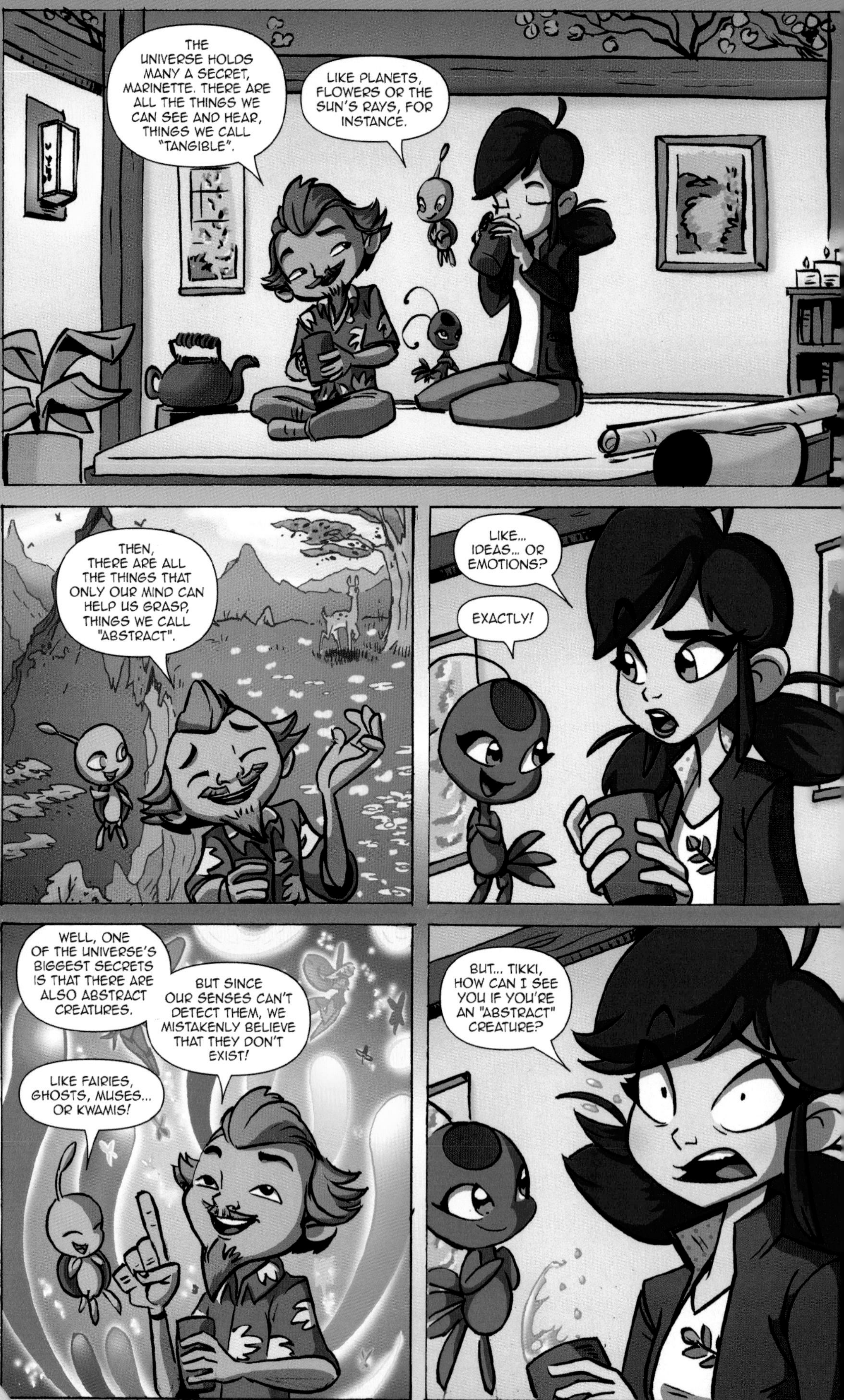

THE UNIVERSE HOLDS MANY A SECRET, MARINETTE. THERE ARE ALL THE THINGS WE CAN SEE AND HEAR, THINGS WE CALL "TANGIBLE".
LIKE PLANETS, FLOWERS OR THE SUN'S RAYS, FOR INSTANCE.
THEN, THERE ARE ALL THE THINGS THAT ONLY OUR MIND CAN HELP US GRASP, THINGS WE CALL "ABSTRACT".
LIKE... IDEAS... OR EMOTIONS?
EXACTLY!
WELL, ONE OF THE UNIVERSE'S BIGGEST SECRETS IS THAT THERE ARE ALSO ABSTRACT CREATURES.
BUT SINCE OUR SENSES CAN'T DETECT THEM, WE MISTAKENLY BELIEVE THAT THEY DON'T EXIST!
LIKE FAIRIES, GHOSTS, MUSES... OR KWAMIS!
BUT... TIKKI, HOW CAN I SEE YOU IF YOU'RE AN "ABSTRACT" CREATURE?

"IN THE PAST, WE USED TO TRAVEL ACROSS THE UNIVERSE WITHOUT BEING ABLE TO INTERACT WITH OTHER LIVING BEINGS."

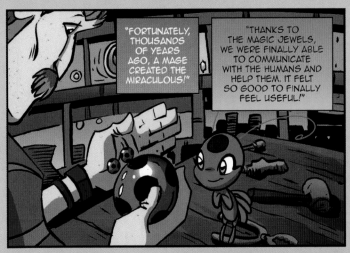

"FORTUNATELY, THOUSANDS OF YEARS AGO, A MAGE CREATED THE MIRACULOUS!"

"THANKS TO THE MAGIC JEWELS, WE WERE FINALLY ABLE TO COMMUNICATE WITH THE HUMANS AND HELP THEM. IT FELT SO GOOD TO FINALLY FEEL USEFUL!"

"YOU NEED TO UNDERSTAND THAT EVERY TIME SOMETHING NEW APPEARS IN THE UNIVERSE, LIKE LOVE, BEAUTY OR EVEN MATHEMATICS, A KWAMI IS FORMED."

"FOR INSTANCE, TIKKI IS THE KWAMI OF CREATION."

"WHICH MEANS THAT SHE APPEARED IN THE BEGINNING."

"TIKKI WAS THE VERY FIRST KWAMI!"

"WOW, THAT'S AMAZING! YOU REALLY DON'T LOOK YOUR AGE, TIKKI."

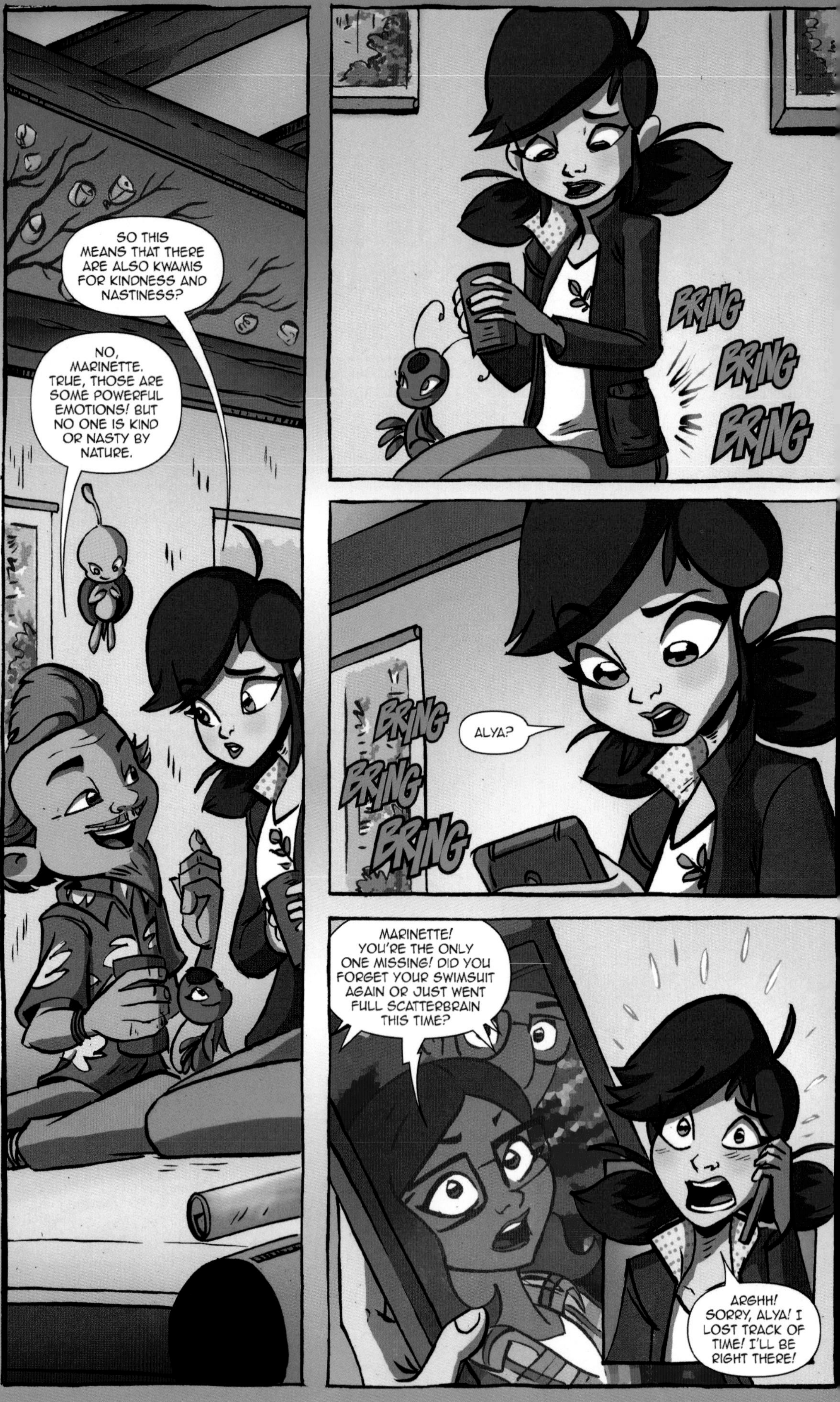
SO THIS MEANS THAT THERE ARE ALSO KWAMIS FOR KINDNESS AND NASTINESS?
NO, MARINETTE. TRUE, THOSE ARE SOME POWERFUL EMOTIONS! BUT NO ONE IS KIND OR NASTY BY NATURE.
BRING
BRING
BRING
BRING
BRING
BRING
ALYA?
MARINETTE! YOU'RE THE ONLY ONE MISSING! DID YOU FORGET YOUR SWIMSUIT AGAIN OR JUST WENT FULL SCATTERBRAIN THIS TIME?
ARGHH! SORRY, ALYA! I LOST TRACK OF TIME! I'LL BE RIGHT THERE!

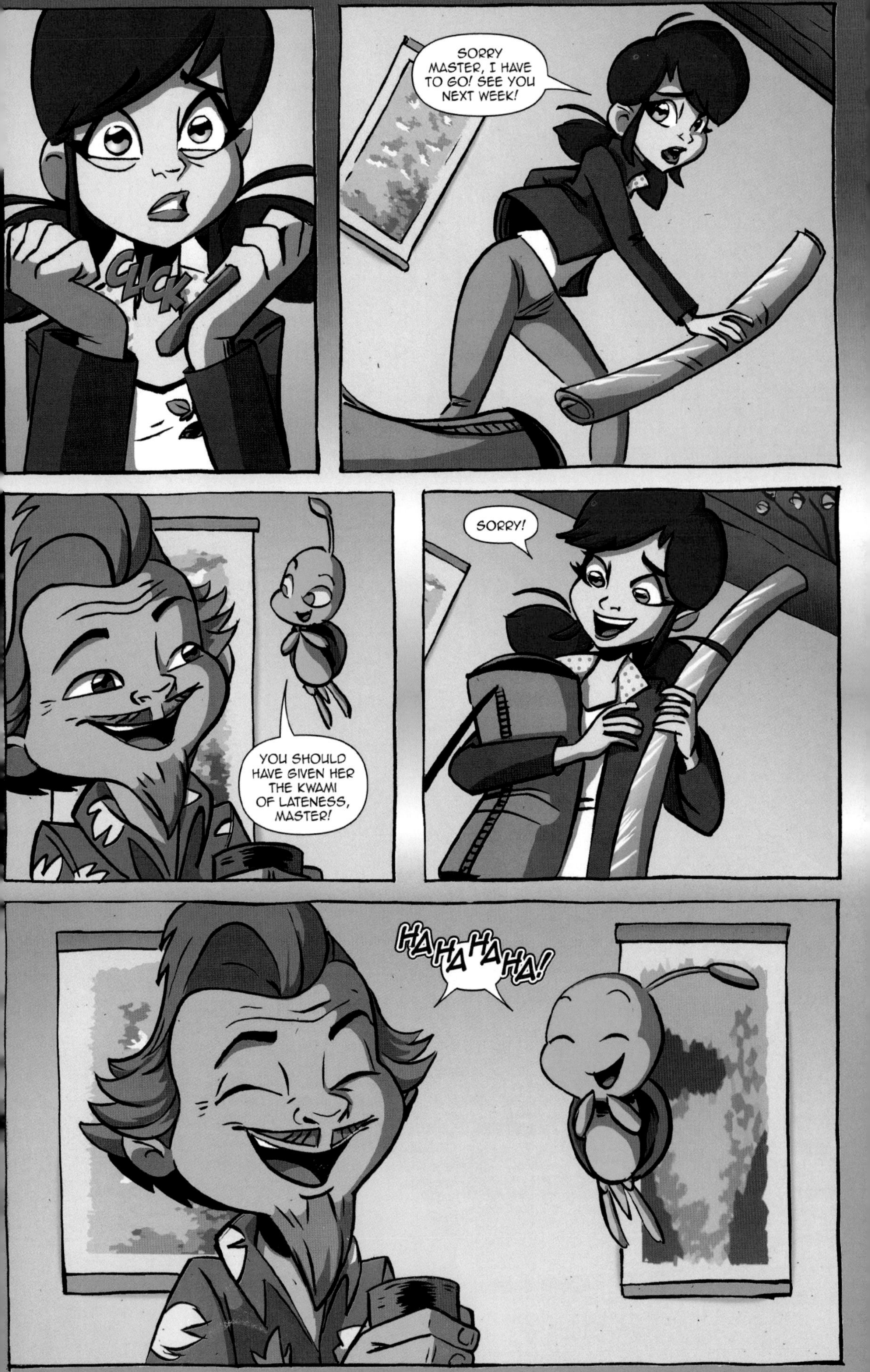
CLICK
SORRY MASTER, I HAVE TO GO! SEE YOU NEXT WEEK!
YOU SHOULD HAVE GIVEN HER THE KWAMI OF LATENESS, MASTER!
SORRY!
HAHA HAHA!

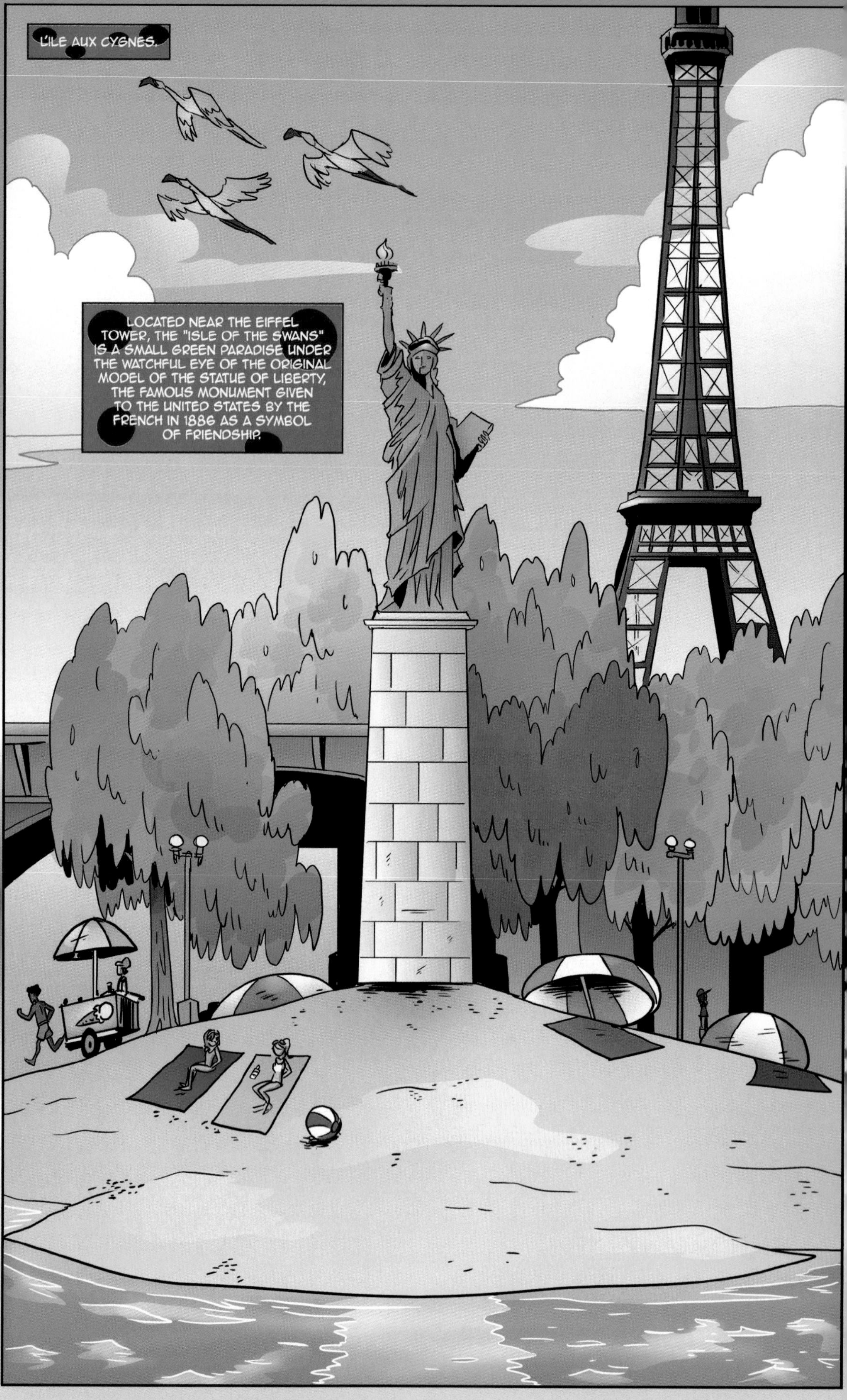
L'ILE AUX CYGNES.
LOCATED NEAR THE EIFFEL TOWER, THE "ISLE OF THE SWANS" IS A SMALL GREEN PARADISE UNDER THE WATCHFUL EYE OF THE ORIGINAL MODEL OF THE STATUE OF LIBERTY, THE FAMOUS MONUMENT GIVEN TO THE UNITED STATES BY THE FRENCH IN 1886 AS A SYMBOL OF FRIENDSHIP.

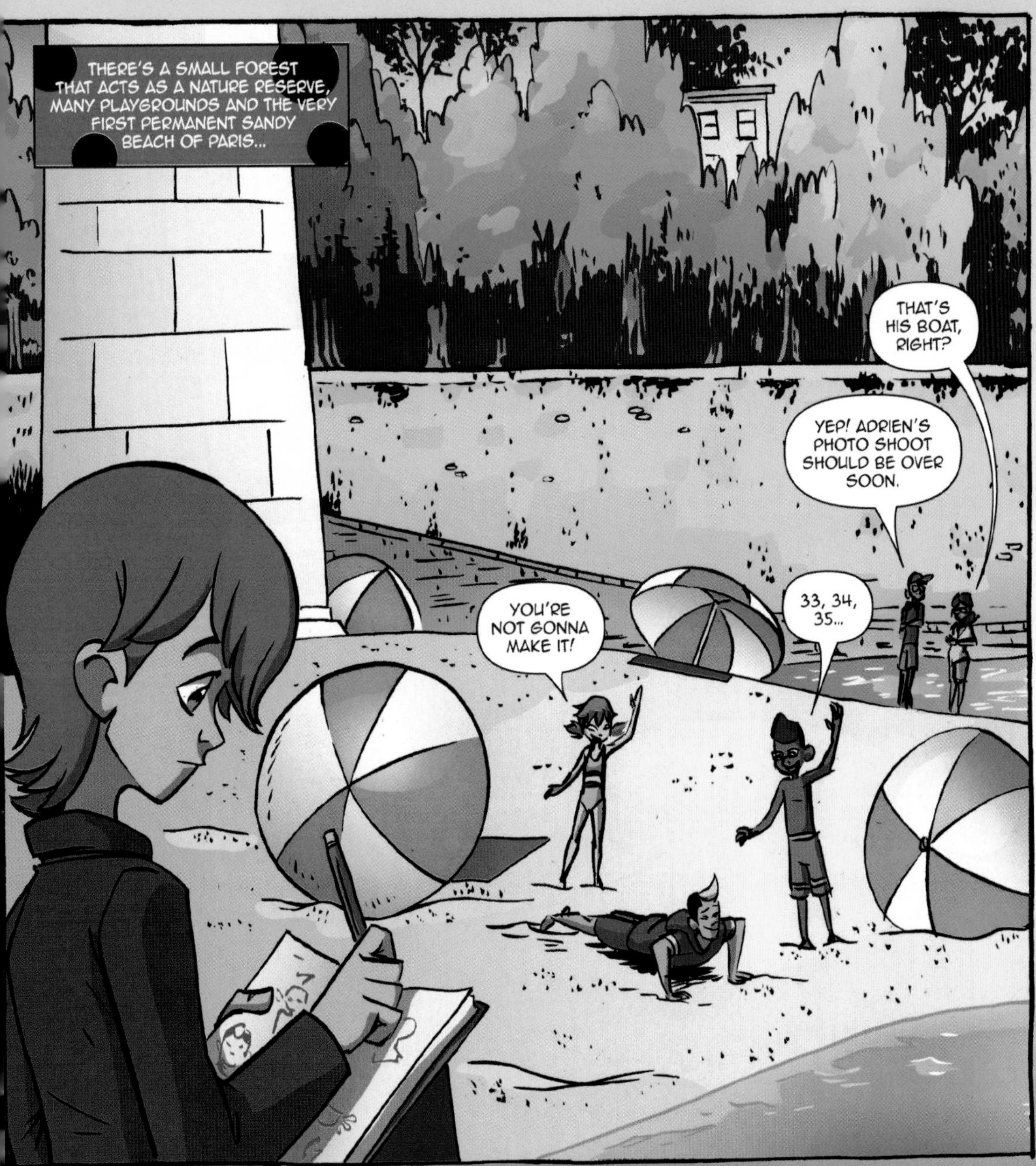
THERE'S A SMALL FOREST THAT ACTS AS A NATURE RESERVE, MANY PLAYGROUNDS AND THE VERY FIRST PERMANENT SANDY BEACH OF PARIS...
THAT'S HIS BOAT, RIGHT?
YEP! ADRIEN'S PHOTO SHOOT SHOULD BE OVER SOON.
YOU'RE NOT GONNA MAKE IT!
33, 34, 35...

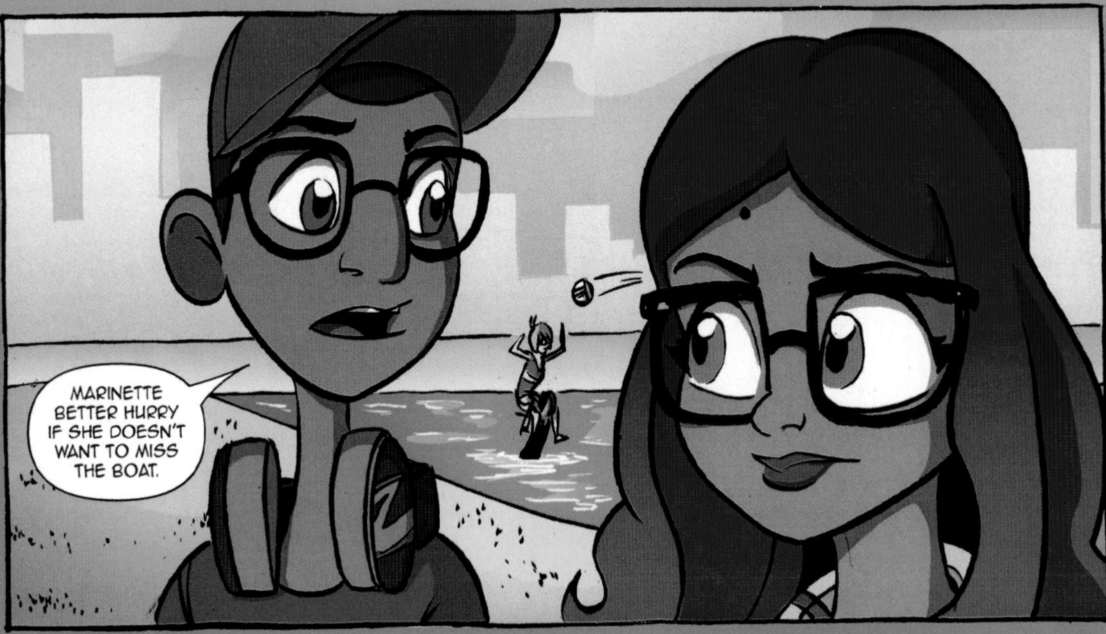
MARINETTE BETTER HURRY IF SHE DOESN'T WANT TO MISS THE BOAT.

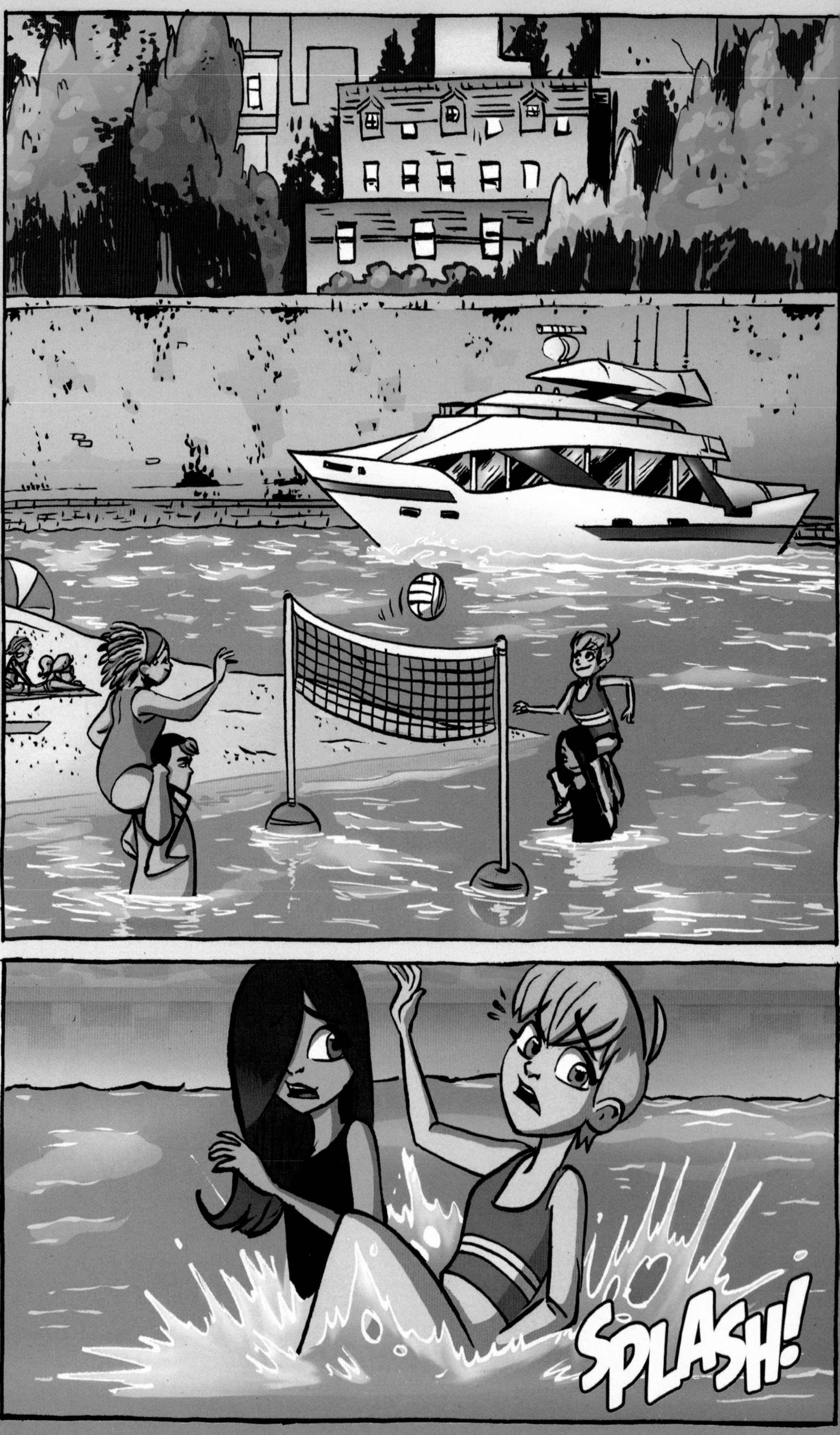
SPLASH!

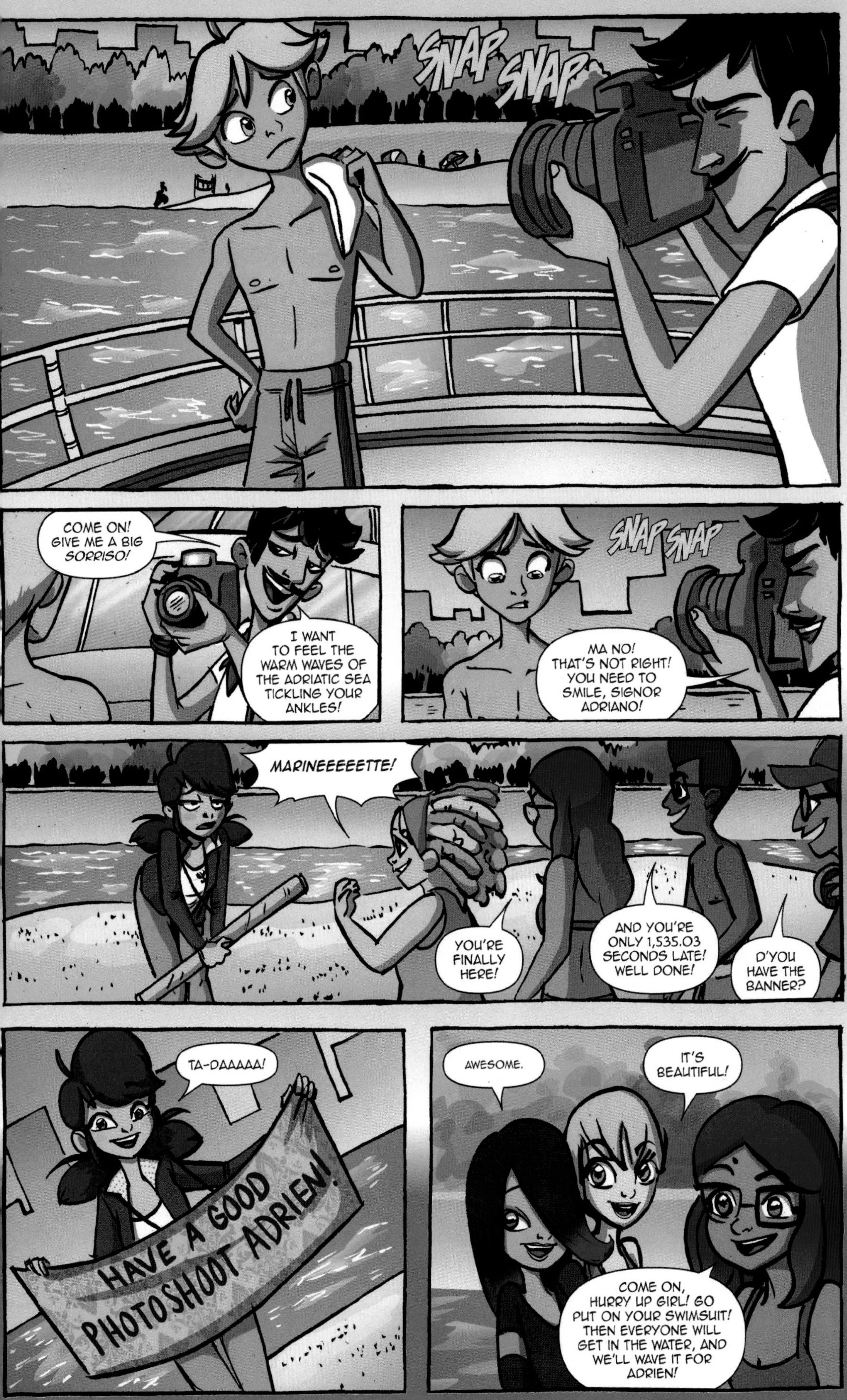
SNAP SNAP
COME ON! GIVE ME A BIG SORRISO!
I WANT TO FEEL THE WARM WAVES OF THE ADRIATIC SEA TICKLING YOUR ANKLES!
SNAP SNAP
MA NO! THAT'S NOT RIGHT! YOU NEED TO SMILE, SIGNOR ADRIANO!
MARINEEEEETTE!
YOU'RE FINALLY HERE!
AND YOU'RE ONLY 1,535.03 SECONDS LATE! WELL DONE!
D'YOU HAVE THE BANNER?
TA-DAAAAA!
HAVE A GOOD PHOTOSHOOT ADRIEN!
AWESOME.
IT'S BEAUTIFUL!
COME ON, HURRY UP GIRL! GO PUT ON YOUR SWIMSUIT! THEN EVERYONE WILL GET IN THE WATER, AND WE'LL WAVE IT FOR ADRIEN!

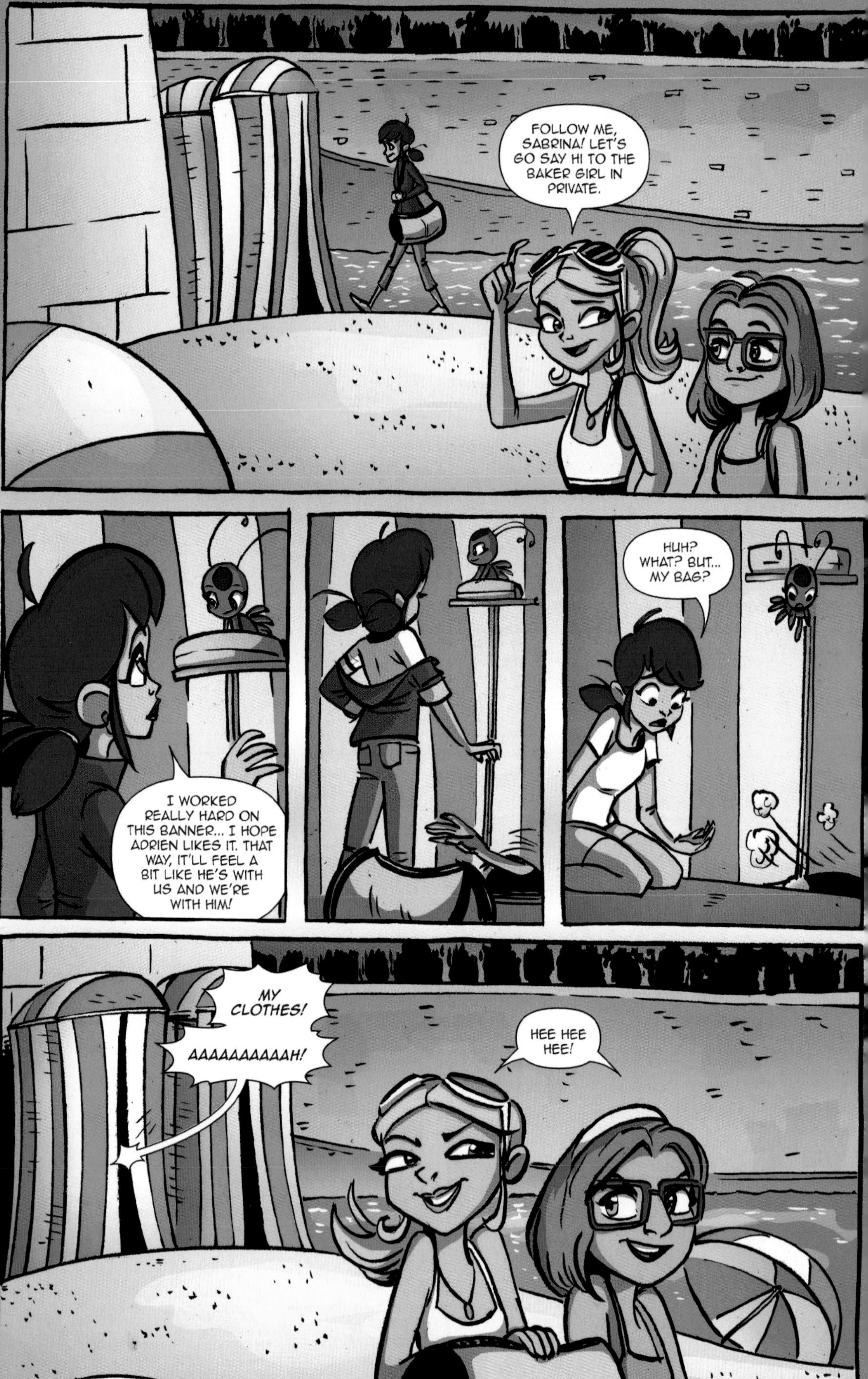
FOLLOW ME, SABRINA! LET'S GO SAY HI TO THE BAKER GIRL IN PRIVATE.
I WORKED REALLY HARD ON THIS BANNER... I HOPE ADRIEN LIKES IT. THAT WAY, IT'LL FEEL A BIT LIKE HE'S WITH US AND WE'RE WITH HIM!
HUH? WHAT? BUT... MY BAG?
MY CLOTHES!
AAAAAAAAAAH!
HEE HEE HEE!

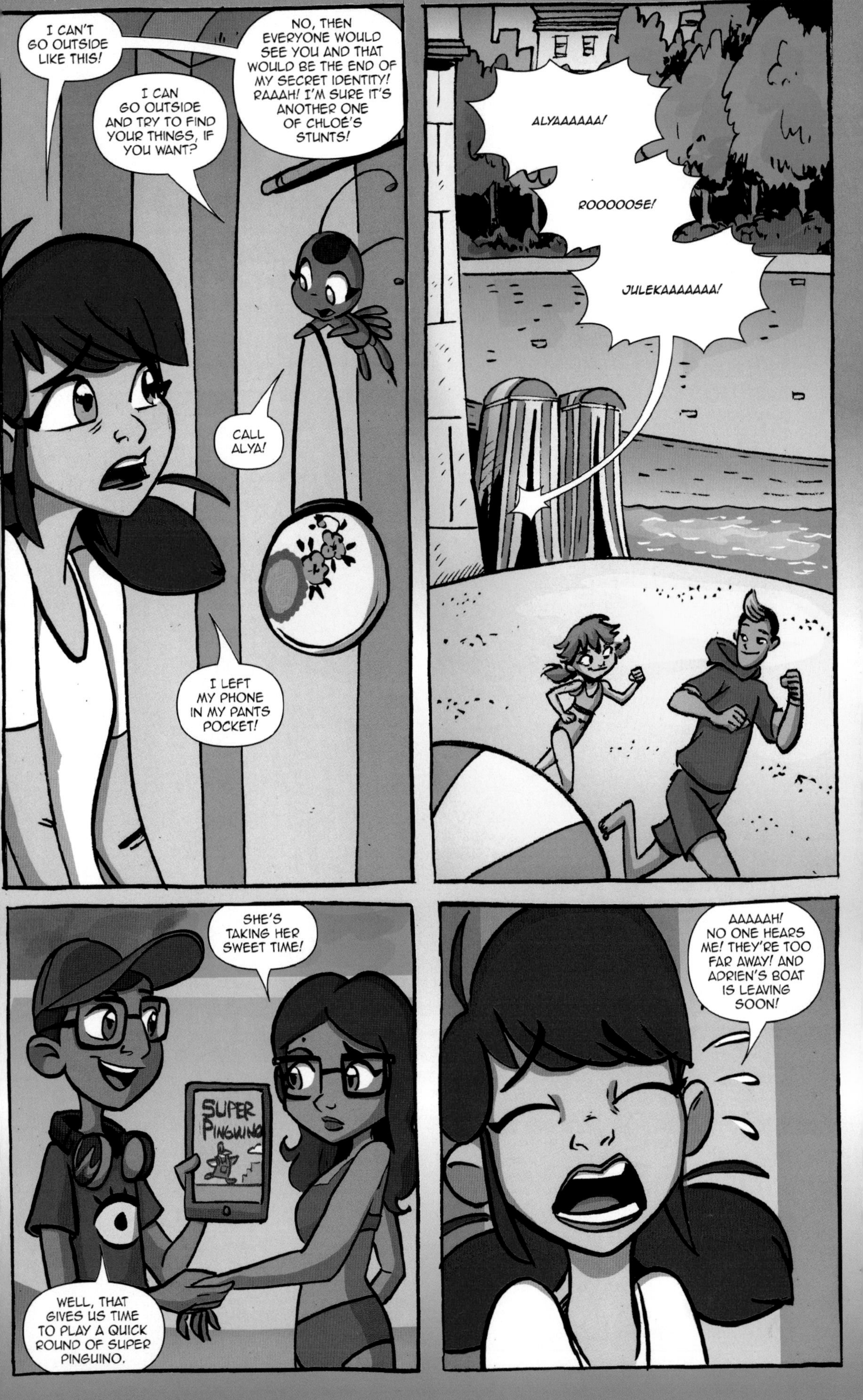
I CAN'T GO OUTSIDE LIKE THIS!
NO, THEN EVERYONE WOULD SEE YOU AND THAT WOULD BE THE END OF MY SECRET IDENTITY! RAAAH! I'M SURE IT'S ANOTHER ONE OF CHLOÉ'S STUNTS!
I CAN GO OUTSIDE AND TRY TO FIND YOUR THINGS, IF YOU WANT?
CALL ALYA!
I LEFT MY PHONE IN MY PANTS POCKET!
ALYAAAAAA!
ROOOOOSE!
JULEKAAAAAAA!
SHE'S TAKING HER SWEET TIME!
SUPER PINGUINO
WELL, THAT GIVES US TIME TO PLAY A QUICK ROUND OF SUPER PINGUINO.
AAAAAH! NO ONE HEARS ME! THEY'RE TOO FAR AWAY! AND ADRIEN'S BOAT IS LEAVING SOON!

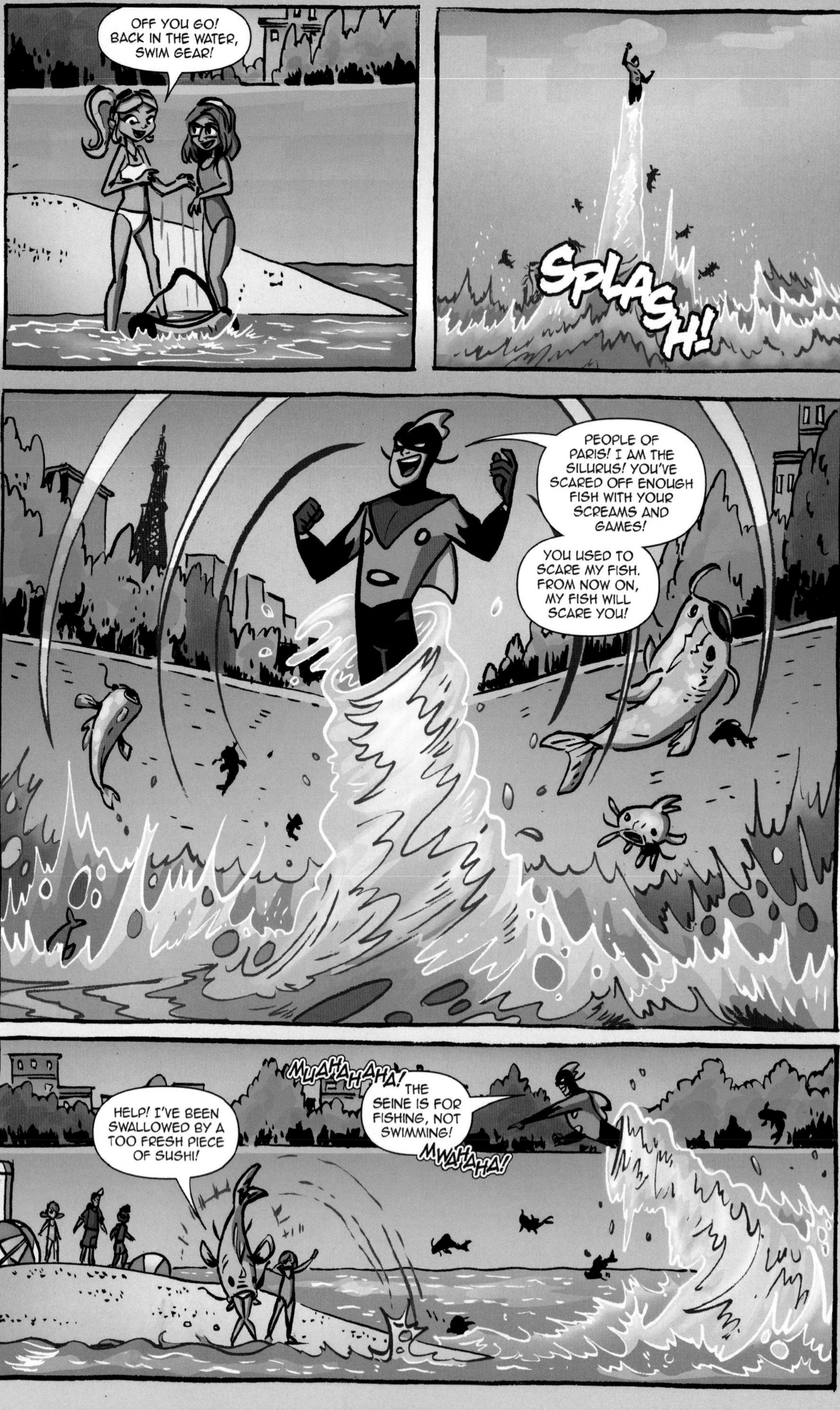
OFF YOU GO! BACK IN THE WATER, SWIM GEAR!
SPLASH!
PEOPLE OF PARIS! I AM THE SILURUS! YOU'VE SCARED OFF ENOUGH FISH WITH YOUR SCREAMS AND GAMES!
YOU USED TO SCARE MY FISH. FROM NOW ON, MY FISH WILL SCARE YOU!
HELP! I'VE BEEN SWALLOWED BY A TOO FRESH PIECE OF SUSHI!
MUAHAHAHA!
THE SEINE IS FOR FISHING, NOT SWIMMING!
MWAHAHA!

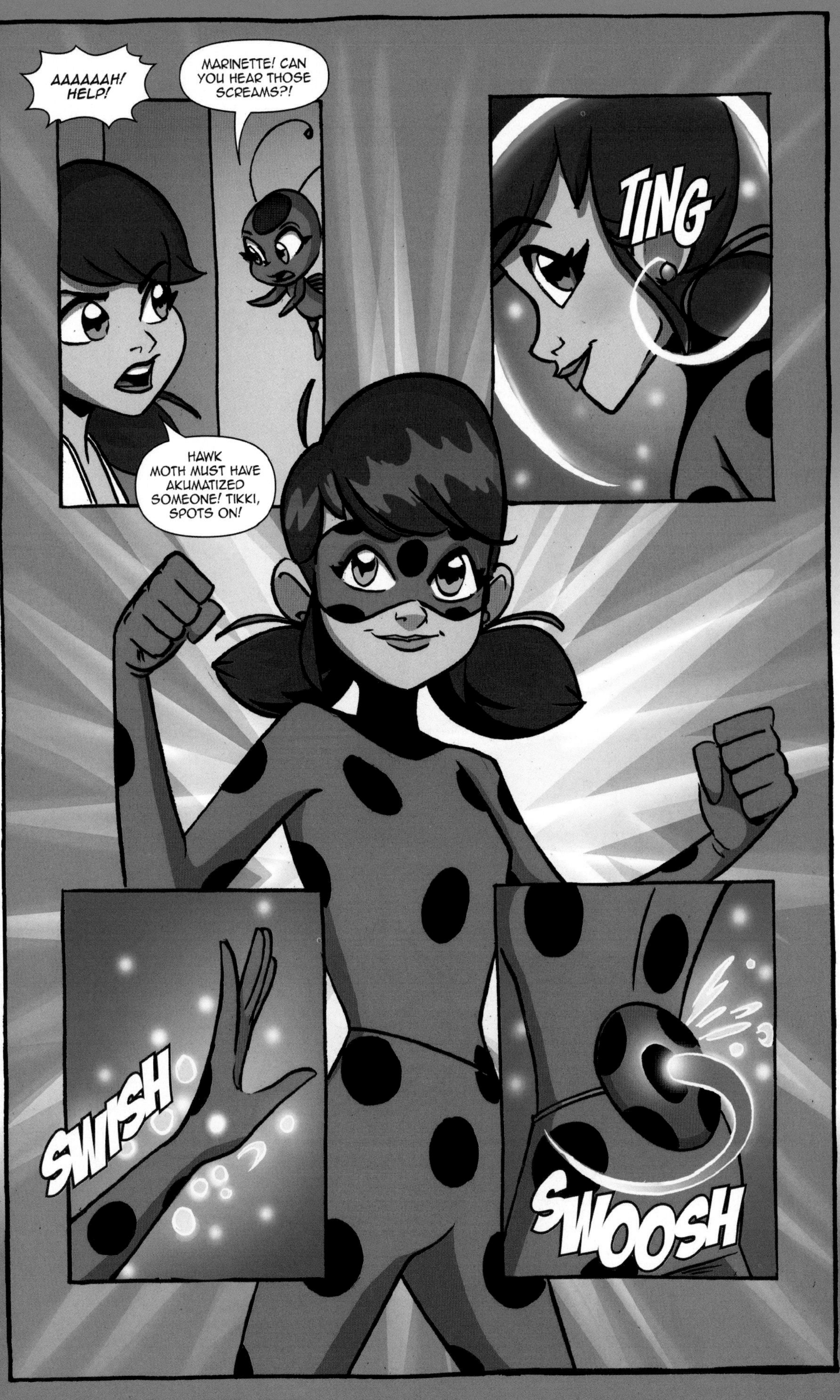
AAAAAAH! HELP!
MARINETTE! CAN YOU HEAR THOSE SCREAMS?!
HAWK MOTH MUST HAVE AKUMATIZED SOMEONE! TIKKI, SPOTS ON!
TING
SWISH
SWOOSH

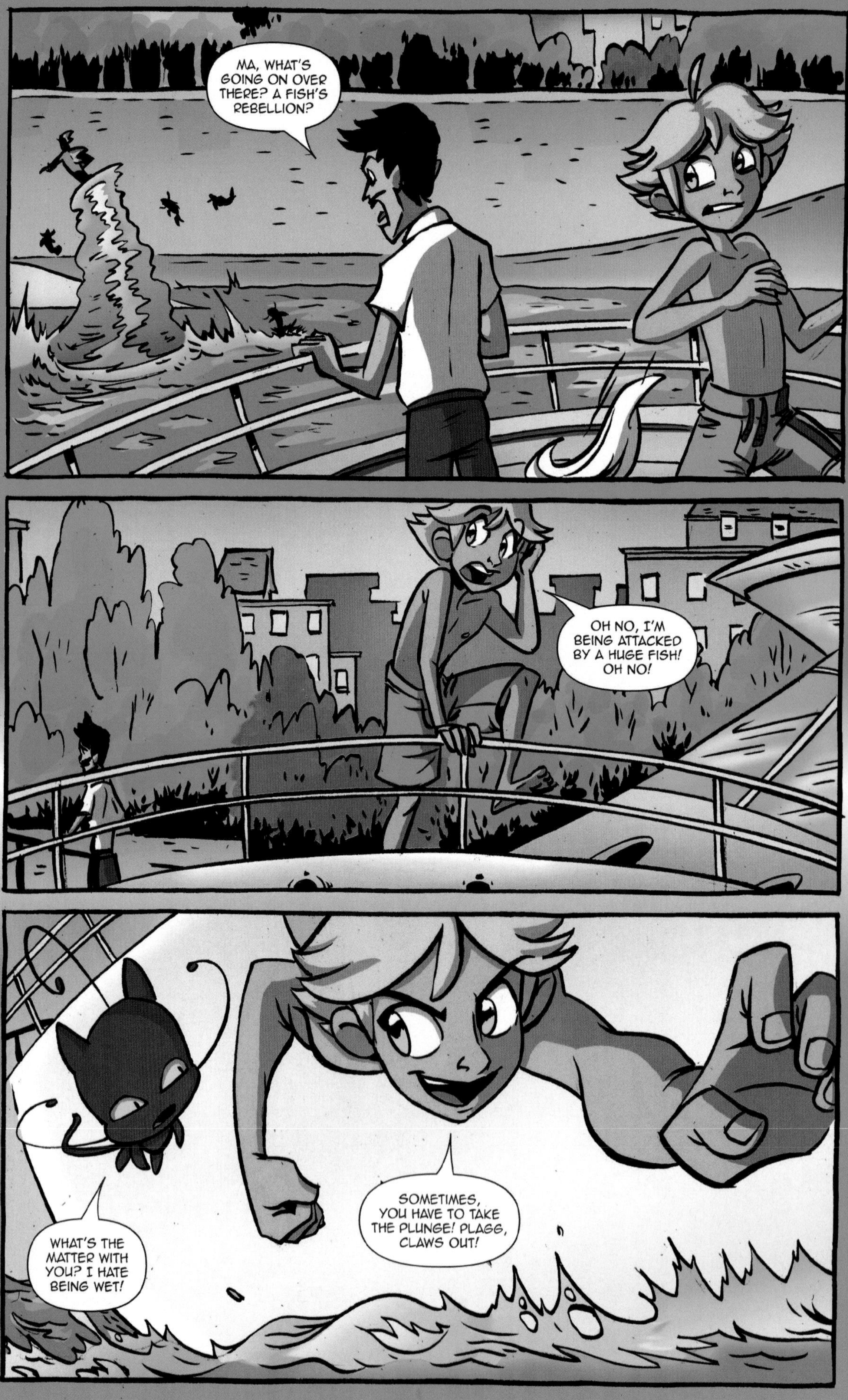
MA, WHAT'S GOING ON OVER THERE? A FISH'S REBELLION?
OH NO, I'M BEING ATTACKED BY A HUGE FISH! OH NO!
WHAT'S THE MATTER WITH YOU? I HATE BEING WET!
SOMETIMES, YOU HAVE TO TAKE THE PLUNGE! PLAGG, CLAWS OUT!

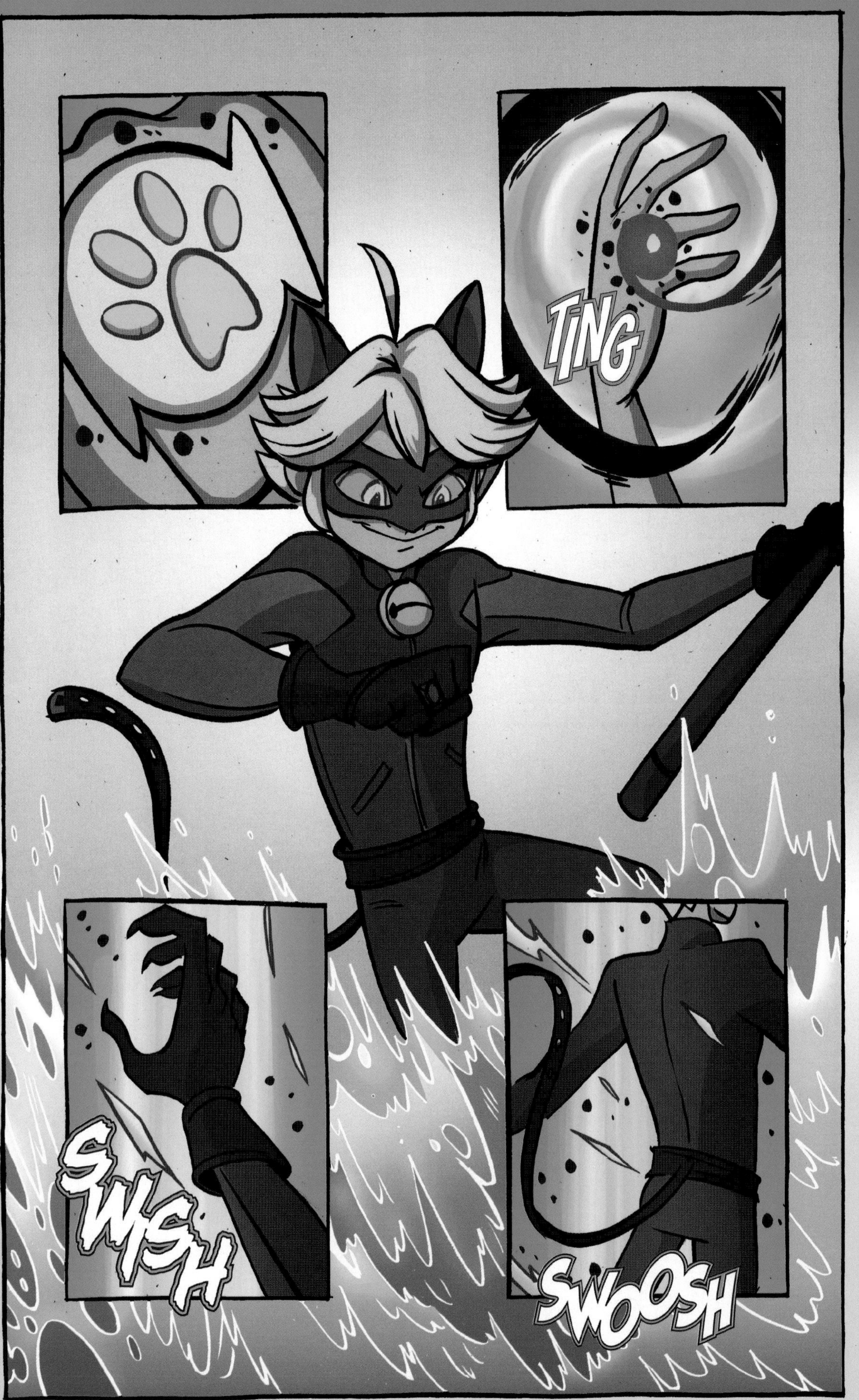
TING
SWISH
SWOOSH

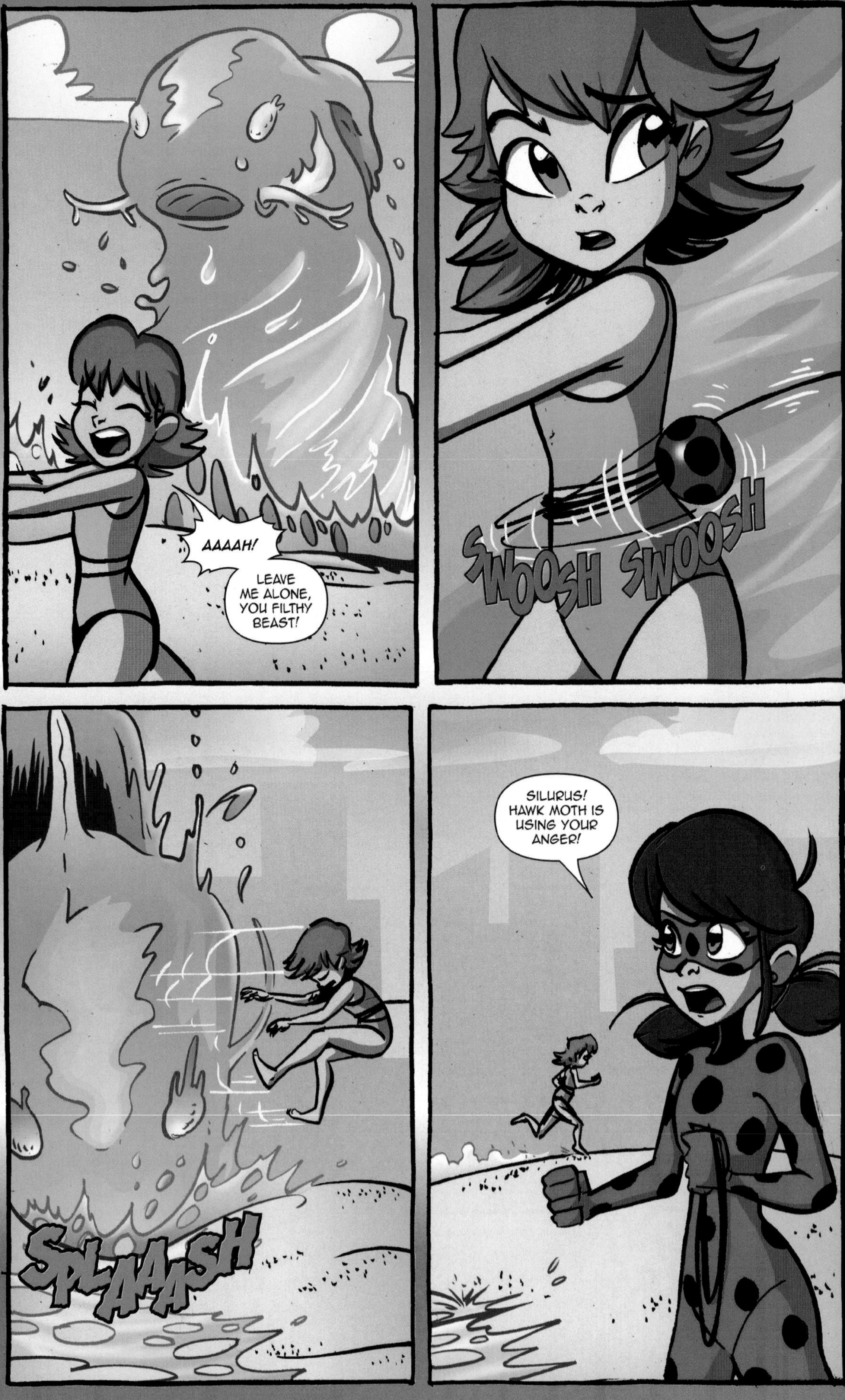
AAAAH!
LEAVE ME ALONE, YOU FILTHY BEAST!
SWOOSH SWOOSH
SPLAAAASH
SILURUS! HAWK MOTH IS USING YOUR ANGER!

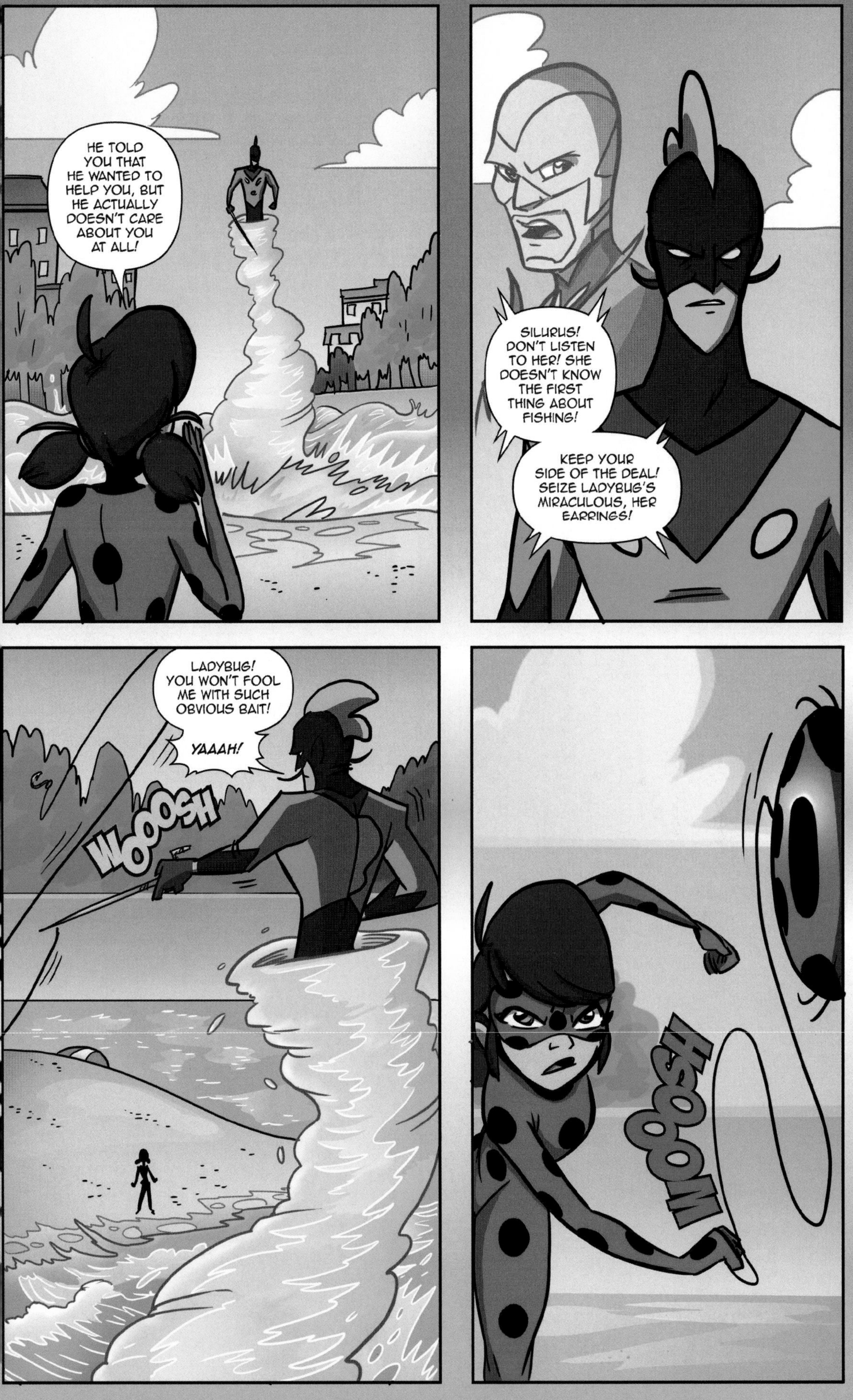
HE TOLD YOU THAT HE WANTED TO HELP YOU, BUT HE ACTUALLY DOESN'T CARE ABOUT YOU AT ALL!
SILURUS! DON'T LISTEN TO HER! SHE DOESN'T KNOW THE FIRST THING ABOUT FISHING!
KEEP YOUR SIDE OF THE DEAL! SEIZE LADYBUG'S MIRACULOUS, HER EARRINGS!
LADYBUG! YOU WON'T FOOL ME WITH SUCH OBVIOUS BAIT!
YAAAH!
WOOOSH
WOOOSH

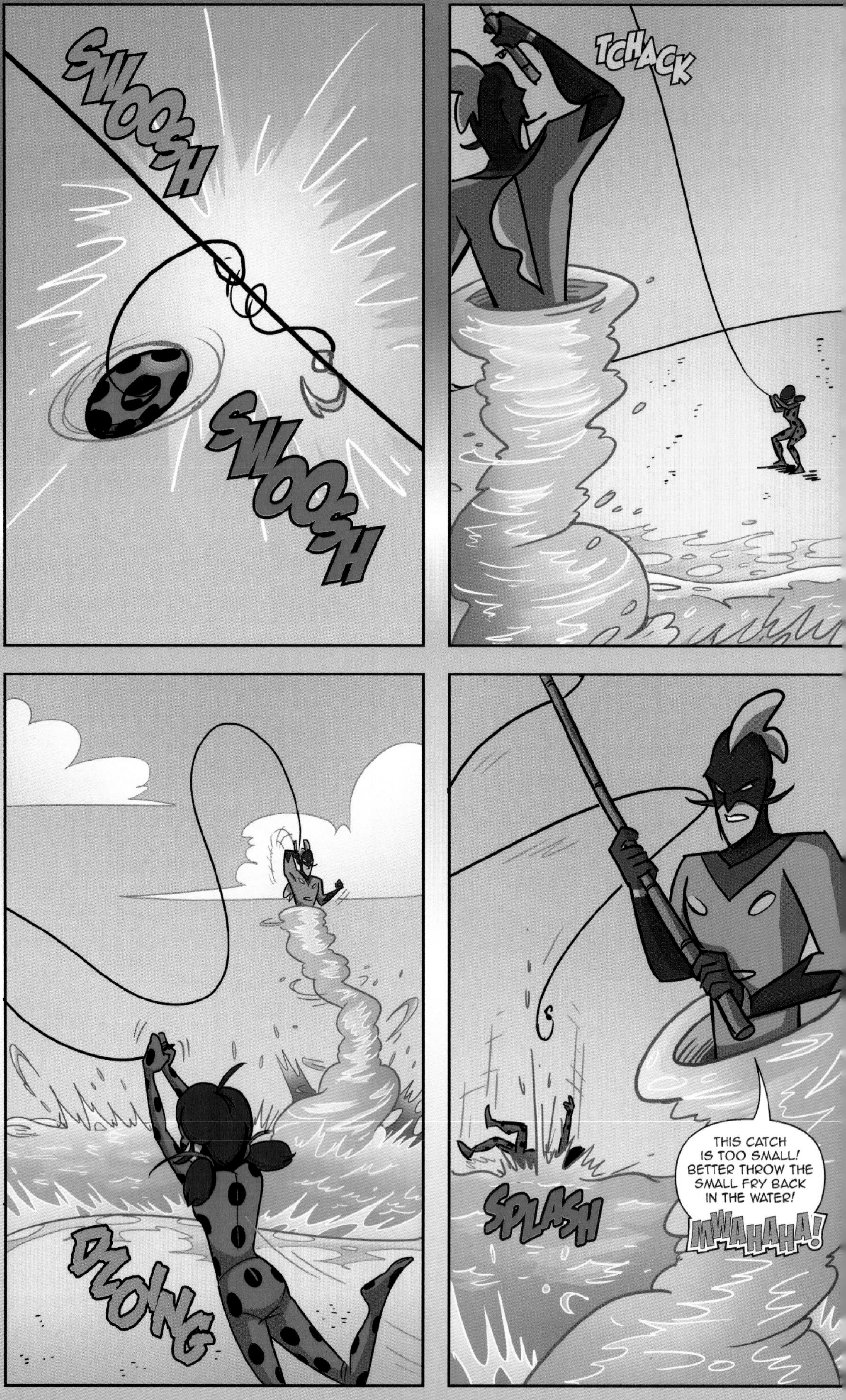
SWOOSH
SWOOSH
TCHACK
DZOING
SPLASH
THIS CATCH IS TOO SMALL! BETTER THROW THE SMALL FRY BACK IN THE WATER!
MWAHAHA!

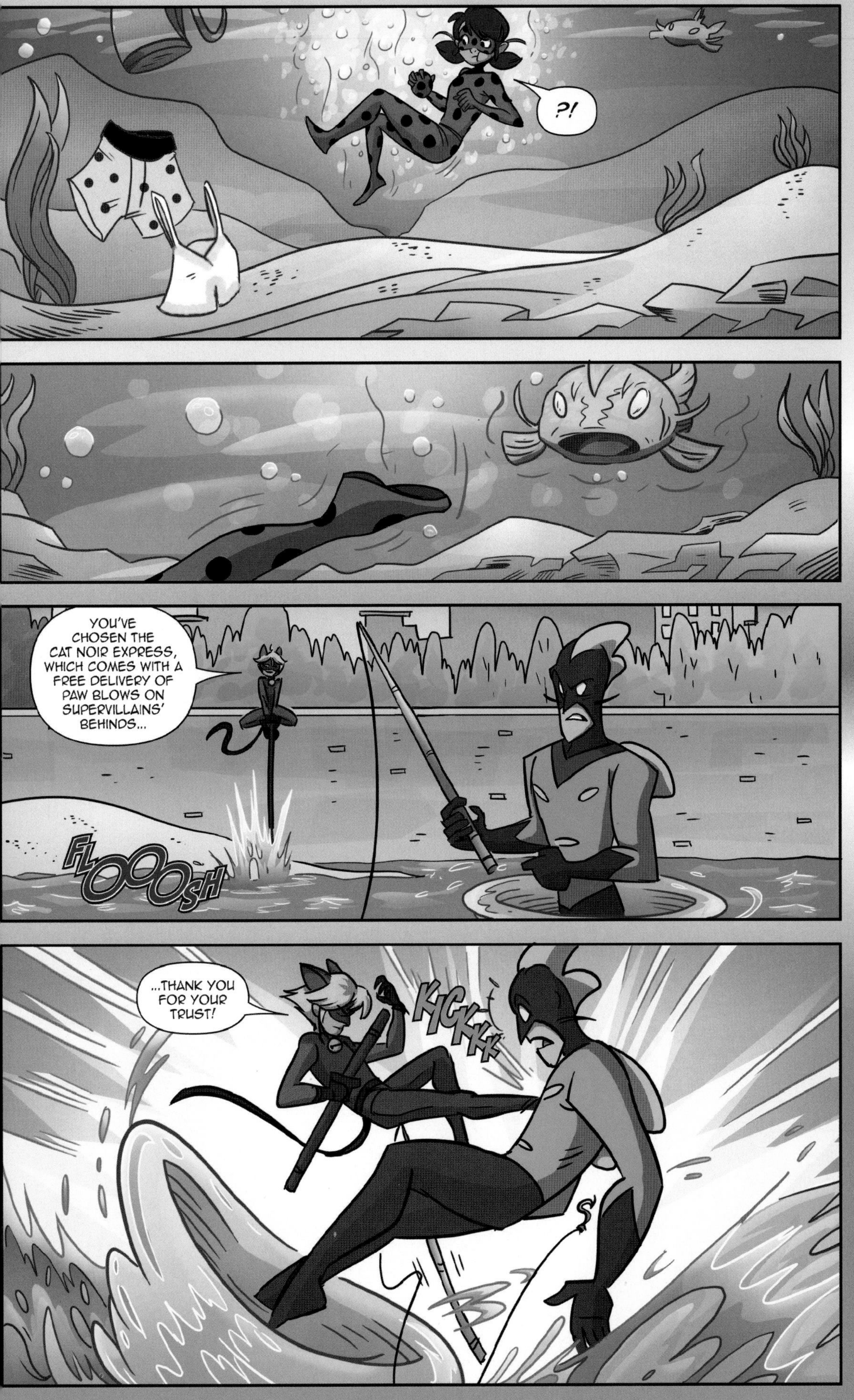
?!
YOU'VE CHOSEN THE CAT NOIR EXPRESS, WHICH COMES WITH A FREE DELIVERY OF PAW BLOWS ON SUPERVILLAINS' BEHINDS...
FLOOOOSH
...THANK YOU FOR YOUR TRUST!
KICKKK

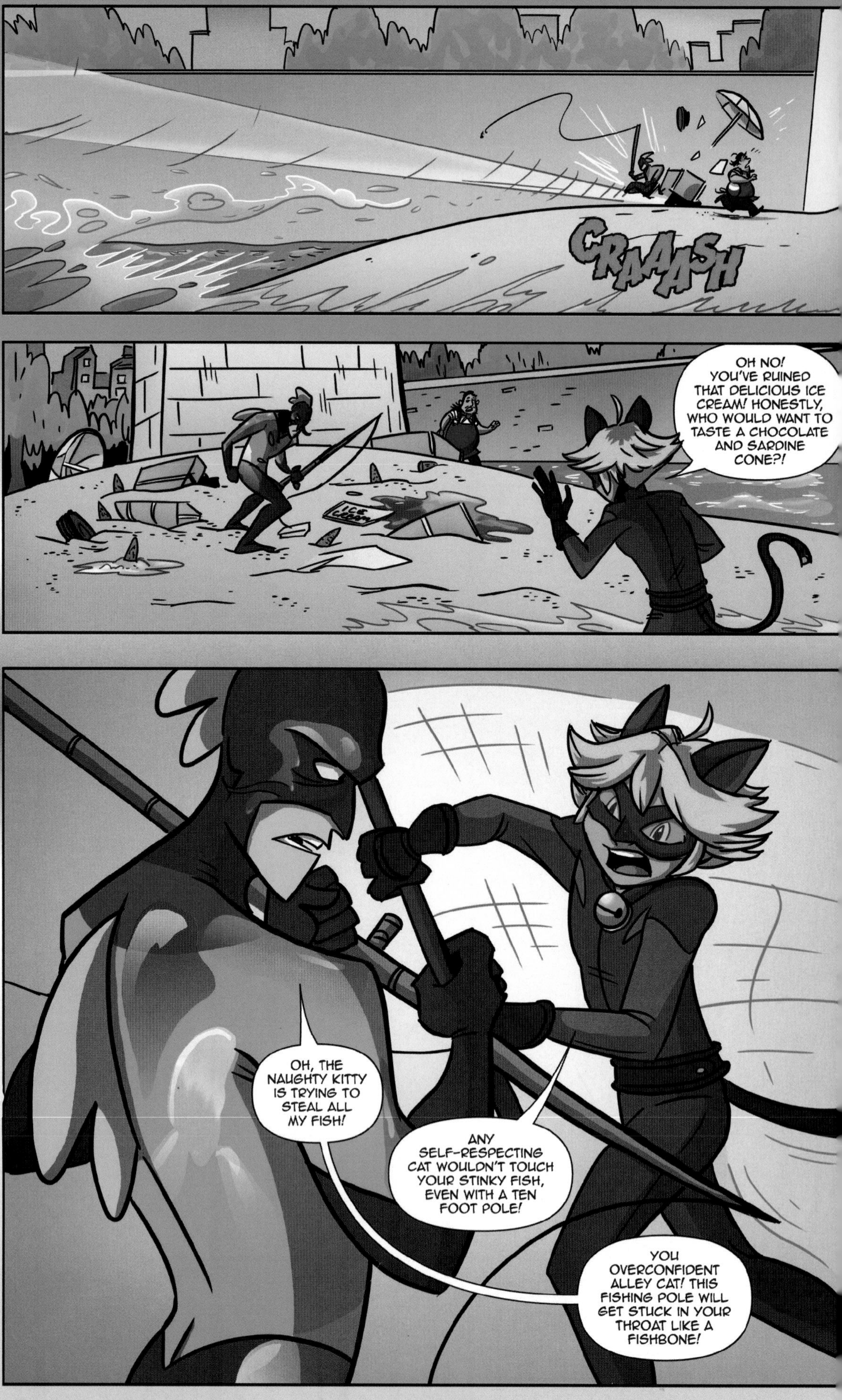
CRAAAASH
OH NO! YOU'VE RUINED THAT DELICIOUS ICE CREAM! HONESTLY, WHO WOULD WANT TO TASTE A CHOCOLATE AND SARDINE CONE?!
OH, THE NAUGHTY KITTY IS TRYING TO STEAL ALL MY FISH!
ANY SELF-RESPECTING CAT WOULDN'T TOUCH YOUR STINKY FISH, EVEN WITH A TEN FOOT POLE!
YOU OVERCONFIDENT ALLEY CAT! THIS FISHING POLE WILL GET STUCK IN YOUR THROAT LIKE A FISHBONE!

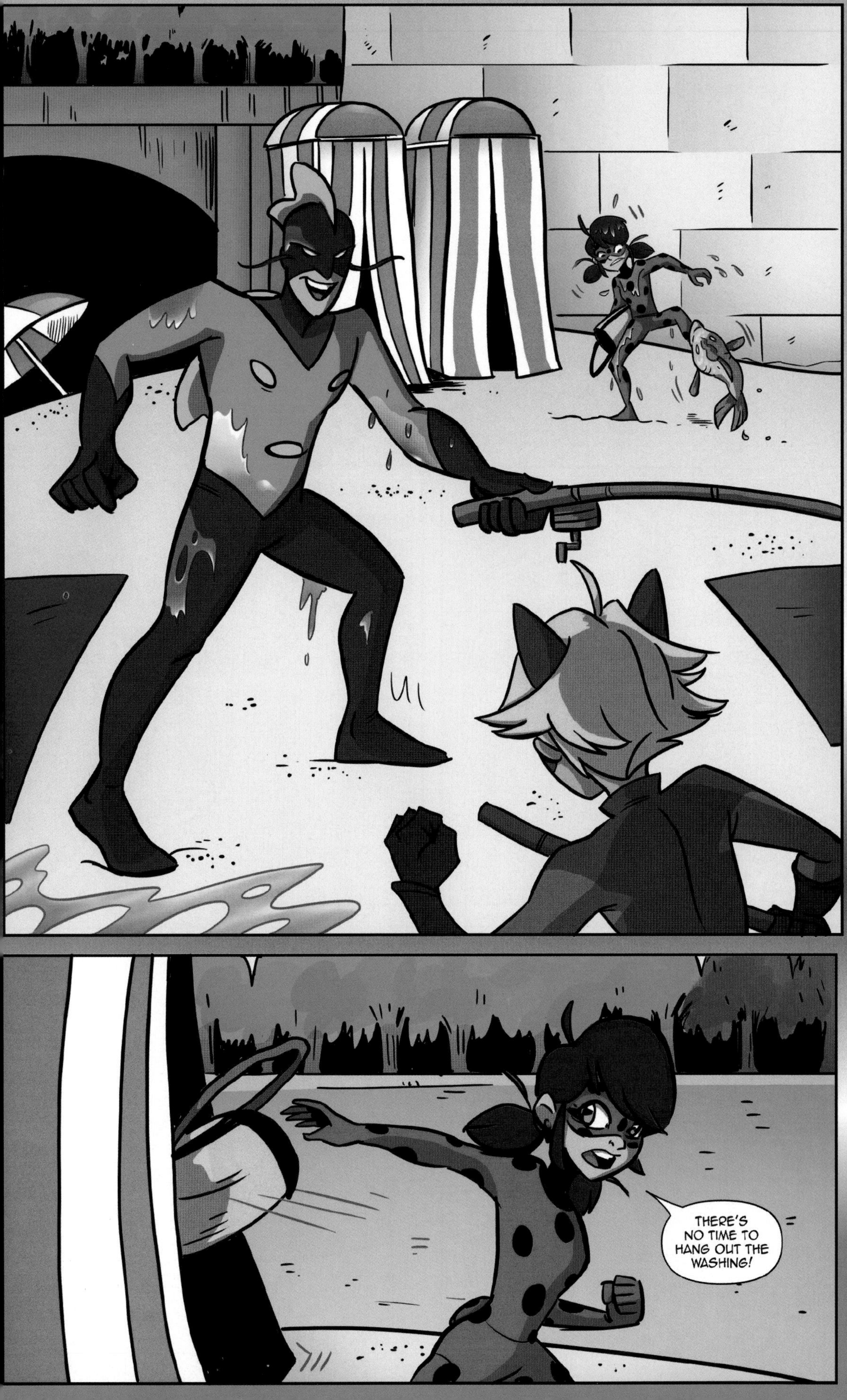
THERE'S NO TIME TO HANG OUT THE WASHING!

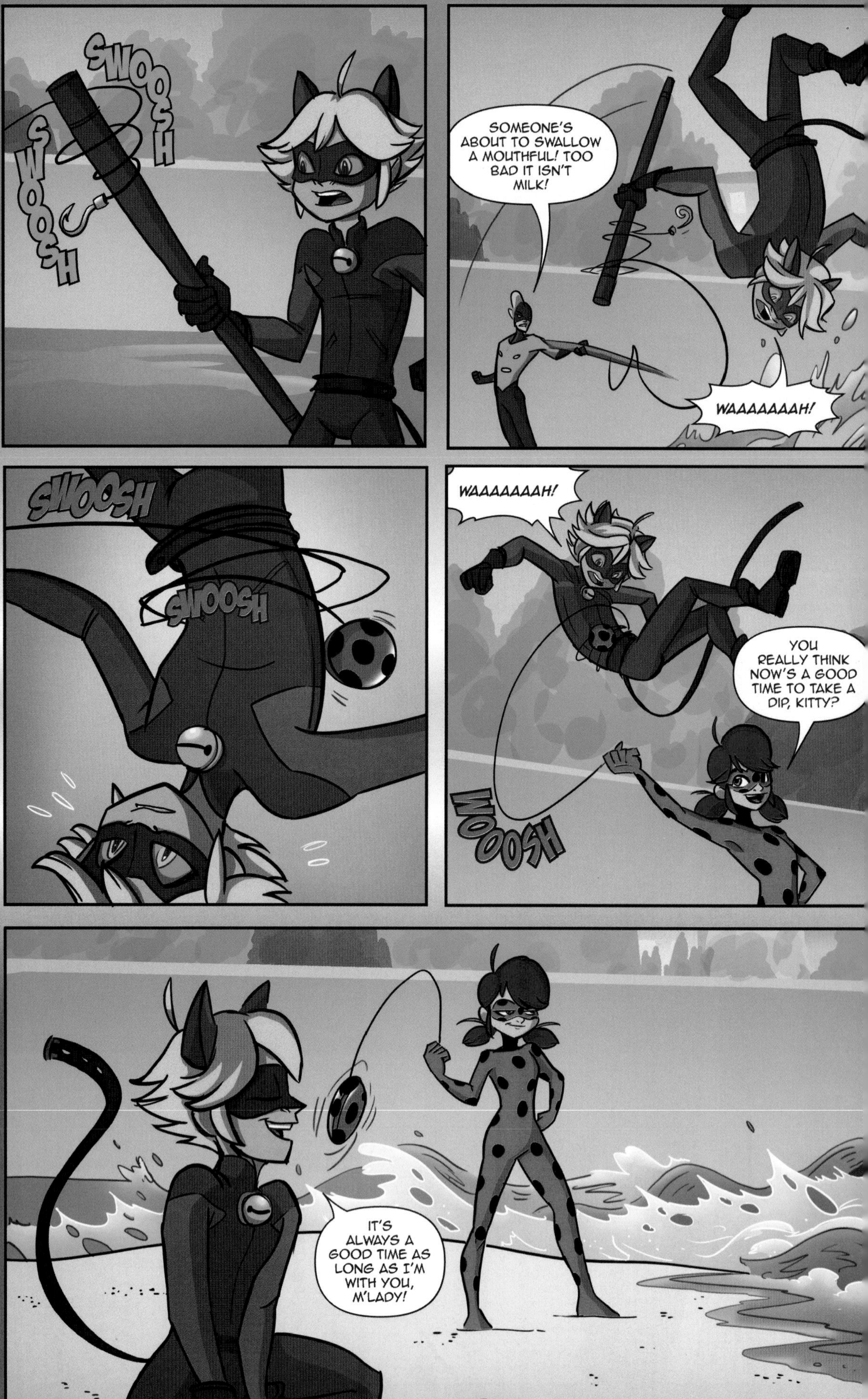
SWOOSH
SWOOSH
SOMEONE'S ABOUT TO SWALLOW A MOUTHFUL! TOO BAD IT ISN'T MILK!
WAAAAAAAH!
SWOOSH
SWOOSH
WAAAAAAAH!
YOU REALLY THINK NOW'S A GOOD TIME TO TAKE A DIP, KITTY?
WOOOSH
IT'S ALWAYS A GOOD TIME AS LONG AS I'M WITH YOU, M'LADY!

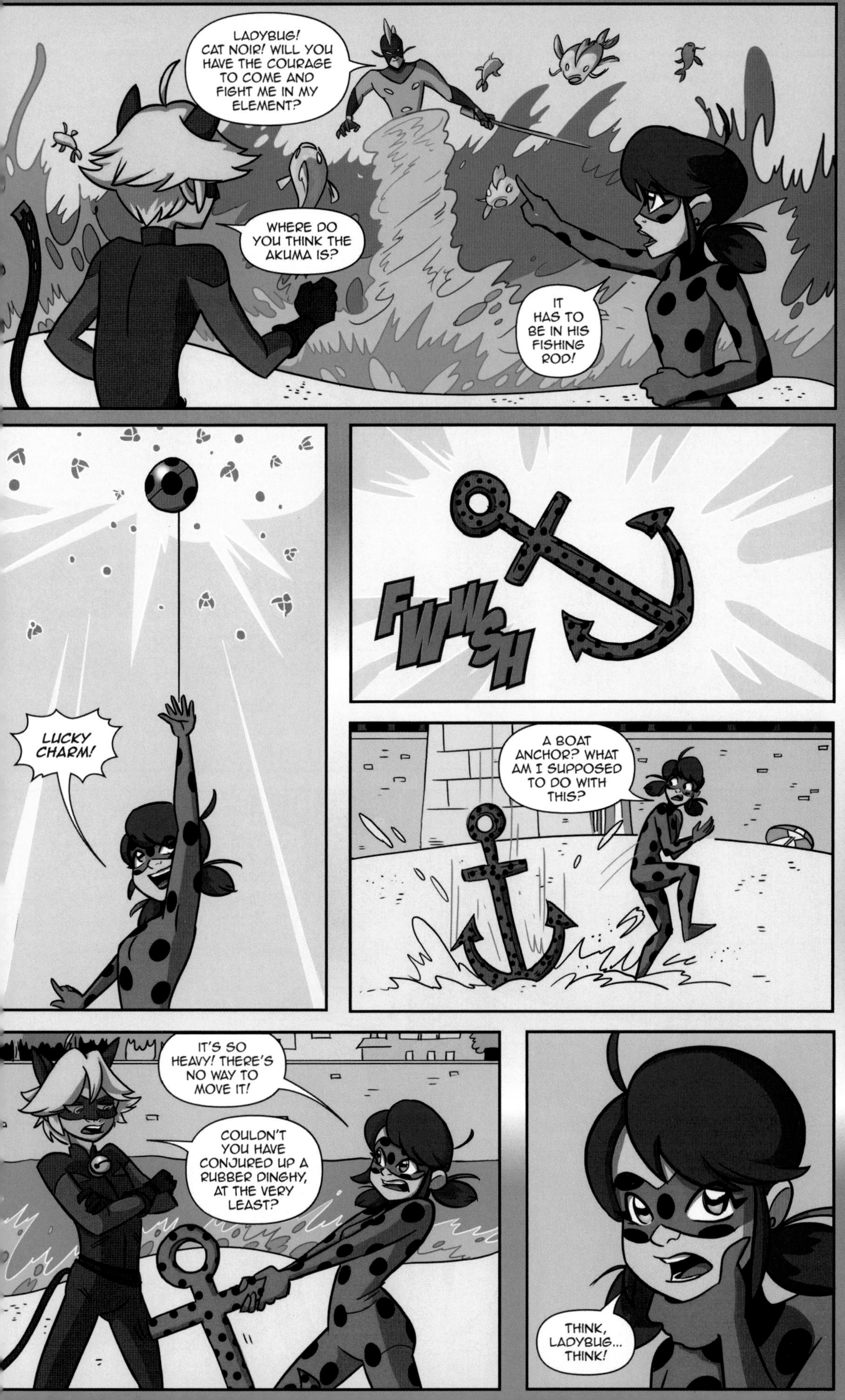
LADYBUG! CAT NOIR! WILL YOU HAVE THE COURAGE TO COME AND FIGHT ME IN MY ELEMENT?
WHERE DO YOU THINK THE AKUMA IS?
IT HAS TO BE IN HIS FISHING ROD!
LUCKY CHARM!
FWWSH
A BOAT ANCHOR? WHAT AM I SUPPOSED TO DO WITH THIS?
IT'S SO HEAVY! THERE'S NO WAY TO MOVE IT!
COULDN'T YOU HAVE CONJURED UP A RUBBER DINGHY, AT THE VERY LEAST?
THINK, LADYBUG... THINK!

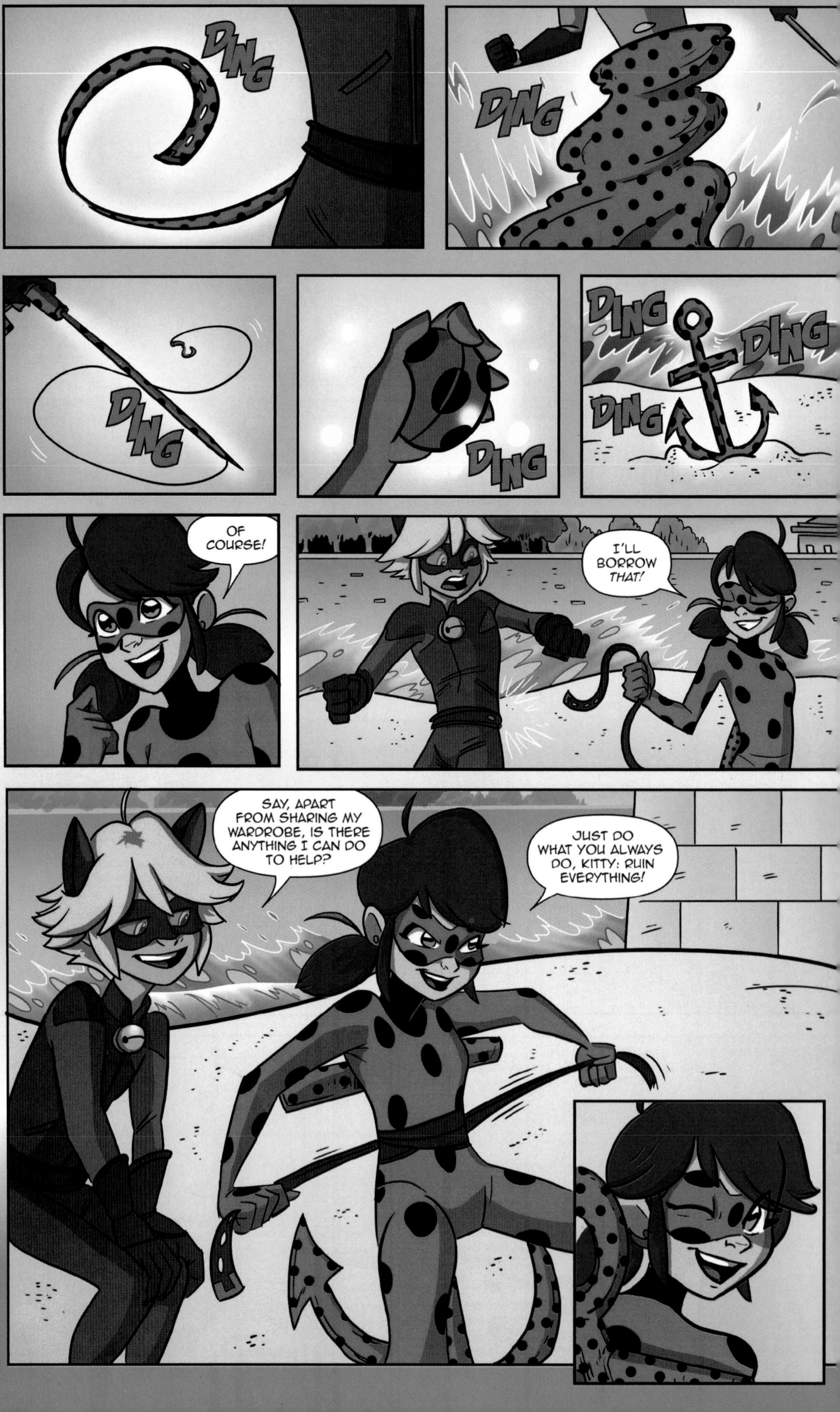
DING
DING
DING
DING
DING
DING
DING
OF COURSE!
I'LL BORROW THAT!
SAY, APART FROM SHARING MY WARDROBE, IS THERE ANYTHING I CAN DO TO HELP?
JUST DO WHAT YOU ALWAYS DO, KITTY: RUIN EVERYTHING!

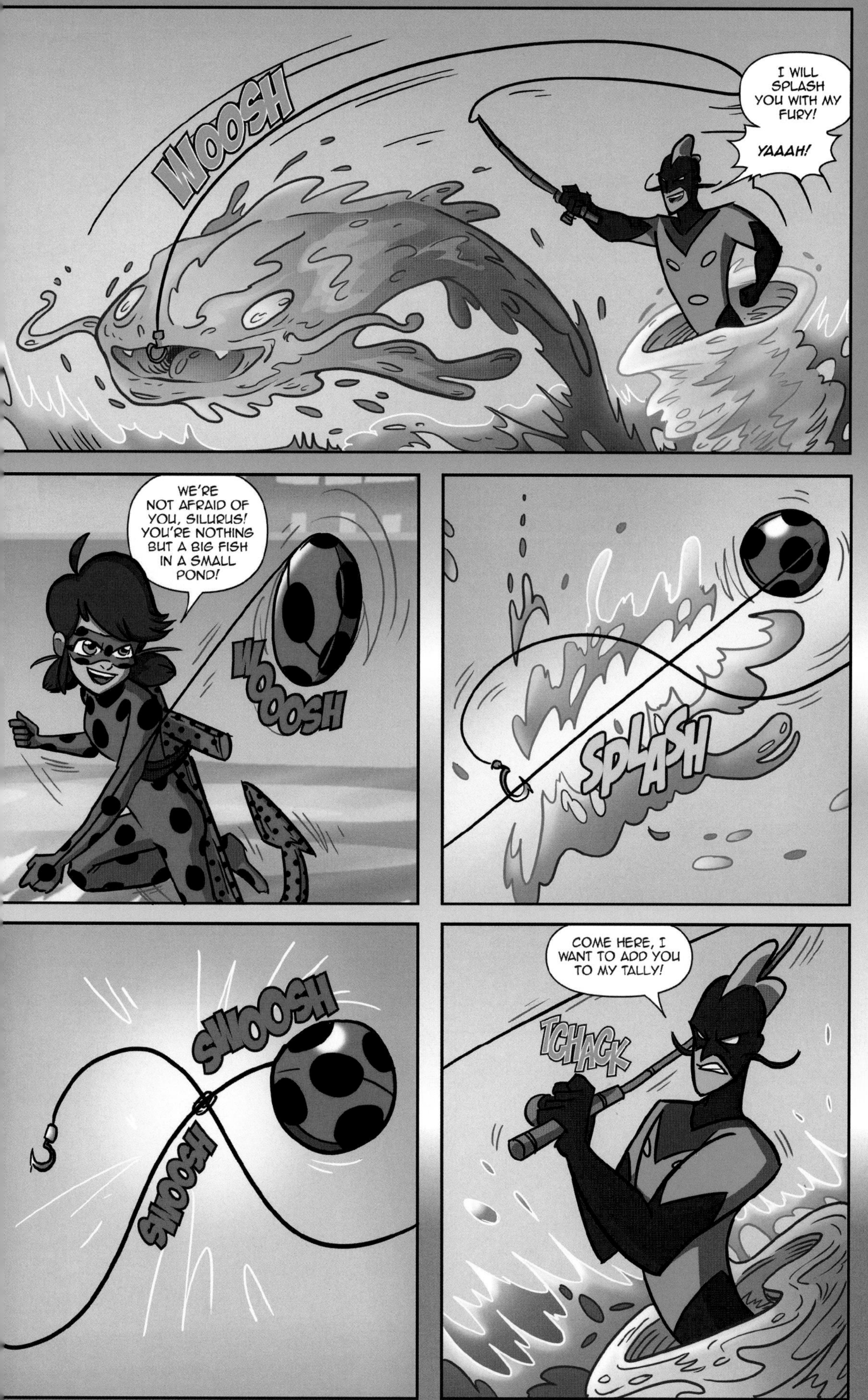
WOOSH
I WILL SPLASH YOU WITH MY FURY!
YAAAH!
WE'RE NOT AFRAID OF YOU, SILURUS! YOU'RE NOTHING BUT A BIG FISH IN A SMALL POND!
WOOOSH
SPLASH
SHOOSH
SHOOSH
COME HERE, I WANT TO ADD YOU TO MY TALLY!
TCHACK

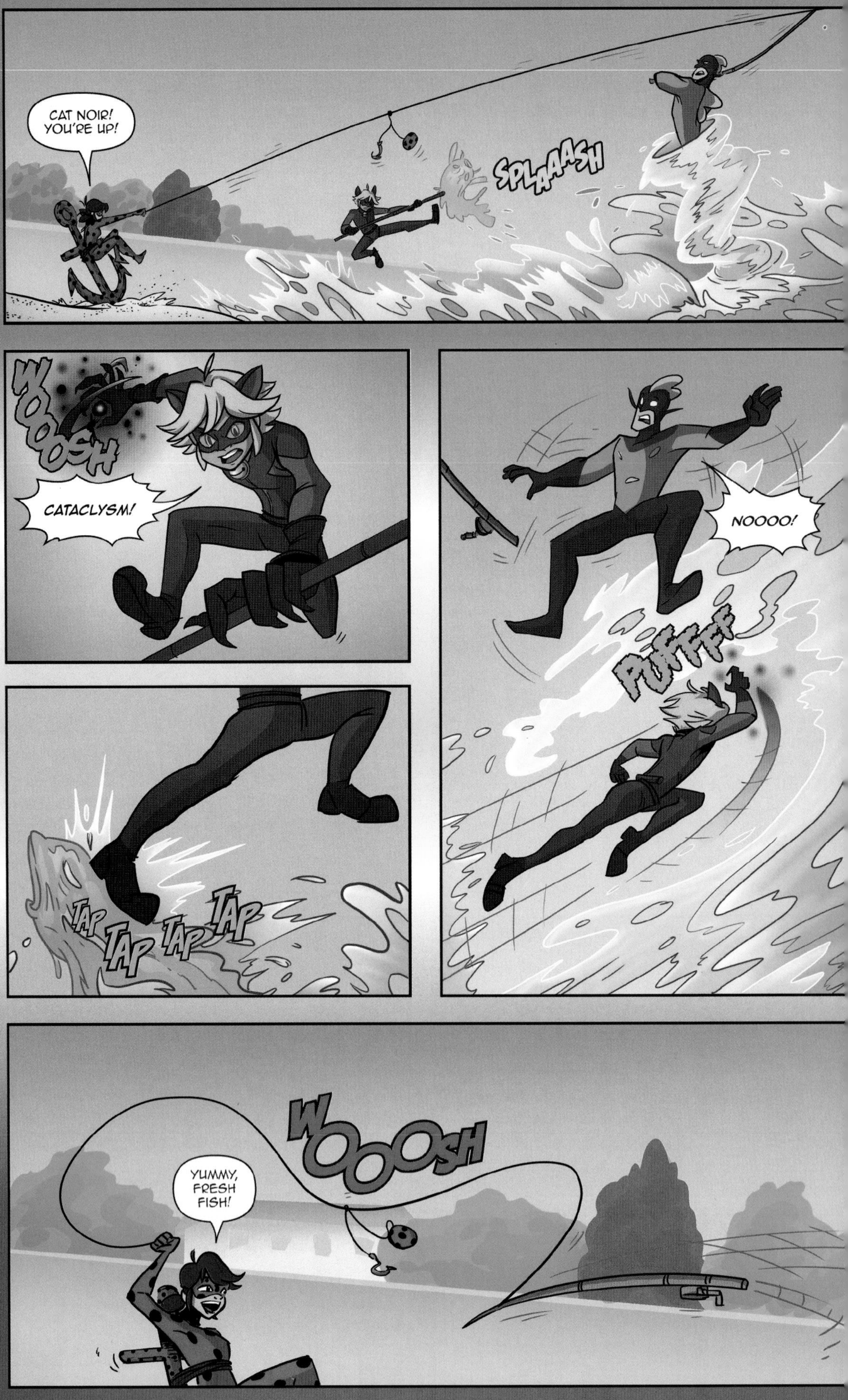
CAT NOIR! YOU'RE UP!
SPLAAASH
WOOOSH
CATACLYSM!
NOOOO!
PUFFFF
TAP TAP TAP TAP
WOOOSH
YUMMY, FRESH FISH!

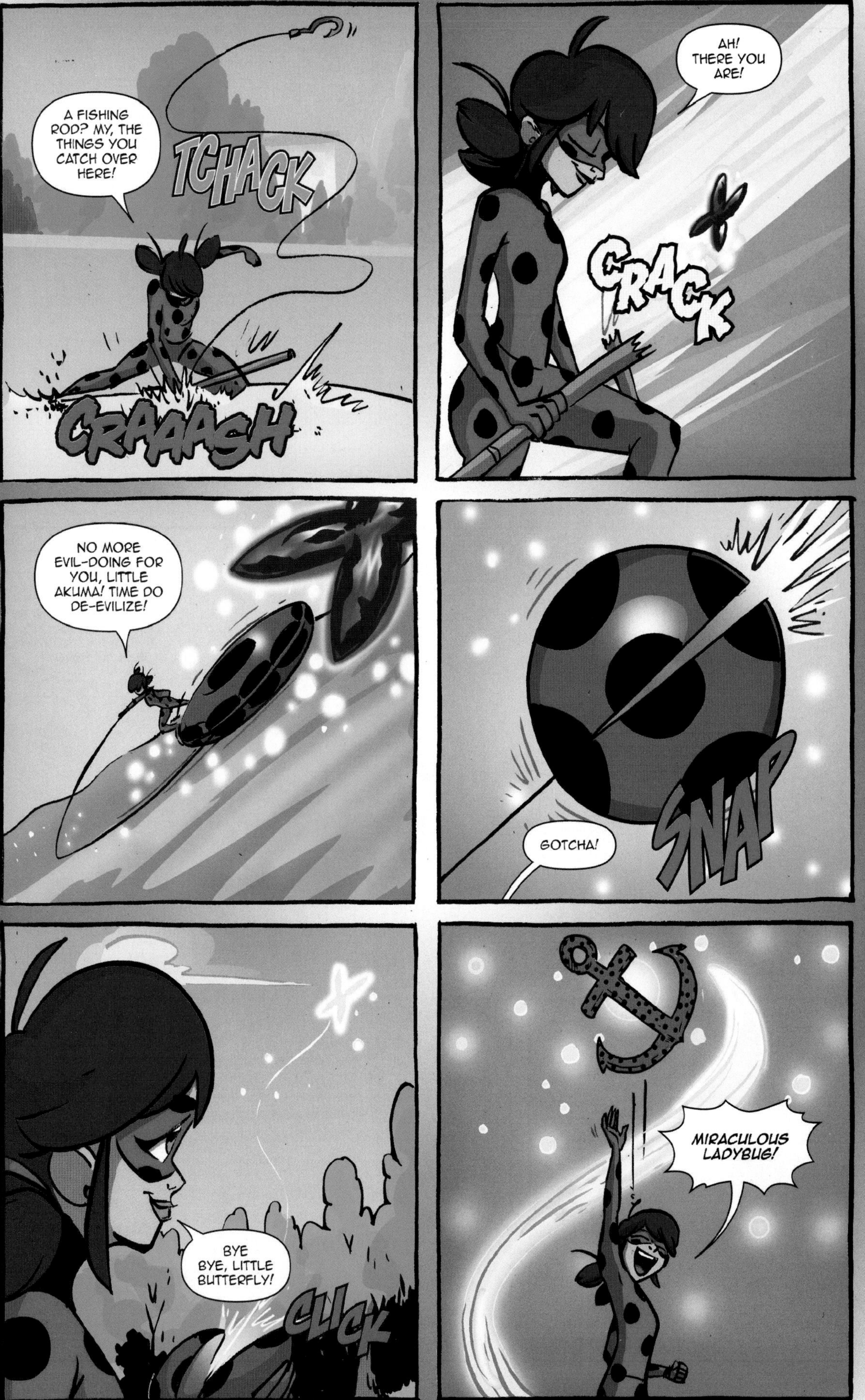
A FISHING ROD? MY, THE THINGS YOU CATCH OVER HERE!
TCHACK
CRAAASH
AH! THERE YOU ARE!
CRACK
NO MORE EVIL-DOING FOR YOU, LITTLE AKUMA! TIME DO DE-EVILIZE!
GOTCHA!
SNAP
BYE BYE, LITTLE BUTTERFLY!
CLICK
MIRACULOUS LADYBUG!

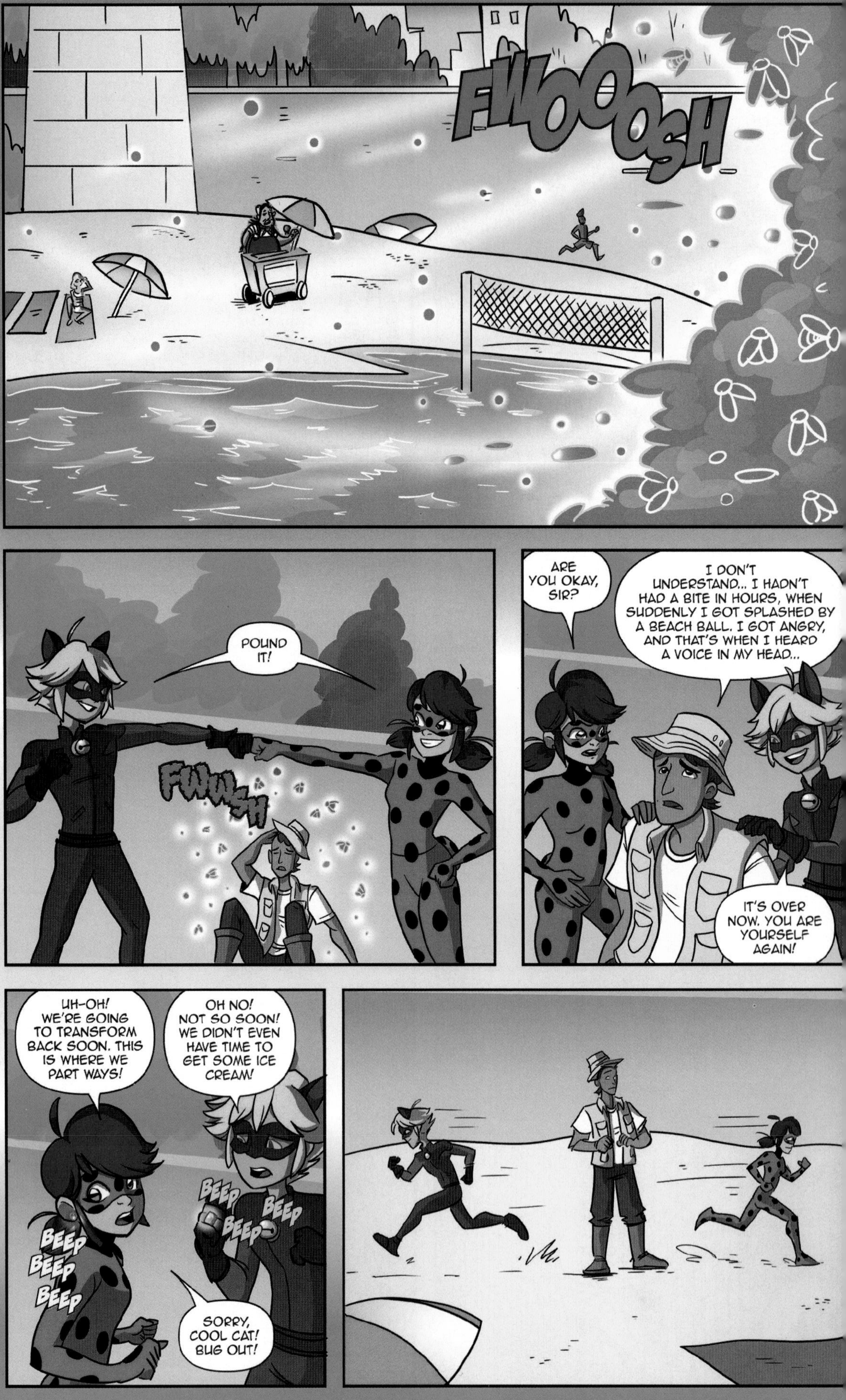
FWOOOOSH
POUND IT!
FWWSH
ARE YOU OKAY, SIR?
I DON'T UNDERSTAND... I HADN'T HAD A BITE IN HOURS, WHEN SUDDENLY I GOT SPLASHED BY A BEACH BALL. I GOT ANGRY, AND THAT'S WHEN I HEARD A VOICE IN MY HEAD...
IT'S OVER NOW. YOU ARE YOURSELF AGAIN!
UH-OH! WE'RE GOING TO TRANSFORM BACK SOON. THIS IS WHERE WE PART WAYS!
OH NO! NOT SO SOON! WE DIDN'T EVEN HAVE TIME TO GET SOME ICE CREAM!
BEEP BEEP BEEP
BEEP BEEP
SORRY, COOL CAT! BUG OUT!

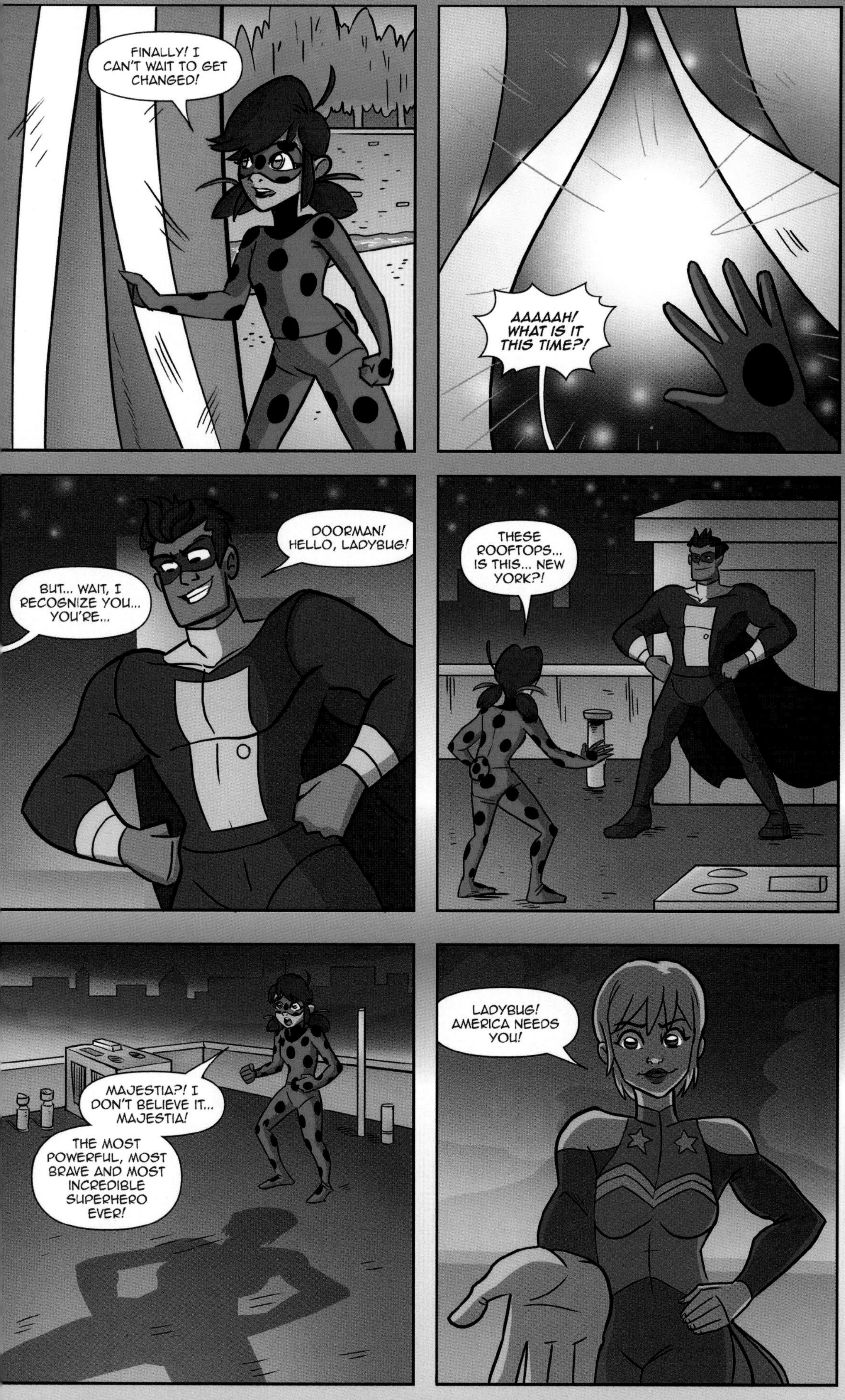

FINALLY! I CAN'T WAIT TO GET CHANGED!
AAAAAH! WHAT IS IT THIS TIME?!
DOORMAN! HELLO, LADYBUG!
BUT... WAIT, I RECOGNIZE YOU... YOU'RE...
THESE ROOFTOPS... IS THIS... NEW YORK?!
MAJESTIA?! I DON'T BELIEVE IT... MAJESTIA!
THE MOST POWERFUL, MOST BRAVE AND MOST INCREDIBLE SUPERHERO EVER!
LADYBUG! AMERICA NEEDS YOU!

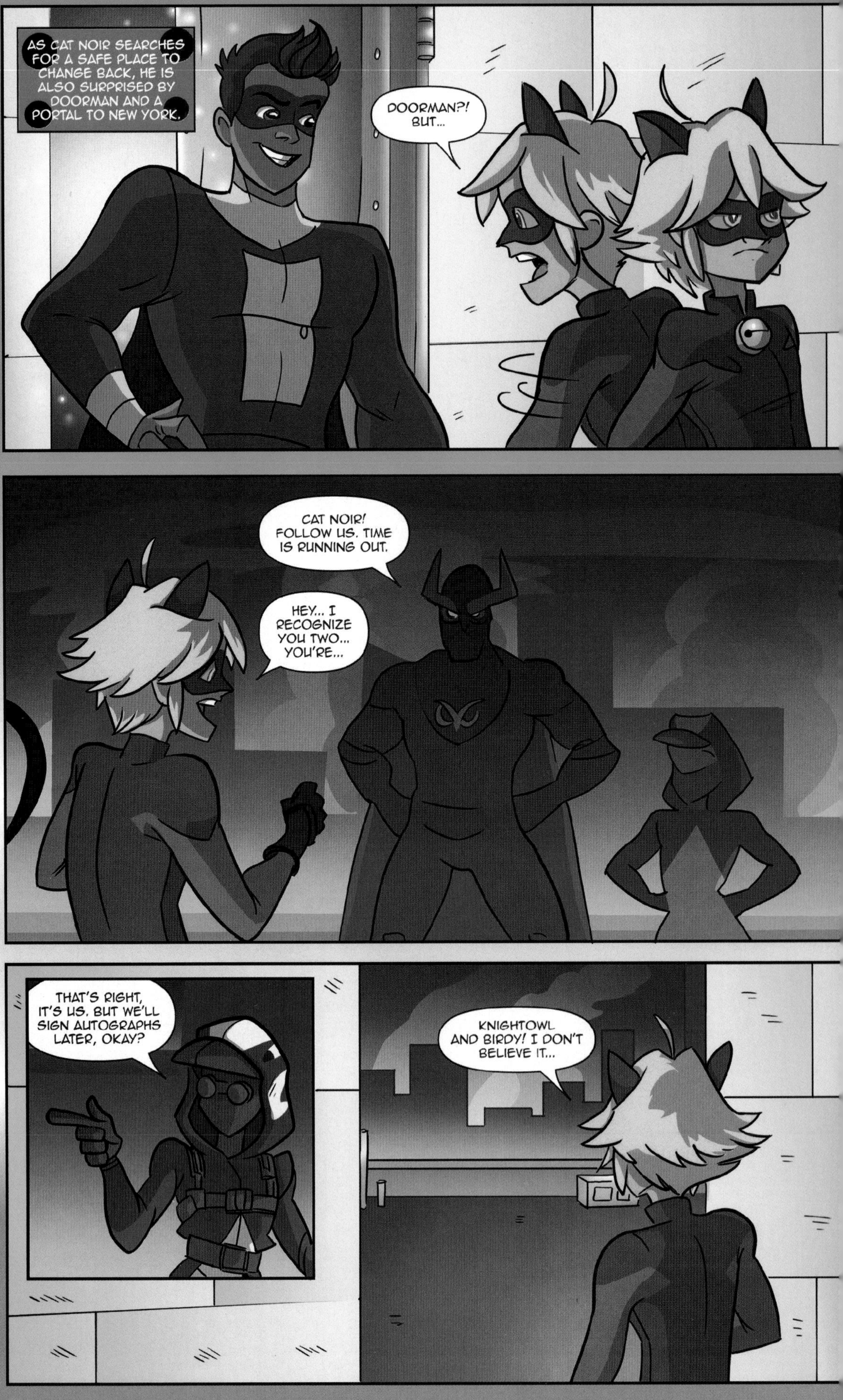
AS CAT NOIR SEARCHES FOR A SAFE PLACE TO CHANGE BACK, HE IS ALSO SURPRISED BY DOORMAN AND A PORTAL TO NEW YORK.
DOORMAN?! BUT...
CAT NOIR! FOLLOW US. TIME IS RUNNING OUT.
HEY... I RECOGNIZE YOU TWO... YOU'RE...
THAT'S RIGHT, IT'S US. BUT WE'LL SIGN AUTOGRAPHS LATER, OKAY?
KNIGHTOWL AND BIRDY! I DON'T BELIEVE IT...

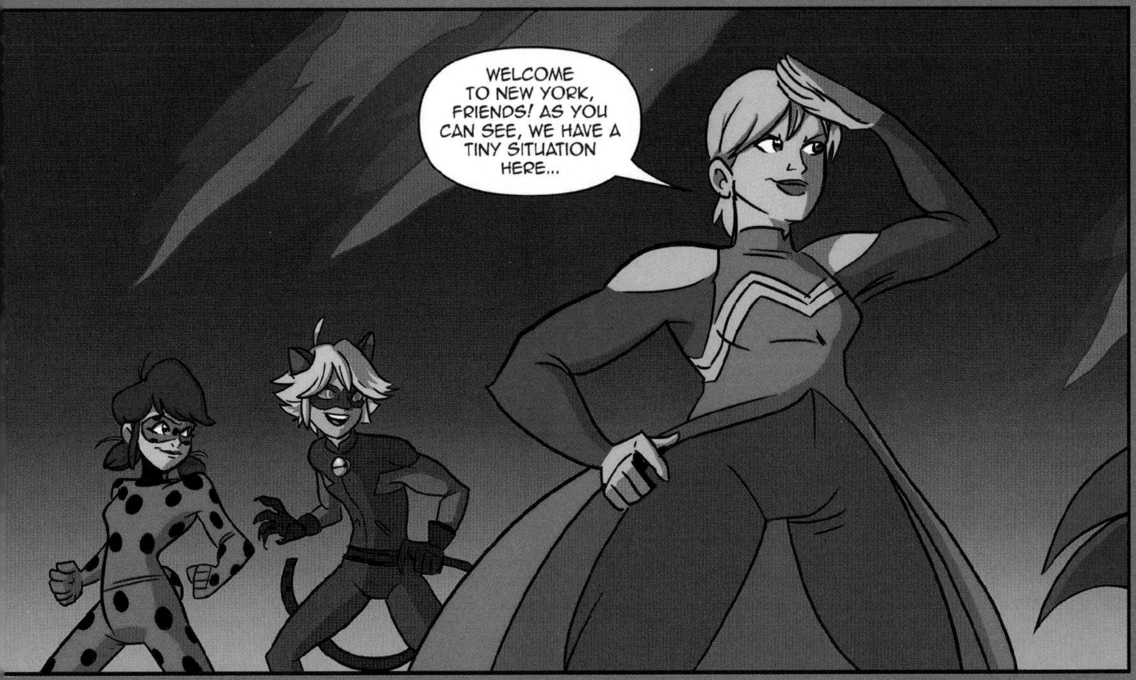
WELCOME TO NEW YORK, FRIENDS! AS YOU CAN SEE, WE HAVE A TINY SITUATION HERE...

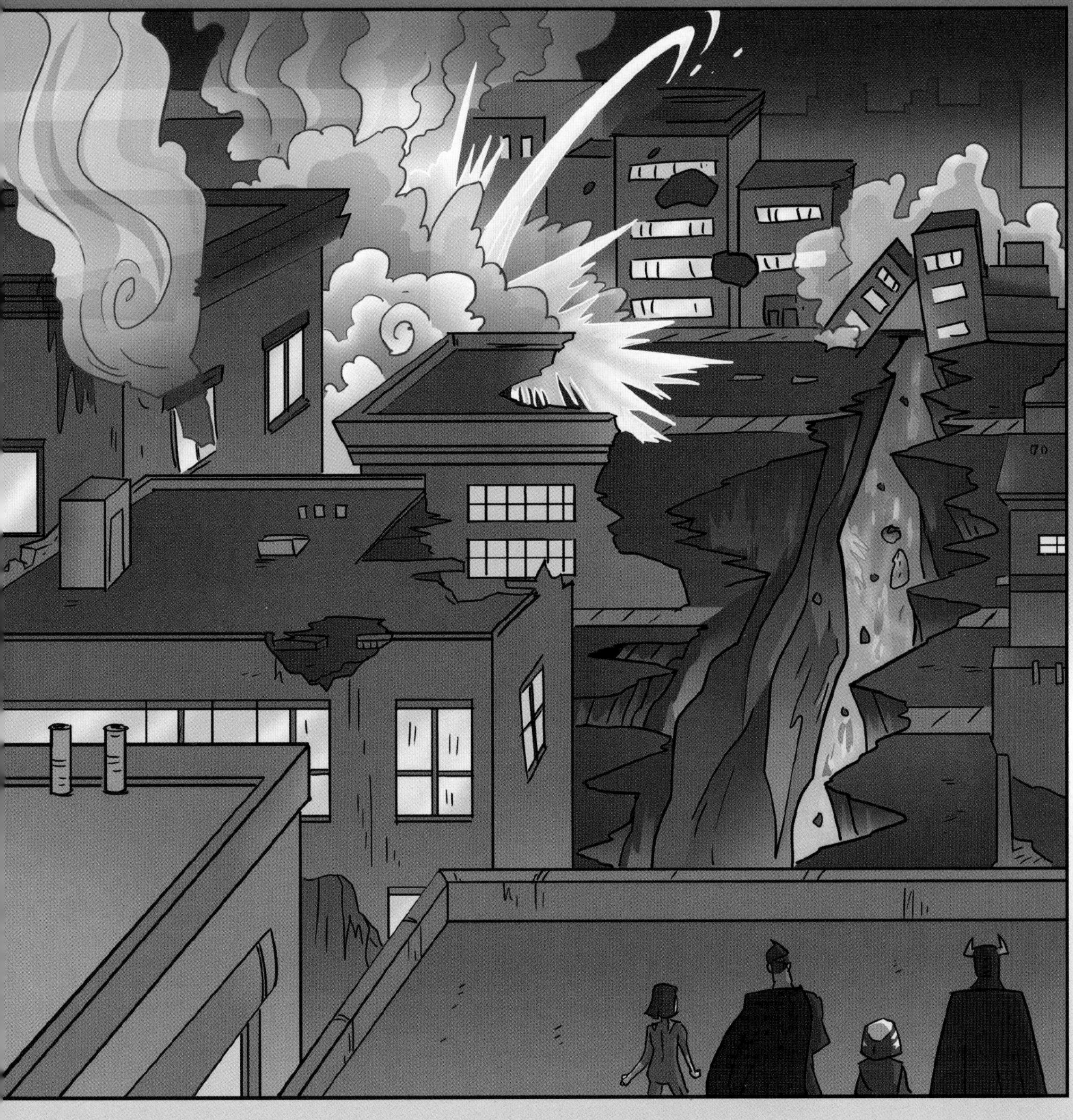

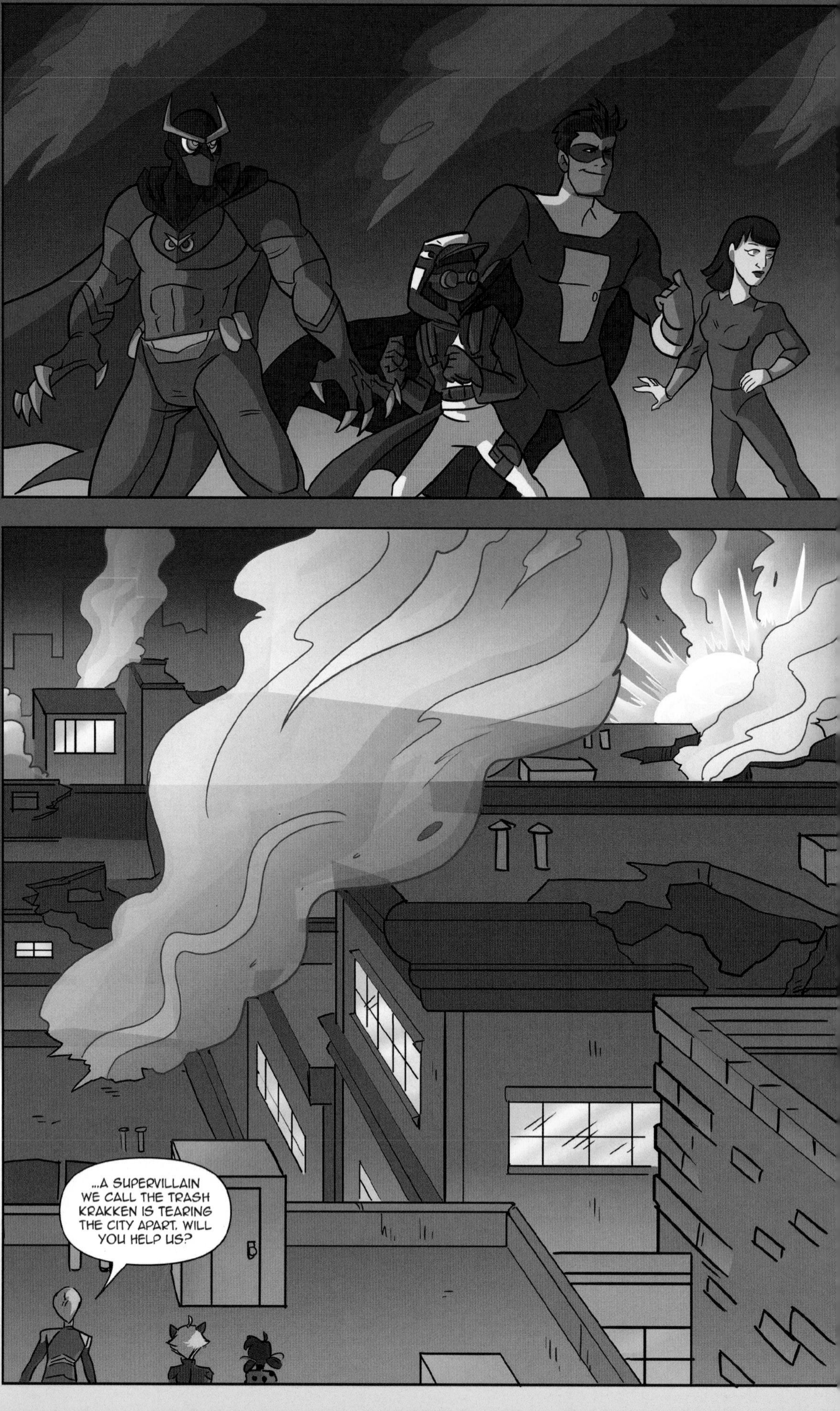
...A SUPERVILLAIN WE CALL THE TRASH KRAKKEN IS TEARING THE CITY APART. WILL YOU HELP US?

CHAPTER 3:
THE TRASH KRAKKEN:
THE BIG LEAGUES

Created by: Thomas Astruc

Written by: Thomas Astruc, Mélanie Duval, Fred Lenoir, Sébastien Thibaudeau & Bryan Seaton

Pencils by: Ellen Cerreta

Inks by: Brian Hess

Letters by: Justin Birch

Colors by: Darné Lang

Editing by: Nicole D'Andria & Bryan Seaton

Cover A: Brian Hess • Cover B: Tony Fleecs

**Comic art style based on the
Webisode art style of Angie Nasca**

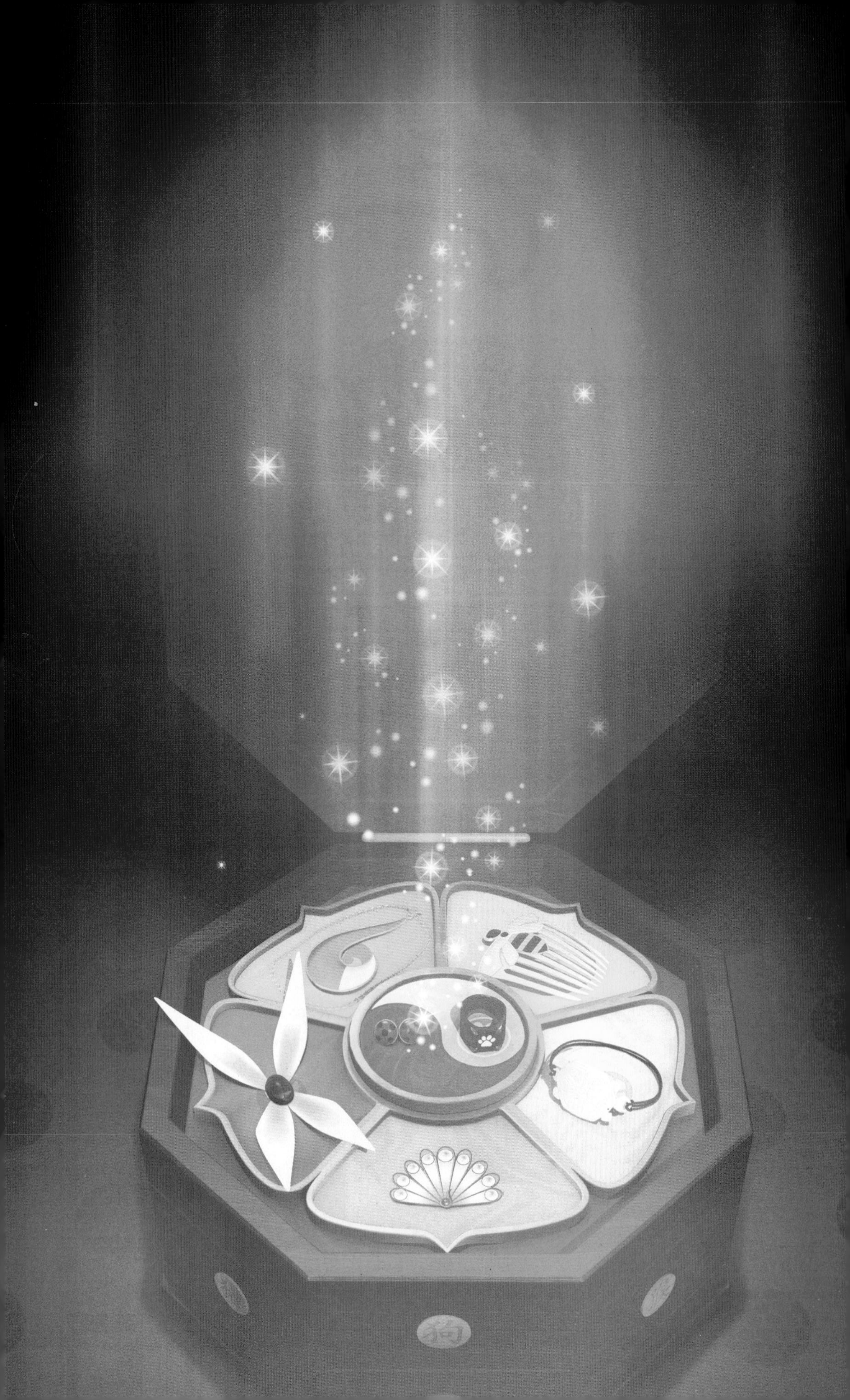
狗

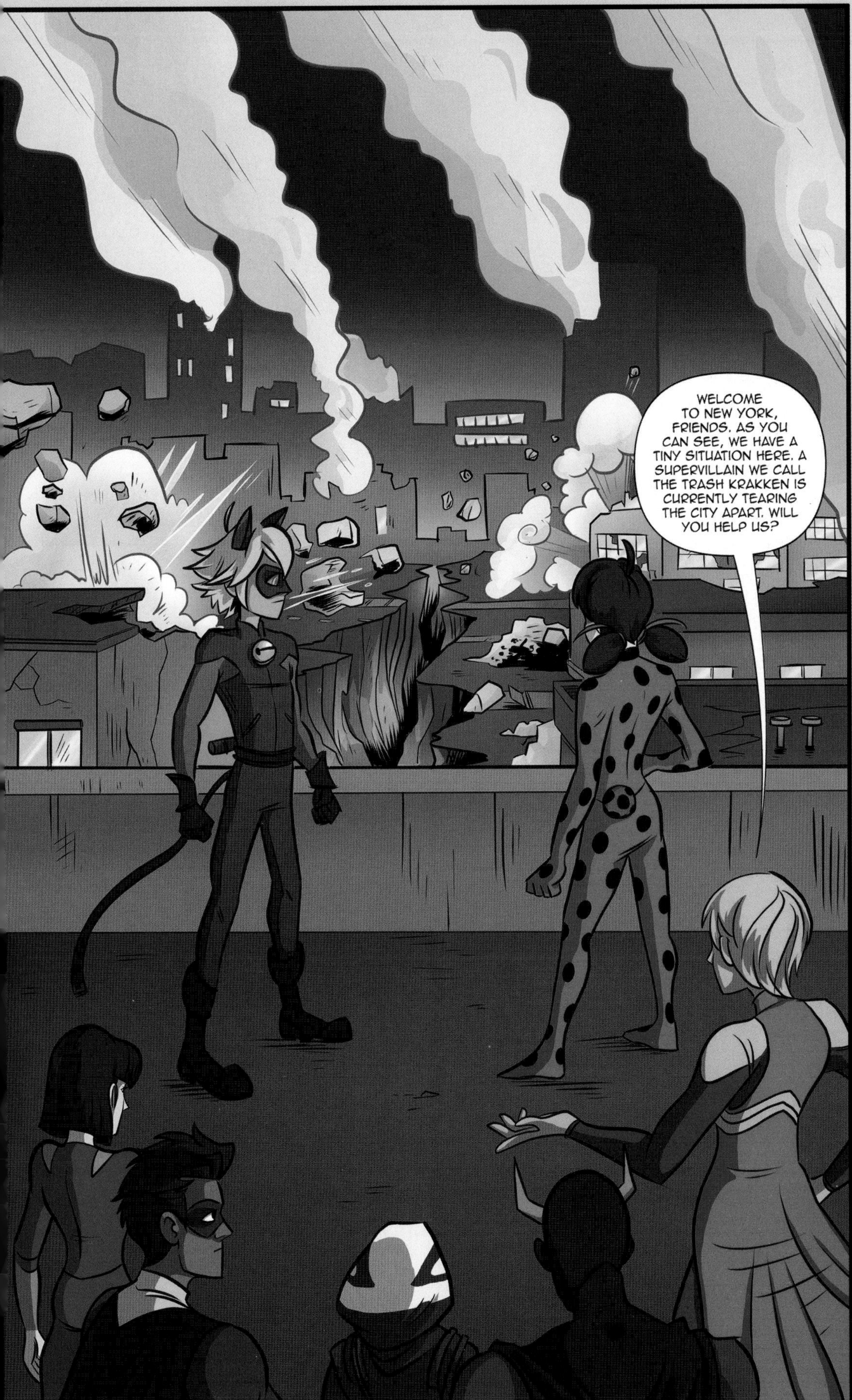
WELCOME TO NEW YORK, FRIENDS. AS YOU CAN SEE, WE HAVE A TINY SITUATION HERE. A SUPERVILLAIN WE CALL THE TRASH KRAKKEN IS CURRENTLY TEARING THE CITY APART. WILL YOU HELP US?

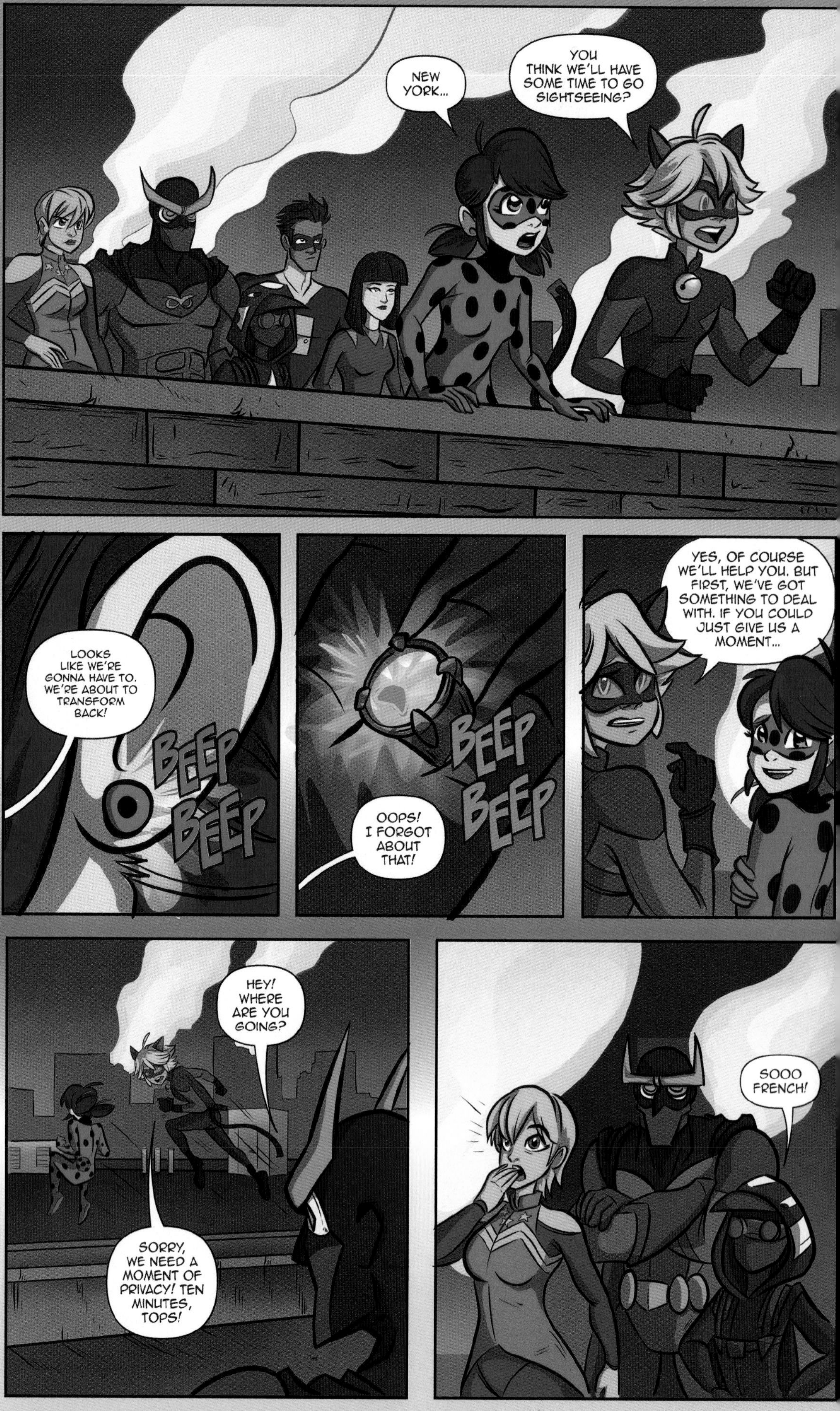
NEW YORK...
YOU THINK WE'LL HAVE SOME TIME TO GO SIGHTSEEING?
LOOKS LIKE WE'RE GONNA HAVE TO. WE'RE ABOUT TO TRANSFORM BACK!
BEEP BEEP
BEEP BEEP
OOPS! I FORGOT ABOUT THAT!
YES, OF COURSE WE'LL HELP YOU. BUT FIRST, WE'VE GOT SOMETHING TO DEAL WITH. IF YOU COULD JUST GIVE US A MOMENT...
HEY! WHERE ARE YOU GOING?
SORRY, WE NEED A MOMENT OF PRIVACY! TEN MINUTES, TOPS!
SOOO FRENCH!

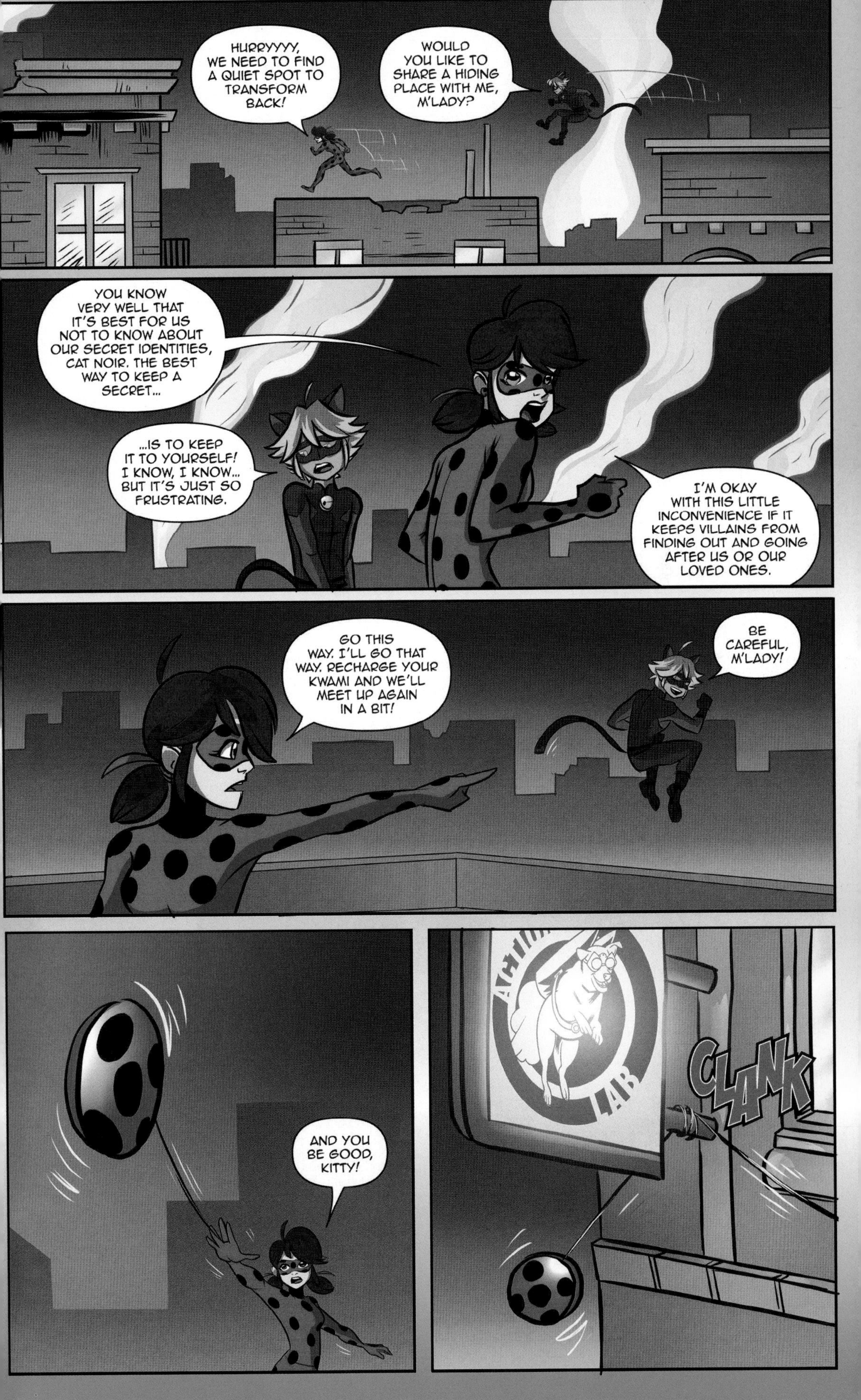
HURRYYYY, WE NEED TO FIND A QUIET SPOT TO TRANSFORM BACK!
WOULD YOU LIKE TO SHARE A HIDING PLACE WITH ME, M'LADY?
YOU KNOW VERY WELL THAT IT'S BEST FOR US NOT TO KNOW ABOUT OUR SECRET IDENTITIES, CAT NOIR. THE BEST WAY TO KEEP A SECRET...
...IS TO KEEP IT TO YOURSELF! I KNOW, I KNOW... BUT IT'S JUST SO FRUSTRATING.
I'M OKAY WITH THIS LITTLE INCONVENIENCE IF IT KEEPS VILLAINS FROM FINDING OUT AND GOING AFTER US OR OUR LOVED ONES.
GO THIS WAY. I'LL GO THAT WAY. RECHARGE YOUR KWAMI AND WE'LL MEET UP AGAIN IN A BIT!
BE CAREFUL, M'LADY!
AND YOU BE GOOD, KITTY!
LAB
CLANK

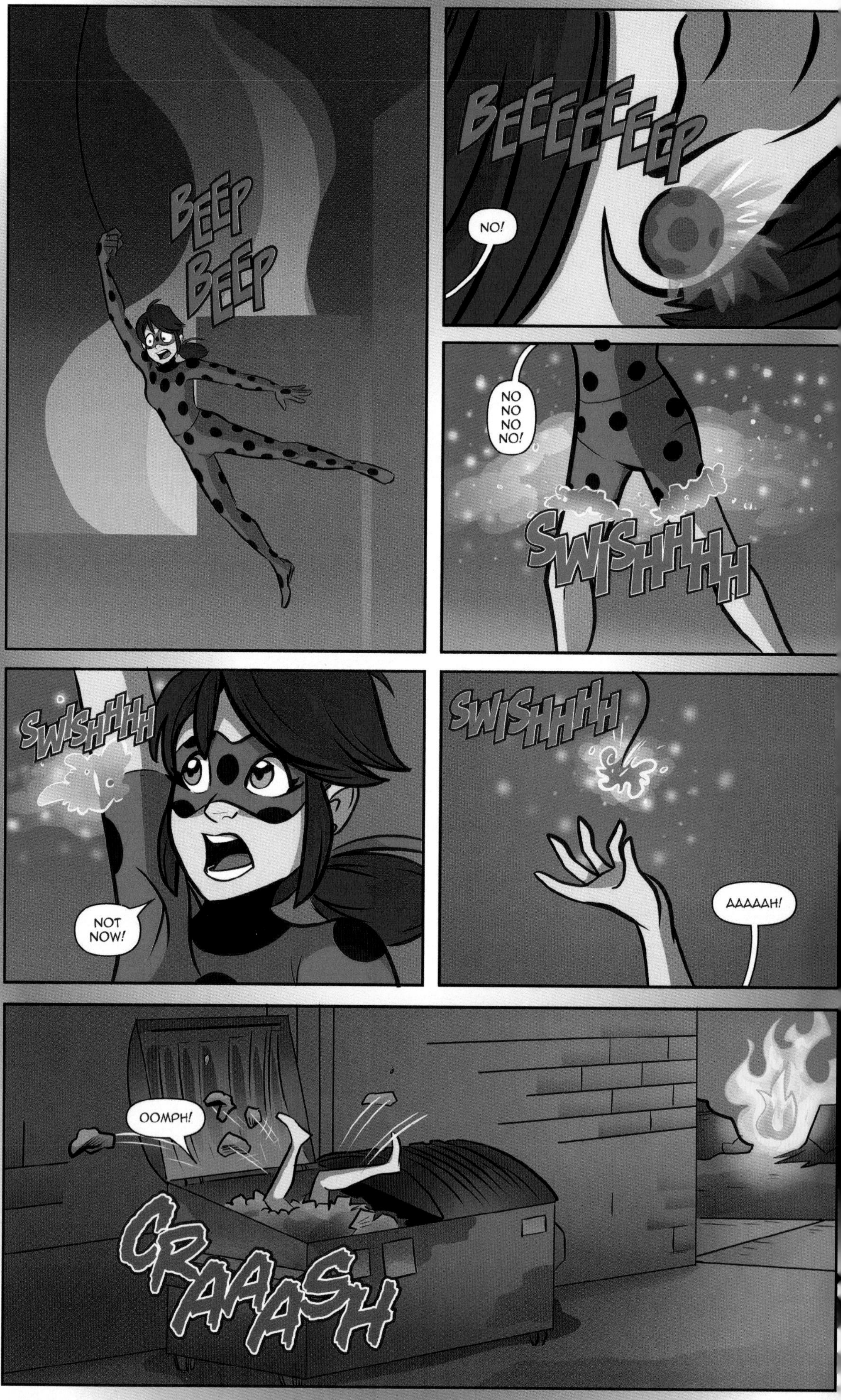
BEEP
BEEP
BEEEEEEEEP
NO!
NO NO NO NO!
SWISHHHHH
SWISHHHH
NOT NOW!
SWISHHHH
AAAAAH!
OOMPH!
CRAAASH

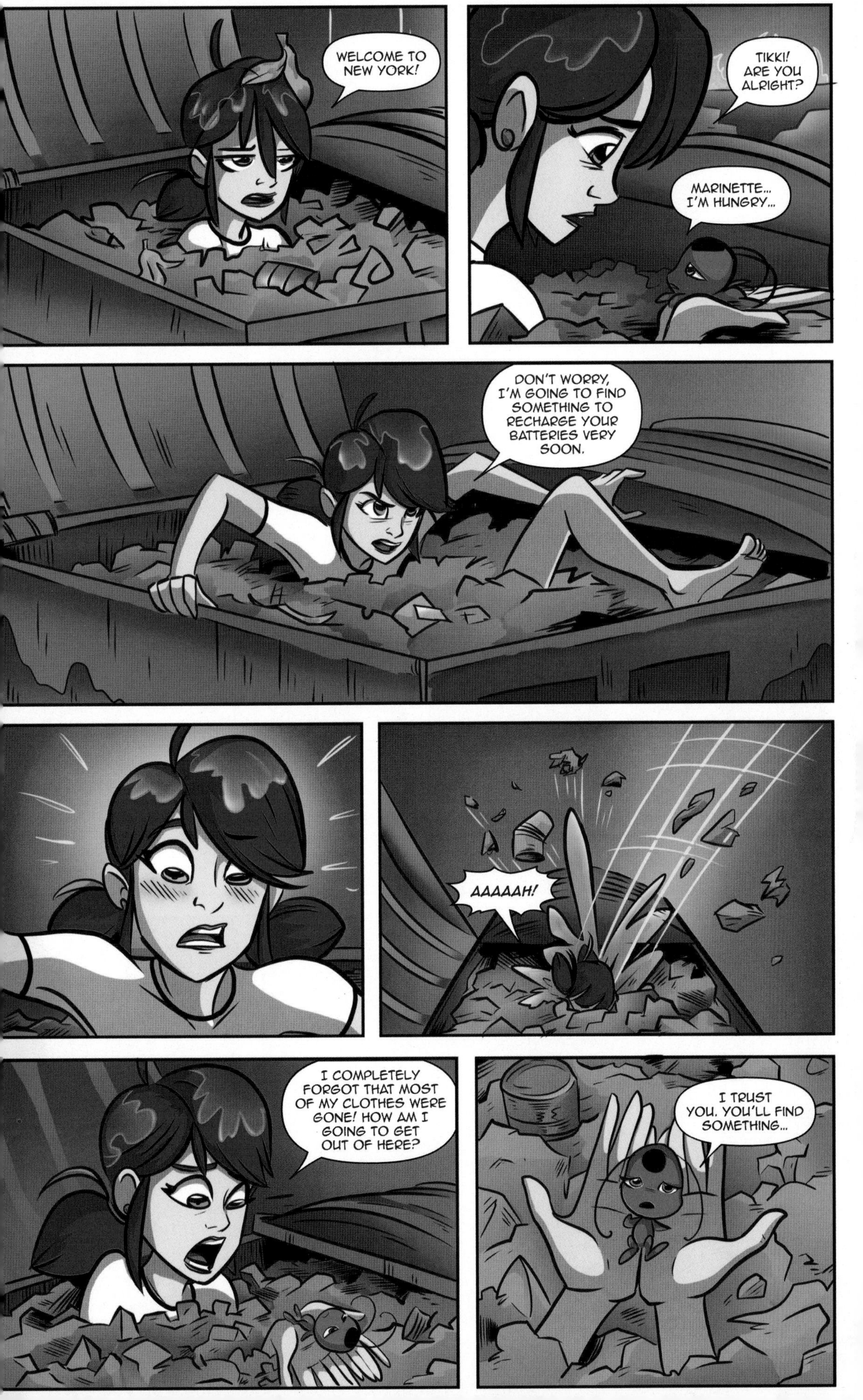
WELCOME TO NEW YORK!
TIKKI! ARE YOU ALRIGHT?
MARINETTE... I'M HUNGRY...
DON'T WORRY, I'M GOING TO FIND SOMETHING TO RECHARGE YOUR BATTERIES VERY SOON.
AAAAAH!
I COMPLETELY FORGOT THAT MOST OF MY CLOTHES WERE GONE! HOW AM I GOING TO GET OUT OF HERE?
I TRUST YOU. YOU'LL FIND SOMETHING...

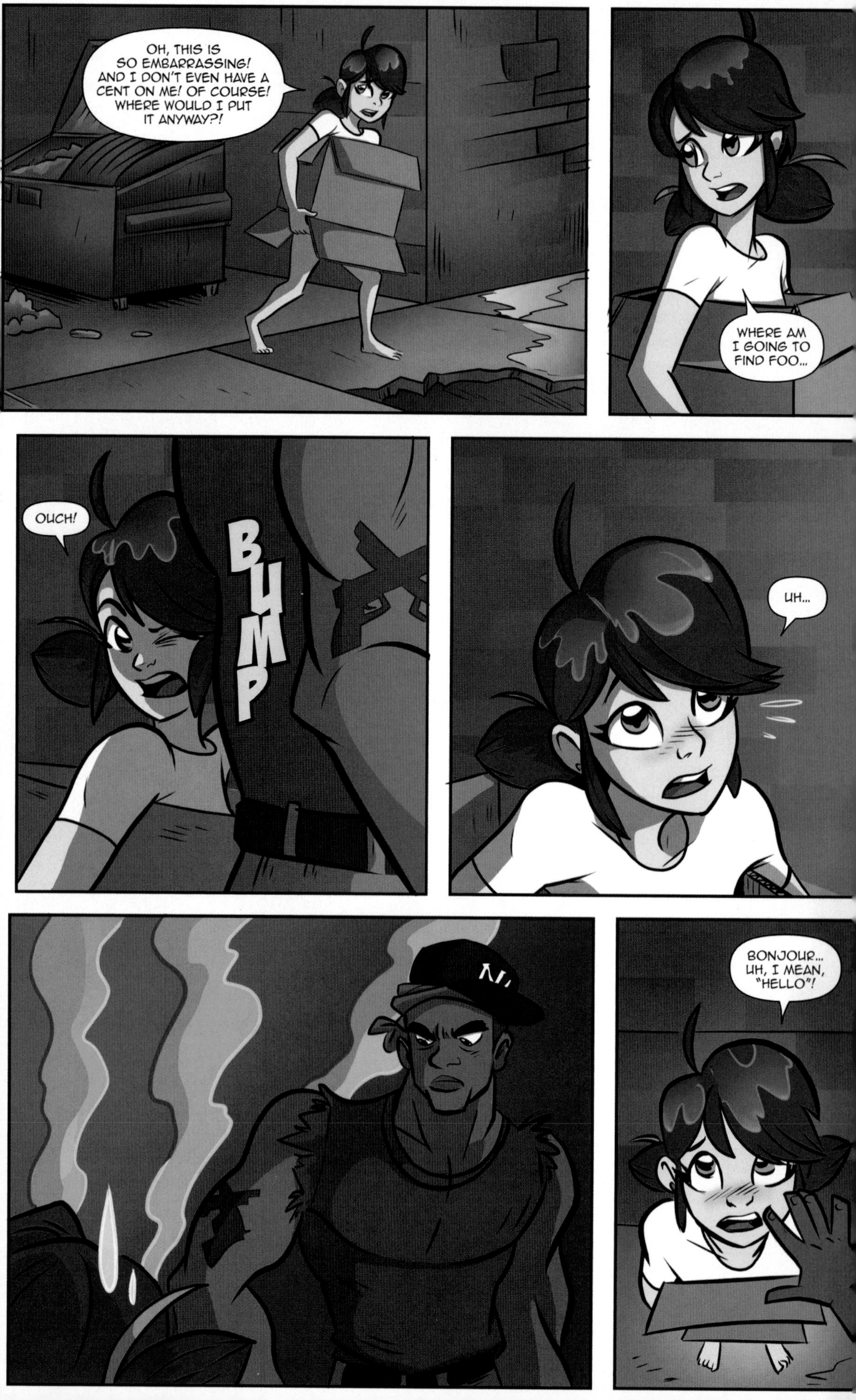
OH, THIS IS SO EMBARRASSING! AND I DON'T EVEN HAVE A CENT ON ME! OF COURSE! WHERE WOULD I PUT IT ANYWAY?!
WHERE AM I GOING TO FIND FOO...
OUCH!
BUMP
UH...
BONJOUR... UH, I MEAN, "HELLO"!

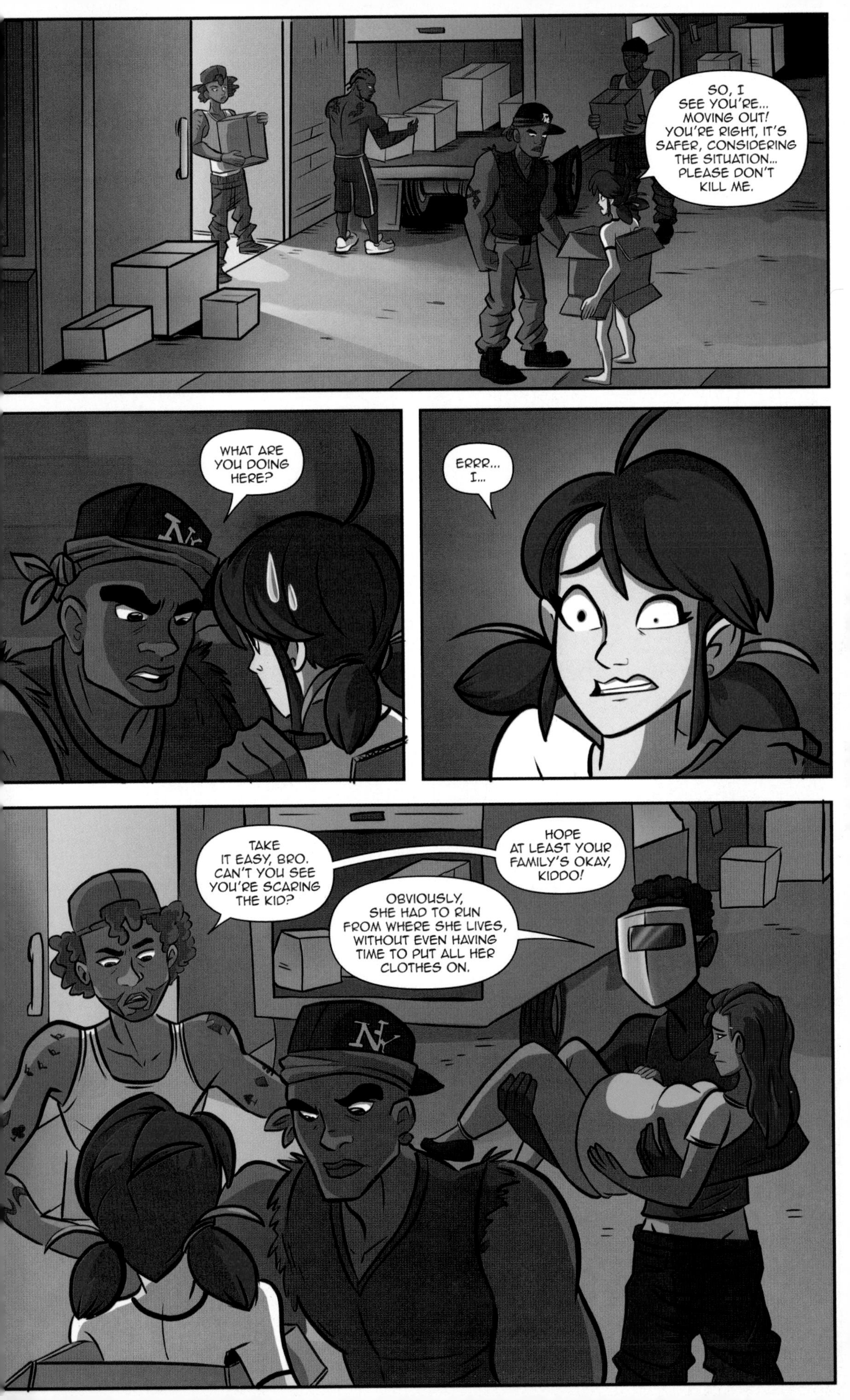

SO, I SEE YOU'RE... MOVING OUT! YOU'RE RIGHT, IT'S SAFER, CONSIDERING THE SITUATION... PLEASE DON'T KILL ME.
WHAT ARE YOU DOING HERE?
ERRR... I...
TAKE IT EASY, BRO. CAN'T YOU SEE YOU'RE SCARING THE KID?
HOPE AT LEAST YOUR FAMILY'S OKAY, KIDDO!
OBVIOUSLY, SHE HAD TO RUN FROM WHERE SHE LIVES, WITHOUT EVEN HAVING TIME TO PUT ALL HER CLOTHES ON.

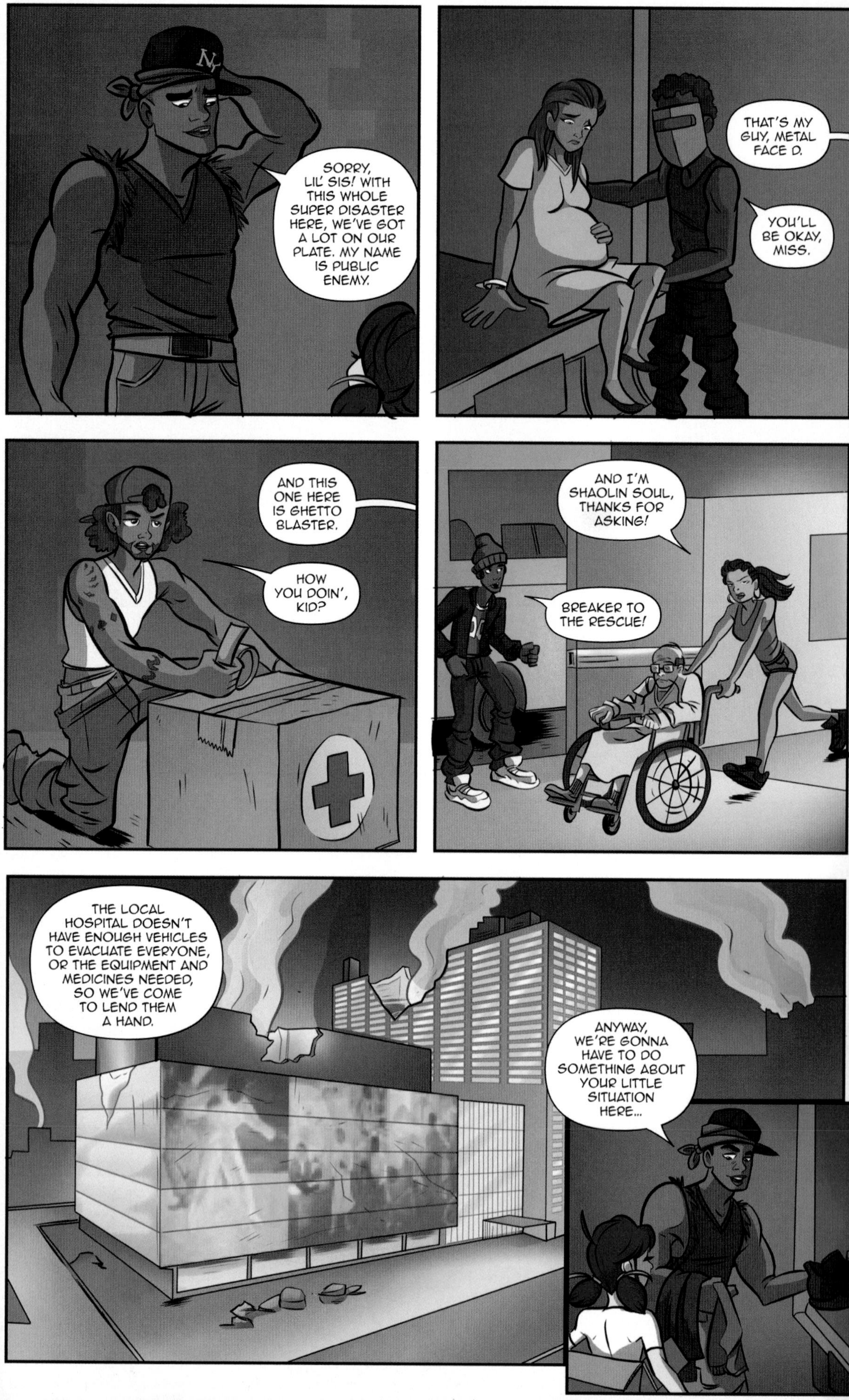
SORRY, LIL' SIS! WITH THIS WHOLE SUPER DISASTER HERE, WE'VE GOT A LOT ON OUR PLATE. MY NAME IS PUBLIC ENEMY.
THAT'S MY GUY, METAL FACE D.
YOU'LL BE OKAY, MISS.
AND THIS ONE HERE IS GHETTO BLASTER.
HOW YOU DOIN', KID?
AND I'M SHAOLIN SOUL, THANKS FOR ASKING!
BREAKER TO THE RESCUE!
THE LOCAL HOSPITAL DOESN'T HAVE ENOUGH VEHICLES TO EVACUATE EVERYONE, OR THE EQUIPMENT AND MEDICINES NEEDED, SO WE'VE COME TO LEND THEM A HAND.
ANYWAY, WE'RE GONNA HAVE TO DO SOMETHING ABOUT YOUR LITTLE SITUATION HERE...

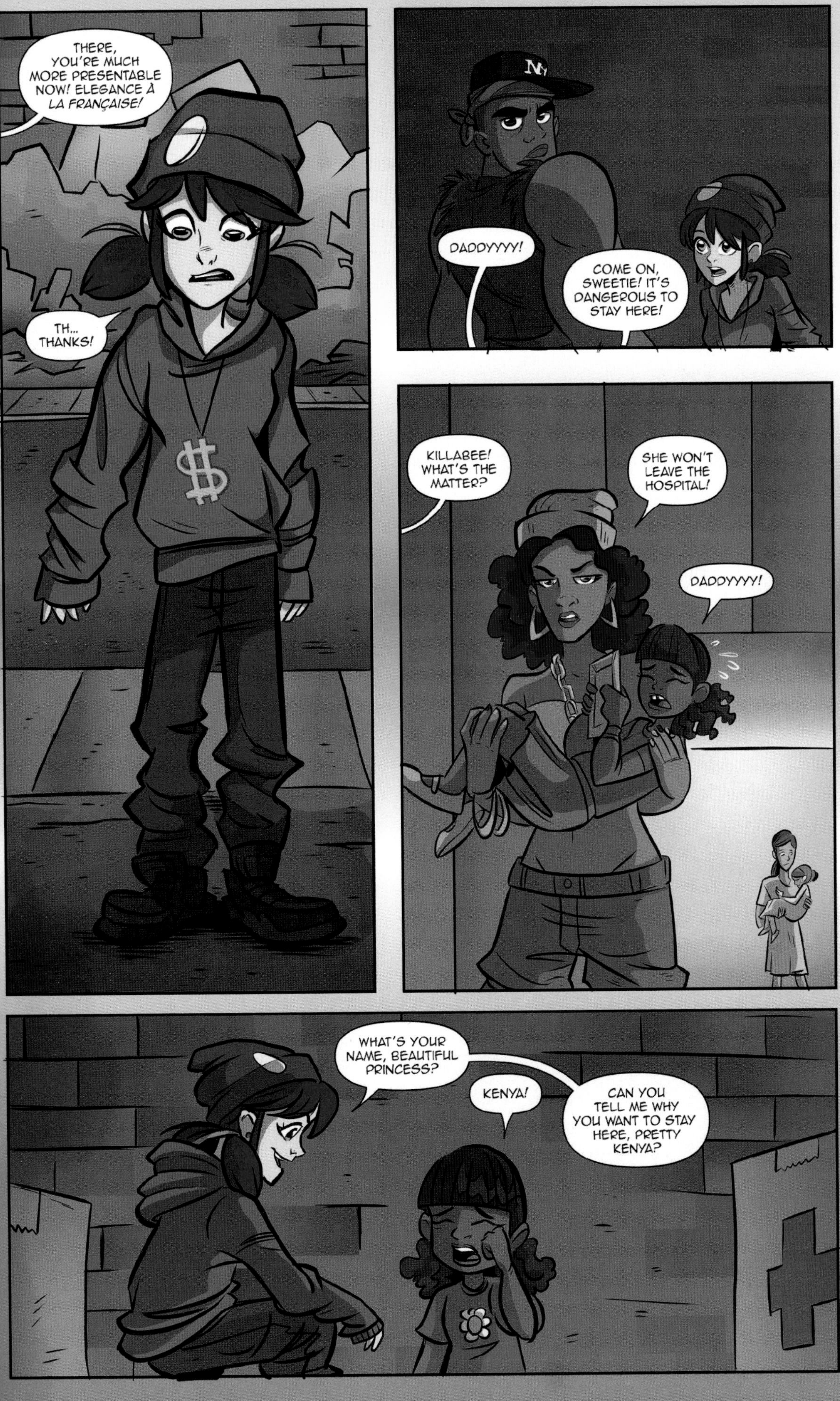
THERE, YOU'RE MUCH MORE PRESENTABLE NOW! ELEGANCE À LA FRANÇAISE!
TH... THANKS!
DADDYYYY!
COME ON, SWEETIE! IT'S DANGEROUS TO STAY HERE!
KILLABEE! WHAT'S THE MATTER?
SHE WON'T LEAVE THE HOSPITAL!
DADDYYYY!
WHAT'S YOUR NAME, BEAUTIFUL PRINCESS?
KENYA!
CAN YOU TELL ME WHY YOU WANT TO STAY HERE, PRETTY KENYA?

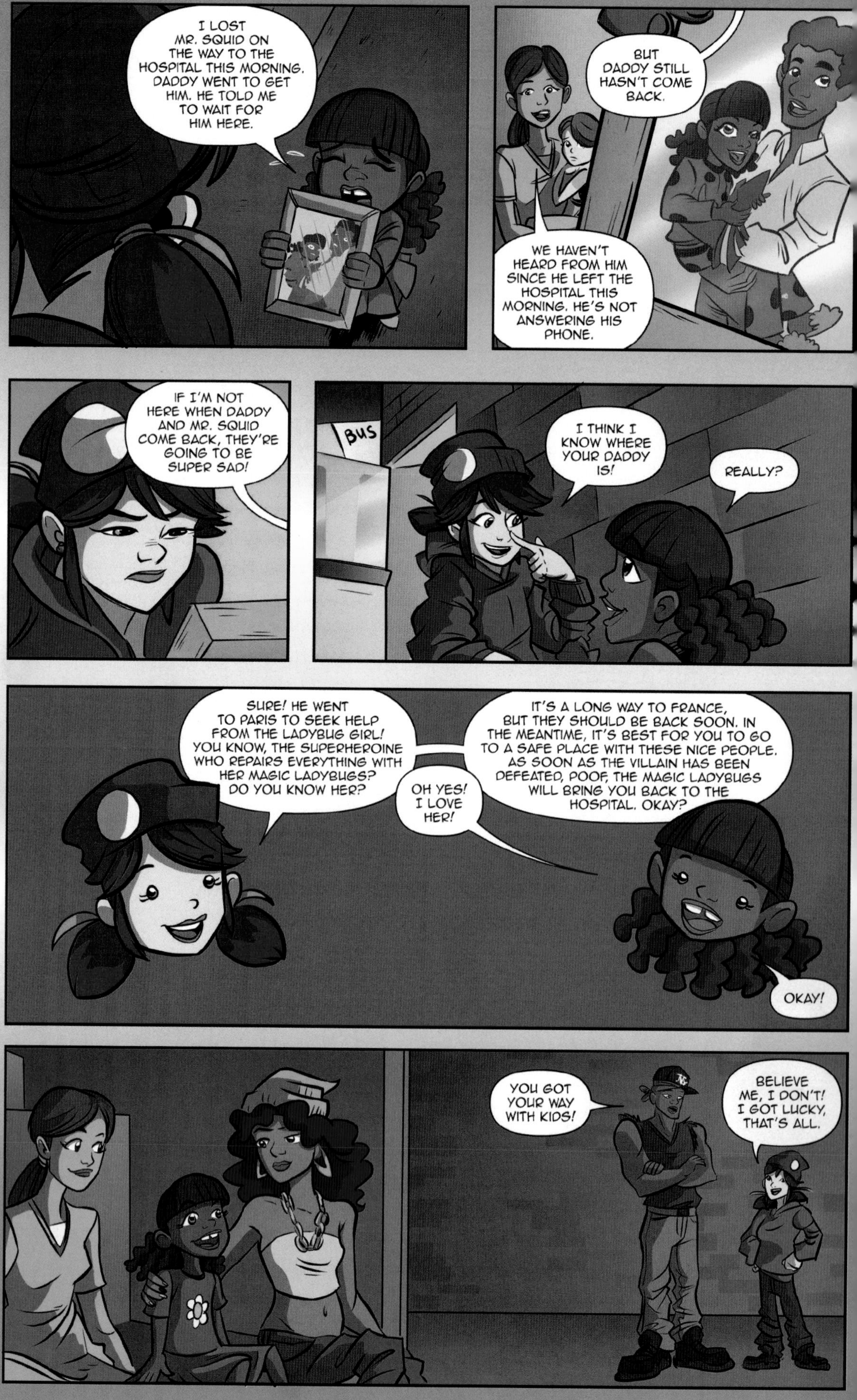
I LOST MR. SQUID ON THE WAY TO THE HOSPITAL THIS MORNING. DADDY WENT TO GET HIM. HE TOLD ME TO WAIT FOR HIM HERE.
BUT DADDY STILL HASN'T COME BACK.
WE HAVEN'T HEARD FROM HIM SINCE HE LEFT THE HOSPITAL THIS MORNING. HE'S NOT ANSWERING HIS PHONE.
IF I'M NOT HERE WHEN DADDY AND MR. SQUID COME BACK, THEY'RE GOING TO BE SUPER SAD!
BUS
I THINK I KNOW WHERE YOUR DADDY IS!
REALLY?
SURE! HE WENT TO PARIS TO SEEK HELP FROM THE LADYBUG GIRL! YOU KNOW, THE SUPERHEROINE WHO REPAIRS EVERYTHING WITH HER MAGIC LADYBUGS? DO YOU KNOW HER?
OH YES! I LOVE HER!
IT'S A LONG WAY TO FRANCE, BUT THEY SHOULD BE BACK SOON. IN THE MEANTIME, IT'S BEST FOR YOU TO GO TO A SAFE PLACE WITH THESE NICE PEOPLE. AS SOON AS THE VILLAIN HAS BEEN DEFEATED, POOF, THE MAGIC LADYBUGS WILL BRING YOU BACK TO THE HOSPITAL. OKAY?
OKAY!
YOU GOT YOUR WAY WITH KIDS!
BELIEVE ME, I DON'T! I GOT LUCKY, THAT'S ALL.

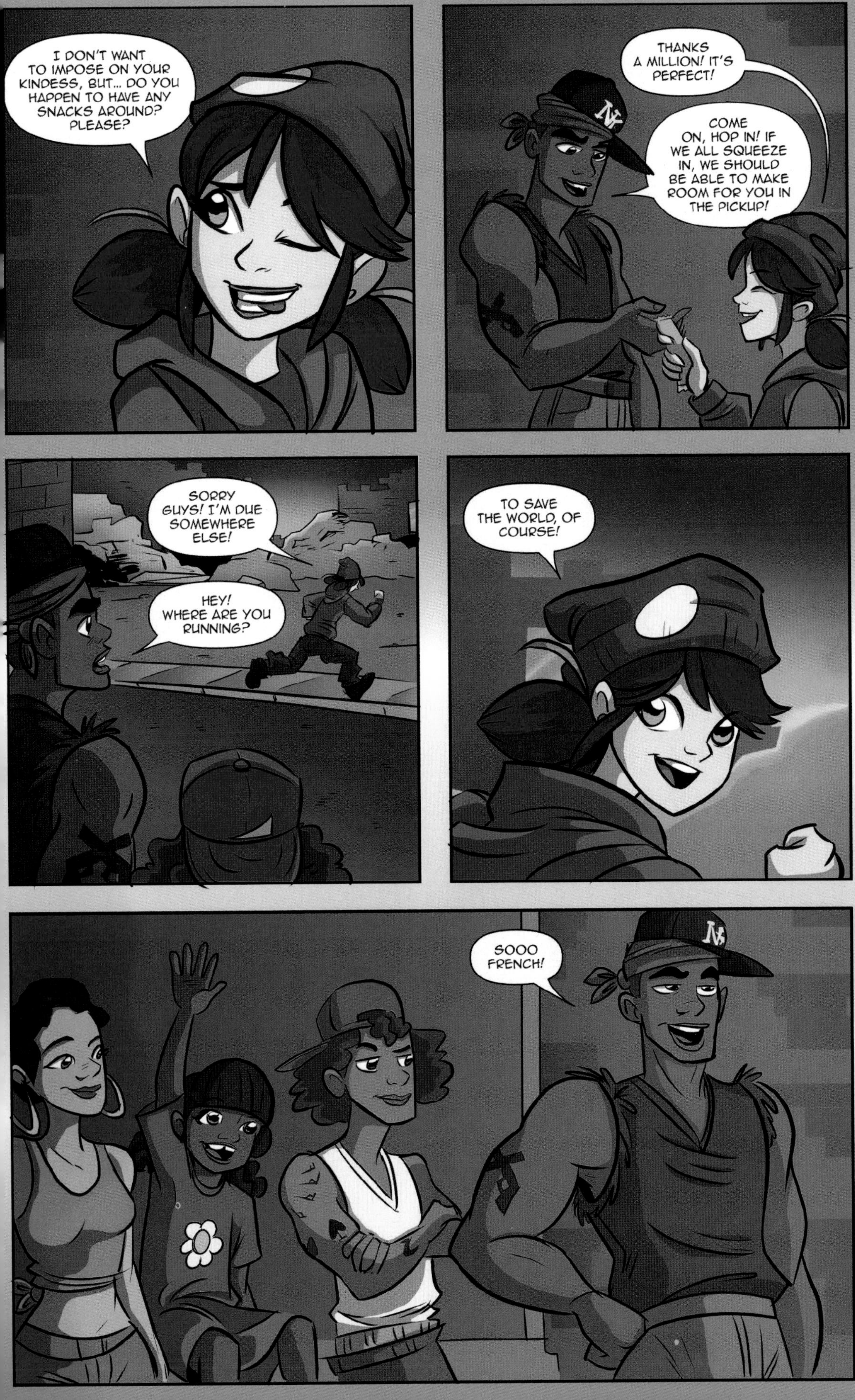
I DON'T WANT TO IMPOSE ON YOUR KINDESS, BUT... DO YOU HAPPEN TO HAVE ANY SNACKS AROUND? PLEASE?
THANKS A MILLION! IT'S PERFECT!
COME ON, HOP IN! IF WE ALL SQUEEZE IN, WE SHOULD BE ABLE TO MAKE ROOM FOR YOU IN THE PICKUP!
SORRY GUYS! I'M DUE SOMEWHERE ELSE!
HEY! WHERE ARE YOU RUNNING?
TO SAVE THE WORLD, OF COURSE!
SOOO FRENCH!

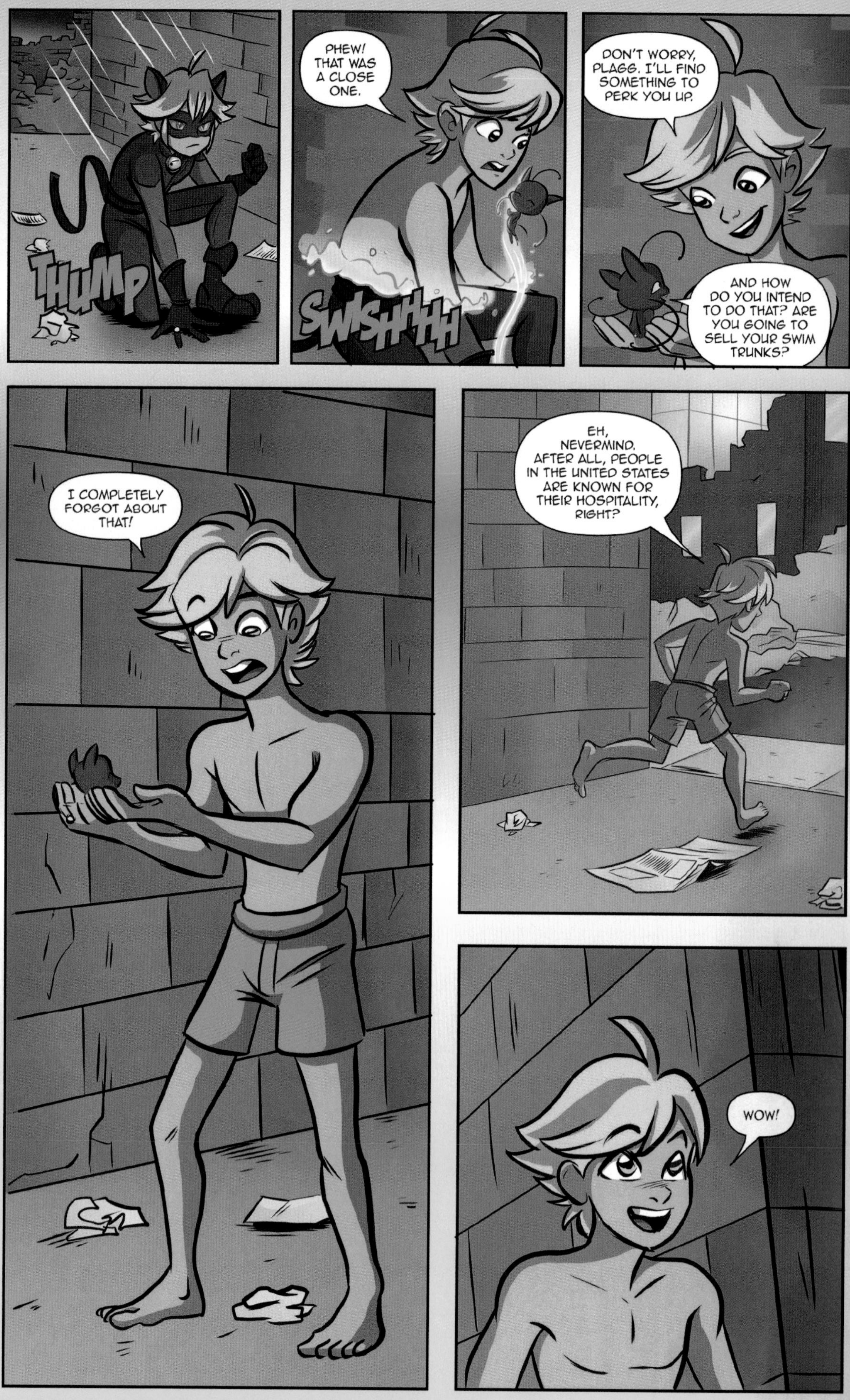
THUMP
PHEW! THAT WAS A CLOSE ONE.
SWISHHHH
DON'T WORRY, PLAGG. I'LL FIND SOMETHING TO PERK YOU UP.
AND HOW DO YOU INTEND TO DO THAT? ARE YOU GOING TO SELL YOUR SWIM TRUNKS?
I COMPLETELY FORGOT ABOUT THAT!
EH, NEVERMIND. AFTER ALL, PEOPLE IN THE UNITED STATES ARE KNOWN FOR THEIR HOSPITALITY, RIGHT?
WOW!

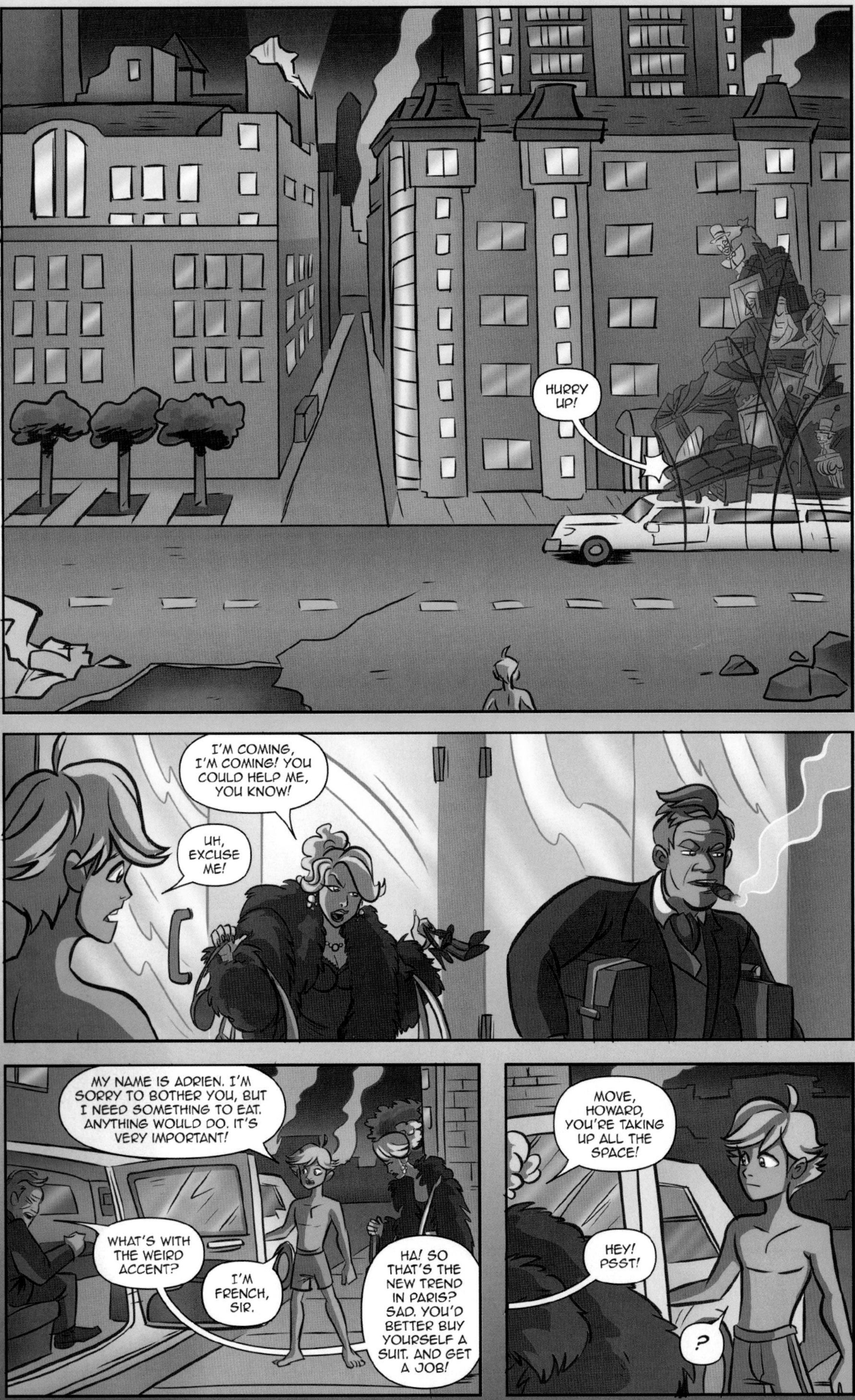
HURRY UP!
I'M COMING, I'M COMING! YOU COULD HELP ME, YOU KNOW!
UH, EXCUSE ME!
MY NAME IS ADRIEN. I'M SORRY TO BOTHER YOU, BUT I NEED SOMETHING TO EAT. ANYTHING WOULD DO. IT'S VERY IMPORTANT!
WHAT'S WITH THE WEIRD ACCENT?
I'M FRENCH, SIR.
HA! SO THAT'S THE NEW TREND IN PARIS? SAD. YOU'D BETTER BUY YOURSELF A SUIT. AND GET A JOB!
MOVE, HOWARD, YOU'RE TAKING UP ALL THE SPACE!
HEY! PSST!
?

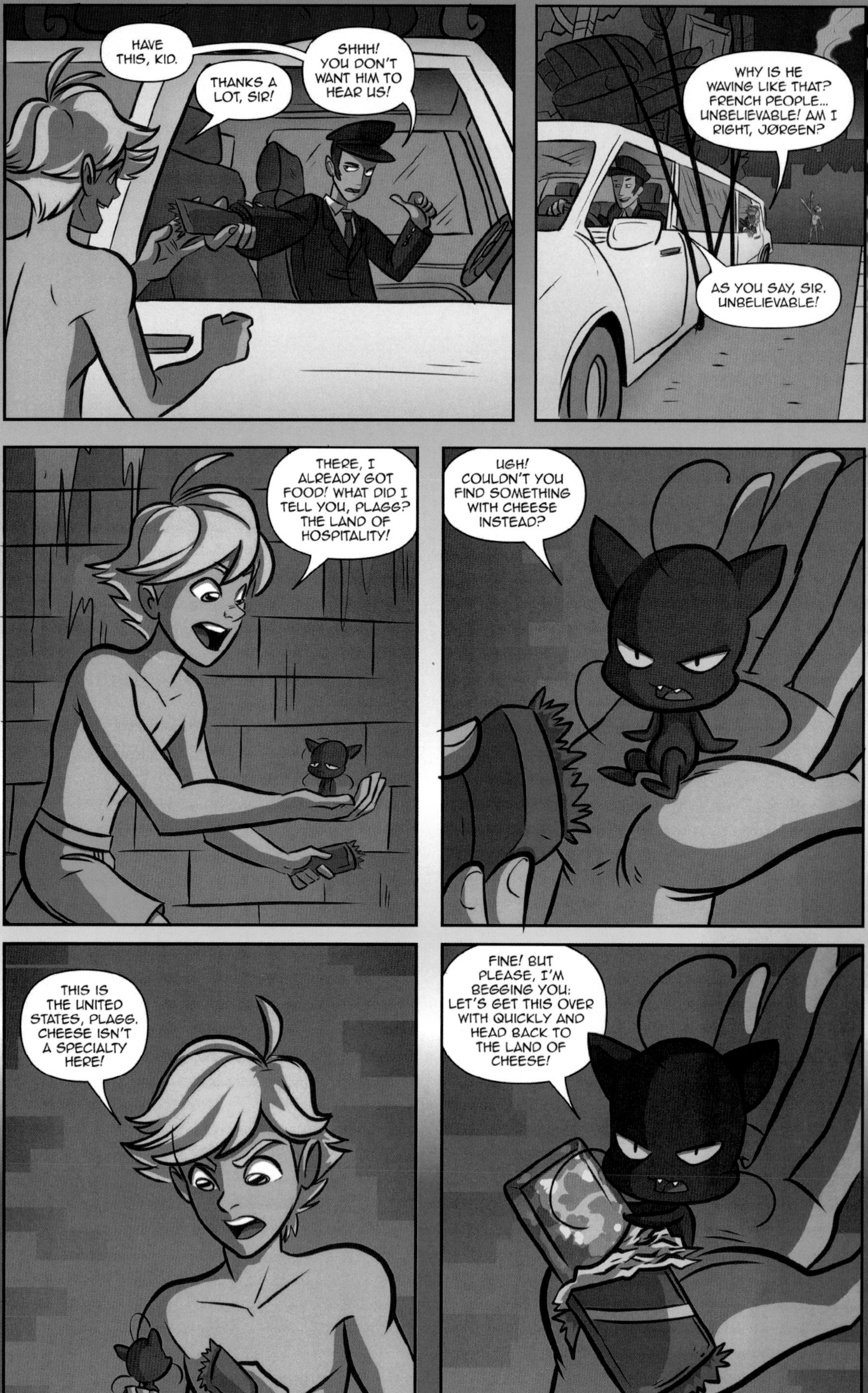
HAVE THIS, KID.
THANKS A LOT, SIR!
SHHH! YOU DON'T WANT HIM TO HEAR US!
WHY IS HE WAVING LIKE THAT? FRENCH PEOPLE... UNBELIEVABLE! AM I RIGHT, JØRGEN?
AS YOU SAY, SIR. UNBELIEVABLE!
THERE, I ALREADY GOT FOOD! WHAT DID I TELL YOU, PLAGG? THE LAND OF HOSPITALITY!
UGH! COULDN'T YOU FIND SOMETHING WITH CHEESE INSTEAD?
THIS IS THE UNITED STATES, PLAGG. CHEESE ISN'T A SPECIALTY HERE!
FINE! BUT PLEASE, I'M BEGGING YOU: LET'S GET THIS OVER WITH QUICKLY AND HEAD BACK TO THE LAND OF CHEESE!

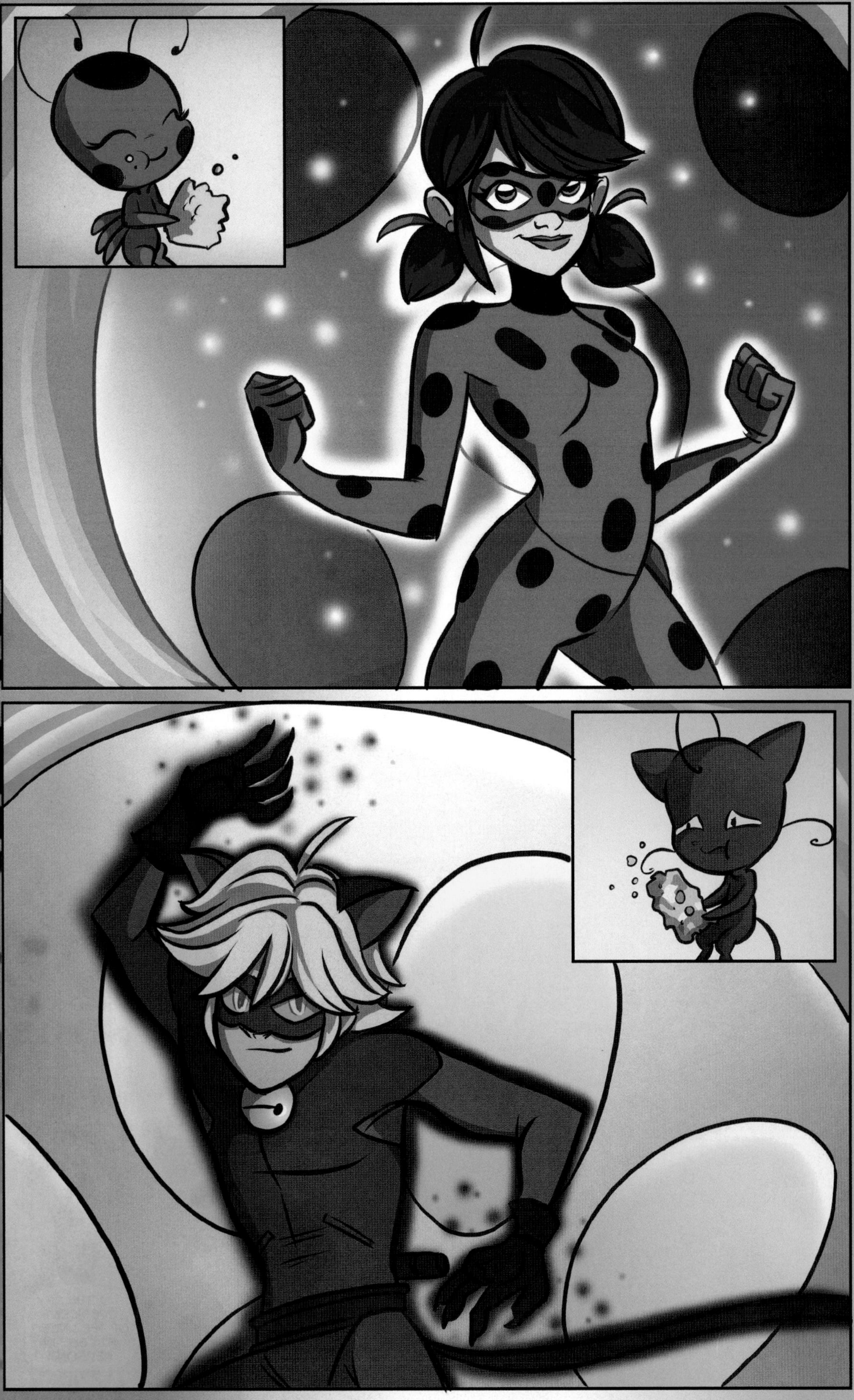

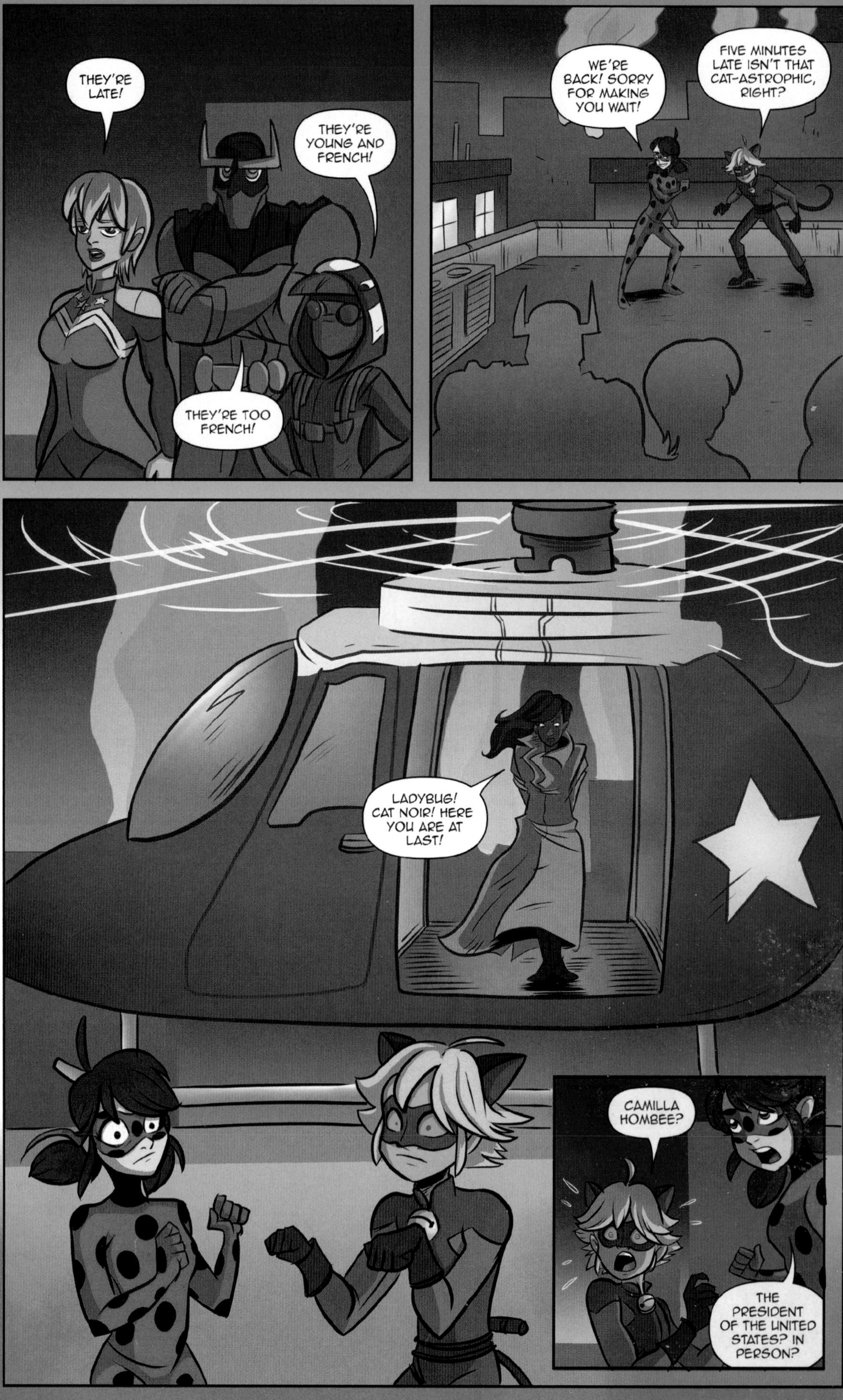
THEY'RE LATE!
THEY'RE YOUNG AND FRENCH!
THEY'RE TOO FRENCH!
WE'RE BACK! SORRY FOR MAKING YOU WAIT!
FIVE MINUTES LATE ISN'T THAT CAT-ASTROPHIC, RIGHT?
LADYBUG! CAT NOIR! HERE YOU ARE AT LAST!
CAMILLA HOMBEE?
THE PRESIDENT OF THE UNITED STATES? IN PERSON?

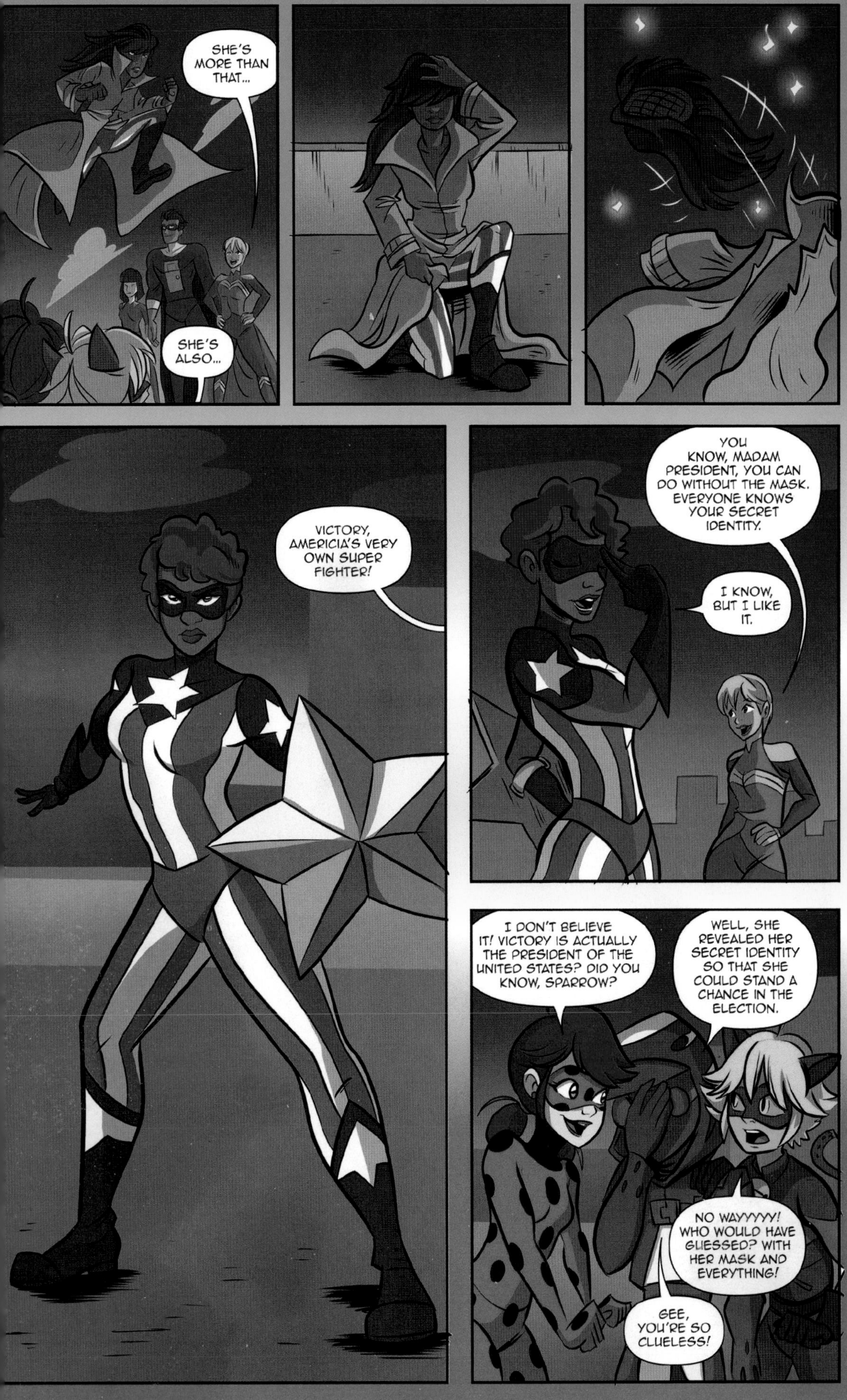
SHE'S MORE THAN THAT...
SHE'S ALSO...
VICTORY, AMERICIA'S VERY OWN SUPER FIGHTER!
YOU KNOW, MADAM PRESIDENT, YOU CAN DO WITHOUT THE MASK. EVERYONE KNOWS YOUR SECRET IDENTITY.
I KNOW, BUT I LIKE IT.
I DON'T BELIEVE IT! VICTORY IS ACTUALLY THE PRESIDENT OF THE UNITED STATES? DID YOU KNOW, SPARROW?
WELL, SHE REVEALED HER SECRET IDENTITY SO THAT SHE COULD STAND A CHANCE IN THE ELECTION.
NO WAYYYYYY! WHO WOULD HAVE GUESSED? WITH HER MASK AND EVERYTHING!
GEE, YOU'RE SO CLUELESS!

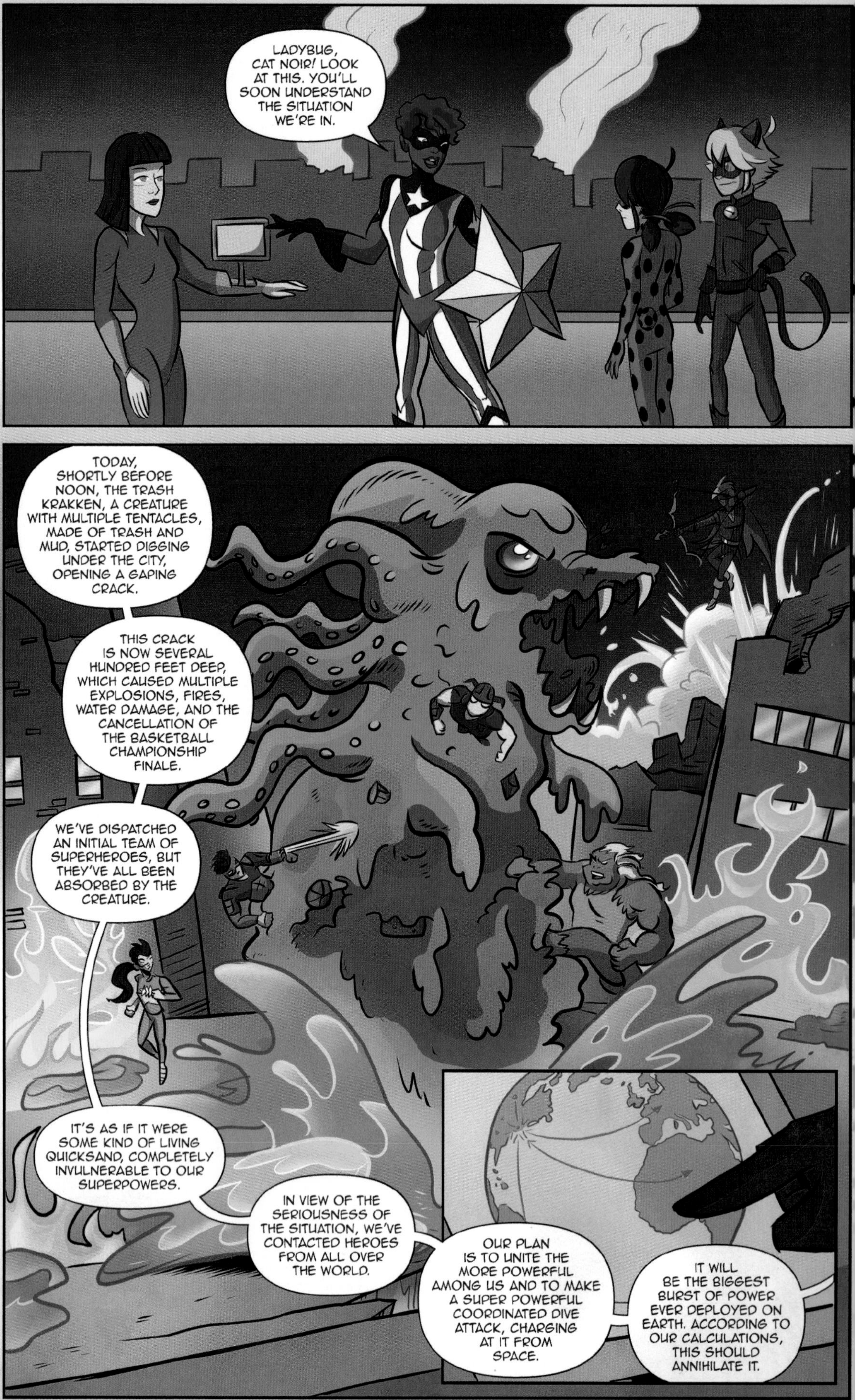
LADYBUG, CAT NOIR! LOOK AT THIS. YOU'LL SOON UNDERSTAND THE SITUATION WE'RE IN.
TODAY, SHORTLY BEFORE NOON, THE TRASH KRAKKEN, A CREATURE WITH MULTIPLE TENTACLES, MADE OF TRASH AND MUD, STARTED DIGGING UNDER THE CITY, OPENING A GAPING CRACK.
THIS CRACK IS NOW SEVERAL HUNDRED FEET DEEP, WHICH CAUSED MULTIPLE EXPLOSIONS, FIRES, WATER DAMAGE, AND THE CANCELLATION OF THE BASKETBALL CHAMPIONSHIP FINALE.
WE'VE DISPATCHED AN INITIAL TEAM OF SUPERHEROES, BUT THEY'VE ALL BEEN ABSORBED BY THE CREATURE.
IT'S AS IF IT WERE SOME KIND OF LIVING QUICKSAND, COMPLETELY INVULNERABLE TO OUR SUPERPOWERS.
IN VIEW OF THE SERIOUSNESS OF THE SITUATION, WE'VE CONTACTED HEROES FROM ALL OVER THE WORLD.
OUR PLAN IS TO UNITE THE MORE POWERFUL AMONG US AND TO MAKE A SUPER POWERFUL COORDINATED DIVE ATTACK, CHARGING AT IT FROM SPACE.
IT WILL BE THE BIGGEST BURST OF POWER EVER DEPLOYED ON EARTH. ACCORDING TO OUR CALCULATIONS, THIS SHOULD ANNIHILATE IT.

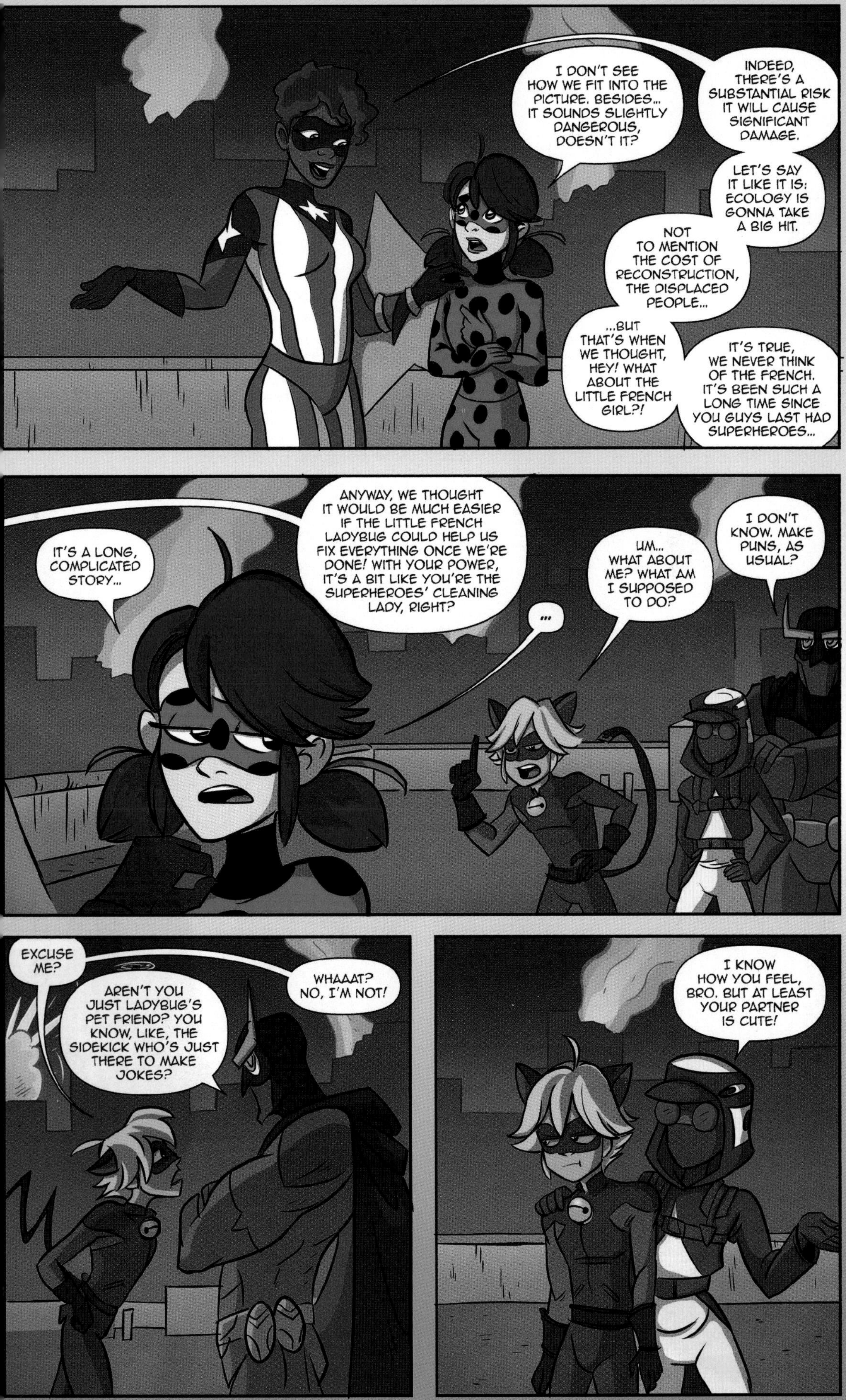
I DON'T SEE HOW WE FIT INTO THE PICTURE. BESIDES... IT SOUNDS SLIGHTLY DANGEROUS, DOESN'T IT?
INDEED, THERE'S A SUBSTANTIAL RISK IT WILL CAUSE SIGNIFICANT DAMAGE.
LET'S SAY IT LIKE IT IS: ECOLOGY IS GONNA TAKE A BIG HIT.
NOT TO MENTION THE COST OF RECONSTRUCTION, THE DISPLACED PEOPLE...
...BUT THAT'S WHEN WE THOUGHT, HEY! WHAT ABOUT THE LITTLE FRENCH GIRL?!
IT'S TRUE, WE NEVER THINK OF THE FRENCH. IT'S BEEN SUCH A LONG TIME SINCE YOU GUYS LAST HAD SUPERHEROES...
IT'S A LONG, COMPLICATED STORY...
ANYWAY, WE THOUGHT IT WOULD BE MUCH EASIER IF THE LITTLE FRENCH LADYBUG COULD HELP US FIX EVERYTHING ONCE WE'RE DONE! WITH YOUR POWER, IT'S A BIT LIKE YOU'RE THE SUPERHEROES' CLEANING LADY, RIGHT?
...
UM... WHAT ABOUT ME? WHAT AM I SUPPOSED TO DO?
I DON'T KNOW. MAKE PUNS, AS USUAL?
EXCUSE ME?
AREN'T YOU JUST LADYBUG'S PET FRIEND? YOU KNOW, LIKE, THE SIDEKICK WHO'S JUST THERE TO MAKE JOKES?
WHAAAT? NO, I'M NOT!
I KNOW HOW YOU FEEL, BRO. BUT AT LEAST YOUR PARTNER IS CUTE!

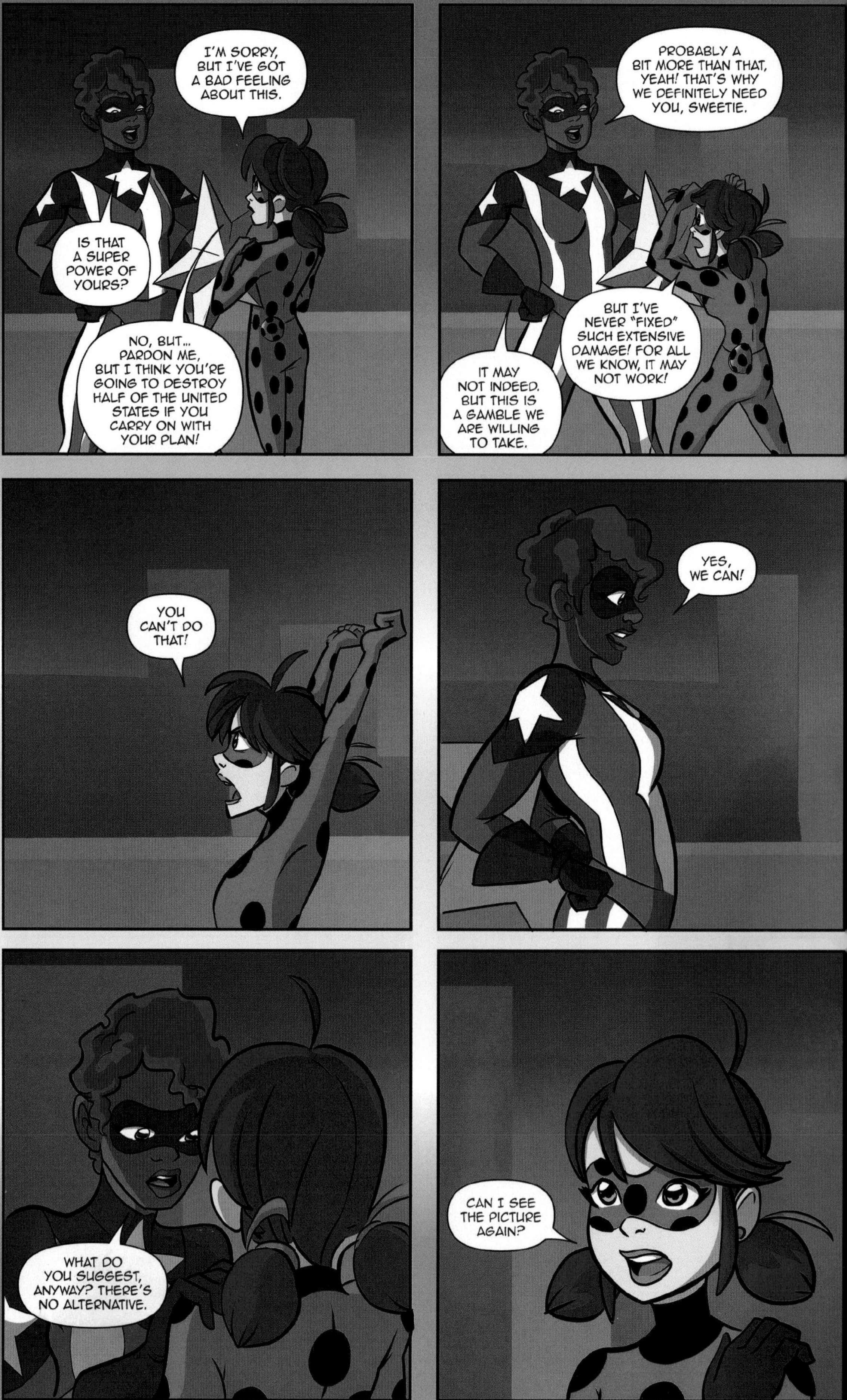

I'M SORRY, BUT I'VE GOT A BAD FEELING ABOUT THIS.
IS THAT A SUPER POWER OF YOURS?
NO, BUT... PARDON ME, BUT I THINK YOU'RE GOING TO DESTROY HALF OF THE UNITED STATES IF YOU CARRY ON WITH YOUR PLAN!
PROBABLY A BIT MORE THAN THAT, YEAH! THAT'S WHY WE DEFINITELY NEED YOU, SWEETIE.
BUT I'VE NEVER "FIXED" SUCH EXTENSIVE DAMAGE! FOR ALL WE KNOW, IT MAY NOT WORK!
IT MAY NOT INDEED. BUT THIS IS A GAMBLE WE ARE WILLING TO TAKE.
YOU CAN'T DO THAT!
YES, WE CAN!
WHAT DO YOU SUGGEST, ANYWAY? THERE'S NO ALTERNATIVE.
CAN I SEE THE PICTURE AGAIN?

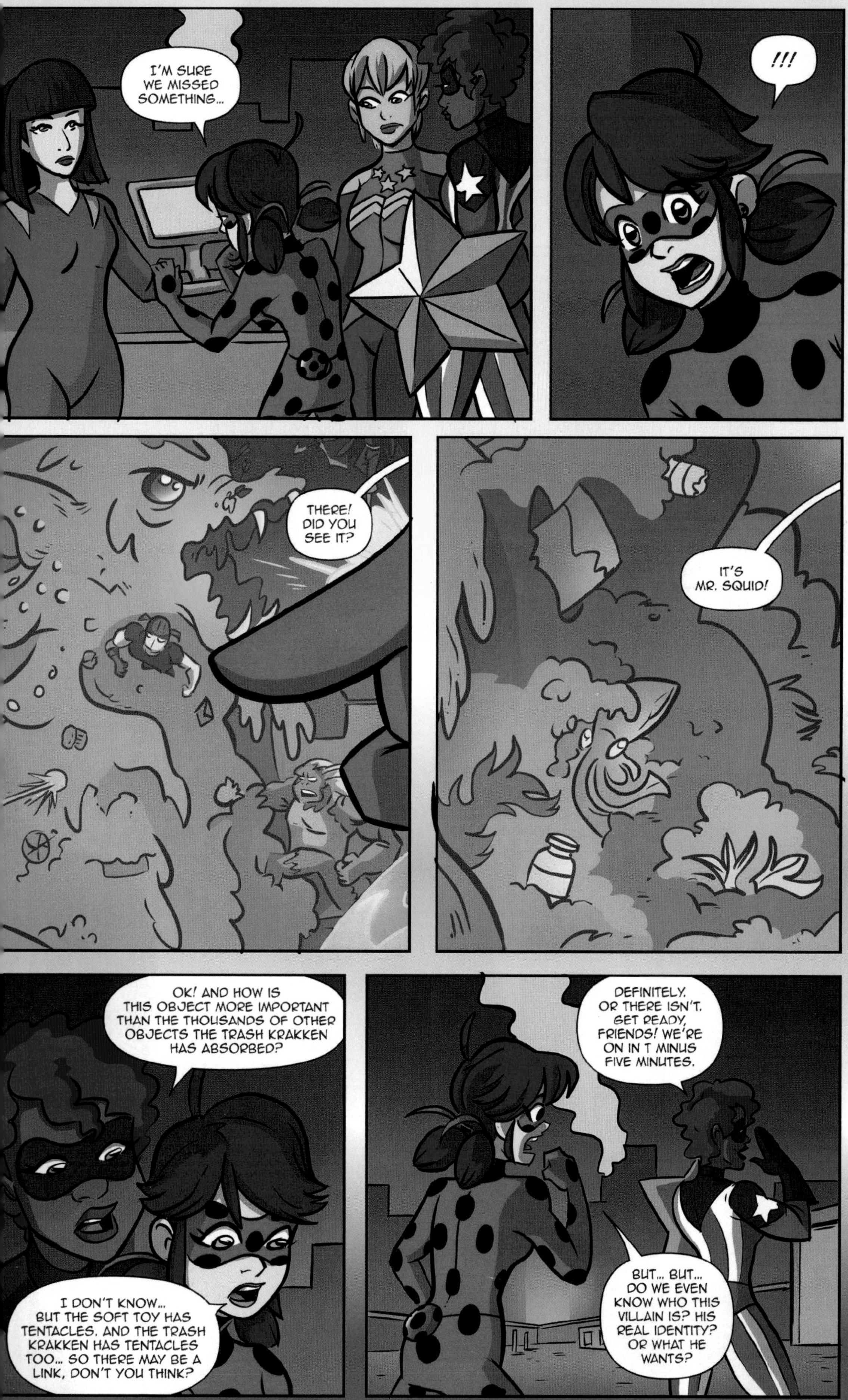
I'M SURE WE MISSED SOMETHING...
!!!
THERE! DID YOU SEE IT?
IT'S MR. SQUID!
OK! AND HOW IS THIS OBJECT MORE IMPORTANT THAN THE THOUSANDS OF OTHER OBJECTS THE TRASH KRAKKEN HAS ABSORBED?
I DON'T KNOW... BUT THE SOFT TOY HAS TENTACLES, AND THE TRASH KRAKKEN HAS TENTACLES TOO... SO THERE MAY BE A LINK, DON'T YOU THINK?
BUT... BUT... DO WE EVEN KNOW WHO THIS VILLAIN IS? HIS REAL IDENTITY? OR WHAT HE WANTS?
DEFINITELY. OR THERE ISN'T. GET READY, FRIENDS! WE'RE ON IN T MINUS FIVE MINUTES.

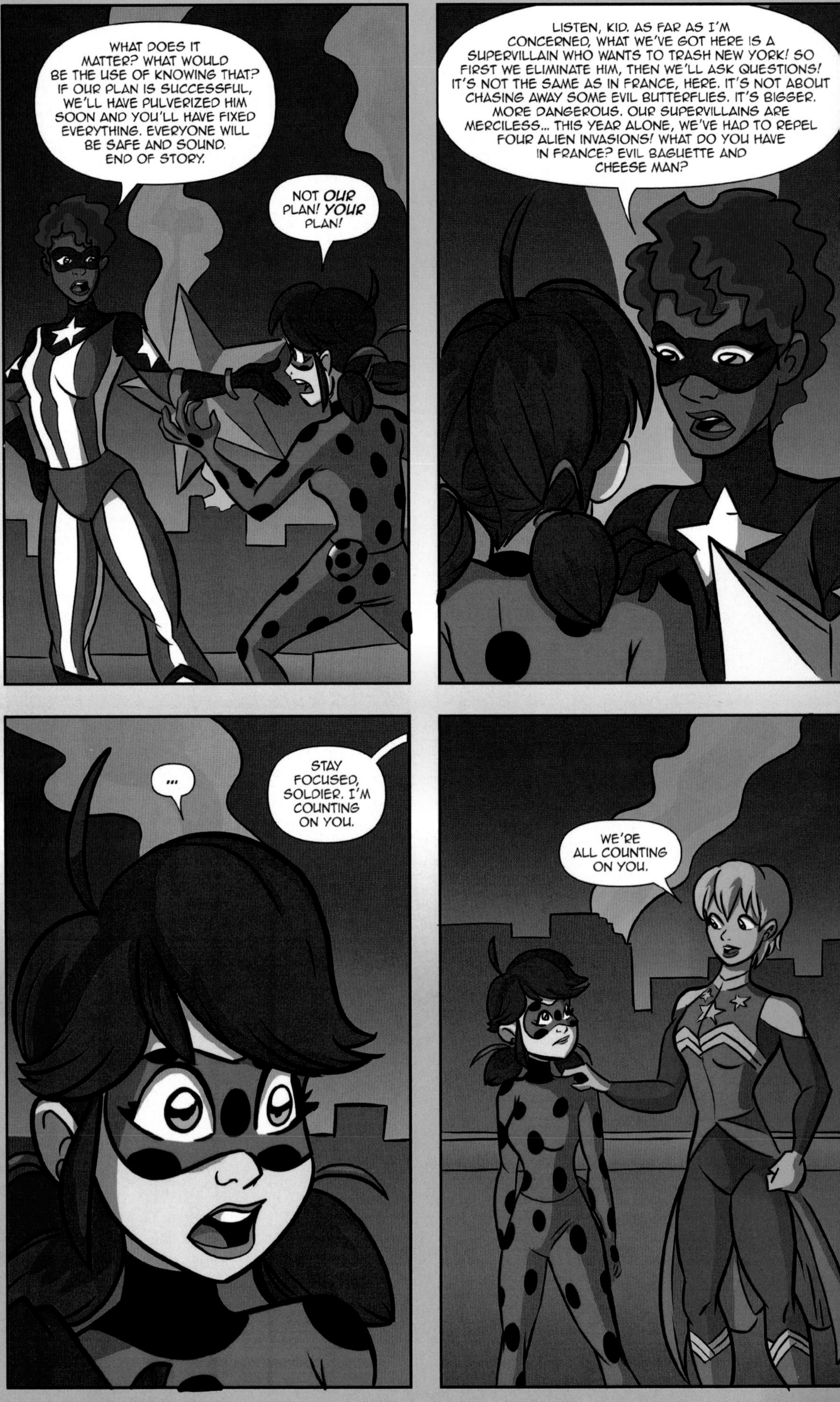
WHAT DOES IT MATTER? WHAT WOULD BE THE USE OF KNOWING THAT? IF OUR PLAN IS SUCCESSFUL, WE'LL HAVE PULVERIZED HIM SOON AND YOU'LL HAVE FIXED EVERYTHING. EVERYONE WILL BE SAFE AND SOUND. END OF STORY.
NOT OUR PLAN! YOUR PLAN!
LISTEN, KID. AS FAR AS I'M CONCERNED, WHAT WE'VE GOT HERE IS A SUPERVILLAIN WHO WANTS TO TRASH NEW YORK! SO FIRST WE ELIMINATE HIM, THEN WE'LL ASK QUESTIONS! IT'S NOT THE SAME AS IN FRANCE, HERE. IT'S NOT ABOUT CHASING AWAY SOME EVIL BUTTERFLIES. IT'S BIGGER. MORE DANGEROUS. OUR SUPERVILLAINS ARE MERCILESS... THIS YEAR ALONE, WE'VE HAD TO REPEL FOUR ALIEN INVASIONS! WHAT DO YOU HAVE IN FRANCE? EVIL BAGUETTE AND CHEESE MAN?
...
STAY FOCUSED, SOLDIER. I'M COUNTING ON YOU.
WE'RE ALL COUNTING ON YOU.

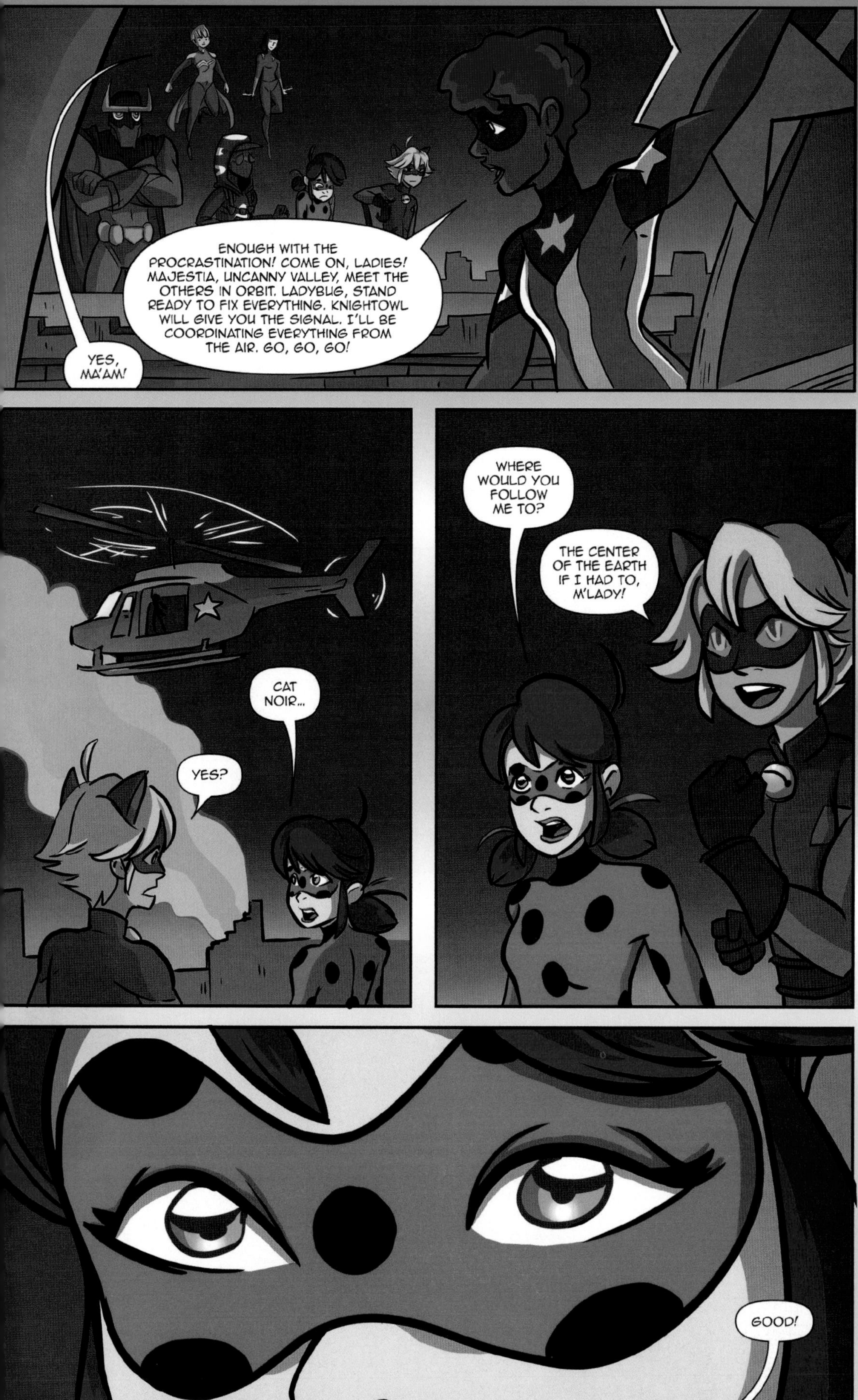
ENOUGH WITH THE PROCRASTINATION! COME ON, LADIES! MAJESTIA, UNCANNY VALLEY, MEET THE OTHERS IN ORBIT. LADYBUG, STAND READY TO FIX EVERYTHING. KNIGHTOWL WILL GIVE YOU THE SIGNAL. I'LL BE COORDINATING EVERYTHING FROM THE AIR. GO, GO, GO!
YES, MA'AM!
CAT NOIR...
YES?
WHERE WOULD YOU FOLLOW ME TO?
THE CENTER OF THE EARTH IF I HAD TO, M'LADY!
GOOD!

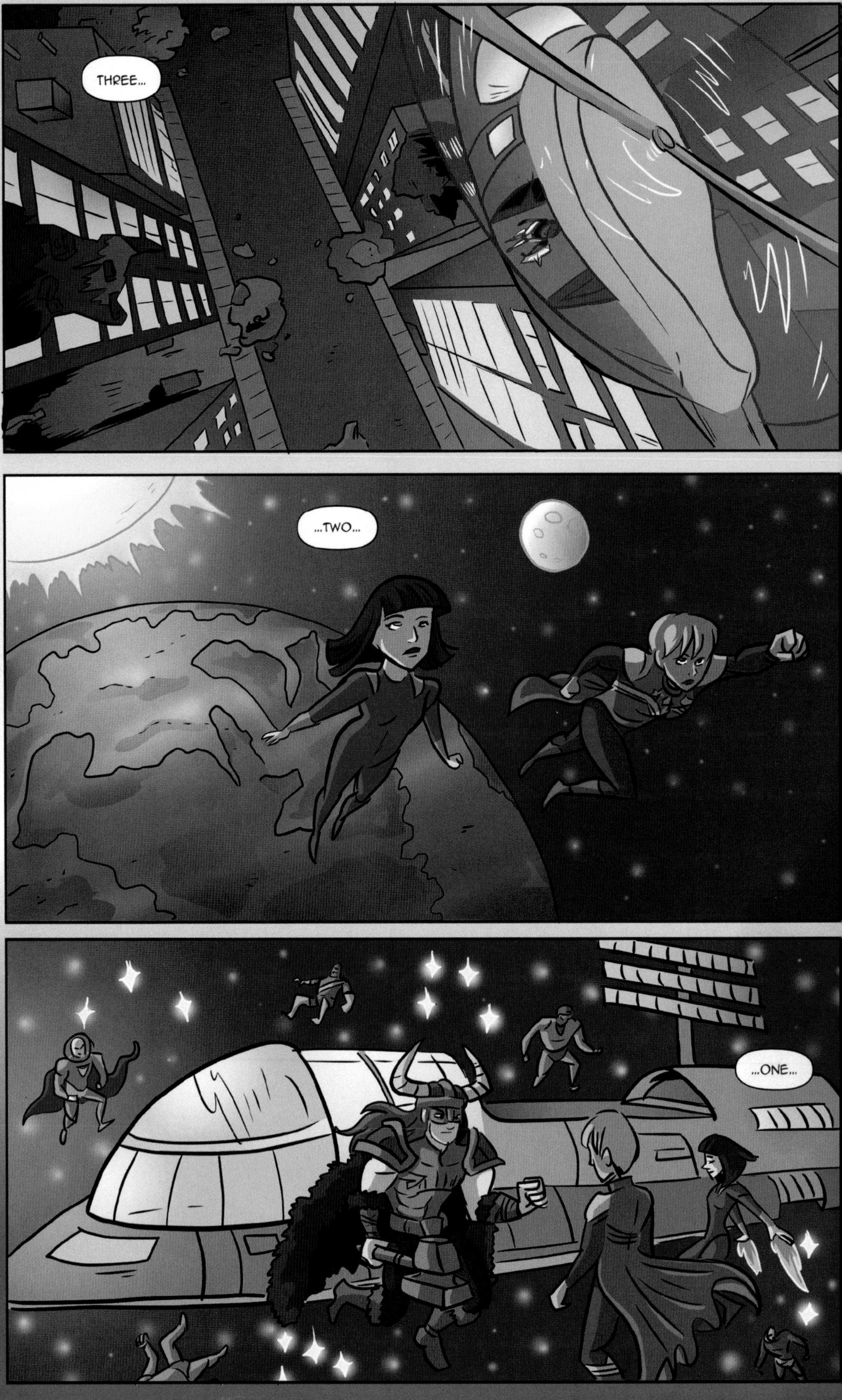
THREE...
...TWO...
...ONE...

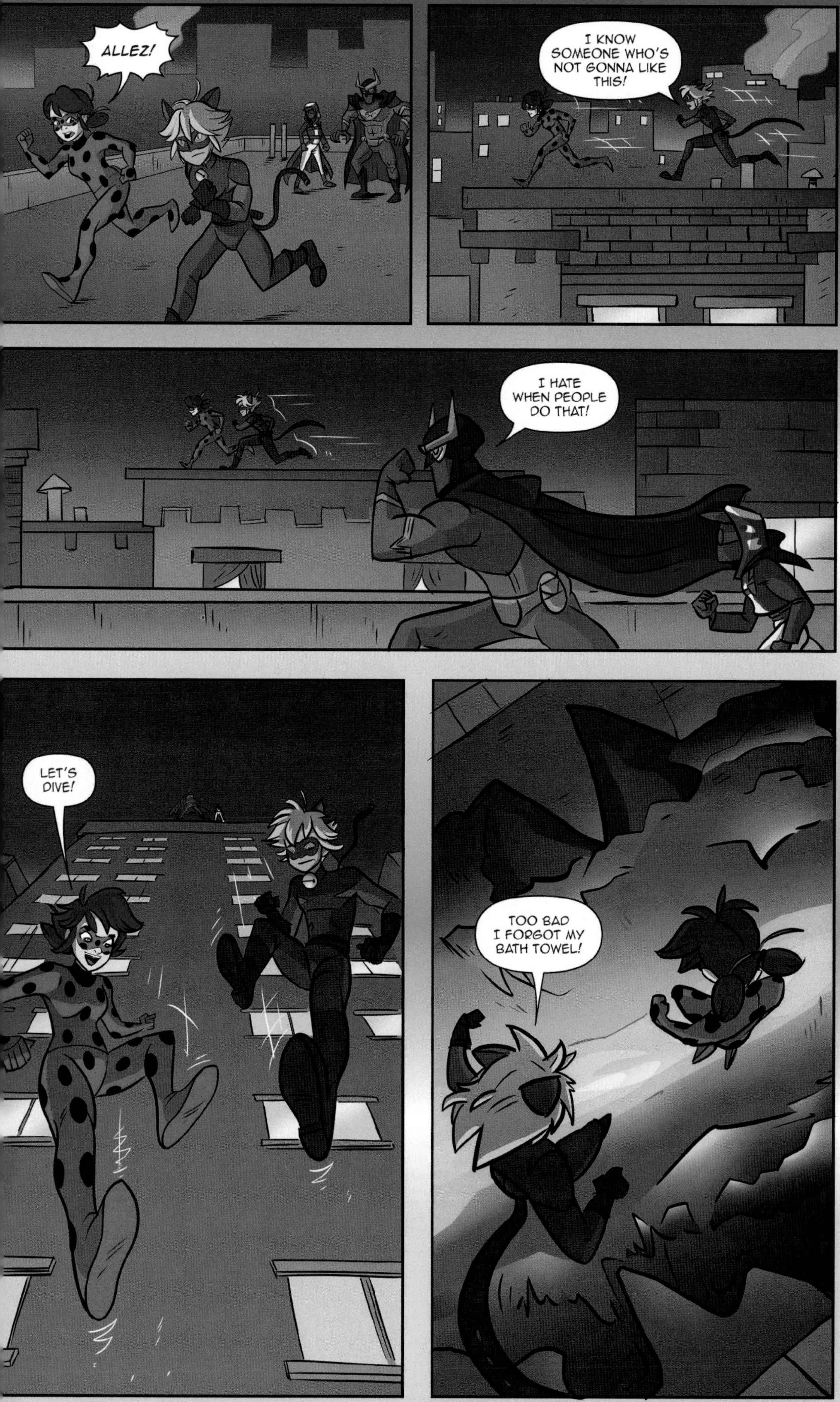
ALLEZ!
I KNOW SOMEONE WHO'S NOT GONNA LIKE THIS!
I HATE WHEN PEOPLE DO THAT!
LET'S DIVE!
TOO BAD I FORGOT MY BATH TOWEL!

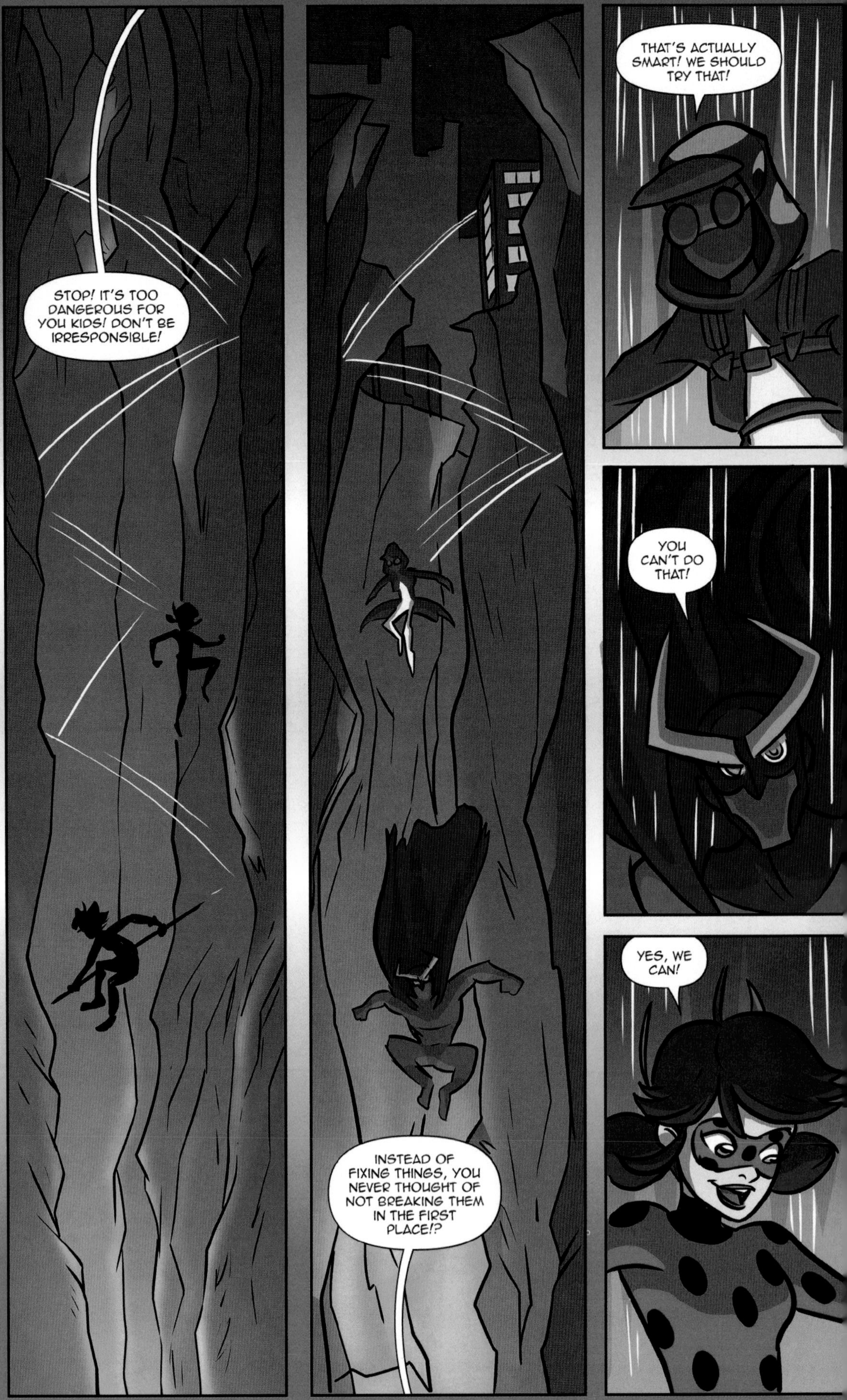
STOP! IT'S TOO DANGEROUS FOR YOU KIDS! DON'T BE IRRESPONSIBLE!
INSTEAD OF FIXING THINGS, YOU NEVER THOUGHT OF NOT BREAKING THEM IN THE FIRST PLACE!?
THAT'S ACTUALLY SMART! WE SHOULD TRY THAT!
YOU CAN'T DO THAT!
YES, WE CAN!

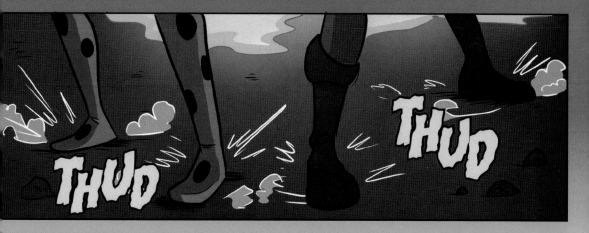

FUNNY, HE LOOKED MUCH SMALLER IN THE PHOTO.

OKAY, I CAN SEE HOW IT'S GOING TO BE COMPLICATED.

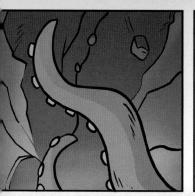

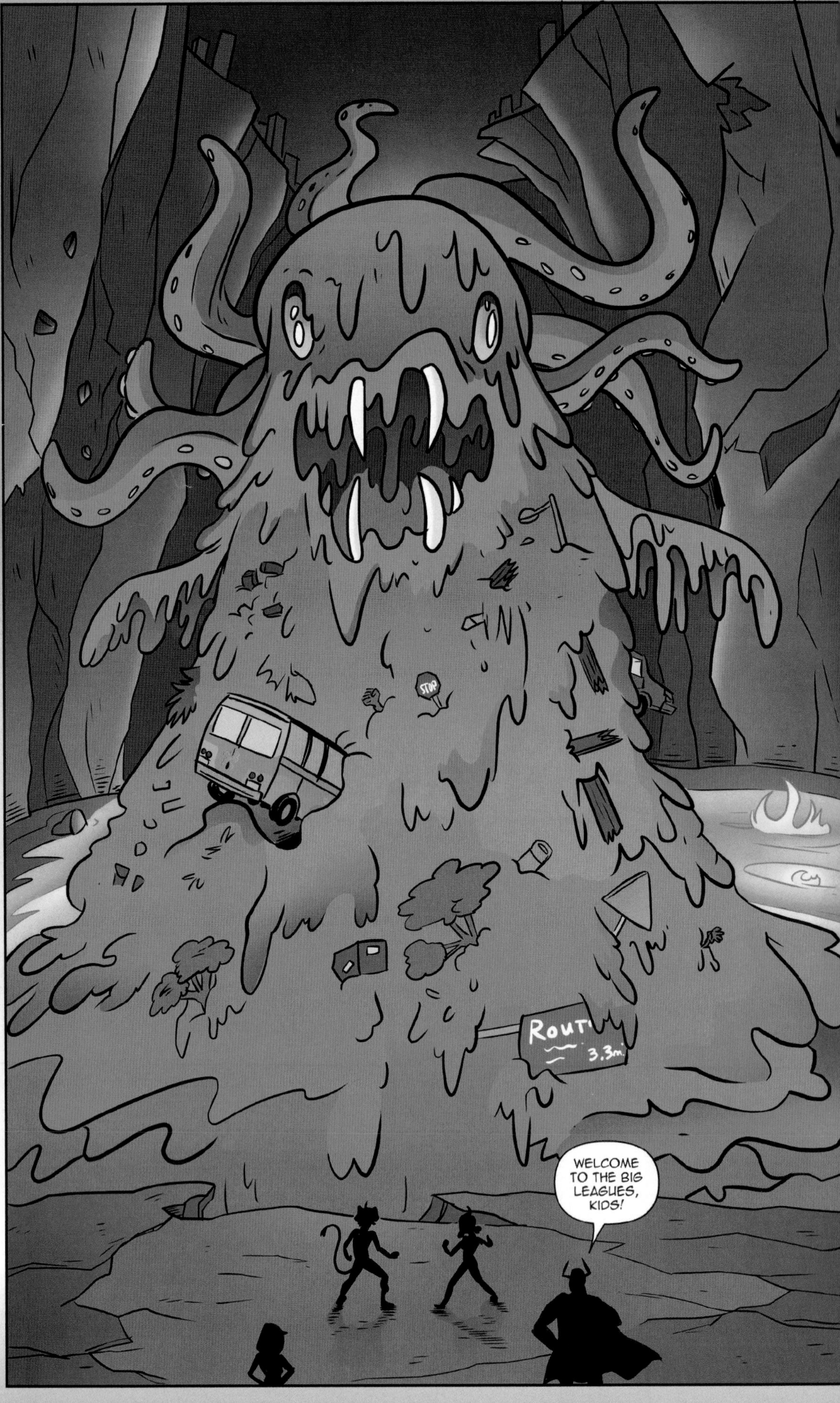
STOP
ROUT
3.3m.
WELCOME TO THE BIG LEAGUES, KIDS!

CHAPTER 4:
THE TRASH KRAKKEN:
BATTLE FOR NEW YORK

Created by: Thomas Astruc
Written by: Thomas Astruc, Mélanie Duval, Fred Lenoir, Sébastien Thibaudeau & Bryan Seaton
Pencils by: Ellen Cerreta
Inks by: Brian Hess
Letters by: Justin Birch
Colors by: Darné Lang
Editing by: Nicole D'Andria & Bryan Seaton

Cover A: Brian Hess • Cover B: Tony Fleecs

Comic art style based on the
Webisode art style of Angie Nasca

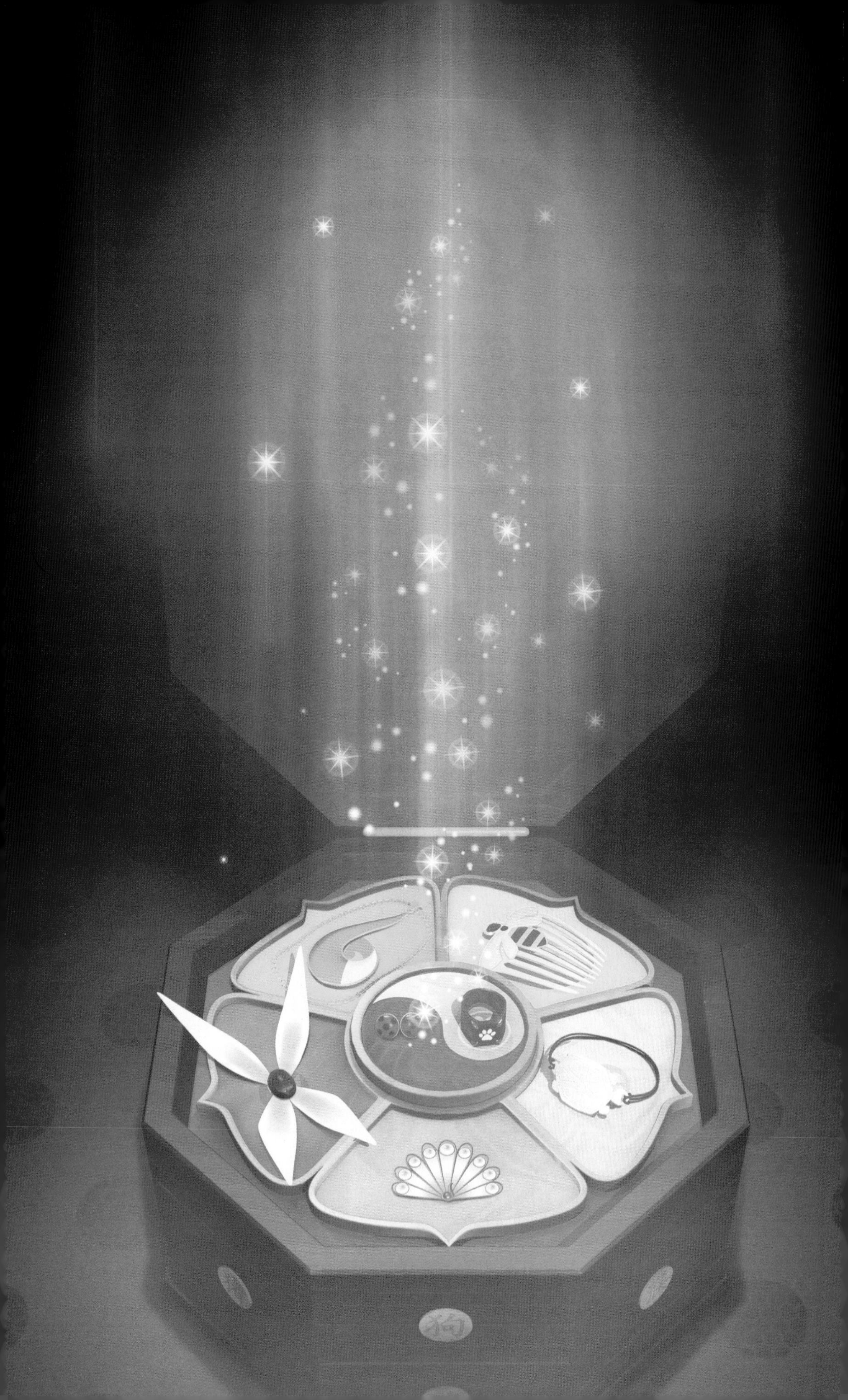
狗

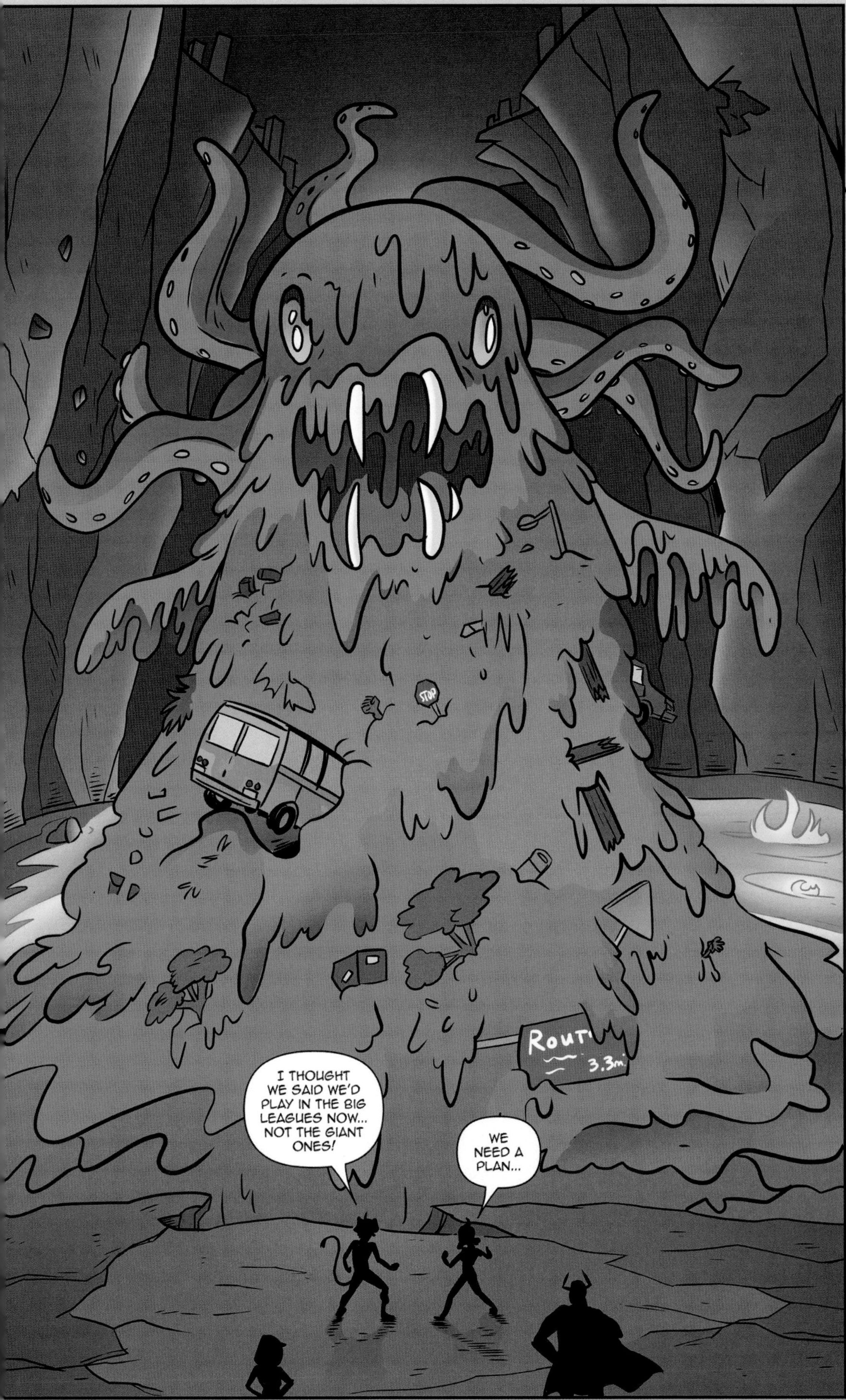
STOP
I THOUGHT WE SAID WE'D PLAY IN THE BIG LEAGUES NOW... NOT THE GIANT ONES!
WE NEED A PLAN...

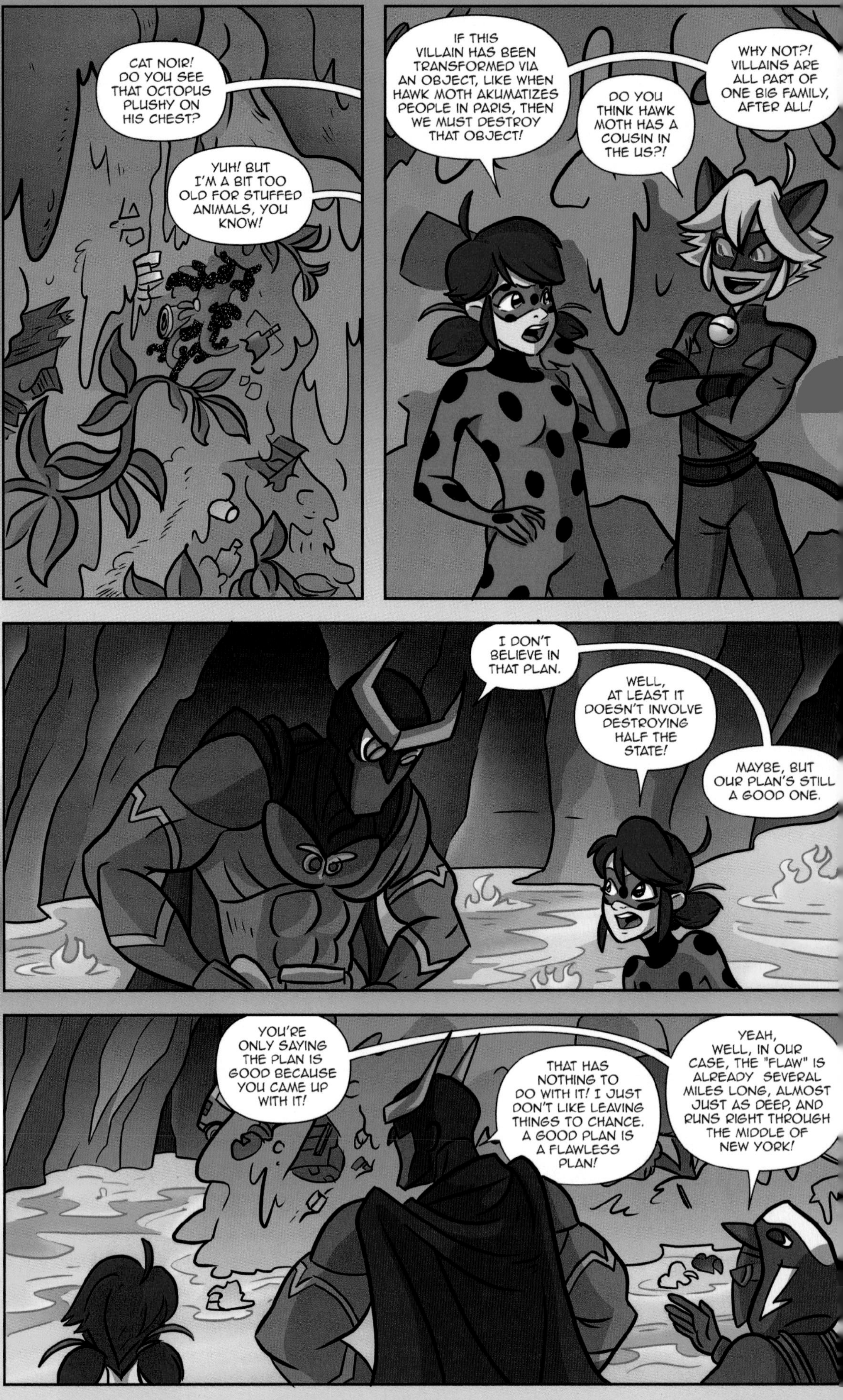
CAT NOIR! DO YOU SEE THAT OCTOPUS PLUSHY ON HIS CHEST?
YUH! BUT I'M A BIT TOO OLD FOR STUFFED ANIMALS, YOU KNOW!
IF THIS VILLAIN HAS BEEN TRANSFORMED VIA AN OBJECT, LIKE WHEN HAWK MOTH AKUMATIZES PEOPLE IN PARIS, THEN WE MUST DESTROY THAT OBJECT!
DO YOU THINK HAWK MOTH HAS A COUSIN IN THE US?!
WHY NOT?! VILLAINS ARE ALL PART OF ONE BIG FAMILY, AFTER ALL!
I DON'T BELIEVE IN THAT PLAN.
WELL, AT LEAST IT DOESN'T INVOLVE DESTROYING HALF THE STATE!
MAYBE, BUT OUR PLAN'S STILL A GOOD ONE.
YOU'RE ONLY SAYING THE PLAN IS GOOD BECAUSE YOU CAME UP WITH IT!
THAT HAS NOTHING TO DO WITH IT! I JUST DON'T LIKE LEAVING THINGS TO CHANCE. A GOOD PLAN IS A FLAWLESS PLAN!
YEAH, WELL, IN OUR CASE, THE "FLAW" IS ALREADY SEVERAL MILES LONG, ALMOST JUST AS DEEP, AND RUNS RIGHT THROUGH THE MIDDLE OF NEW YORK!

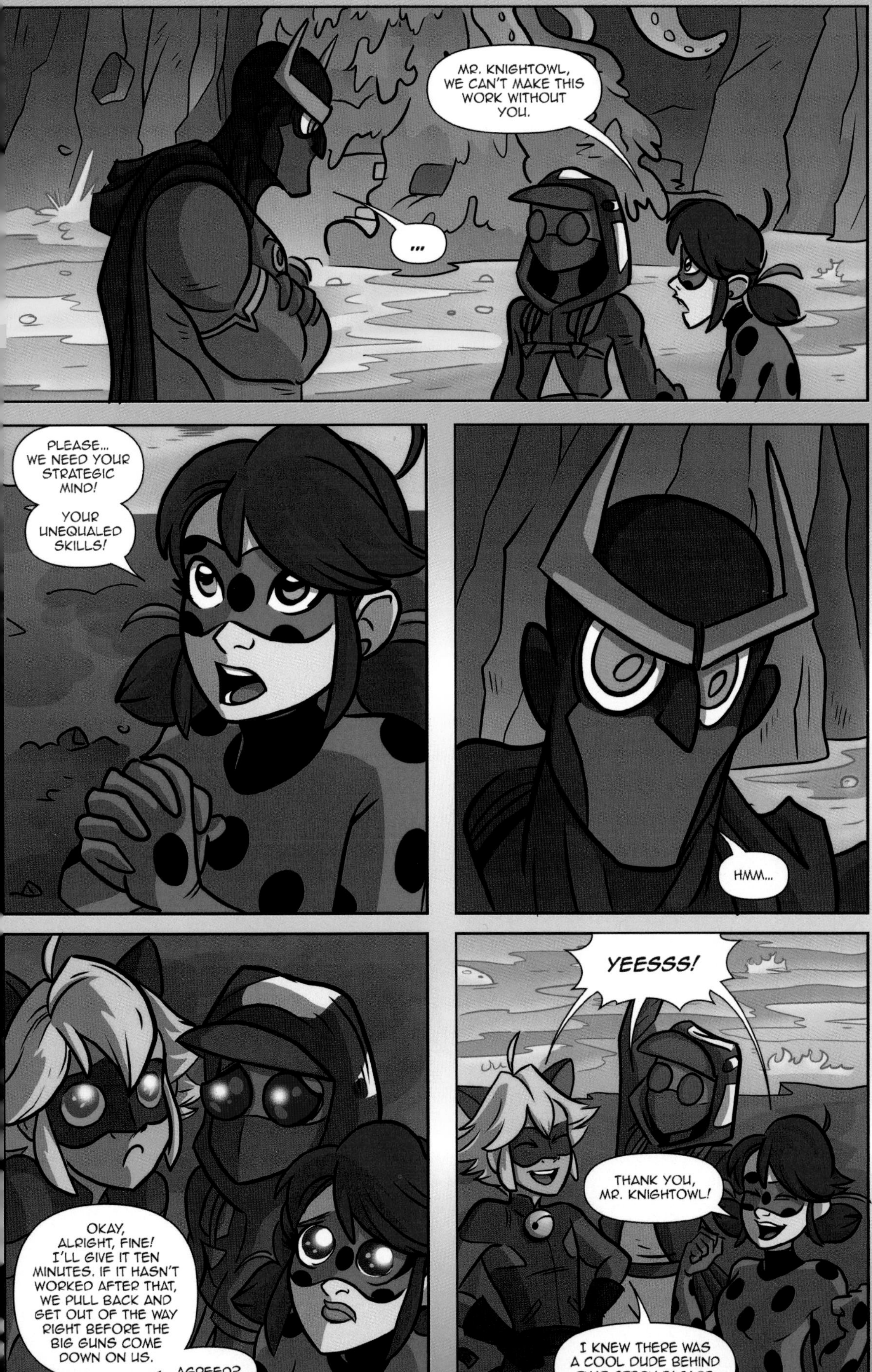

MR. KNIGHTOWL, WE CAN'T MAKE THIS WORK WITHOUT YOU.
...
PLEASE... WE NEED YOUR STRATEGIC MIND!
YOUR UNEQUALED SKILLS!
HMM...
OKAY, ALRIGHT, FINE! I'LL GIVE IT TEN MINUTES. IF IT HASN'T WORKED AFTER THAT, WE PULL BACK AND GET OUT OF THE WAY RIGHT BEFORE THE BIG GUNS COME DOWN ON US.
AGREED?
YEESSS!
THANK YOU, MR. KNIGHTOWL!
I KNEW THERE WAS A COOL DUDE BEHIND THAT STERN FACADE OF YOURS...

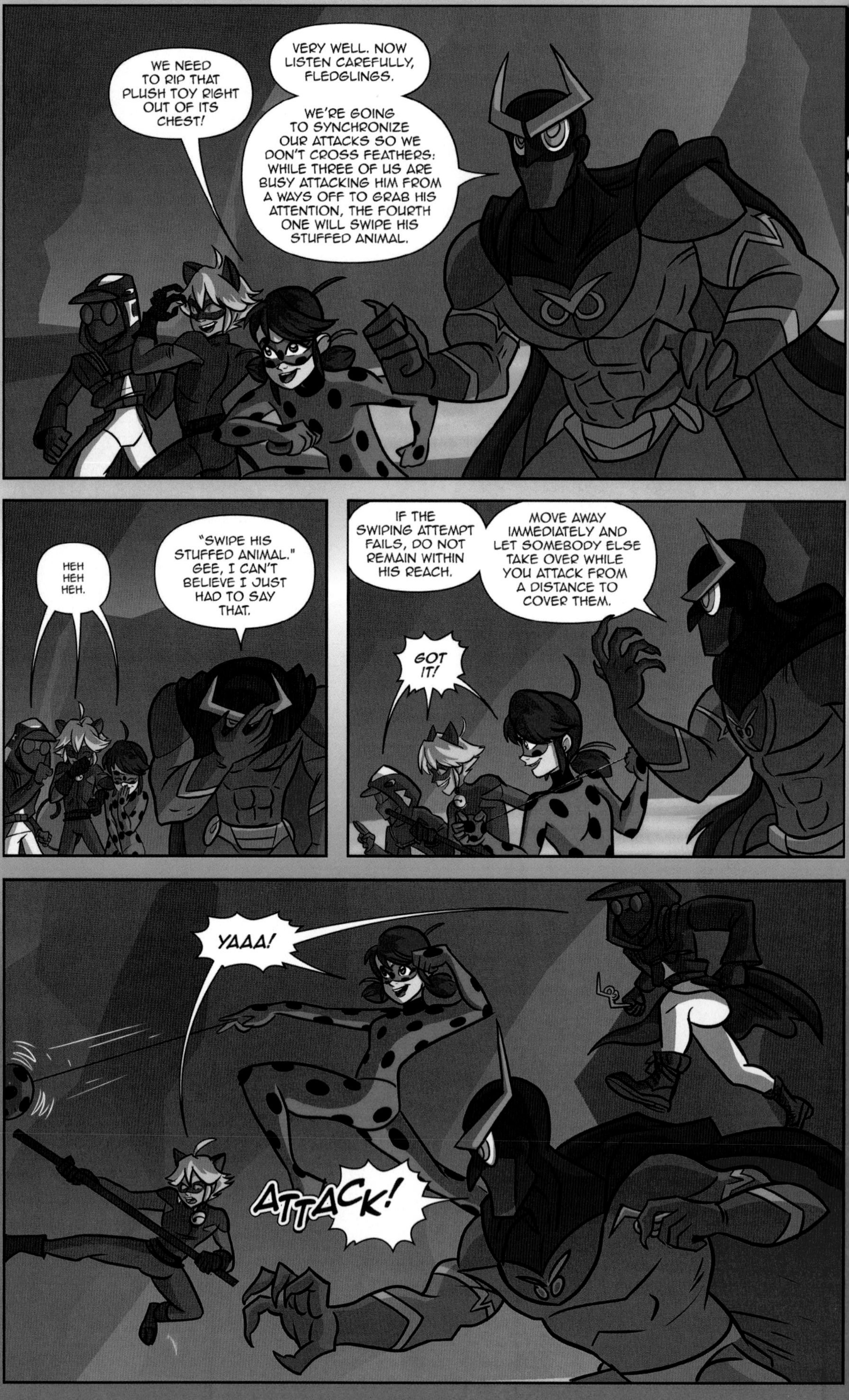
WE NEED TO RIP THAT PLUSH TOY RIGHT OUT OF ITS CHEST!
VERY WELL. NOW LISTEN CAREFULLY, FLEDGLINGS.
WE'RE GOING TO SYNCHRONIZE OUR ATTACKS SO WE DON'T CROSS FEATHERS: WHILE THREE OF US ARE BUSY ATTACKING HIM FROM A WAYS OFF TO GRAB HIS ATTENTION, THE FOURTH ONE WILL SWIPE HIS STUFFED ANIMAL.
HEH HEH HEH.
"SWIPE HIS STUFFED ANIMAL." GEE, I CAN'T BELIEVE I JUST HAD TO SAY THAT.
IF THE SWIPING ATTEMPT FAILS, DO NOT REMAIN WITHIN HIS REACH.
MOVE AWAY IMMEDIATELY AND LET SOMEBODY ELSE TAKE OVER WHILE YOU ATTACK FROM A DISTANCE TO COVER THEM.
GOT IT!
YAAA!
ATTACK!

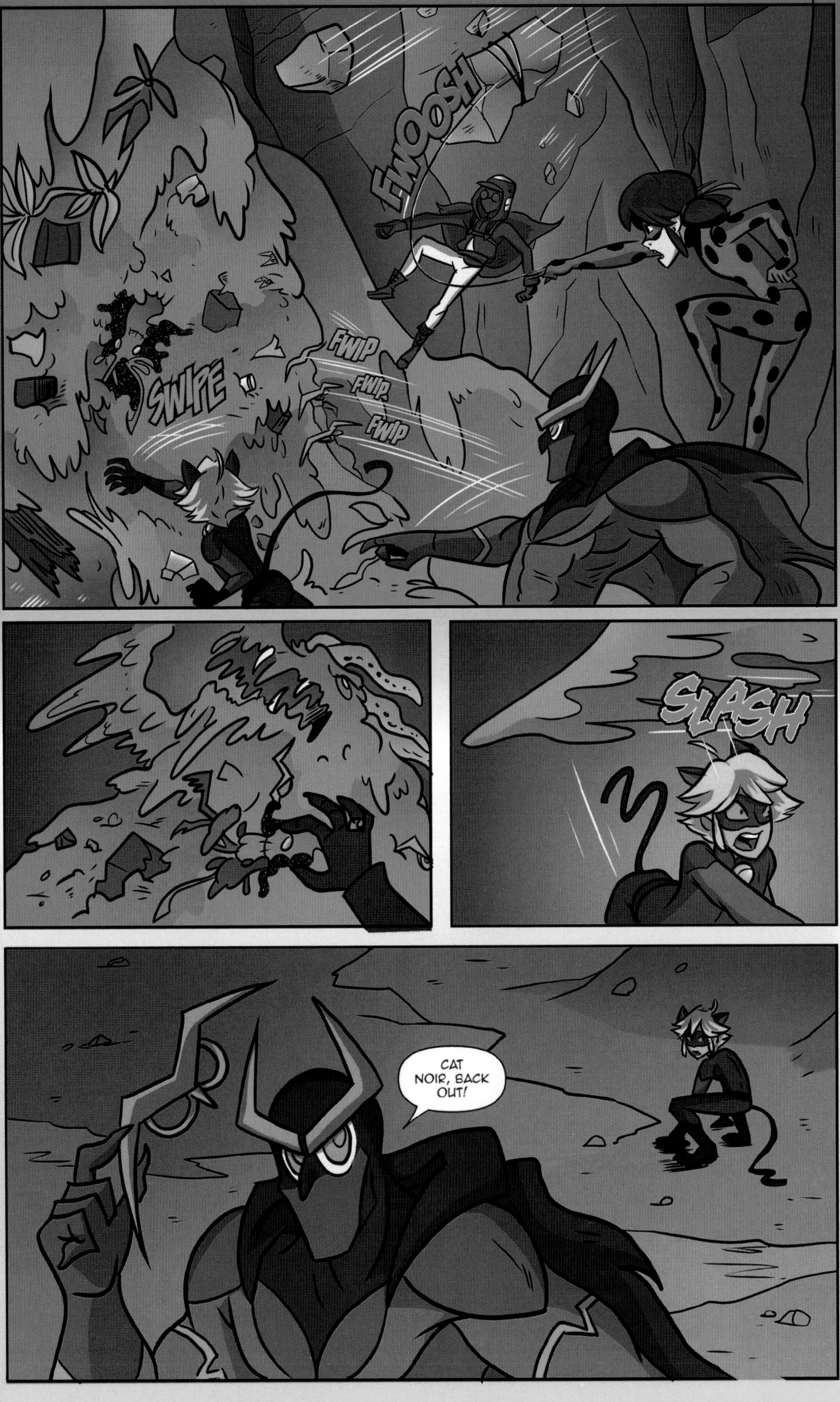

FWOOSH
SWIPE
FWIP
FWIP
FWIP
SLASH
CAT NOIR, BACK OUT!

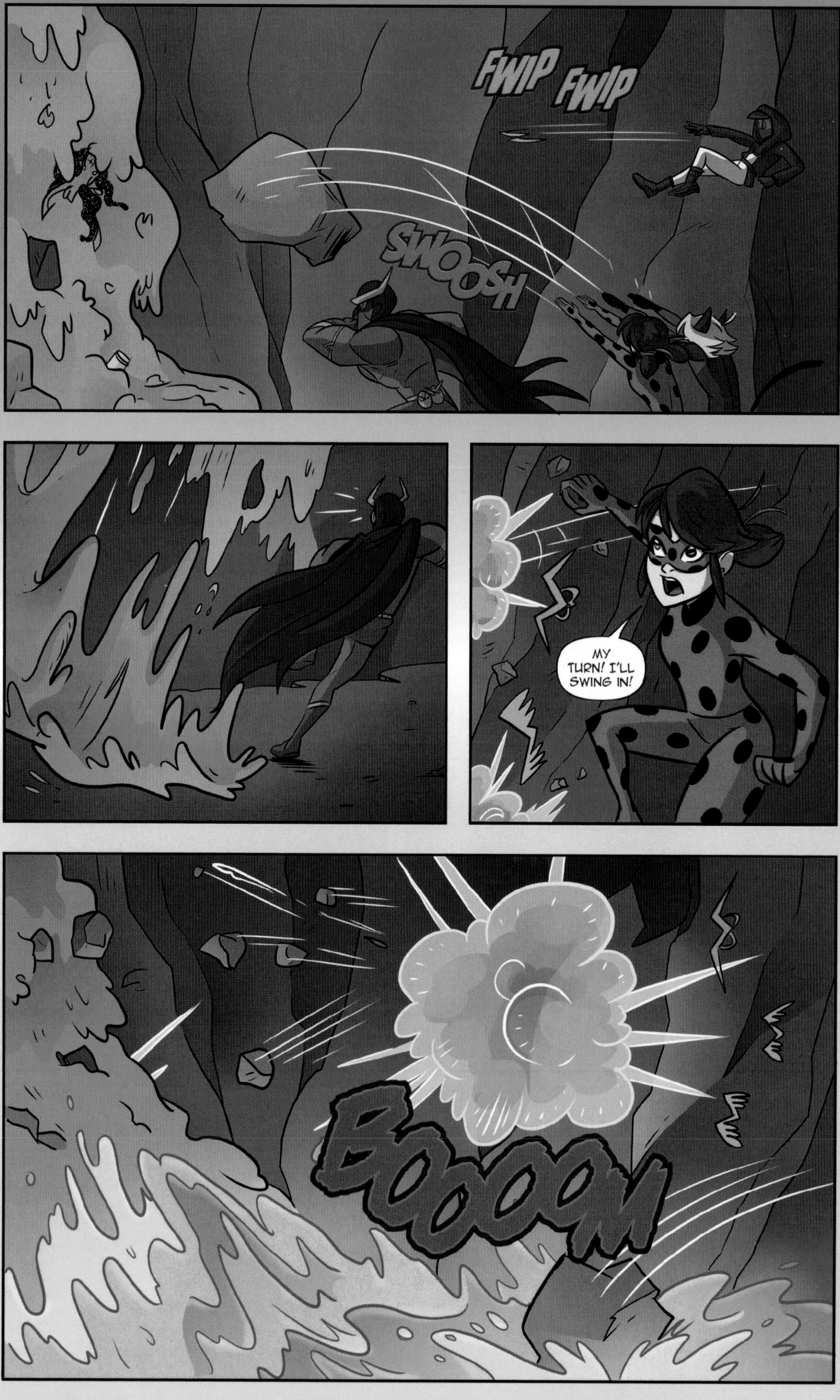
FWIP FWIP
SWOOSH
MY TURN! I'LL SWING IN!
BOOOOM

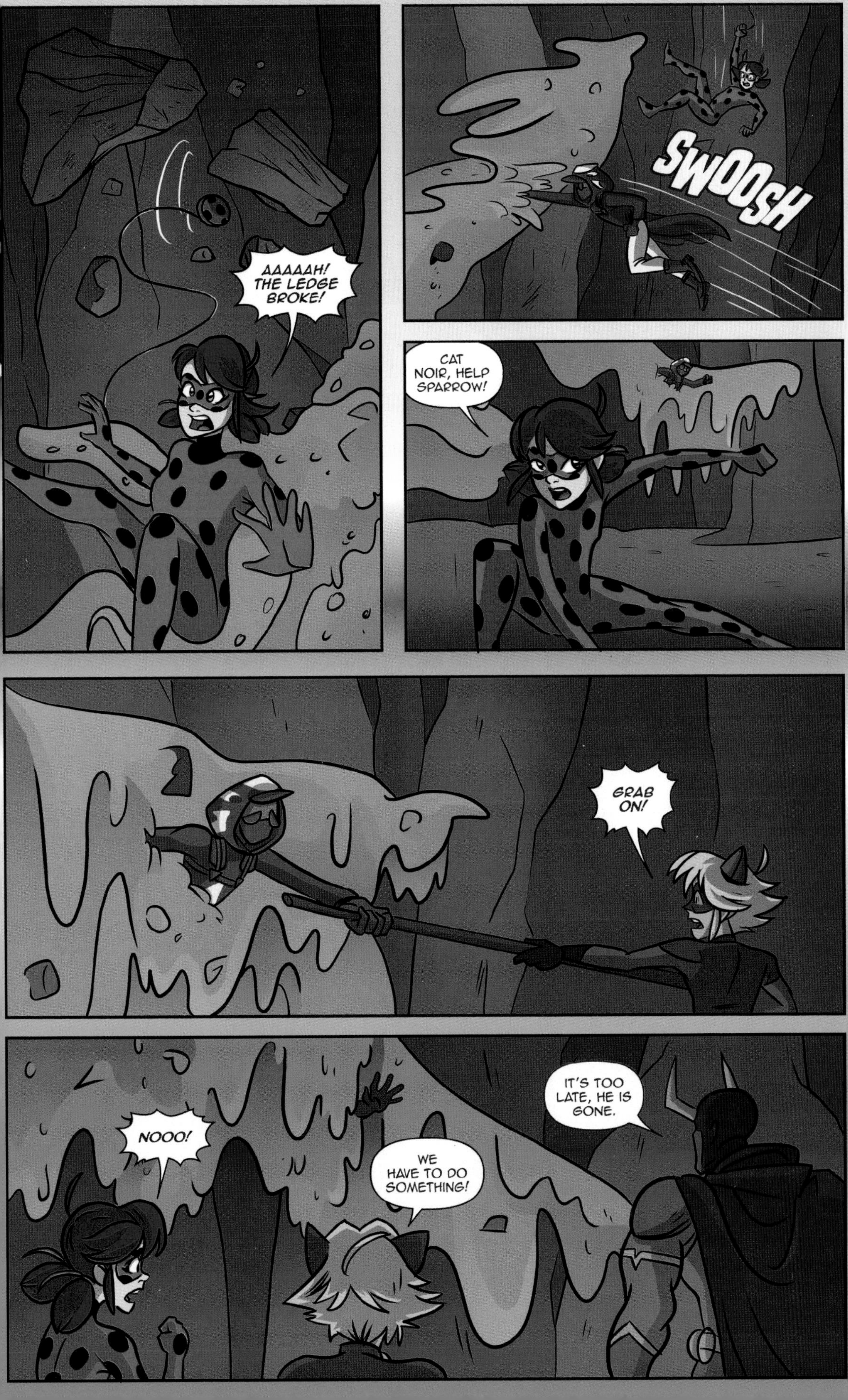
AAAAAH! THE LEDGE BROKE!
SWOOSH
CAT NOIR, HELP SPARROW!
GRAB ON!
NOOO!
WE HAVE TO DO SOMETHING!
IT'S TOO LATE, HE IS GONE.

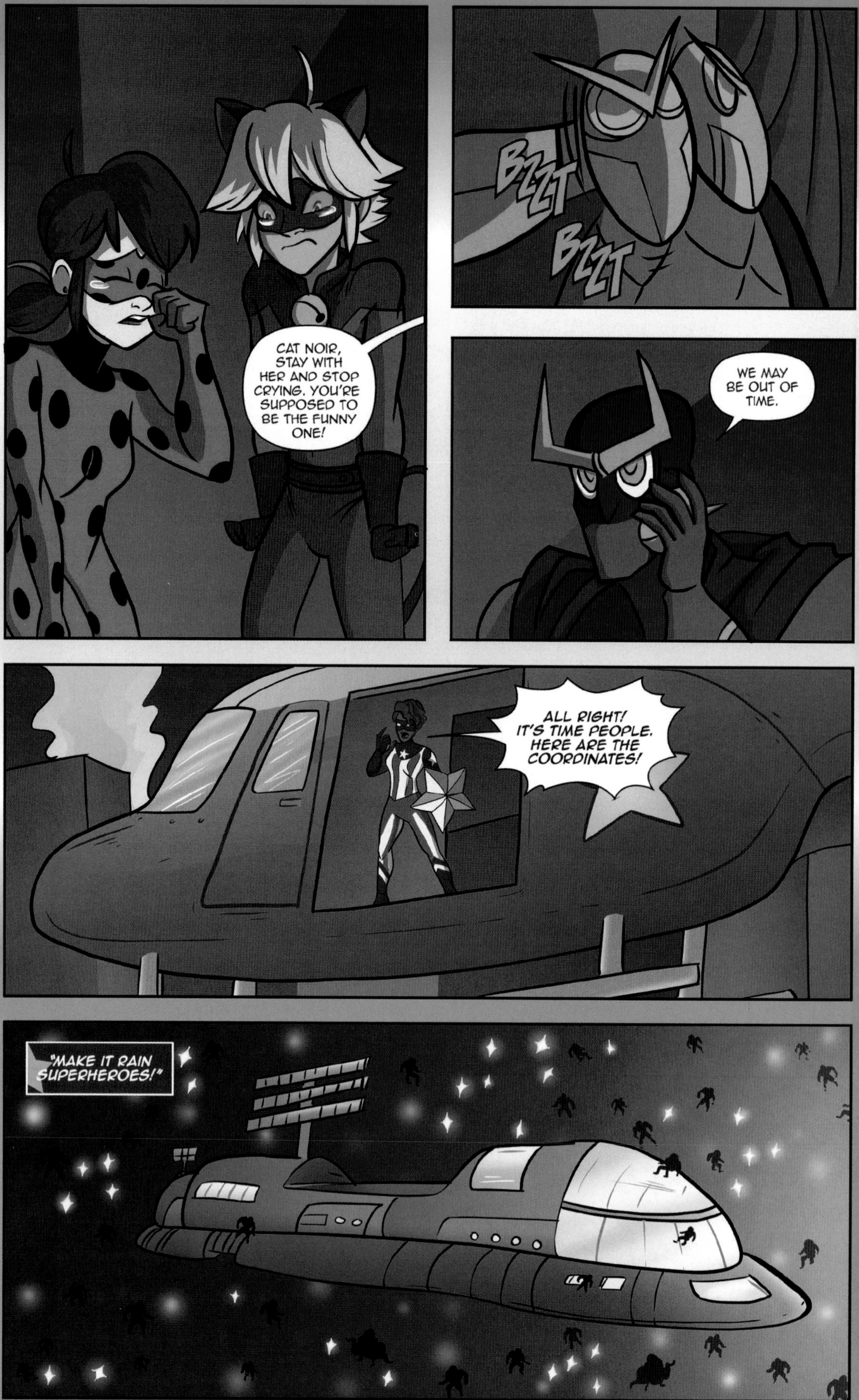
CAT NOIR, STAY WITH HER AND STOP CRYING. YOU'RE SUPPOSED TO BE THE FUNNY ONE!
BZZT
BZZT
WE MAY BE OUT OF TIME.
ALL RIGHT! IT'S TIME PEOPLE. HERE ARE THE COORDINATES!
"MAKE IT RAIN SUPERHEROES!"

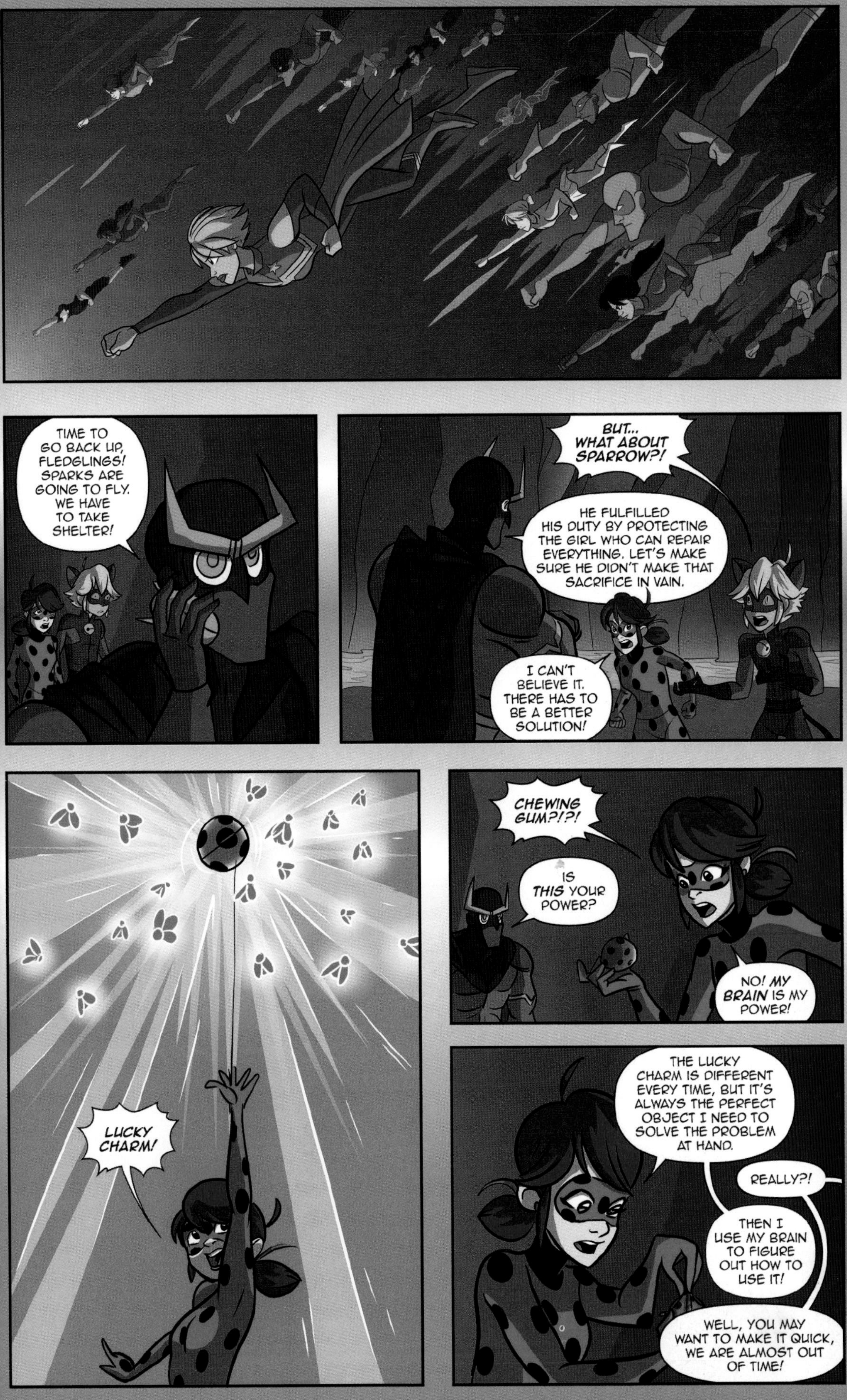
TIME TO GO BACK UP, FLEDGLINGS! SPARKS ARE GOING TO FLY. WE HAVE TO TAKE SHELTER!
BUT... WHAT ABOUT SPARROW?!
HE FULFILLED HIS DUTY BY PROTECTING THE GIRL WHO CAN REPAIR EVERYTHING. LET'S MAKE SURE HE DIDN'T MAKE THAT SACRIFICE IN VAIN.
I CAN'T BELIEVE IT. THERE HAS TO BE A BETTER SOLUTION!
LUCKY CHARM!
CHEWING GUM?!?!
IS THIS YOUR POWER?
NO! MY BRAIN IS MY POWER!
THE LUCKY CHARM IS DIFFERENT EVERY TIME, BUT IT'S ALWAYS THE PERFECT OBJECT I NEED TO SOLVE THE PROBLEM AT HAND.
REALLY?!
THEN I USE MY BRAIN TO FIGURE OUT HOW TO USE IT!
WELL, YOU MAY WANT TO MAKE IT QUICK, WE ARE ALMOST OUT OF TIME!

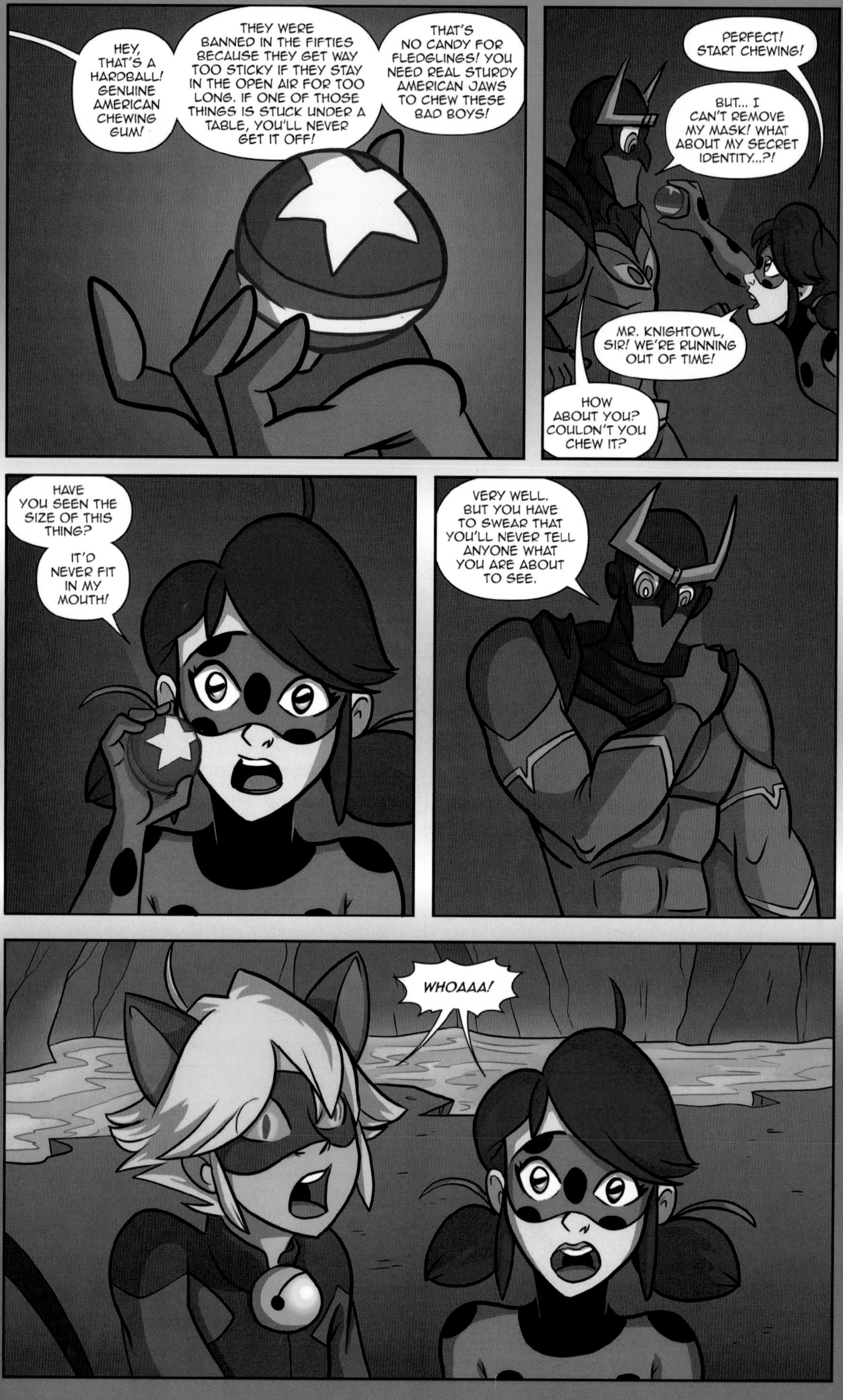
HEY, THAT'S A HARDBALL! GENUINE AMERICAN CHEWING GUM!
THEY WERE BANNED IN THE FIFTIES BECAUSE THEY GET WAY TOO STICKY IF THEY STAY IN THE OPEN AIR FOR TOO LONG. IF ONE OF THOSE THINGS IS STUCK UNDER A TABLE, YOU'LL NEVER GET IT OFF!
THAT'S NO CANDY FOR FLEDGLINGS! YOU NEED REAL STURDY AMERICAN JAWS TO CHEW THESE BAD BOYS!
PERFECT! START CHEWING!
BUT... I CAN'T REMOVE MY MASK! WHAT ABOUT MY SECRET IDENTITY...?!
MR. KNIGHTOWL, SIR! WE'RE RUNNING OUT OF TIME!
HOW ABOUT YOU? COULDN'T YOU CHEW IT?
HAVE YOU SEEN THE SIZE OF THIS THING?
IT'D NEVER FIT IN MY MOUTH!
VERY WELL. BUT YOU HAVE TO SWEAR THAT YOU'LL NEVER TELL ANYONE WHAT YOU ARE ABOUT TO SEE.
WHOAAA!

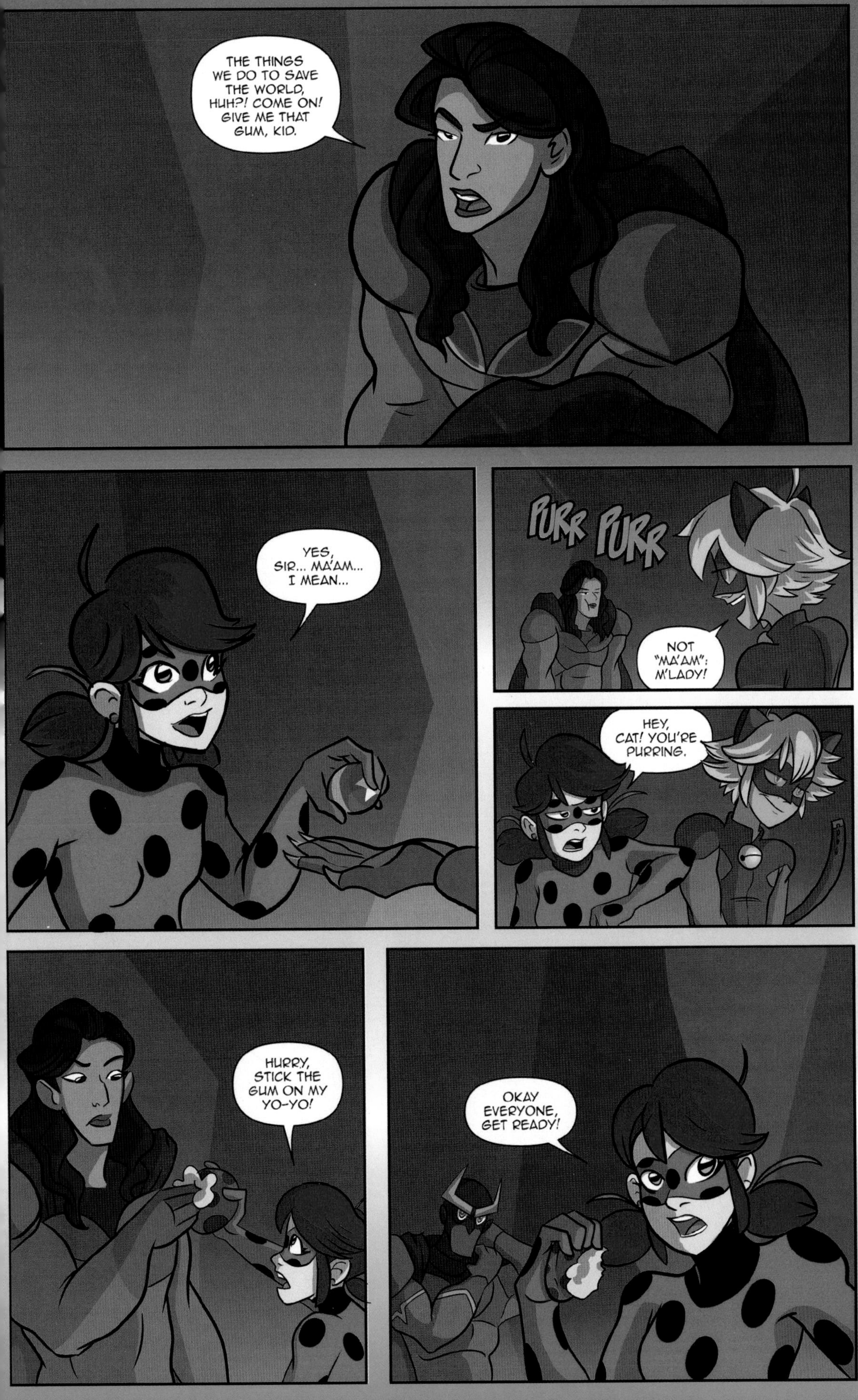
THE THINGS WE DO TO SAVE THE WORLD, HUH?! COME ON! GIVE ME THAT GUM, KID.
YES, SIR... MA'AM... I MEAN...
PURR PURR
NOT "MA'AM": M'LADY!
HEY, CAT! YOU'RE PURRING.
HURRY, STICK THE GUM ON MY YO-YO!
OKAY EVERYONE, GET READY!

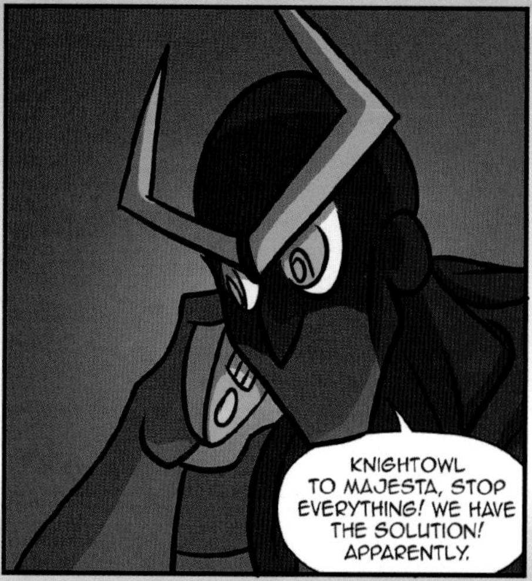
KNIGHTOWL
TO MAJESTA, STOP
EVERYTHING! WE HAVE
THE SOLUTION!
APPARENTLY.

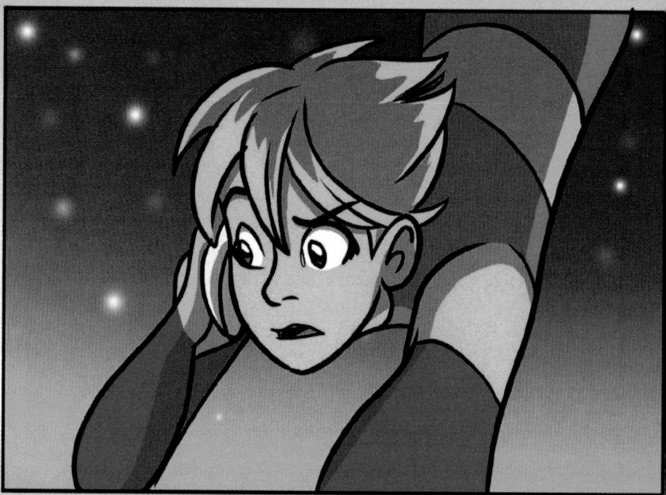

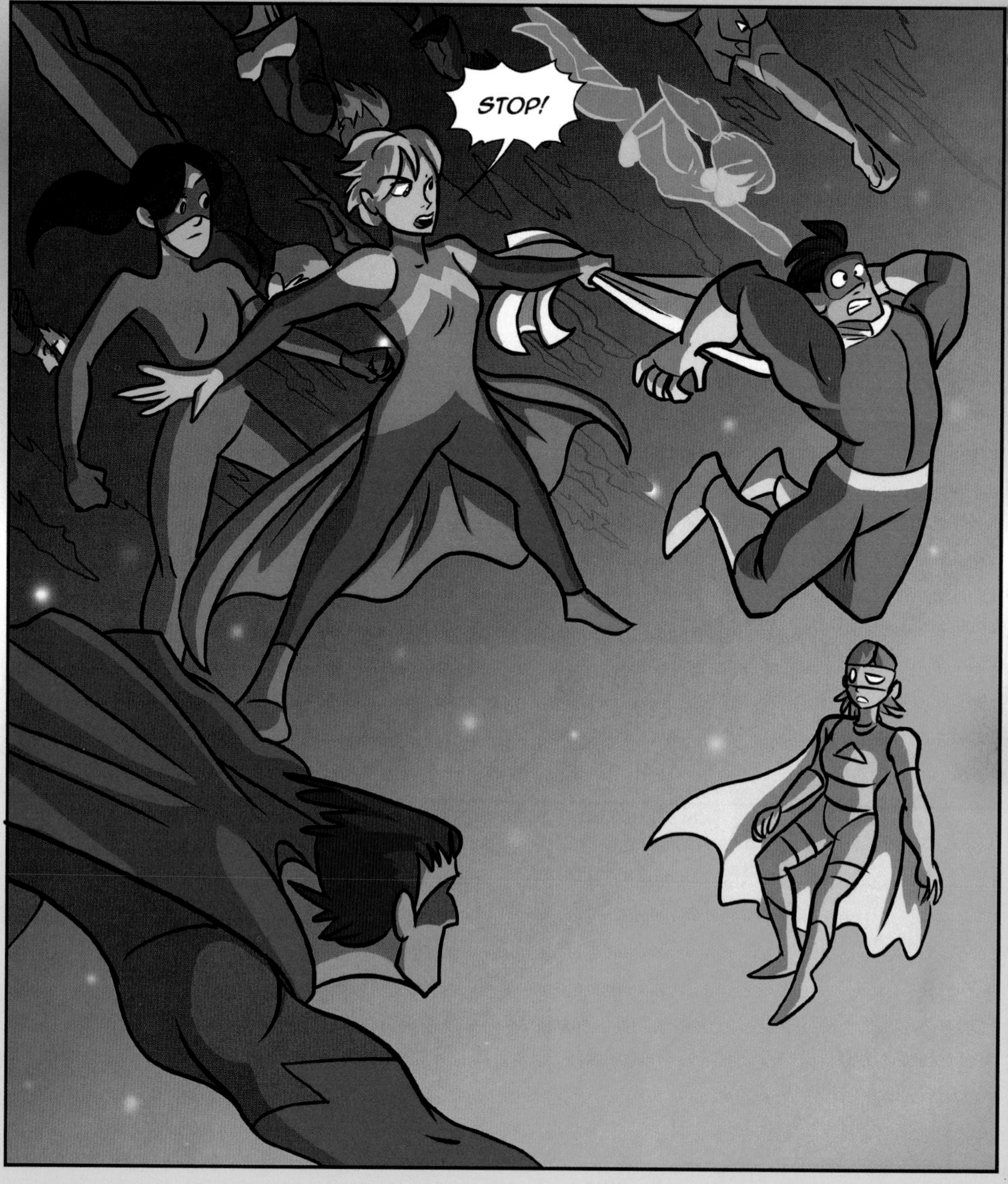
STOP!

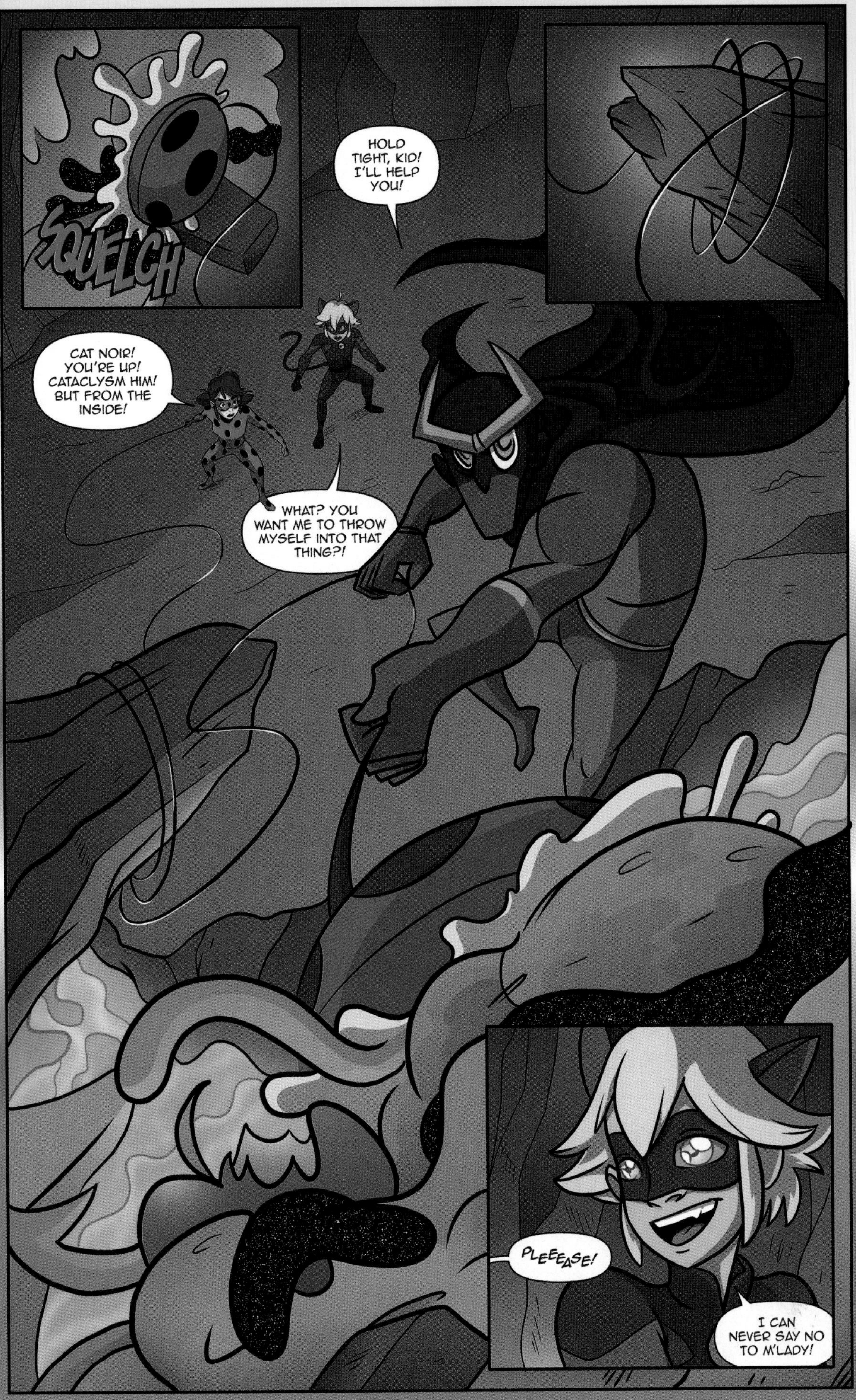
SQUELCH
HOLD TIGHT, KID! I'LL HELP YOU!
CAT NOIR! YOU'RE UP! CATACLYSM HIM! BUT FROM THE INSIDE!
WHAT? YOU WANT ME TO THROW MYSELF INTO THAT THING?!
PLEEEASE!
I CAN NEVER SAY NO TO M'LADY!

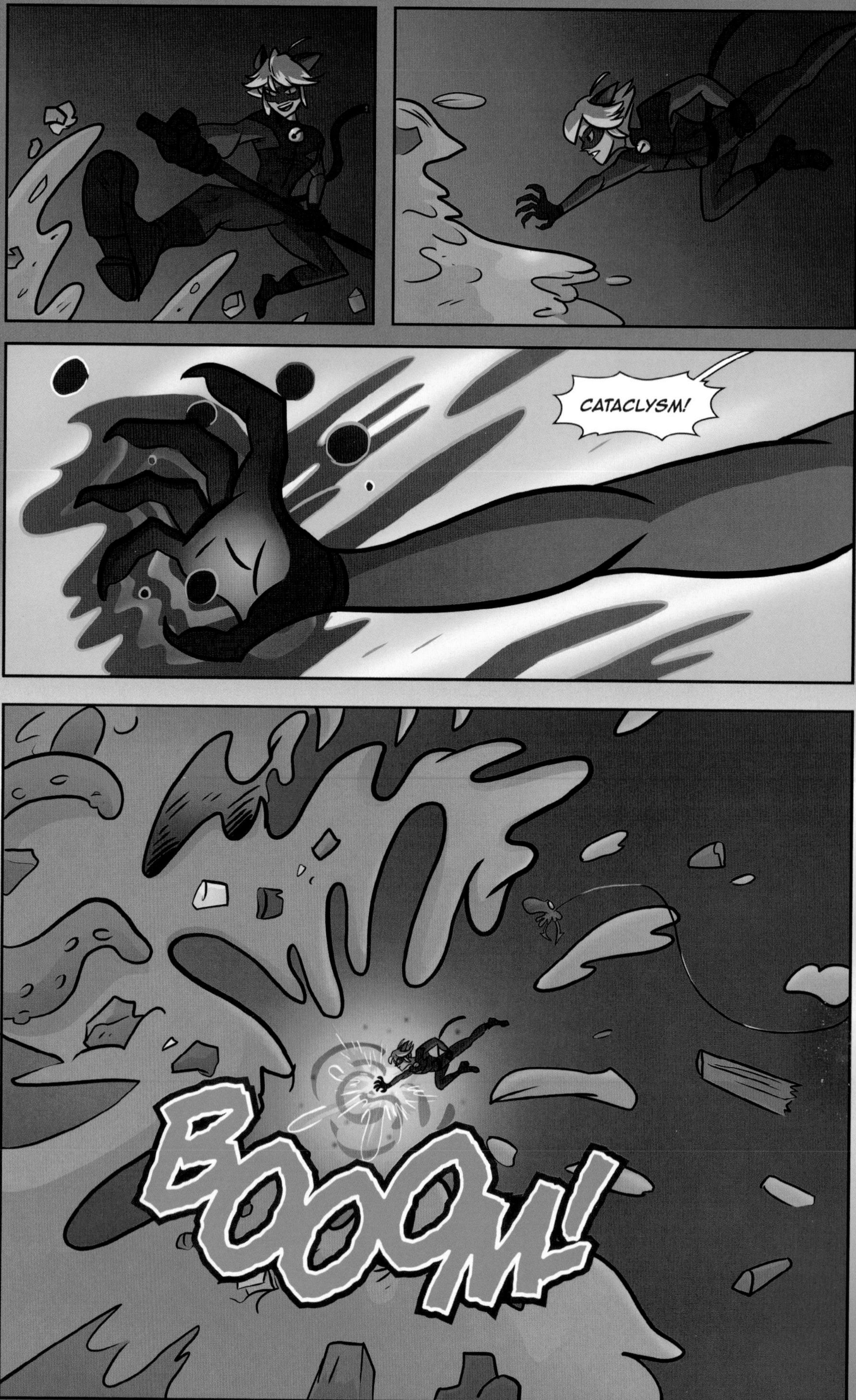
CATACLYSM!
BOOOOM!

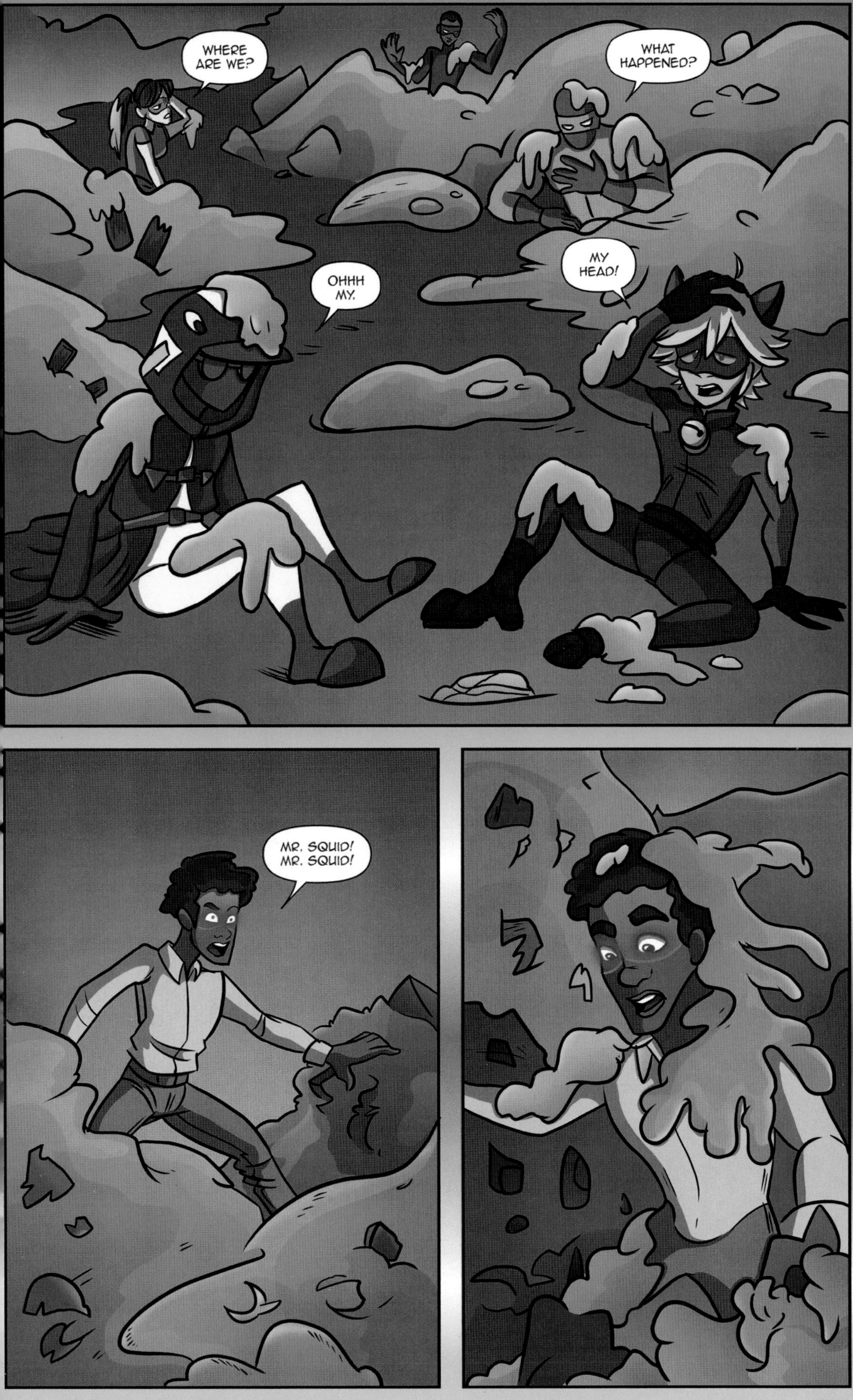
WHERE ARE WE?
WHAT HAPPENED?
OHHH MY.
MY HEAD!
MR. SQUID! MR. SQUID!

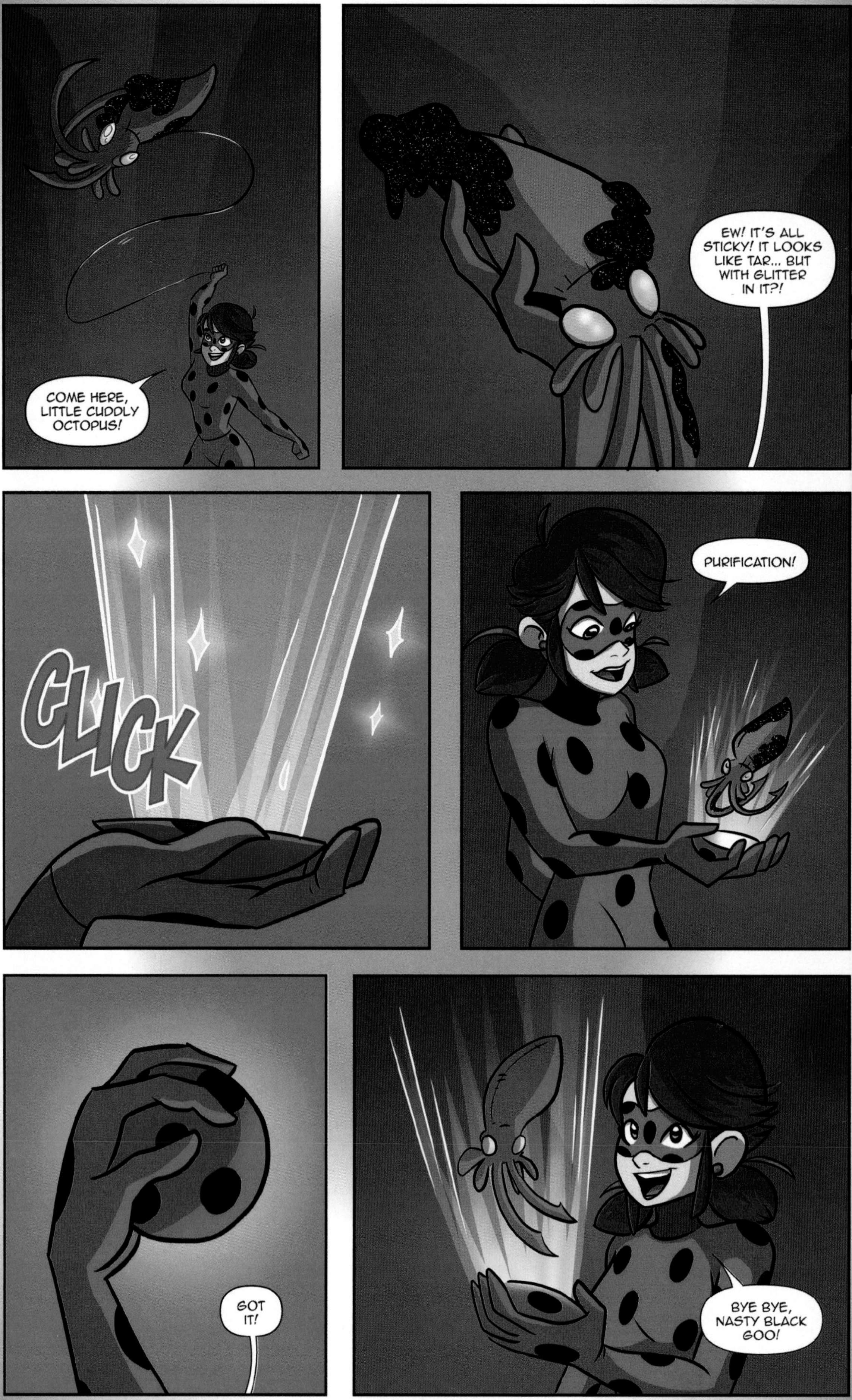
COME HERE, LITTLE CUDDLY OCTOPUS!
EW! IT'S ALL STICKY! IT LOOKS LIKE TAR... BUT WITH GLITTER IN IT?!
CLICK
PURIFICATION!
GOT IT!
BYE BYE, NASTY BLACK GOO!

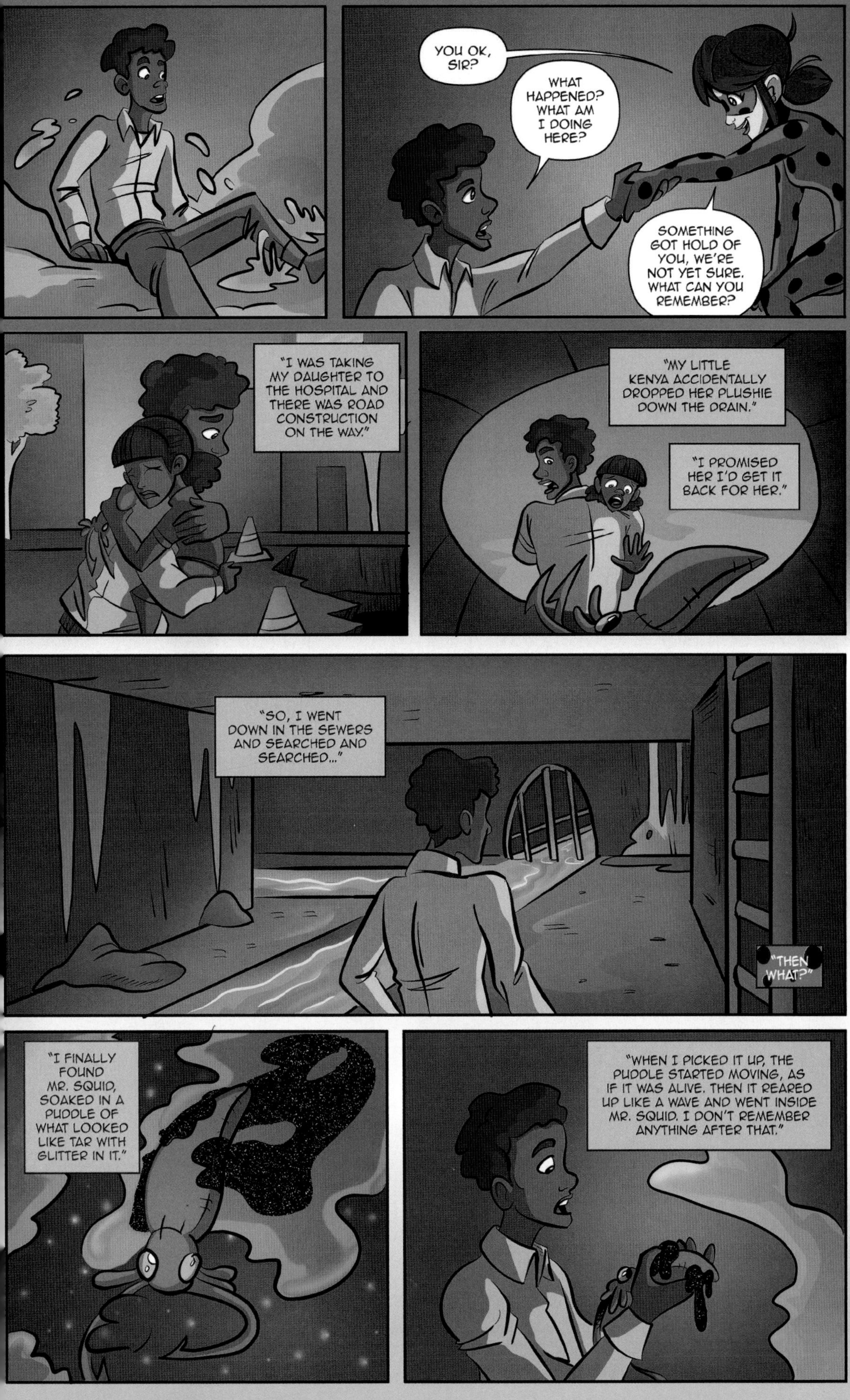
YOU OK, SIR?
WHAT HAPPENED? WHAT AM I DOING HERE?
SOMETHING GOT HOLD OF YOU, WE'RE NOT YET SURE. WHAT CAN YOU REMEMBER?
"I WAS TAKING MY DAUGHTER TO THE HOSPITAL AND THERE WAS ROAD CONSTRUCTION ON THE WAY."
"MY LITTLE KENYA ACCIDENTALLY DROPPED HER PLUSHIE DOWN THE DRAIN."
"I PROMISED HER I'D GET IT BACK FOR HER."
"SO, I WENT DOWN IN THE SEWERS AND SEARCHED AND SEARCHED..."
"THEN WHAT?"
"I FINALLY FOUND MR. SQUID, SOAKED IN A PUDDLE OF WHAT LOOKED LIKE TAR WITH GLITTER IN IT."
"WHEN I PICKED IT UP, THE PUDDLE STARTED MOVING, AS IF IT WAS ALIVE. THEN IT REARED UP LIKE A WAVE AND WENT INSIDE MR. SQUID. I DON'T REMEMBER ANYTHING AFTER THAT."

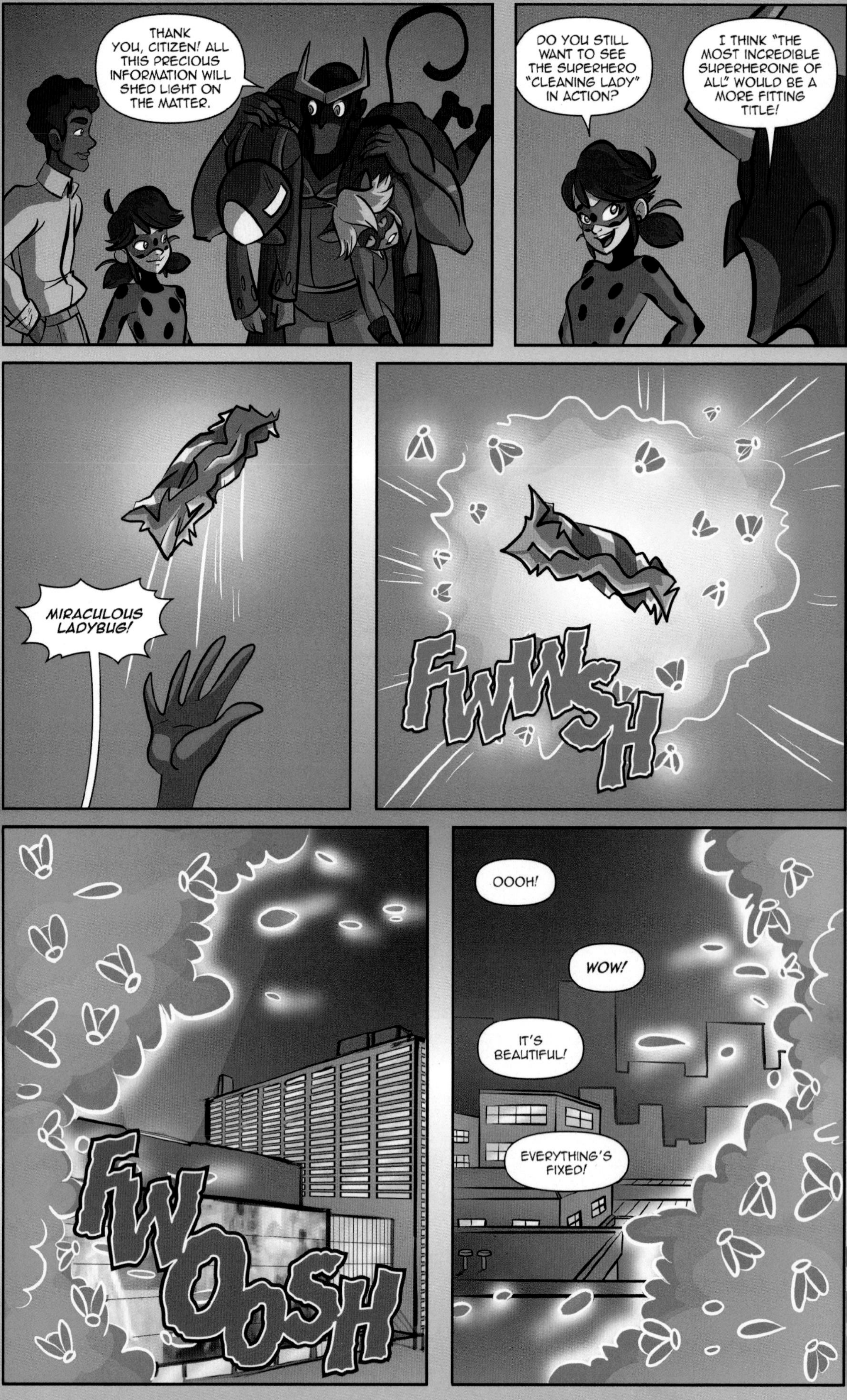
THANK YOU, CITIZEN! ALL THIS PRECIOUS INFORMATION WILL SHED LIGHT ON THE MATTER.
DO YOU STILL WANT TO SEE THE SUPERHERO "CLEANING LADY" IN ACTION?
I THINK "THE MOST INCREDIBLE SUPERHEROINE OF ALL" WOULD BE A MORE FITTING TITLE!
MIRACULOUS LADYBUG!
FWWSH
FWOOSH
OOOH!
WOW!
IT'S BEAUTIFUL!
EVERYTHING'S FIXED!

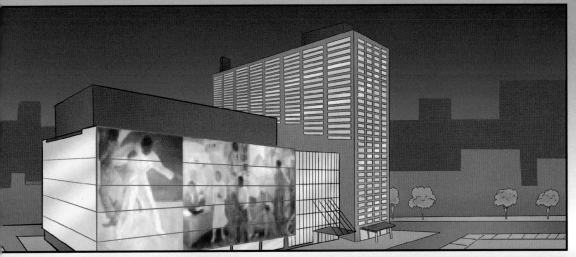

DADDY!

SWEETIE!, I FOUND MR. SQUID!

I KNEW YOU WOULD FIND HIM!

THEY WERE INCREDIBLE. THAT GIRL IS NOTHING SHORT OF MIRACULOUS!

AND CAT NOIR'S NO CLOWN EITHER. IF IT WEREN'T FOR THEM, A LOT OF US WOULDN'T BE HERE NOW. THEY MAKE AN AWESOME COUPLE!

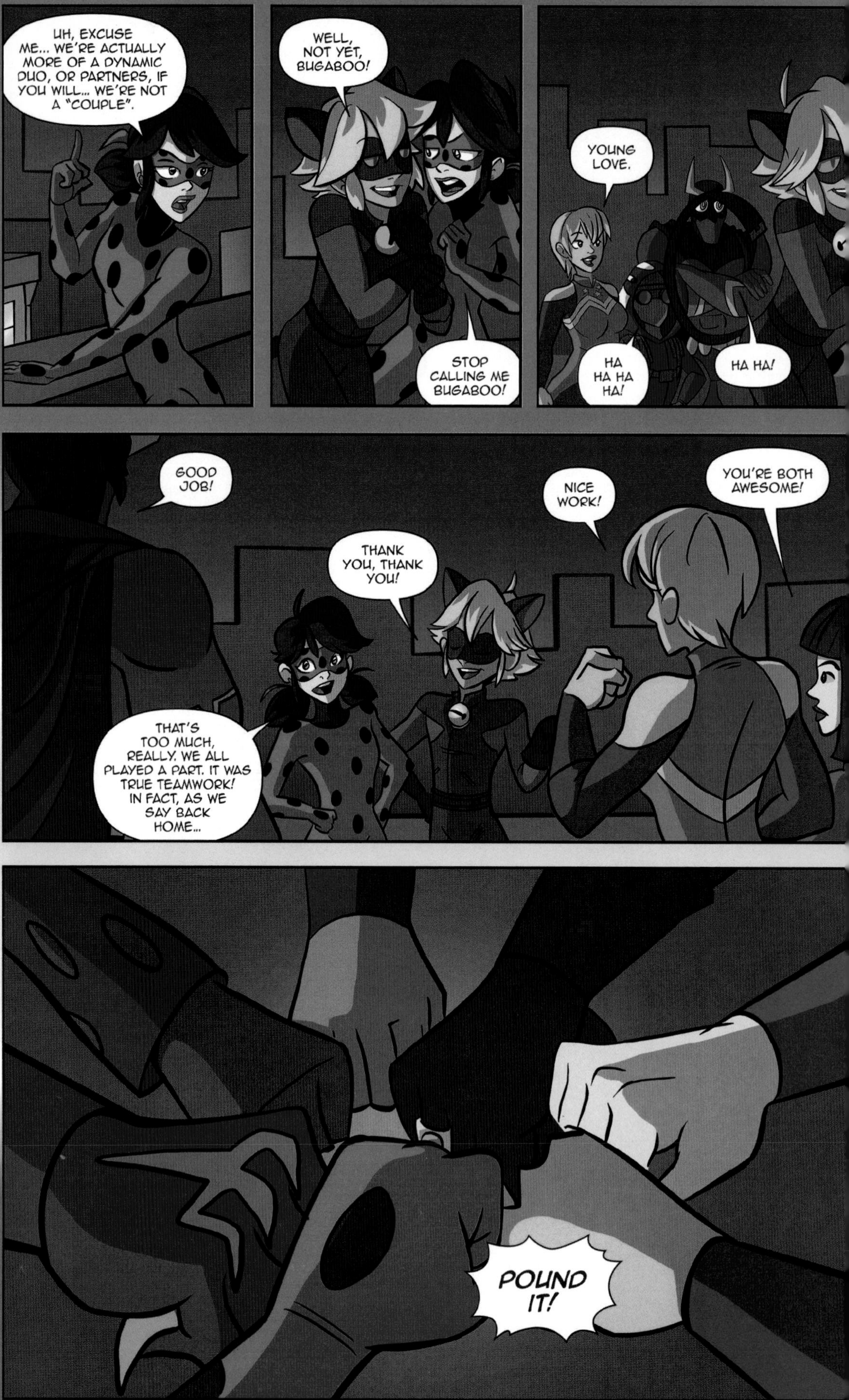
UH, EXCUSE ME... WE'RE ACTUALLY MORE OF A DYNAMIC DUO, OR PARTNERS, IF YOU WILL... WE'RE NOT A "COUPLE".
WELL, NOT YET, BUGABOO!
STOP CALLING ME BUGABOO!
YOUNG LOVE.
HA HA HA HA!
HA HA!
GOOD JOB!
NICE WORK!
YOU'RE BOTH AWESOME!
THANK YOU, THANK YOU!
THAT'S TOO MUCH, REALLY. WE ALL PLAYED A PART. IT WAS TRUE TEAMWORK! IN FACT, AS WE SAY BACK HOME...
POUND IT!

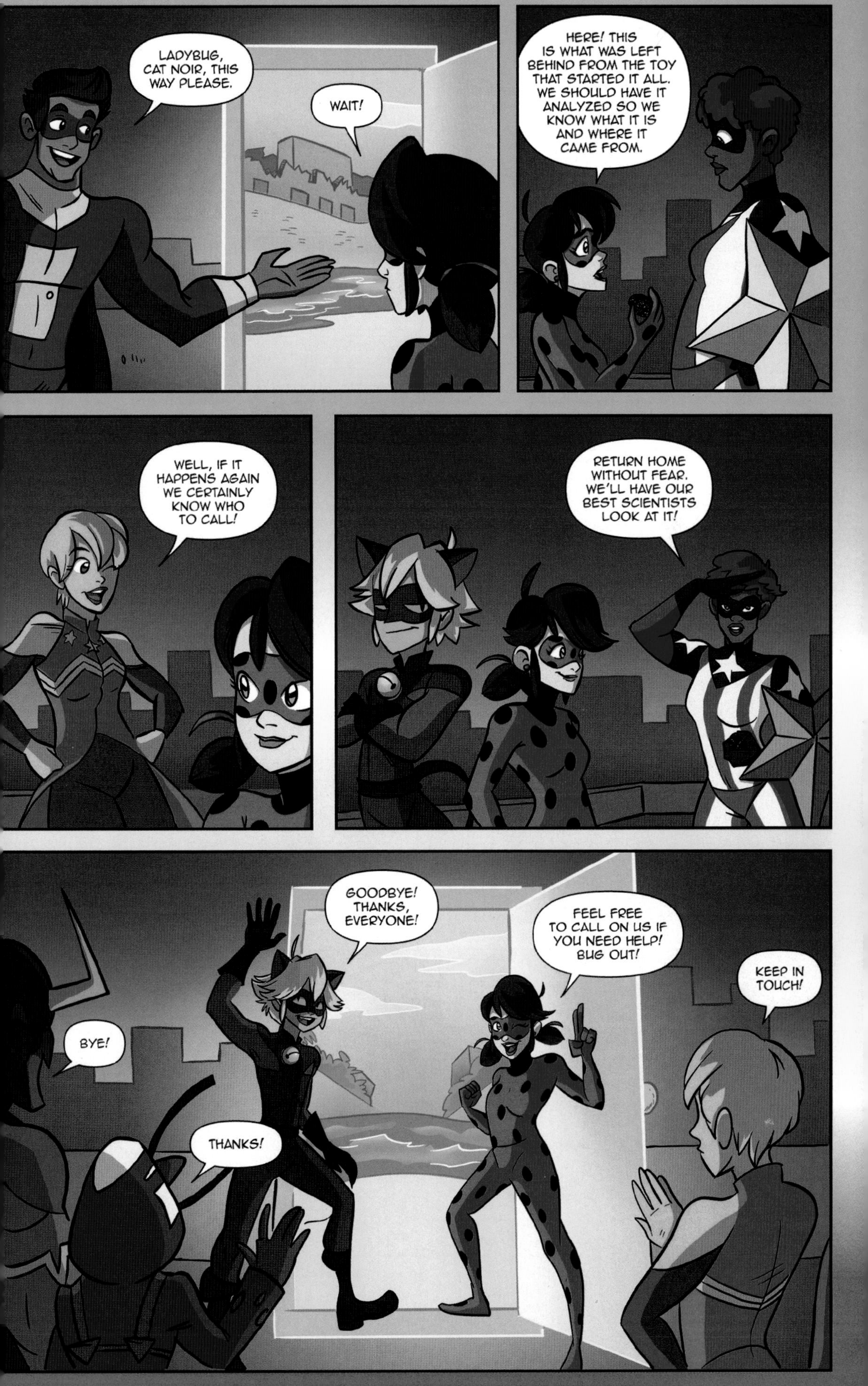
LADYBUG, CAT NOIR, THIS WAY PLEASE.
WAIT!
HERE! THIS IS WHAT WAS LEFT BEHIND FROM THE TOY THAT STARTED IT ALL. WE SHOULD HAVE IT ANALYZED SO WE KNOW WHAT IT IS AND WHERE IT CAME FROM.
WELL, IF IT HAPPENS AGAIN WE CERTAINLY KNOW WHO TO CALL!
RETURN HOME WITHOUT FEAR. WE'LL HAVE OUR BEST SCIENTISTS LOOK AT IT!
BYE!
THANKS!
GOODBYE! THANKS, EVERYONE!
FEEL FREE TO CALL ON US IF YOU NEED HELP! BUG OUT!
KEEP IN TOUCH!

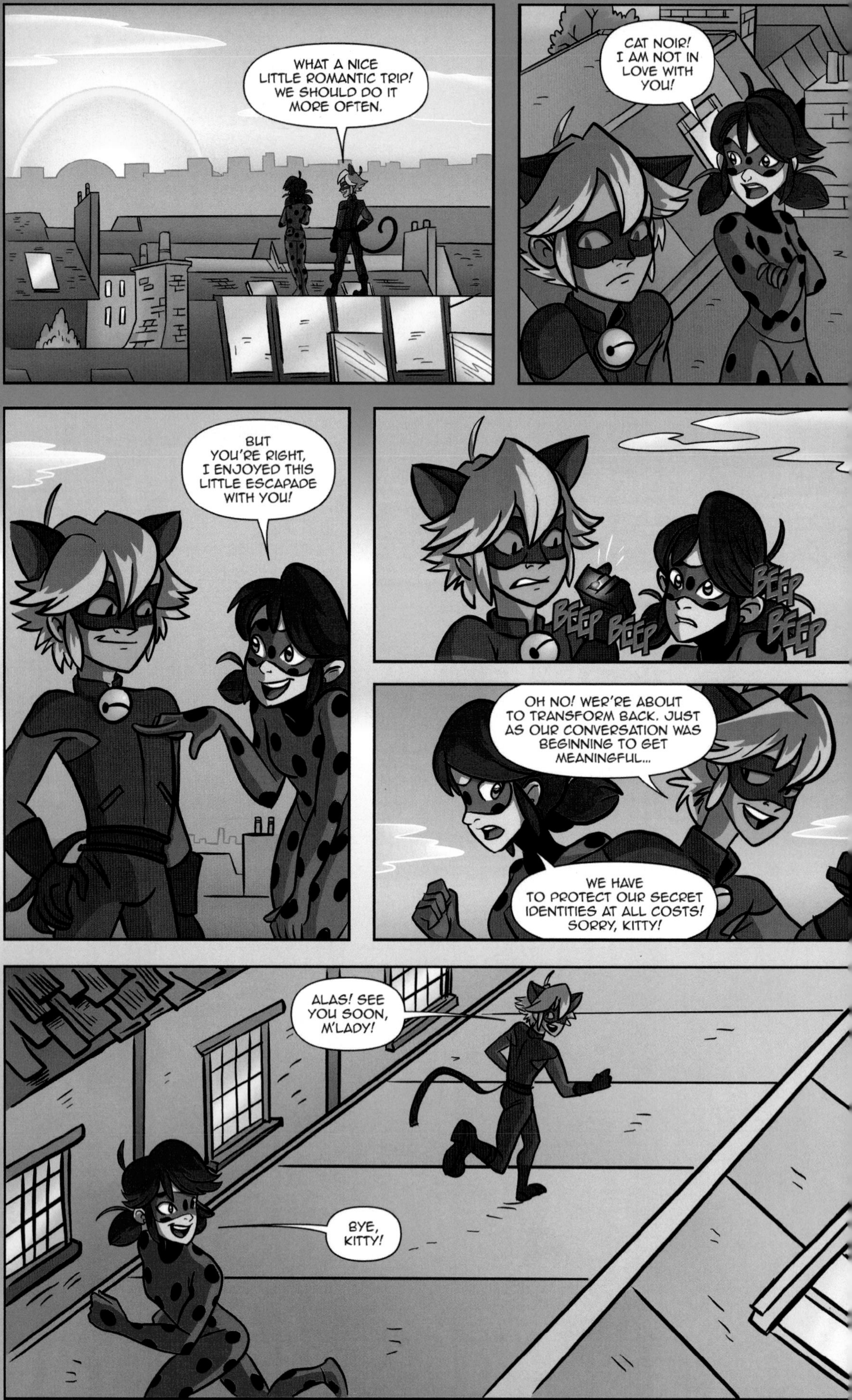
WHAT A NICE LITTLE ROMANTIC TRIP! WE SHOULD DO IT MORE OFTEN.
CAT NOIR! I AM NOT IN LOVE WITH YOU!
BUT YOU'RE RIGHT, I ENJOYED THIS LITTLE ESCAPADE WITH YOU!
BEEP BEEP BEEP BEEP
OH NO! WER'RE ABOUT TO TRANSFORM BACK. JUST AS OUR CONVERSATION WAS BEGINNING TO GET MEANINGFUL...
WE HAVE TO PROTECT OUR SECRET IDENTITIES AT ALL COSTS! SORRY, KITTY!
ALAS! SEE YOU SOON, M'LADY!
BYE, KITTY!

PAGE 1 PROGRESSIO

PAGE 1 – PANEL

Splash page – You can use the last page of issue 3 page 28 to save time
In the foreground, very small, the little French heroes along with KnightOwl and Sparrow finally discover the villain. In the background, his feet in the lava that's beginning to show, destroying the earth's crust, the 33-foot-tall Trash Krakken is pushing the walls with tentacles coming out of his back to enlarge the crack. The Trash Krakken turns around to face them. It's an impressive sight.
Please note: he's gotten much bigger than on the photo. Indeed, in the meantime, he's absorbed new objects and as such, has grown.

The credits should read as follows:
The Trash Krakken Part 3
Created by Thomas Astruc
Written by Thomas Astruc, Mélanie Duval, Fred Lenoir, Sébastien Thibaudeau & Bryan Seaton
Pencils by Ellen Cerreta
Inks by Brian Hess
Letters by Justin Birch
Colors by Darné Lang
Editing by Bryan Seaton and Nicole D'Andria

CAT NOIR: I thought we said we'd play in the big league now... not the giant one!
LADYBUG: We need a plan...

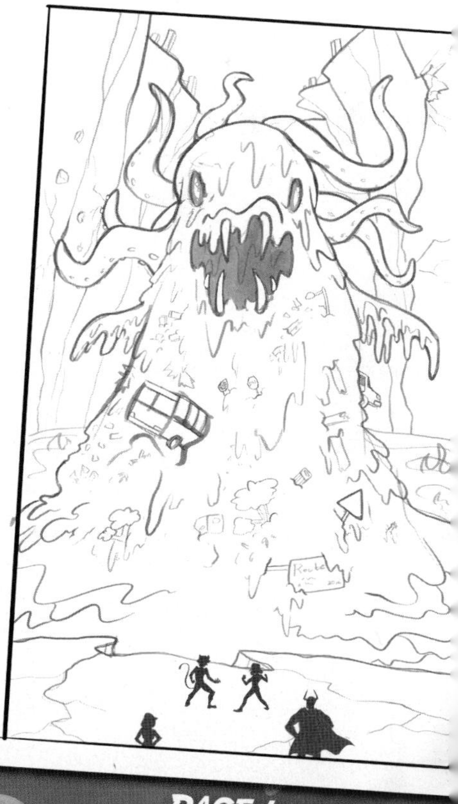

PAGE 1 THUMBNAIL

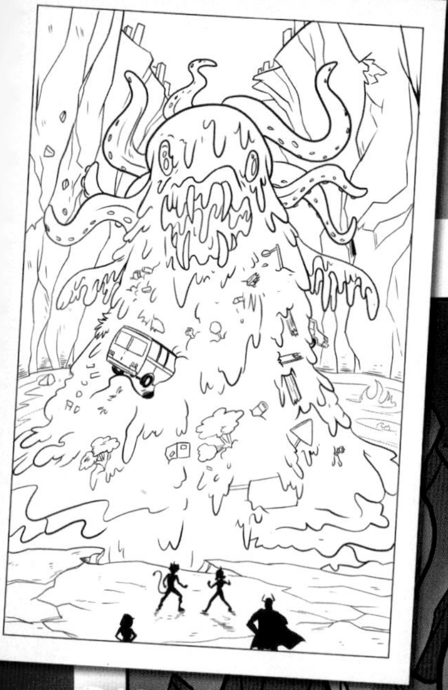

PAGE 1 INKS

PAGE 1 COLORS

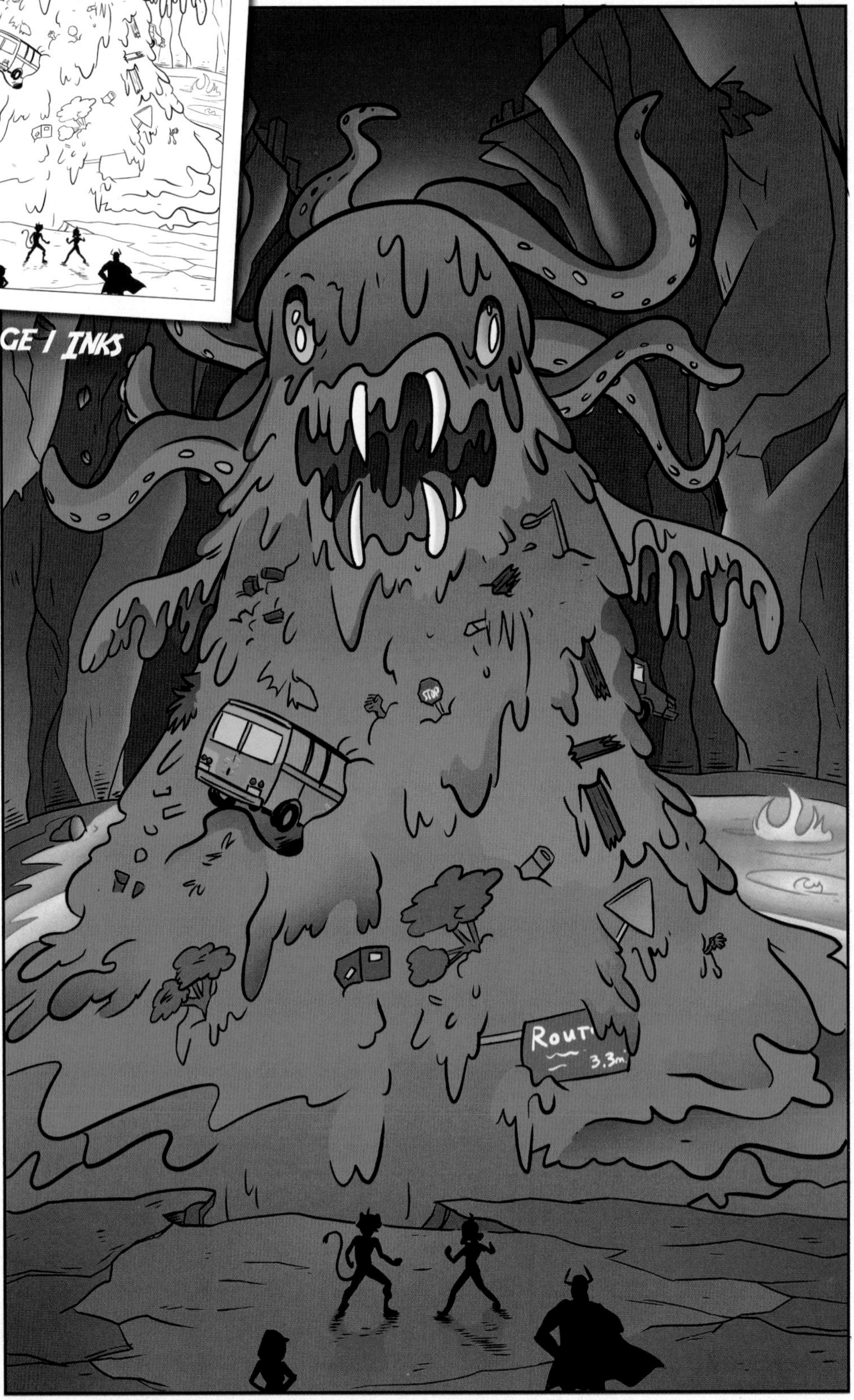
STOP
ROUT
3.3m

PAGE 13-14 PROGRESSIO

PAGE 13 – PANELS
Full page of the trash Krakken with Ladybugs yoyo attached to the plush and going over an overhang, in the center and Knighowl helping her pull the string, Cat Noir is protesting against his orders
KNIGHTOWL: Hold tight, kid! I'll help you!
LADYBUG: Cat Noir! You're up! Cataclysm him! But from the inside!
CAT NOIR: What? You want me to throw myself into that thing?!
Smaller panels around edges of full page image:

Panel One
Close-up of ladybug yoyo hitting the plush and the gum sticking it tight

Panel Two
She wraps the string over an overhang to protect her from the Trash Krakken thrashing movements.

Panel Three
Close-up of Cat Noir looking all "gooey eyed"
LADYBUG(from off screen) PLEEEASE!
CAT NOIR: I can never say no to M'Lady!

PAGE 14 – FOUR PANELS
Panel One - Three
Cat Noir doing a series of leaps, dives and rolls to reach the Trash Krakken ending in panel 3 with hand out stretched ahead of him leaping into the Trash Krakken
CAT NOIR: Cataclysm!

Panel Four (rest of page, at least 1/2 or more)
Big explosion of the Trash Krakken all around Cat Noir with Trash and anything else absorbed raining down everywhere.
SFX: BOOM!

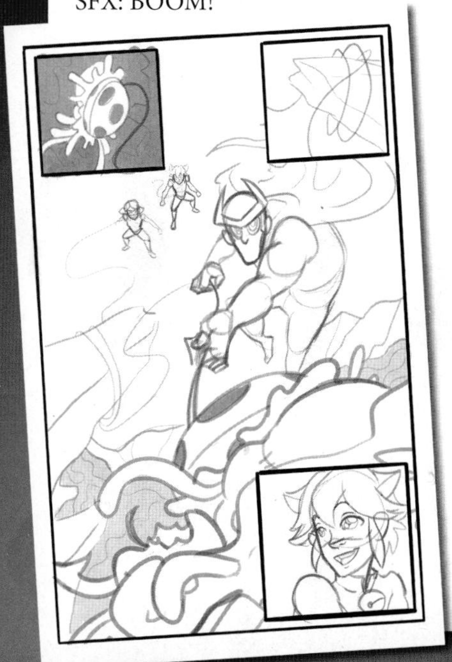

PAGE 13 THUMBNAIL

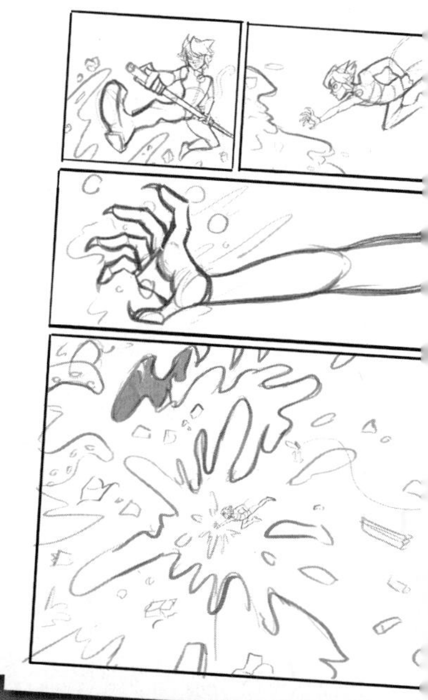

PAGE 14 THUMBNAIL

PAGE 13 COLORS

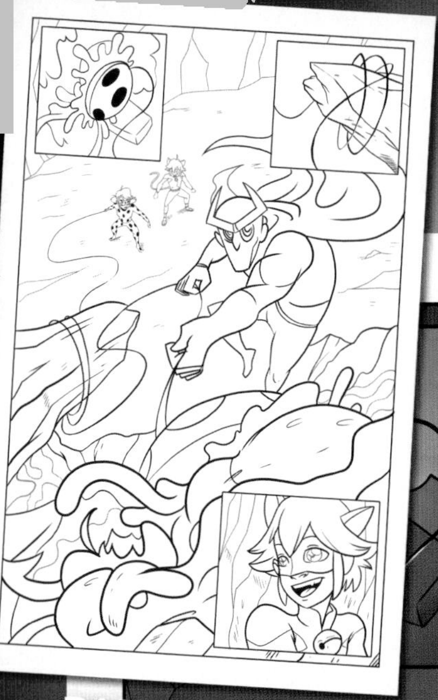

PAGE 13 INKS

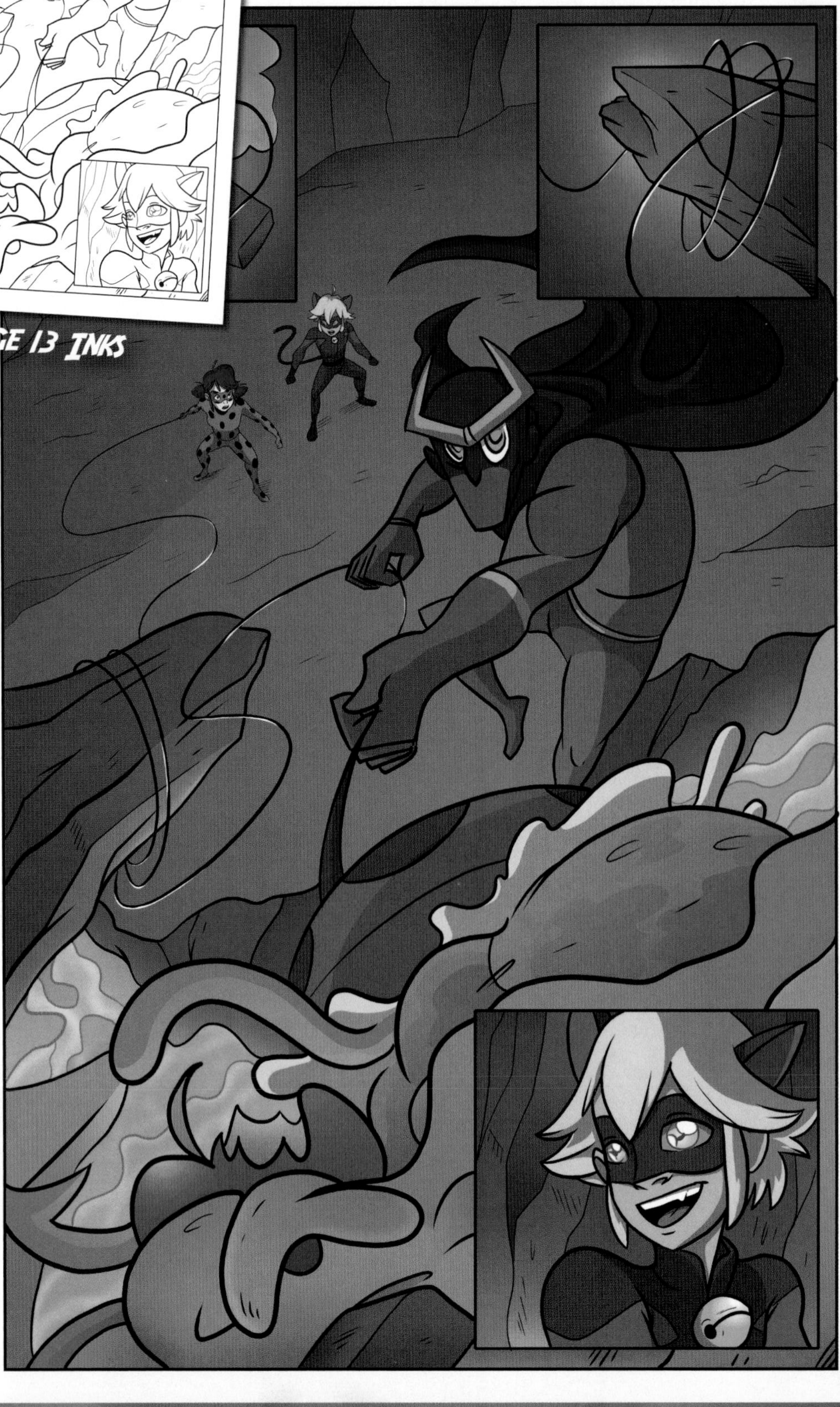

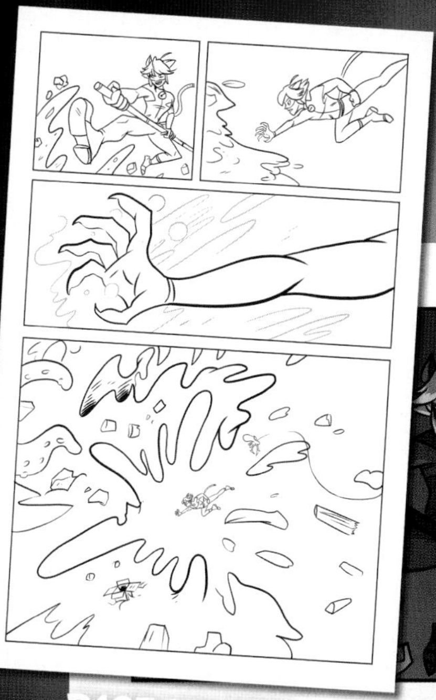

PAGE 14 INKS

PAGE 14 COLORS

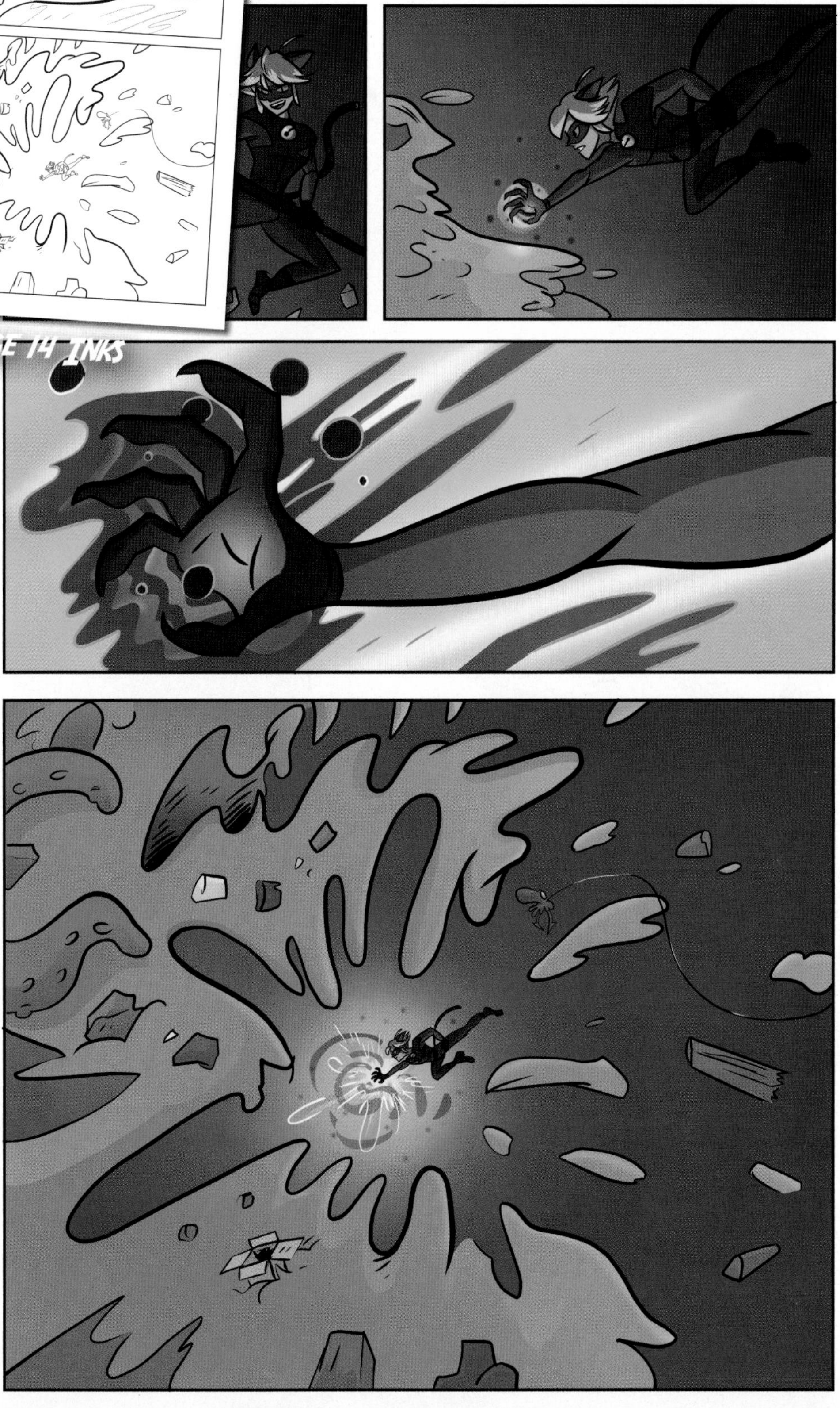

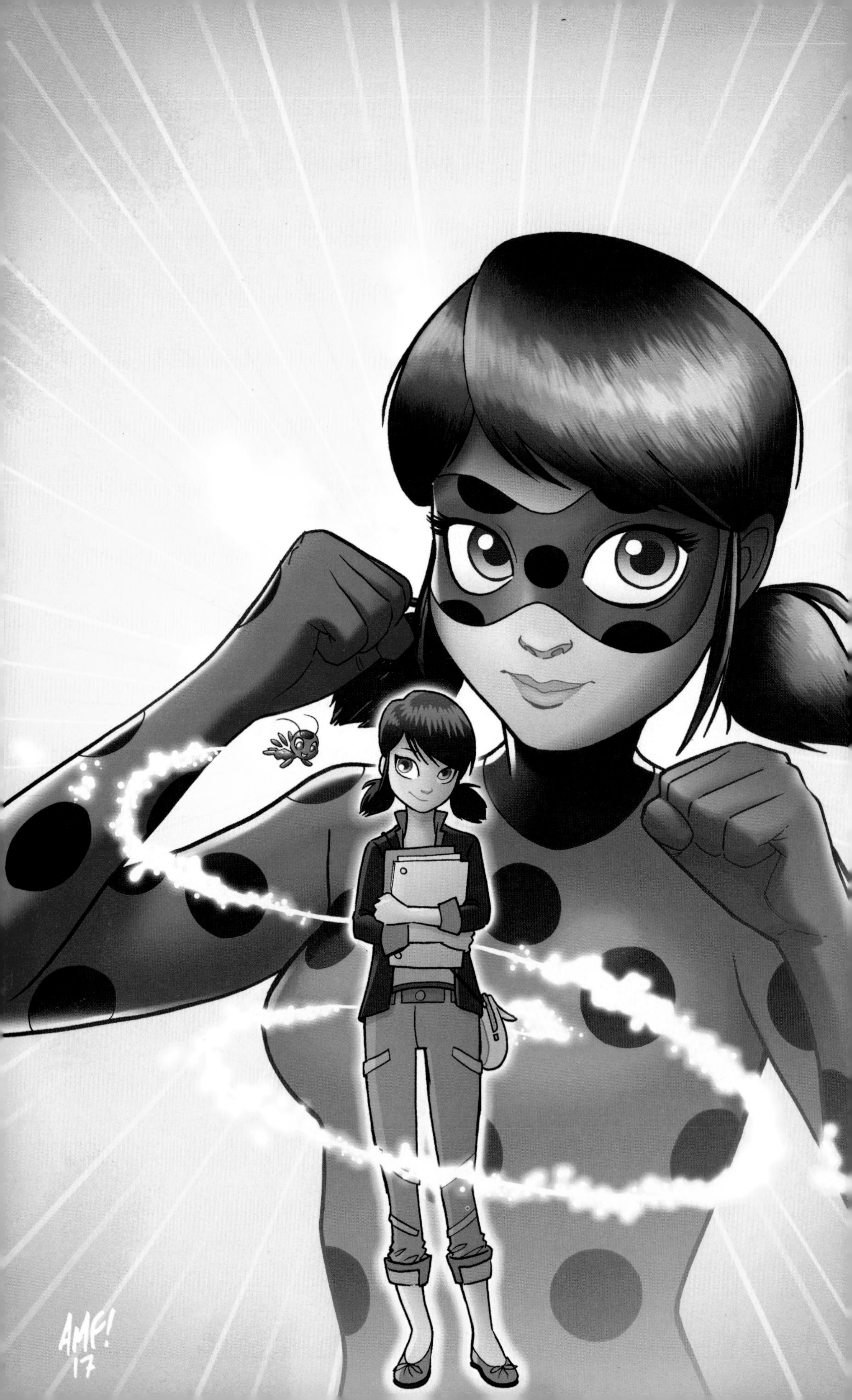
AMF!
17